THE DEMARKIANS

By

CHIDI METU

Copyright 2021

CHIDI METU

All rights reserved. No part of this book/novel, The Demarkians, may be used or reproduced by any means, graphic, electronic, or mechanical, including photocopying, recording, taping or by any information storage retrieval system without the written permission of the publisher except in the case of brief quotations embodied in critical articles and reviews.

OTHER WORKS BY THE AUTHOR

- *ENFANT TERRIBLE*
- *DEVIL'S NEXT OF KIN*
- *ELEGANT EVIL*

Table of Contents

Dedication..ii

Preface..iii

Chapter 1...1

Chapter 2...27

Chapter 3...69

Chapter 4...97

Chapter 5...141

Chapter 6...160

Chapter 7...180

Chapter 8...186

Chapter 9...208

Chapter 10...222

Chapter 11...252

Chapter 12...276

Sequel...285

About the Author..288

DEDICATION

THIS BOOK IS DEDICATED TO THE MEMORY OF MY PARENTS, CHIEF DAVID METU AND GRACE METU. THIS IS MY ETERNAL CANDLE TO YOUR BEAUTIFUL SOULS. MAY YOUR SOULS REMAIN IN ELYSIUM.

PREFACE

This book is about the Demarkians, a very powerful satanic cult that permeated the societies where they were located. The ladder of the cult leadership was well-articulated and organized. Their members were very ardent in conforming to the cores and ethos of the fraternity. They could go to any length to project and protect the ideals of the fraternity. The Demarkian cats, dogs and birds were very dedicated allies used to perpetuate their evil and draconic agenda. The members and the operative animals were very resilient and unwavering in the pursuit and realizations of the Demarkian principles. They had a hierarchy of seniority and order which was strictly observed and adhered to. The Damarkians were very daring and they didn't make no excuses for that. Marching on the toes of a Demarkian was viewed as an act of war and they were very unforgiving. They go all out to fight and win. In the evil world of the dark, they ruled and they destroyed. The members lived and died Demarkians.

The cult was as old as the planet earth and beyond. Membership in the cult provided powers, privileges, material wealth and subjugations. What made the cult essentially dangerous was that the society was oblivious of their existence and powers, which was beyond massive. They thrived in the dark but they destroyed in the ominous powers of the dark. Nothing obstructed them from achieving their objectives. Membership in the cult was an exhibition of the fallibility and vanity of mankind. It showcased the zeal and determination of a typical human to oppress, intimidate, conquer and rule the world. Man is wolf to man, as an adage, was portrayed clearly by this story.

This story is a conflict of civilization and the spiritual vestiges of the dark ages. It is a story of the war of faiths. The Demarkians were engaged in what appeared to be an unflinching war, power tussles, that left trails of casualties and defeat. The world is inundated with demons and evil powers but this cult seemed to transcend the mundane knowledge of an evil spirit. The Satan himself was directly involved in their battles. He appeared in in his full glamour to fight for the members, if need be.

The anthropology of the Demarkians was that it was a satanic cult having its origin in the bible and other holy books. The devil/ Satan/ evil/ Lucifer, seeking for rivalry and dominion over the earth, had this brotherhood of followers, that fought and protected each other.
The book of Isaiah says of Satan:
"How art thou fallen from haven, O Lucifer, son of the morning"
How art thou cut down to the ground, which didst weaken the nations".

The biblical Dragon in the book of revelation seeking followership and dominion. The devil in testing the holiness and determination of Jesus took him to the top of mountains and offered him the entire earth if he could renounce God but Jesus declined. Adam fell the ploy and test of the devil and humanity was banished from the garden of Eden.
The beast with or without the mark of the numbers 666 has willing followers who seek earthly possessions and powers. From the time of the creation of earth and the time of the existence of devil, the tussle of powers started and leaves everyone with a choice to follow.

The Lithuanian stone of Svendubre also known as devil's stone is located in different parts of the world. The Demarkians have the stones. As Legends has it, the stone has been split inadvertently in different places by different civilization and continues to wreak havoc. The power of the Demarkians is not exclusively connected to the stone but a thing of creation with mysterious origin. The brotherhood has also untraceable origin as the mystery of nature.

The book, if it appeals to you, will keep you on the edges of the chairs till the end. This book, and eventually, a screenplay version, will elevate your adrenalin and blood pressure. It could be very scary and frightening though but storyline is designed to achieve that effect on you. Reader's discretion is advised strongly in making the decision to read the book. It is a very engaging and interesting piece of work. When the movie comes out, watch it with others, to avoid prolonged nightmares. It is targeted to be in the Oscar list of the horror movie world. Enjoy the story.

The Demarkians   Chidi Metu

CHAPTER ONE

In the state of Connecticut, on the eastern plains of the great United States of America, is a town known as Newtown. A very quiet, peaceful place without any fanfare. A town of about two thousand inhabitants, most of them college educated and polished individuals. And the history and pedigrees of almost all the families follows the same pattern. Inhabitants minded their businesses but fraternizes with each other communally. Everyone knows everyone by first name. That was very encouraging considering the culture of the United States of everyone by himself or herself. The New towners were great people that embraced peace and tranquility. The buildings were very aristocratic and mostly single family residences consisting of duplexes and bungalows. The tallest buildings were located on the deep south of the town and none of them exceeded three levels in height.

The neighborhood was adorned with beautiful flowers that bloomed incredible colors in the spring. Newtown was one of the cleanest city in the whole country. The neighbors devoted more time in maintaining that than even their own compounds. The city was washed twice a week and the trash was removed twice a week too, unlike most other cities in the United States. The buildings were maintained by the supervision of the city office and tickets were issued to delinquent occupiers. The ambience of the city was very appealing to the inhabitants. The city was administered like a home owners' association and all the rules strictly maintained. Neighbors were seen walking their dogs from dawn to dusk, with cheerful countenances, waving at each other, extending honest pleasantries, stopped in pockets to talk and gossip about everything from politics to infidelity. They seemed to love each other and they lived that in an exemplary way. The city had two beautiful parks at the both north and south ends of the town. The bigger park was the Newtown Park located in the southern part, which is a little more aristocratic than the northern part of the town.

Majority of the Newtowners were retired civil servants and their families. The Newtowners don't sell their homes as they always come back to spend their last days in those homes. They were very religious as most of them, especially in their twilight ages, were seeking the face God. The crime rate in the town was zero, all year round. Houses were left unlocked all day and night. The quietude of the entire city was mind boggling. You could only hear the birds crying or singing all through the day and night. There was nothing ominous about the cries of any animal in Newtown. There were no stray animals except the antelopes, rabbits, and multi-colored ducks seen ubiquitously in the Newtown Lake swimming joyously around the lake.

The town had a small sheriff station with two squad marked black and white cruisers that patrolled the city now and then. The sheriffs would pull up to drink coffees with happy families that offered some to them. The sheriffs were also members of the community professionally and socially. Sheriff Godson, from a neighboring town, the chief sheriff of Newtown, loved Newtown and decided to move into the town to live. He embraced the town ardently and kept praying not to be transferred out before his retirement in five years. He had been in Newtown for six years and there had never been any recorded crime since he got there. He knew everyone by their first names and he cherished that a lot. His wife and kids loved Newtown too and they were never ready to leave the town.

There were two major churches in Newtown, both located at the two ends of the town. There were few other little places of worship scattered around the perimeter of the town. Everyone practiced his or her own religion in peace. Sundays were very busy days as it offered the inhabitants the golden opportunity to meet and interact with each other. The sermons were unusually long but very engaging. The parishioners didn't really mind the long time they spent in the church because they didn't have much to do with their time. They listened, appreciated, commented, joked, with the preaching priests. Newtown, in harmony, represented the true biblical body of Christ. The communions and the church activities were cohesively very impressive. Most of the inhabitants were practicing Christians, trying to abide by the injunctions of their faiths. The biggest church was the Aristorian church of the Anglican Communion known as the Aristorian Church of Christ located at the southern part. A huge and magnificent building, always immaculately white, clean to the core, with a huge cathedral window at the two ends of the building, adorned with cully-flowered windows dented with the pictures of Jesus Christ and the Angels at the sides. The building had a huge lighted cross mounted at the frontal elevation of the building. The lawns of the church looked well -kept and manicured every two days. The entire compound depicted the biblical heaven with only a small portion paved in cement and gravel. The interior of the church held more beauty than the outside, with medieval oak chairs and podium, red carpets adorning the hallways and a huge live crucifix of Jesus Christ mounted at the altar. The tables were all decorated with spotless immaculate white cloths. The church depicted the Newtown, both in appearance and substance.

The two priests and their staffs lived at the two bungalows located at the back of the church. The church was fenced, except the frontal part abutting the major street known as Lincoln Street where the church was located. Services were held twice on Sundays and once on Wednesdays. Father Angelus, in his mid-fifties, was the archdeacon in charge of the church. Having been there for ten years, understood the town very well, knew his parishioners, their families and their abodes very well. He visited them at their homes and interacted socially too with them. He even knew their phone numbers off handedly, in most cases. Fr.

Angelus was married with two teenage kids that were off to college in New York.

Fr. Montenegro, was a young priest, single, very pious, determined to serve God. He lived and breath the church. He spent almost all his time working in the church, stepping beyond his duty bounds to serve the parishioners. His teaching cornerstone was engraved on the Christian faith of the teachings of Christ. He loved the parable of the mustard seeds, and always made references to it in all his sermons. He believed and taught that, as a Christian, a follower of Christ should be able to move the mountains with his faith. He called on all parishioners to remind them of the need to pray all the time. He offered them prayer points and prayed over the phone with them. He believed in the power of fasting and abstinences to things that he considered impure and dirty. His overzealousness is sometimes found irritating by some parishioners who avoided him.

***

There was a new mortgage and loan financial business opened in Newtown last year, called Optimum mortgage and loans, Inc. The business was averagely big with about 5 staffs that were very efficient and dedicated. They served Newtown and other nearby towns efficiently. Most residents of Newtown had their loans and mortgage finances conducted at Optimum. Few months ago, a new manager, Mr. Oliver Winterbrush, a young man in his early forties, newly married to a beautiful wife, Philomena, in her late twenties, took over the running of optimum. The Winterbrush, appeared regular initially, had a beautiful three- year old daughter that received dotting attention from them endlessly. Oliver and his wife, in their college days, attended the prestigious Ivy league Princeton University and graduated highly in flying colors. Both of them were not in the college at the same time but met later in life and started dating and eventually tied the knots. Mr. Winterbrush is from an average family in Connecticut, son of retired farmers. Philomena was a daughter to a relatively rich but very private family from Delaware. Her parents lived the life of pariahs, raised their kids with that culture and attitude. Their community did not understand their lifestyles which were inundated with oddities.

They were never involved with the community in all activities of their community at Delaware, including attending church service. They were rich and well to do but that was the end of what anyone could say about them. They were closed out to the world in a disturbing reclusion lifestyle.

The Winterbrush came to Newtown and rented an apartment in the northern part. Initially, neighbors did not notice them but after a few months, their weird lifestyles became pronounced. You could only have a glance of them with their huge black dog that never seemed to have stepped out of the house. Unlike other normal dogs, it was never taken out for a walk. The Winterbrush, for their ages, were very conservative and withdrawn. They defied the culture of the town by not interacting or cared about anyone. They drove their Mercedes Benz cars, with tinted back windows and fully closed windows all the time. Their only interaction with the community was during their work times at their offices. Philomena Winterbrush got a job as a postal manager in the only post office in the town. Her office was administratively located inside the building, with perimeter surveillance cameras in the interiors and exteriors. She was a very private person that chose to stay by herself and talked less. Her relationship with any staff was job-related only. She was very pleasant at her job but could hardly recognize and wave at anyone outside the office. She and her husband were in the world of their own. The entire town started noticing that and stayed away from them as they called them weirdo. For Philomena, at her age and year of graduation from college, it became even more perplexing that she could be in such a high position in the US postal system. But she was a demarkian and that made a lot of differences in how she attained such a pivotal job in such a short time. Her parents and her husband were demarkians too.

Societal ladder doesn't mean much to them in terms of attaining pivotal positions. The demarkian was an extremely very powerful satanic cult that transcends the society. They had very unique lifestyles as a dictate of the fraternal order of the cult. They left trails of woes and agonies on all their activities. A march on the toes of a demarkian is a dance of death for the marcher. Demarkians were usually quiet and withdrawn in their lifestyles, overly ambitious and ruthless in their pursuits. They were palpably destructive and unrelenting in their act of wars. They permeated all the sectors of the government and private industries and there was no compromise in looking out for their members. They were usually the cream and shot-callers of the society. They were anti-Christ, not affirmatively but defensively. The demarkians were evil incarnates and ardent followers of Lucifer. They never accepted defeat or submit to a loss. They were very resilient in their acrimony and retributions. When they bite, they suck blood.

The Winterbrush, feeling that their private lives were not protected in their current rented apartment, tried to move into a secured private, stand-alone single home but couldn't secure one for more than 6 months of their living in Newtown. They were somewhat frustrated because they couldn't walk their dog out of the house or freely walk outside themselves to stretch their legs a little. As a final resort, they put a phone call to their local Demarkian prefect in the region and a land was purchased in the southern Newtown and a beautiful bungalow built up within two months and they moved in. The building was oddly painted with dark colors, fenced high, with beautiful ground-paved compounds. The compound was paved instead of having a lawn to avoid the gardeners coming into their compound to attend to the lawns. The frontal part of the compound was left open in compliance with the city building plans. Despite their efforts to conform the building per the city code, the city authorities did a compliance site visit and mandated them to change the color of the building from the dark color to a bright color. They resisted a little bit but followed the cult's prefect instructions to abide and change the color. The Demarkians never fought a de minimis war and the city code regulations was considered one of them. The Winterbrush were very happy with their new independence and privacy. They were allowed by the city to alter and install a small electronic white cottage gate that worked with an access key, and of course a remote control. Their new community in the south were perplexed by this beautifully young but odd couple that avoided everyone since they moved in.

They would never look at anyone or wave. They drove exotically in their Mercedes Benz cars, zoomed in and out. They seemed to wallow in affluence and grandeur, in their closed world. Everything about them depicted evidence of good living. There were surveillance cameras installed at the perimeter of the compound and the building. The monitor for the cameras were huge 48- inch screens located at their sitting room, den and their master bedroom. Two of the cameras were positioned to see the full street from both angles.

The community started gossiping about them at the markets, church and little sit-out family events hosted sporadically by residents. Voices were hushed talking about them and why they chose to work in such a small town that doesn't offer a lot of career opportunities for their youthful generation. But they seemed very affluent and successful! They brought that to the attention of the Sheriff but nothing could be done about that, being that they were not violating any laws. On the church part. Fr Angelus decided to reach out to them but couldn't find their name in the phone registry to call them. Noting that they didn't have house phone and not knowing their number, decided to visit them unannounced. He drove up to their gate but couldn't get in. There was no bell at the gate, Fr. Angelus started yelling: is anyone at home!! Hello, Hello…The Winterbrush saw him at the gate in his full priestly regalia and ignored his calls. Their dog, pinto, was very restless and quietly aggressive, looking through the window towards the gate where the priest was standing. The winterbrush were very troubled and upset by this visit for reasons that would be revealed later. They were puzzled as to a nosy community where a priest visit residents unannounced, as in this case. Do they want a war with the Demarkians? Do they really know what they were up against? They turned off their television and went inside their room, ignoring the priestly irritant, taking the restless pinto with them into the bedroom. Pinto couldn't stay in the room as it was pacing the hallway and the window facing the street watching the priest trying to get the attention and an invitation into the compound. The ominous sound started playing at the background. Fr Angelus left and decided to check back another time, his inquisitiveness having been heightened now by his own personal observation of this weird couple with a huge dog peeping through the window without barking at him!

The Winterbrush house was very poorly lit at the outside, with limited lightings inside too. The windows had thick curtains, a signature décor for the Demarkians. Their tv and music system has their volumes turned down very low in aristocracy. Their little daughter, Bridget, have been raised in their lifestyles, doesn't ask much questions and did not behave like a typical 5 year -old kid. Avery beautiful brown-eyed princess with the maturity of a ten-year-old. She liked to play with pinto. She attended the local elementary school and interacted like a normal child. Apart from her maturity, there was no oddity about her behavior

The community started picking on the Winterbrush family who were there to work and live their lives in peace. community Kids started knowing about them too, based on the adult gossips trending in the Newtown. To avert the pressure and distress, Bridget was taken off public school to a private school with very high tuition which wasn't a problem for the Winterbrushes. Bridget initially was doing well until the students started attacking her and calling her child of the weirdo and other derogatory names. That was very troubling to the Winterbrushes and they kept putting up with it for a while until Bridget refused to attend school anymore. Philomena had to stay at home by taking a few days off to situate her daughter's problem. First, she took the child back to the school to discuss with the principal which helped a little bit but the harassment continued and they removed her from the school temporarily. Philo was very upset as well as Oliver. They found this town quiet and fulfilling and intended to live there and raise their family there. They intended to live here for as long as it took, raise their family and attend to their lovely jobs. But the activities of the members of the community was deemed an invitation and courting the trouble of the powerful Demarkian cult, and their reprisals could be very voracious and vicious. This small community, in the middle of nowhere, should just let the sleeping dog lie.

✱✱✱

Last Sunday, in the Newtown church, the sermon was prolonged and dwelt more on the secret lives of human beings in relation to the church and their faiths. The Winterbrushes were even mentioned by the priest on the pulpit. After church services, almost everyone was engaged in talking about the Winterbrushes, which topic was very inflammatory and generated extreme keenness from the entire parishioners. Mr. Stokes was the chief gossip monger. He spearheaded the most attentions on the Winterbrushes. He had discussed the Winterbrushes with the sheriff and the church.

Tension started building up in the town, between the Winterbrush family and the entire local community.
Oliver again took his troubles to the prefect of the order of the demarkians in that region. The prefect asked them if they would like to move out of the town for another job elsewhere but the Winterbrushes vehemently said no. They wanted to stay back and fight to destabilize the nosy town for their incursions into their private lives. The prefect promised to call them back with a decision on their issues. Few days later, the prefect informed Oliver that the Demarkians have declared subtle but intense war on the Newtown. Knowing the reach and powers of the cult, this battle line would have raised the hairs on the bodies of the community but they were oblivious of that fact, as would be discovered later. They were sticking their hands in the mouth of a lion and they were to find out the hard way.

Oliver was able to secure admission for his daughter in another town 45 miles away which created a stress on them taking her to school and bringing her back home daily. Their anger became aggravated for that but they kept quiet and continued to live their normal lives. Few months later, Newtown started noticing some changes in terms of the quietness and ambience of the town. Black crows and ravens were seen flying around the town, making weird noises. Some ominous sounds of animals were heard all through the nights, every day, especially in the midnights.

Mr. Stokes, a seventy-five-year-old retired teacher, a longtime resident of Newtown, was at the forefront of the residents noticing the changes. He heard the growling and cries of animals, woke up in the nights to search for the animals. On this particular night, he noticed a huge black crow perching at the tree across from his house crying in high tone and refused to fly away even when stones were thrown at it. The huge bird's eyes were glowings in the dark and seemed ready to attack Stokes. Stokes positioned his flashlight on the bird and kept throwing objects at the bird. Another black crow flew over and joined the other, as they continued hollering at Stokes. Stokes was surprised about these birds and their activities, their resilience and fearlessness and the weirdness of their behavior. There were other ominous sounds, totally weird, heard loudly within that vicinity which woke few more members of the community from their night sleeps.

It was a spectacle as few of them walked over to their porches and following stokes flashlights and seeing the black birds who were not making any attempts to fly away. It was 3 am in the morning. In the morning for God's sake! One of the resident rushed in and brought out a telescope, ardently watching these weird and fearless birds that were terrorizing the community at this odd time of the night. At some point they seemed to have flown away for twenty minutes. Stokes sat in his porch watching the poorly lit street, the beautiful shrubs and the park, about two hundred and fifty yards away. Stokes kept on flashing his flashlights but couldn't find anything disturbing. He felt relaxed and dozed off on the patio couch for a minute. Suddenly, he felt a strangling hard grip on his neck, opened his eyes but everywhere was so dark and he couldn't get his flashlight which was placed on the ground by his side. The two black birds had their legs intertwined on his neck, extraordinarily strong for a normal birds, so strong was their grips that he couldn't get out any sound to yell for the neighbors' help. He was strongly trying to fight off the birds but they were out to subdue him as the birds started puncturing his face with their powerful beaks which felt like stabs of a dagger. One of bird, like a lion, gripped on his mouth and nose suffocating him while repeatedly plunging their beaks into his eyes, causing severe vision damages to both eyes. His eyeballs were shattered in less than five minutes. Blood was all over the place as the birds flew away quietly into the darkness of the night. Stokes regained his voice and yelled out to the community and his neighbors, some of them still awake from the observations of the birds, ran over and beheld the shocks of their lives. Stoker's eyeballs were practically hanging out of the sockets with his tongues badly cut and severed as if it was mutilated by a knife. Stokes was in so much pains and in agony struggling to stay alive. The 911 and the sheriff were called in immediately. An ambulance came over and took Stokes to the nearest hospital. Everyone, including the staffs in the hospital was overwhelmed by what they saw.

Stokes was three quarter dead and comatose when he arrived the hospital. An ophthalmologist was summoned and couldn't do much to help stokes. His face was mashed up inexplicably bad, with heinous mutilations. The question that was in everyone's mouth was, what and who could have caused these measure of damages to a human being, and within the given time? What kind of weapon was used to achieve that? The eyeballs were surgically patched up and sewn back into the sockets but the retina and lens were totally and irretrievably damaged. The tongue was sewn up too and pushed back but it was more of a cosmetic panacea. Stokes was in the ICU unit for two months, utterly out of the world. Tons of fellow parishioners and neighbors thronged the hospital daily to console with the family of Stokes and prayed for him. The priests were always there, as stokes was the church Deacon and was heavily involved with the activities of the church. Stoker's situation was so bad that he was in and out of life support for a while. He struggled to live and he eventually did but permanently lost his eyes and was literally dumb because he could not make any decipherable statement. His hands were very shaky and his brain worked at a half mast to even articulate the event of that night. He might never be able to do that. The demarkians just set an example with him, believing that the community should learn from that but they didn't.

Phillip, a grandson of Stokes, resident of Phoenix, Arizona, heard what happened to his grandpa, flew in the next day. He was jolted by what he saw in the hospital. His Grandpa's almost lifeless body was lamely lying on the bed with thick eye patches covering his two eyes, a feeding intubation pipes inserted into his mouth, and his heart connected to a life machine. The sight was very pathetic and Phillip decided that he would do whatever it took to revenge on whoever did this to his grandpa. He started crying uncontrollably for a long time and later left the hospital.

Phillip was the oldest grandson of Stokes and stokes' most favorite of all the grandchildren. Phillip was a handful who couldn't get on well with his parents, especially his dad, Stokes jnr. He was a truant through secondary school and his grandpa was always there to pull him out of trouble. In some cases, he was to be retrieved from the police stations as he was falling out of line in almost everything. He was a full renegade of a son and granddad was the only member of his family to tolerate his indiscretions. Grandpa did everything possible for him to attend college but it was an arduous task that failed. He used his connections in the US Army via one of his ex-students, a US marine Brigadier to get Phillip into the Army. He went through the training and passed out honorably and was commissioned.

He went through US Army college but the demon in him never left him even after all these accomplishments. He was violating a lot of the rules and was dishonorably dismissed from the army and the college too. The family was not surprised but Grandpa, very disillusioned, accepted him back. Stokes continued to pray for Phillip and holding church services for him. He brought him back home to Newtown and nurtured him back to civility and responsibility, gave him all his pensions and 401k to start a new life in Arizona. Phillip turned his life around, with the beast in him remained dormant. That beastly part of him was awakened by this attack on his most revered grandpa. He wouldn't mind to die in his quest for retribution against whoever did this to grandpa.

The sheriffs, all of them were dumbfounded and angry as to what happened to Stokes. This attack, the ferocity and the damages, were too much to comprehend. Stokes had been a very serious neighborhood watchman, a strong liaison between the sheriff and the Newtown community. A respected retired teacher with incredible resume and integrity. A church deacon and a friend of everyone. He held special barbeques for the sheriff and the church every summer at the back of his house. He invited the sheriff for coffee every day and was ready for discussions on any issue pertaining to the town. He understood the US political landscape very well and was ready to educate anyone who had time for his political lectures. At some point, residents were routing and gingering him to run for the US congress in their district but he didn't have the stamina to deal with that, at his age and a little failing health. Stokes was a perfectionist and he wouldn't want to do a haphazard job at Washington, if elected.

The Aristorian Church, stokes' church, was in a bigger travail because of the pivotal role Stokes played in the church. Lately, he started taking piano classes to help the church in having a pianist and solve the problem of borrowing or having per diem pianist for their busy church services. Stokes was ready to be the pianist for free and for as long as he could. He was that kind and caring, especially to the church. Stokes' wife died of cancer two years ago and he was just getting out of the devastation of his bereavement when this happened. This was a huge tragedy and the entire crux of Newtown was getting ready for war.

The sheriff invited everyone who was awake that night to relay what they may have witnessed. Three neighbors that lived a few houses away from Stokes relayed the ominous birds cry at 3 a.m. in the morning when birds were supposedly sleeping. Their observations of the crows, their sizes, their fearlessness, the flashlights on them, the stones to scare them aware and their resilience. The neighbor with telescope relayed what he saw and the creepy nature of the birds. They saw the birds flew away for a while as Mr. Stokes went back to his patio and they didn't see him again. It was assumed that Stokes went back inside. They didn't hear anything anymore until he yelled for help with a muffled voice and they ran over and saw him gruesomely attacked. There was no struggle as the chairs on the patio were not ruffled and nothing appeared disheveled. The witnesses did not have much to say really beyond these.

The sheriff looking for more physical evidence, looked at the injuries on the face of stokes, the marks of the birds' nails even though appearing unusually deeper, the marks of the beaks permeating his eyes and nose but too pointed and narrow to be from a dagger, knife or weapon. The puzzle continued throughout the investigations. Everything was pointing to the black birds but how could a bird or birds maim a human being like that? The puzzle became more compounded because, Stokes had a solidly and weaponized police flashlight which could knock off the birds with only one strike. Was a human being involved in this attack? There were no human finger marks on Stokes who was unusually very light skinned. There was no mark on his neck area or a rumpled shirt. Stokes did not fall to the ground as there was no evidence of such struggle. His hands were not bound from fighting back as there was no indication of that too! There was also no proof of strangulation and the fact he couldn't call for help became more puzzling. How could he had called for help after the attack? Even if someone with a glove was holding his neck, there would have been marks on the neck. The sheriff continued their investigation by inviting many members of the church and the community and interviewing them for days. The case was beginning to get cold and the sheriffs didn't want to stop.

Philip decided to stay back in Newtown for as long as it took to avenge the mayhem on his grandpa. He started investigating on his grandpa's possible enemies in the town or the church? Does anyone have an issue with the prominence of stokes in the community and the church? Was it about him assuming the pianist position? Phillip kept on running into dead end in his frustrating investigations because his grandpa was an impeccable man. There was nobody with a motive to harm him in Newtown and beyond. When he was about to give up, a parishioner, an old lady, stokes good friend, hinted to Phillip about the weird new neighbors in their mist and gave detailed information as much as she knew to

Phillip. Phillip was enraged again but at least he has a little opening. He went and located the Winterbrush residence, found their job locations and decided to pay a visit to Oliver at his office.

He called and made an appointment and falsely claimed that he was seeking for an equity line of credit for his house, gave grandpa's address, which house was already actually willed to him. He went over to Optimum property and met with Oliver. Phillip was disappointed when he met Oliver, a tall, young good looking white male with a confident personality. Oliver was very courteous and professional to Phillip. They talked about few things and got into the credit issues and the details. At this point, Phillip was disarmed vowing that this young man, who didn't know or pretended not to know of his grandpa, couldn't have hurt him like that. He didn't even know the location of their home. Phillip wanted to cut the meeting short and leave but broached up the attack on his grandpa and noticed a surprising change in the countenance of Oliver, his face turned red and blushed for a few minutes and the smiles dried up on his face.

Phillip started looking into his eyes but he looked away. Phillip kept mentioning the black birds and/or individual that might have attacked and grievously damaged his grandpa. Oliver denied any knowledge of that and advised Phillip coldly to seek the help of the police. Phillip got up, shook his hands, walked away by the door and stopped briefly to look at his watch. Oliver thinking that he was already on the hallway blurted out this: "stupid old man, he got what he deserved. The war is getting started". Phillip stood still and peeped through the door to make sure that Oliver was not on the phone. He walked back in and confronted Oliver with the statement which, of course, Oliver denied vehemently. Phillip was sure of what he heard, kept on pressuring Oliver to admit that he said that and why did he say that? Did you have a problem with my Grandpa? Are you behind the attack on him? A lot of questions were thrown at Oliver. Phillip was getting more enraged and Oliver was asking him to leave or he would call the police on him! The demon in Phillip was trying to break out but Phillip who was trained in judo and karate, a black belt Judoka, was restraining himself greatly. The crescendo of his anger was building strongly and fast, he looked through the window and noticed a huge black crow bird, fitting all the descriptions given by the witnesses on the night of the incident, perched protectively at the outside of the window fervently and fearlessly focused on Phillip. In a few seconds, another sister bird flew in and perched next to that one and they were focused on Phillip as if daring him to act. Phillip walked towards the window, wanted to smack it open and grab the birds and strangle them, Oliver yelled at him, with his eyes popping out, in a beastly outlook, asked Phillip to leave and leave now!!

The ominous evil sounds started playing in the immediate vicinity and Phillip was confused and a little scared. He started looking at Oliver, astonished. Phillip asked Oliver: who the hell are you? Are you a human being or are you a demon? What are these birds and where are they from? These were the same birds that possibly attacked my grandpa! Oliver looked at him calmly and admonished him to go home, pack his stuff and go back to Arizona. Phillip responded to Oliver to get ready for war. Oliver laughed demonically and retorted to Phillip that he is a really piece of shit. Don't stick your stupid hands in the mouth of a lion!! Wise up and get out and tell your community to leave us alone!

Oliver went to the Sheriffs straight from there and relayed his chilling interactions to the chief at the stations. The chief was stupefied and short of words. His confusion was further compounded by this information. He called the finance house and got connected to Oliver. They spoke for a while and he invited Oliver to his office. Later in the evening Oliver went over there and met with him. They went over his interactions with Phillip. Oliver denied knowledge of any connotations relating to the presence of the birds. Oliver denied the statement credited to him by Phillip. Reminded the Sheriff that he shouldn't have invited him here for this absurdity. He requested from the sheriff to tell the residents to leave them alone! He asked the sheriff to warn the Church or any of their clergy to stop disturbing them. Oliver reiterated that he and his wife are just law abiding civil servants who found a home in Newtown. Finally, to let them know that they may start a war that would consume them. He angrily exited the office and walked back into his car and drove off.

Phillip was very confused and he kept talking to the neighbors who corroborated his observations in Oliver's office, the black birds, their fearlessness, the ominous sounds, the rage and the beastly appearance of Oliver all of a sudden, his confidence and threats in asking him to leave the town. Paying with his credit card, he ran his name on Zaba search and LinkedIn, found him surely, Oliver Winterbrush, his schools, residences, family, jobs, nothing standing out particularly about him. Same with his wife Philomena, impeccable records, respectable members of the society, no criminal records, went to distinguished Princeton college, no scandals. Why are they here in this middle of nowhere with very limited career growth? Why are they so arrogant and misanthropic? They are too young for the life they live here. There must be something about them that needed to be unraveled.

The Sheriff took the story to the superior court Judge and sought for a search warrant. The Judge knew Stokes and loved him too, like the whole community but the law has to be followed to the tee. What is the probable cause for the search? Who was to sign the affidavit of the search warrant? Was there going to be a return on the warrant? There were strong dialogue and arguments between the judge and the Sheriff but eventually the Judge signed the warrant. Armed with it, the Sheriff called for back-up from the neighboring county and stormed Oliver's home the next morning by 7 a.m. when Oliver and Philo were just about to leave to take their daughter on the long drive to school. A very strenuous argument ensued as to the timing of the warrant, as follows:
Oliver: we can't do this now, too early and we are about to leave for school in another town. We will be late to school and our jobs.
Sheriff: We choose when we execute search warrants and not you and you are strongly advised to allow us or we will arrest both of you for obstructions. I will not say that twice! Open the door and barricade your dog or other pets so that we can start the search.

Oliver: Can my wife take our daughter to school so that I can stay back?

Sheriff: Nope, both of you stays. We are investigating an attempted murder and we don't need to remind you of the seriousness of such allegations.

Oliver: We are peaceful people and do not have any idea what you are talking about. You and I have talked about this in your station. I find it surprising that you are still bringing this up and pursuing it any further. My wife and I do not even know the victim.

Philo brought out her cell phone and wanted to call in late to her job but the sheriff took the phone from her, asked her to sit down at the couch quietly until the end of the search.

Oliver went to their dog, which was sitting quietly at a corner and walked it into the balcony and barricaded it away. The Sheriff started the search to every nook and crannies of the house but couldn't find anything that triggers suspicions.

Oliver and Philo were heavily interrogated by the sheriff completely on the circumstances surrounding the attack and injuries on Mr. Stokes. Their hands were physically examined again and nothing was observed. The Sheriff left, after 4 hours of intense search, disappointed. The Winterbrushes were too upset to do anything including taking their daughter to school. They stayed back at home and Oliver called the prefect and detailed him out on the activities in the town. He was instructed to be calm and let the cult deal with all the involved residents of the erring town in their own way.

Life continued normally in Newtown. Phillip was wallowing in his confusions, seething in anger as to the evil that befell his grandpa, and the town seemed to have moved on so soon. The church and sheriff were not ready to give up. The church gathered the community in the park and decided to create placards and lead a peaceful protest in front the Winterbrush residence asking them to leave. The Sheriff was not in support of that but again the community has their rights of free speech. The Sheriff detested the Winterbrush anyways. A procession was organized and picketing was done as planned but the Winterbrush didn't blink. They watched the 3 hour picketing via their surveillance cameras. Pinto as usual was restless but the community later walked away in anger. The cult saw this as a final act of war declared against the Demarkians. The war has now started formally.

* * *

The city of Newtown had a beautiful city hall located at the major prime street of Lincoln Blvd. The Aristorian church and Sheriff's Department were also located in that street. Mr. Stokes' house was located in Lincoln too. It was the major hub connecting other streets in this small, beautiful and formally quiet town. They had a one-hundred-year-old city clock with an inbuilt loud bell donated by one of the last century resident. The bell was strikingly beautiful and worked with perfection. The city regularly serviced the clock for precision time keeping. It rang every hour with the classic bell ringing tone until 10 p.m. everyday. It had a public announcement system built next to it. They were collectively well taken care of. On this fateful Sunday night, the bell sounding twice its volume in decibel went off by 12 midnight non-stop and got the whole city freaking out and yelling, cursing at the city managers. It stopped for 60 minutes to give the impression that the error has been corrected, and went off again at about 2a.m in a deafening sound level. The city manager Mr. Allison heard it and this time decided to run over there and fix the bell. Armed with the small tower key, he drove crazily to the city center, and met with half of the city standing in the area with their hands covering their ears. He quickly opened the tower, climbed up and looked at the bell but everything seemed ok. He was confused as to why the bell was going off at this time of the night. He unplugged the bell from the power socket and the bell chiming stopped. He came down, locked up the door to the bell tower with the two keys and apologized to the residents who were fuming, and that was very bad with the election coming up early next year. He drove off and everyone went to sleep. At about   4a.m. the bell came back alive with the same ferocious ringing like prior. Now, the whole city, including kids, were awake. Everyone except the Winterbrush was confused as to what was going on. The city manager, scared and concerned drove back to the tower again, called his assistant and they both climbed up the tower together to inspect the bell. They got up there and found that the bell still unplugged but was ringing relentlessly. What in the world is going on here?!! The city manager yelled. They climbed down and explained all their discoveries to the crowd who were practically yelling for their heads. The crowds asked them to remove the damned bell and they agreed to do that. They climbed back up and took out the bell and the public announcement systems. The city manager, in the presence of most residents, loaded the bell and the system into his truck and drove off. The tower door was locked up securely and the residents dispersed.

After about an hour, at about 5 a.m., the bell went off again, and few neighbors that were able to sleep woke up and came out to their patios confused, some of them knowing that the city manager removed the bell home. The question was: which bell is now ringing? And why was it ringing when it was unplugged? The city manager from his home heard the ringing and rushed over to where he placed the clock an hour ago but it wasn't there anymore. The public address system disappeared too. He drove back to the city center again and ran into angry mob that threatened to lynch him. He accessed the tower again by opening the doors in the full glare of the residents, took one of the residents to see him dismantle the clock and system. He handed them over to Mr. Emory, an elderly well respected resident. He locked up the tower again and drove off. By 6.15 a.m. in the morning, while Emory had the clock and the system in his possession, the same ringing went off in the tower. Emory panicked, dropped off the clock ran out in front of his house and yelled for neighbors who assembled, saw the clock system, were moping at the clock and the system. While converged there, the daylight started showing gradually and the public address system came on with a deeply demonic laughter and jumbled announcements, in legion, informing the community that they have started a war they will lose. The deep hoarse voice, emitting evil, was stern in informing the residents that the war has started and they should not expect it to end anytime soon. Now, fully daylight, 4 menacing looking crows were seen flying around and towards the residents and there was a stampede as everyone was rushing to enter his or her house and lock the door. Some elderly residents couldn't make it in time but the crows didn't attack them. Some sprained their foot in the stampede.

$$* * *$$

Phillip have not been sleeping well and the activities of the last night and this morning clearly shows that the Winterbrush are evil people and he was determined to find out who they are and why they chose to live in Newtown. Meanwhile, his grandpa had been discharged from the hospital in a vegetative state and he had been assigned a state nurse and caregiver round the clock for one year. Phillip was worried about a lot of things, including folding his prosperous business in Arizona and moving back home to take care of grandpa. He was also concerned how best to approach the challenges of this evil family decimating their beautiful homeland. He was also concerned about the extent of their powers and whether he could withstand it. He came back with unregistered police special. 38 that he bought off the street in Arizona. He oiled the gun and made sure that it was working well. He checked on his military style knife that he stole from the military armory before his discharge. He rekindled his training on suppressing or killing a charging dog or animal as he was taught by a reputable US marine instructor. He brought out his enhanced pepper spray and other combat paraphernalia. He decided that he will pay the Winterbrush a visit and search their home. He monitored their schedule and found out that they worked Monday to Friday, 9 a.m. to 5.p.m., Philo gets home a little late after picking Bridget from school. He monitored them for a week and picked a day to jump into their house and pick their keys. He was also an expert locksmith, having learnt all that in a rescue training exercise in the military. He waited for the day of reckoning. He had decided to handle the evil family and possibly destroy them single handedly. He does not have an inkling about the powers he was planning to confront. The whole of a US Marine squad in combination with the US Navy seal that took out Osama Bin Laden, could not have achieved what he was embarking on. The Demarkians would destroy him in a heartbeat but he doesn't know that.

***

The two Reverend fathers were thoroughly disturbed of the developments in their beautiful quiet town. Fr. Angelus met with Montenegro and the church council were summoned for emergency meeting that lasted for hours, discussing the evil powers that had invaded the community. The church should get involved in prayers and fasting to defeat the satanic forces that was hell bent on destroying them. They agreed to hold a night vigil every Friday from midnight to morning, in prayers and worships. They agreed to start on the next day which was a Friday. The congregation assembled as agreed and started singing and worshipping, praying, binding whatever spirit that was tormenting the town. By 1 a.m. the public address system which had not even been reinstalled came on, with the same ominous sounds of the devil speaking in tongues, laughing deeply and mimicking the songs of worship by the Aristorian church. The whole town went amok, as people woke up and was yelling at the devil. A very heavy wind came on unannounced crescent almost to a tornado level, uprooting some trees in the street, some of the trees smashing into some homes and parked vehicles including that of the church members; followed by a heavy rain in the middle of summer, that lasted for close to 3 hours. The church undeterred continued their spiritual crusade till the next morning. The members with destroyed vehicles were undeterred and their vehicles were towed away. The church promised to seek for donations to replace their vehicles.

This practice continued for another one week but the satanic cult seemed to be winning the war because residents started migrating into neighboring towns for shelter and peace of mind. The Winter-brushes, unperturbed, were living their normal life. They took sleeping pills and ear plugs to enable them sleep at the chaotic nights. The entire town were scared as the peace that they enjoyed were severely disrupted. The evil crows flew around once in a while to let the residents know that they were still being watched. The greatest of it all was that the residents, who hitherto, thought that they were deep in their Christian faith, found themselves failing spiritually.

Phillip decided to carry out his mission tomorrow morning at 10 a.m. He had perfected his wall scaling skills that he also learnt from the military. The Winterbrush lived behind a 7 foot wall but that won't pose any problem for Phillip. On the said time, Phillip, walked carefully to the back street, Olive Street, sat by the tree for a few minutes, made sure nobody was watching him, briskly brought out his emergency military rope already twisted into a ladder and flipped on top of the wall, climbed over and descended into the compound very quietly and pulled down his rope. He walked to the back door, brought out his picking keys and was about to open the door when he started hearing that evil ominous sound again. He was temporarily distracted by it, got a little scared but with the keys anyways, he opened the back door. He wore a soft-padded shoes. He tiptoed into the hallway and behold the giant pinto dog was standing there looking at him, with a little nonchalant attitude. He brought out his gun equipped with a powerful silencer and pepper spray aiming to shoot pinto. The dog got upset, opened its mouth to show its huge fanged tooth, with its hairs standing out, not looking like a regular dog anymore, with eyes that turned blood red, started approaching Phillip. Phillip aimed and fired multiple shots at the dog but the dog stopped and allowed Phillip shoot it more. The dog remained unscathed and was ferociously and briskly coming at Phillip but Phillip ran out of door and jammed the door. Breathing very hard and deeply scared now, he was hoping to get out of there alive. He locked back the door with the keys and turned to run to the fence for escape but ran right into the dog standing few feet away from the him. He was confused as to how the dog got there knowing that he locked back the exit door, and was transfixed in fear as he stood face- to- face with Satan. He accepted at that point that he was going to be killed by this beastly evil. But surprisingly, Pinto just looked at him for few minutes, walked away and disappeared from the other side. Phillip climbed the wall with the rope fearfully and jumped to the street and started running away. On getting home, same two black birds were perched on their patio looking at him and not blinking. He stopped and wanted to run back down the street but the birds flew away quietly.

Phillip ran to the church and relayed all his experiences with the priests. They scolded him seriously, calling his mission juvenile and completely senseless. You couldn't have used your military trainings against the spiritual principalities. The fight is not against flesh and blood but an optimal spiritual warfare that had to be concerted. It was now very clear that the Winterbrush were not humans but satanic agents sent to destroy the city. The only thing that Phillip achieved in this trip was that there was an evil dog that seemed to have much more powers than the birds. The fraternity deliberately decided not to hurt Phillip so that he would inform the community as to what they were up against. Phillip's escapade was shared with the sheriffs who informed him to desist and refrain from such conduct or he would be arrested next time.

In the midnight of today, Mr. Stokes peacefully died in his sleep. Phillip woke up in the morning, went over to hug him, sat and talk to him as usual hoping that he was healthy enough to hear and understand him. He held his hands and felt the coldness. The nurse was sleeping as she could only get a little sleep in the morning before the next shift. Phillip ran over and woke the nurse up and informed her of his findings. They both, very agitated, ran into the room and checked for purse but it was clear that Stokes had passed on. Phillip was devastated and started crying hard and incessantly. He was asking a lot of questions as to why this evil people killed him. Did he have any problem with them? Maybe he discovered their evil activities and challenged them. Stokes was such a fine man that nobody that knew him would hurt him. The coroner's office came and removed him for processing. The church and the whole community, including the Sheriffs were distraught. The whole town assembled in the city center, with the mayor, city officials, the church, and the sheriffs, and the funeral was planned and fixed.

The city hall was repainted and decorated to lay Stokes in state in it. Balloons and flowers were everywhere. Everyone wore white attires, undertakers wheeled the body into the hall, with the entire city hall staffs present, Fr Angelus and Montenegro officiated the death sermon, speeches were made by the sheriffs, the mayor and some city council members. Mr. Stokes jnr. made a resounding tribute for his father. Other family members, brothers, cousins, nieces, nephews, grandchildren, all rendered eulogies. In continuing with the obsequies, Phillip was given an ample time to deliver his eulogy. He did for more than an hour, laid out his life and struggles starting from his primary school up to the military. He continued in his epistle post military and the relentless staunch support he received from the grandpa who turned his life around to a successful man that he is today. He recalled in his tearful speech how he heard about the attack and what he saw when got to Newtown. He relayed his visit to the office of Oliver Winterbrush and detailed out his interactions with the satanic man. He continued to the travails that the whole town had been going through recently and declared it publicly that the Winterbrush were agents of the Satan. He talked about the city clock, the bells, the public address system, the warning issued by Oliver to him in his office, the birds that appeared again in the first morning of the city bell disruptions. He paused, stated that he loved his family and most particularly, grandpa and owed him his life. He paused gain, looked at the chief Sheriff for a quick second and in full detail, informed the whole congregation about his criminal visit to the Winterbrush's home.

The whole crowd was dead quiet as everyone was moping at him for multiple reasons, first his stupidity in relaying a home burglary to crowd that included law enforcements, except that he did not mention telling this to the Sheriff a day before; secondly, his great courage in undertaking such a suicide mission; thirdly, his undying love for his grandpa and his conviction to put his own life on the line in seeking for retribution. He quickly chipped in that he only wanted to find out who the Winterbrush were. He didn't go in when they were around but rather to conduct his own search. He was allowed to get out alive to inform the town who they were really. He relayed the black birds waiting for him at home when he got there and how they flew away. He broke down again and cried profusely and family members led him off the stage.

The casket was closed and wheeled into the hearse and everyone dispersed except family members and others who desired to be part of the brief graveside ceremony performed by Montenegro. Not Surprisingly, a lot of the attendees were present at the graveside to bid stokes final farewell.

At Stokes' home, a repass was done with a lot of foods and beverages donated by church members and family friends. The church held a singing services singing hymns of consolations for the Stokes family. Fr. Angelus made a final speech and the gathering dispersed. The Stokes family, for the first time, sat together, relaxed and exchanged pleasantries. Started talking about their life challenges, their joys and sorrows, kids' educations, who was down and who was up.

Phillip retreated to the back of the house, sat in a quiet corner, fighting tears, in retrospect, reminiscence on his grandpa, the tributes today, a city burial for a non-city official, the outpouring of love by the church and he felt relieved and hoping that he was in a better place. Just as he was about to get up, he looked up at the electric pole in the street and saw one of the crows starring directly at him. He became infuriated again but held himself back and walked into the room.

CHAPTER TWO

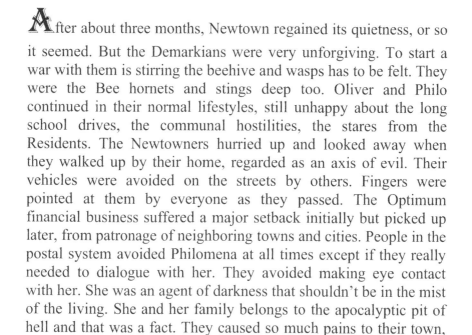

After about three months, Newtown regained its quietness, or so it seemed. But the Demarkians were very unforgiving. To start a war with them is stirring the beehive and wasps has to be felt. They were the Bee hornets and stings deep too. Oliver and Philo continued in their normal lifestyles, still unhappy about the long school drives, the communal hostilities, the stares from the Residents. The Newtowners hurried up and looked away when they walked up by their home, regarded as an axis of evil. Their vehicles were avoided on the streets by others. Fingers were pointed at them by everyone as they passed. The Optimum financial business suffered a major setback initially but picked up later, from patronage of neighboring towns and cities. People in the postal system avoided Philomena at all times except if they really needed to dialogue with her. They avoided making eye contact with her. She was an agent of darkness that shouldn't be in the mist of the living. She and her family belongs to the apocalyptic pit of hell and that was a fact. They caused so much pains to their town, so soon. Oliver experienced the same treatment in his job. Being humans after all, they were concerned and they remained angry. They were not the rubble rousers, the community were. They considered moving out of town to a neighboring town but struck the idea as it portends weakness. Demarkians are stronger than lions and so shall it remain. The big shit will come at the appointed time, as they waited. He who fights and run away will live to fight another time.

Phillip stayed back in Newtown for another month, bought a telescope to monitor the activities of the Winterbrushes but there was nothing much to see or observe. Their home was highly and secretively enclosed. He spotted the dog a few times, just lying by itself unceremoniously. The crows were not seen anymore. Phillip decided that he had to go back to Arizona as soon as possible to continue with his life.

The city bell was reinstalled and the old practice continued. The ran- away residents returned to Newtown. The small businesses picked up. The snag was that the city had a long session and had a proclamation advising the residents to avoid the Winterbrushes in their businesses and in their homes hoping that they would be frustrated and leave their town. The church repeatedly reminded the residents to avoid the Winterbrushes as per the city proclamations and they heeded the injunctions even though they were non-mandatory. Gossips kept on growing in the town as to what brought these evil people in their quiet and peaceful town. A lot of queries and concerns were raised as to whether they have given up or was something brewing? The clergy found the whole thing embarrassing noting that they could not, so far, defeat the evil ones. It was an affront on their faith and their relevance. They were concerned that the residents might have introverted disappointments on their spiritual failures.

The Demarkians were a direct test of their Christian powers and values and they seemed to have failed. Fr. Angelus was deeply troubled about that. He would wake up in the middle of the night to pray, cry and asking God to intervene, to save them and to remove the shame hoisted on them by the travail. His wife and kids, who were visiting from schools, were troubled too and they joined in the spiritual crusade. The peace and tranquility continued but the city's actions and the continued reiterations of that by the church and the community was seen as an act of continued war, by the powerful Demarkian confraternity. They were enraged and they were determined to unleash the fire and brimstone on this stupid and ignorant community. The National leader of the cult was informed and he decided to get involved in the war.

Fr. Montenegro usually sleeps very late because of his midnight prayers and spiritual rejuvenations. This young priest was one of three kids of his parents.

REMINSCENCE: Montenegro was pious from very young age. His attachment to their family church from his catechism age was a little puzzling to the parents. He was so deeply interested in the bible and teachings of Jesus Christ. At the age of 5, he could recount the ten commandments in a minute. He was prone to reminding everyone around him what commandment they were violating by any conduct at any given time. He would always let any listener know that the kingdom of God is real and hell is not a good place to be. In Primary two, he was already preaching to the fellow classmates which violated the school non-secular rules. The parents were called in a few times but it continued and they sent him to a private catholic school which infuriated his dad. The monthly school fees were a strain on the family and this young toddler appears unrelenting. Unlike other kids, he never fought back, reminding his attackers that God is his fortress and will fight all his battles. In fourth grade, a knucklehead student that hated him so much slapped him during a physical education class and he looked at him for a few seconds and turned the other cheek for him.

The teacher who observed that summoned them to the office and asked the attacker why he slapped him and all that he said was that he hated him for so long. The attacker claimed that he should be a kid like all others and play with them. His premature exhibition of wisdom was not resonating well with the school student community. He was not a nerd in its truest form but he was adjudged annoying. In responding to the teacher, Montenegro said that Jesus asked them to turn the other cheek when slapped and that's all he did. When asked about the mosaic law that requires him to rub sand in his hand and slap back the aggressor, he laughed and said that the coming of Jesus was a usurpation of new rule and practices. That the advent of our lord Jesus Christ imposes that old things has gone away and all thing has become new. That new wines are now in the new wineskins and a rejuvenating spirit was born. He looked at the teacher and asked him: do you know how many times that this my brother will slap me before I slap him back? The teacher answered no. He said seventy times seven, which is four hundred and ninety times! By then I should have graduated college. He laughed for a quick few seconds and asked the teacher, do you think that this my brother will beat me to a fight if I engaged him? With all these muscle in my biceps? He pulled up his shirt and showed his tiny biceps, little and flabby. The teacher, in utter amazement, started laughing and was dumbfounded to say anything further. He scolded the aggressor and informed him that he would report his activities to his parents if he touched another student again. He excused them but recalled Montenegro and sat him down. The teacher himself was a seminarian and had an incisive theological inclination. The teacher's interest was in noticing what he considered a biblical proclivity of Montenegro, popularly called Monte. He asked about his family background, their religious inclinations, whether any of his parents was a clergy, which church they attended, where they lived, how he got this early exposure to Christian faith and practices.

Monte, sat down and listened to the questions and intelligently rendered answers to all the queries as follows, backing some of them with biblical quotes. First of all, my grandparents and my parents have never been clergy and they are all still alive. My great paternal grandfather, named Montenegro, was a catechist in a local church. He devoted his time to the church until he died. He desperately wanted to be a reverend father but the lack of school education thwarted that ambition which he regretted till he passed but he vowed to correct it in his next life. He had a noticeable mole at the side of his neck and when I was born, I had and still have the mole at the same exact location. I was named Montenegro after him. According to my father, my grandfather was in town when I was born and he came to the hospital with my father to see me.

When they walked in, I was crying down the ward, as usual. My father, in ecstasy and jubilation of a parent, lifted me up and then my grandfather screamed out and jumped up! Give me the child, hand me my father. He is back, and he exclaimed "Montenegro, my Daddy" and started crying hard in happiness. He started yelling, "welcome back daddy, I love you!!!" He touched my mole and his face lit up. He was incredibly lucky and kept on shouting: oh he said it all through his life that he was going to be back for us, that he will be very educated, deeply into the service of Christ. And that he will be an ardent fisher of men. When the nurse came to shower and feed me, they could not retrieve me from him. He was kissing me and hugging me and calling me his father. He kept on touching my mole and thanking God. He was yelling out that he was going to devout his life and time to serve me as I was a good father to him. He started praying and thanking God for making him see this day. May your kindness and glory to my family stays till the end of time. He stood up and started dancing our traditional Irish song. He kissed my mole and handed me over to my mum. He looked into my mother's eye and called her Grandma and said this to her: "you gave birth to my father. You are now my mother in all intents and purposes. You will never do wrong in my eyes. Goodness and mercy shall follow you till the end of time. Anything that you touch moving forward shall turn to gold. The depth of the ocean or the height of the sky cannot keep your prosperity. I bless you and my son, my father today and forever more. This boy, my father, shall be named Montenegro, without a junior added to the name because he is my father!" All through the day, I was crying but as soon as my grandfather noticed the mole and called me father, I stopped crying abruptly and started laughing heartily, from that day moving forward. The only way to stop me from crying was to call me
"Catechist Monte" and it worked like magic.
Monte continued his story, as relayed to him by his family:
The nurses and other hospital staffs rushed over to observe the spectacles and were crying in joy too, like my parents after they were intimated of what was going on. They jointly sang the hymns extolling God.

Monte pulled his shirt collar aside and showed the mole to the teacher. He continued in the discourse by asking the teacher whether he believed in reincarnation? The teacher was confused for a minute and said no. Monte asked him: do you agree, according to the biblical old testament that Prophet Elijah reincarnated as John the Baptist? As a seminarian, the teacher is supposed to know and understand that but it was a difficult question to answer and he tried to parry it over but Monte wouldn't allow him to. The teacher said yes and that he believed that he was a reincarnated great grandparent. Monte continued by explaining to the teacher that his religious calling was inexplicable to him considering his age. He lamented about the loss of his childhood as a result of that but reminded the teacher that the multitude were called but only few were chosen. Jesus Christ started his evangelism few years into his 30s but I will start earlier, Monte stated. Sometimes, he felt like being a child and play with other kids but he found himself too grown to fraternize with them. He told the teacher that he was expelled from public school as a result of pocket missionary practice few years ago which brought him here but incurred a financial strain on his struggling parents. He was not happy about it and hoped that God would continue in his mercies until he graduates and leave for his priestly trainings. He further informed the teacher that he sleeps by 1 a.m. every day to enable him do the midnight prayers. Of course he inherited his well-preserved Great Grandfather's bible, which remained his greatest possession all through his life. Being awake by midnight was a serious battle with his parents initially but his grandfather got involved by reminding them that Monte was his dead father and that they should leave him alone! Everything Monte was doing was a replication of senior Monte's lifestyle as an adult.

Monte continued: I read the bible a lot and I comprehend my readings a lot too, considering my age. I live and practice the bible and I never planned to deviate from it. I will be a catholic father, intends to obtain a theological doctorate degree. Teacher, I will be a fisher of men, all through my life. When he said that, the teacher developed goose pimples, astonished at this little boy's depth of Knowledge and wisdom. He asked him how he came to know about doctorate degree at such a young age? Monte responded: Teacher, I have said enough here to let you into my world. I am not your regular child as I am endowed with inexplicable knowledge that you can only explain as a mystery of life. I am already developing my doctoral thesis in theology as a loose idea. I am hoping to skip a class and jump into the seventh grade next year. That's why I am doing everything within my powers to maintain my current grade and I will like the school to assist me. I am guarded and guided by the teachings and the divine powers of our Lord Jesus Christ and so shall it remain. When I lived the first time, I couldn't do a lot but I am now back to accomplish all that. So getting slapped by another student, who was being a child of his age, doesn't mean much to me. Kids are always going to be kids not minding how we feel about it. I will try the best I can to mingle with them as my peers but they are not really my peers. I will be treated like pariah because I am not going to be doing the things that they expect of me and hence the attacks and the hates. I am not perturbed Teacher. Jesus Christ, as a prince of peace, represented humility and diligence. He was hated, vilified, tortured and heinously murdered for the salvation of mankind. I am here, back in this world to assist Joseph of Arimathea in carrying that cross through the Golgotha. We live in a world of Golgotha and I am not going to be deterred by the skulls.

Monte graduated and went straight to seven grade Seminarian school, at the age of 11 years. Monte was exceptionally outstanding and continued to dazzle the world. Being a catholic, he vowed not to be married and to devout his entire life in the service of God. He graduated and went to theological college where he continued to excel up to his doctorate degree, on a thesis he developed and nurtured from primary school. His grandfather was still alive when he graduated. The whole family attended his doctoral graduation in style. From his birth, the grandfather took over for all his needs, never scolded him and attended to him with reverence. He could go out of his way to provide Monte's needs. He took him to live with him in Phoenix, Arizona. Called him Daddy all the time and pampered him with all his good desires. He personally drove him to all his schools and picked him back. He bought him flight tickets to and fro anywhere. Monte loved everything that his father liked. He was growing up and looking more like him. His face, laughter, idiosyncrasies, behavior, were a replication of his father's. He was a child of destiny and was fervently protected.

Monte himself seemed, sometimes to remember somethings about his prior life, like a deja vu. Some places looked familiar as well as some activities but he couldn't get a full hang of it. The grandfather would take Monte to the Grand canyons in Arizona which Monte Snr loved, having been there a few times with them as his kids. He loved the beauty, the stone formations, the mountain and ranges of the Grand Canyon. Monte senior believed that the Grand Canyon is the most beautiful thing that God created. He found it breathtaking and astonished by its beauty. He was there a good number times in his life before he died. When Monte junior, called junior only for clarification purposes, was taken there the first time, his grandfather took him to the same exact spots that his father, Monte snr liked, Monte jnr. looked a little disoriented but seemed to remember the place and asked a weird question: grandpa, haven't we been here before? The grandpa answered to him: yes, we had and you brought us here a few times as your kids. Remember when I almost ran and fell over this cliff and you rushed and caught my leg and dragged me back! You were very upset and for the first time, you beat me! We didn't come back here again for a long time until I was older and appreciated danger and you flew us in the viewing helicopter while we were all eating ice cream. Monte asked him: was I wearing a green khaki short pant? And his grandfather started crying again and answered him: Yes, yes, daddy!!! He started hugging him again, kissing him and screaming to everybody's surprise. His grandfather explained to him that he loved the green short pant a lot and that his wife, my mum, bought it for him from a discount store and that she used to tease him about it. He reminded him how much he loved that pant and wore it to all their summer outings and barbeques. He never washed it but rather dry-cleaned it to preserve its color. When it got ripped, you practically re-made it. It had multiple pockets and zippers. You always wore it with your different sandals. You were a very devoted dad to us. Your life was just for us and your church services. Out of the blues, in your late 60s of age, you fell sick… [Grandfather, at this point, couldn't hold back the tears, he cried unrestrained again for a few minutes while being consoled by Monte and others], recollected himself and continued in his story. He informed Monte that he developed this sickness which seemed weird initially but it later turned out to be a liver problem. The family was extremely devastated, most especially your great grandmother, my mother.

We were so scared and troubled, as well as other members of the family. The Doctor informed us that you had only 6 months to live and that was the worst day of my life. I was your first son and you taught me all the virtues of life including Christian values. You provided all my needs and to all of us too. As a father, you never failed in anything. We were there with you, praying for a last minute miracle which never came. You lost a lot of weight and your eyes turned yellow by jaundice, you emaciated almost to a skeleton but you kept your faith always. You were obsessed with the story of Job and you fought the fight and kept your faith. You believed that you have served God as best as you could and that God would heal you at the end. The Hospital took you to a hospice to prepare your death but you remained adamant, continued within the little strength left in you, to preach the word of God, advising us and friends not to mourn you. You explained that death is a cross that we all will carry someday and that it is a transition. You believed that, from the point that you accepted Jesus Christ, you maintained purity of Life and that God will put you in a better place. You admonished us not to relent in seeking and embracing Jesus even at moments of distress. You repeatedly promised us that you will come back and continue from where you stopped. You vowed that you will get your doctorate and that you would be a priest, not catechist anymore and you laughed. You looked into my life and said: my son, I love you more than you will ever know. I will be with you till the end of time. When I get to haven, I will beg God to protect my family. If reincarnation is true, I will seek to come back to your lineage. You said to me: you are my oldest child, please remember that you are now the new sheriff in town and that you should follow my footsteps and be a good shepherd. If I come back, you will see my neck mole in the exact same location. He died few weeks later and was buried with fanfare. The devastation was incredible to all of us but we were consoled by who he was, the life he lived and the stellar legacies he left behind. My Grandfather promised to tell me more as we live and he did.

Rewound to his prior dialogue with teacher, at this point the Teacher was completely freaked out and couldn't know what to make of this young oddly-intelligent young man but he got an insight into who he was now. The school bell rang; break was over as students filed back into the class. The student that slapped Monte came back to apologize and Monte was thrilled and hugged him tightly and whispered to him, God bless you my brother. The teacher was further puzzled!

The class continued and school dispersed. A test was done and Monte scored very high as usual. The teacher asked him to explain the essay that the class was tested on. Monte boldly and confidently stood in front of class and made a wonderful presentation of the essay, to the amazement of the whole class and the school principal who was in the class by accident and decided to watch. This little boy appeared to be a better teacher than the adult teachers. His elucidation and comprehension was mind-boggling. Monte was churning out examples and demonstrations to support and explain the purports of the essay. Being a fellow student, he was able to connect with the students faster.

When the school dispersed, the principal had a meeting with the teacher about Monte. The teacher laid out everything he knew about the boy. His parents were invited to school and a full positive discussion about the boy were held. With the approval of the parents, Monte was made the official school valedictorian.

Fast-forward to Newtown, Monte, as a priest continued in his devotions. He was troubled by the ugly incidence happening in this town and church he came to love so much. Sometimes, he held vigils and prayed from midnight to daybreak. He cried out to the lord to take over and heal the town.

This night, he went to sleep by 3 a.m. and had a troubling dream about Newtown. In the dream, he saw the entire Newtown in total darkness, citizens trapped into their homes, in awe and fear, city surrounded by what looked like an oceanic waters and mountains trapping the residents in. There were beastly beings, ugly to the core, some of them very gigantic, dogs with fangs, cats with fangs, black crows and ravens with more than usual beaks, all animals have bloodshot eyes and menacing. The beasts were seen roaming the city and seemed firmly in control.

Wind and rainfalls were incessant and seemed to be choking the city. There were very heavy rains, trees were uprooted, fell on houses, vehicles and destroyed them, as has happened before. This huge beast, devil itself, seemed very vicious and upset, growling loudly, with creepy and loud ominous music which were heard in the darkness of the city. Children were crying for help but the parents who were very subdued, couldn't help them. The Winterbrushes were the only occupants of the city living well with electricity and their compound remained unaffected. They were seen laughing, jubilating and doing a victory lap. The church building took a big hit as the building was damaged by what looked like a tornado mishap. There were endless thunders plummeting the already desolate town. His own building started vibrating so hard that he woke up sweating heavily and exclaimed: No! Satan is a liar! Started praying hard for an hour, stopped and looked over to Fr. Angelus section, found out that he was still up, called him and they started praying together.

On this beautiful summer evening in Newtown, the weather was excellent and fine. Everyone was out having fun and sunbathing. The sun sets by 8 p.m. every day and sometimes, beyond that. By about 7.45 p.m., Ms. Ruth, was taking a walk with his dog and her two small daughters in the park. Initially they didn't see anyone and was giggling around the park, doing run and catch with their dog. It started getting a little dark and Ruth noticed that her daughters were waiving at something with fixated looks. She looked over and up on the hilly end of the park, she noticed two well-kept beautiful kids, with noticeable blue eyes, even from that distance, which Ruth found odd, dressed impeccably in white and clean sandals. Ruth walked up to her kids and inquired who the kids were? Were the kids in this part of the park before? They answered no, and that they just noticed them now. Do you know where they walked out from? The kids nodded that they didn't know and stated that they just saw them now. Did you see them with their parents or any adult? The kids answered in the negative. Ruth continued to get more puzzled and she looked up to see that the kids were still there smiling and waving at them. The kids were beckoning on Ruth's kids to come over to their side of the park. Ruth taught about walking over to the kids to inquire as to who brought them to the park.

Ruth looked around for her dog which was playing with another dog further down away from them and completely oblivious of what was going on. The dog has not been taken out for few days because of the busy schedule of Ruth's family. Ruth called the dog, decided to walk over there with the kids to meet with these beautiful but odd kids who could come to the park without any adult supervision and it was getting dark too! Her mother's instinct kicked in and she called on her dog again and shouted at it to come. The dog ran over to her, looked up and saw those kids and hell broke loose. Ruth grabbed it by the neck to stop it from running over to attack the kids. Ruth hung the leach on her dog, held it strongly, beckoned on her kids and they started walking over to meet the kids on the hilly side of the park. The kids stayed and waited for them until they got to about 300 yards, the kids started walking towards the shrub located near the park. Ruth was yelling at them to stop but they didn't. Ruth's kids were walking faster to meet up with these mystery kids who kept walking away from them. At this point their dog was completely cuckoo and was barking abnormally hard and unrestrained. The dog stopped making any effort to chase after the kids but was barking and looking frightful. Ruth, surprised, was still walking faster to meet the kids who walked into the shrubs and disappeared. Ruth got to the shrubs and the looked beyond the cleared rear of the shrubs and the open field there but she didn't find the kids. She was perplexed as to their whereabouts. Even if they were to have walked into this shrub, they could still be seen in the open slope which flattened as a field fifty feet away. She looked into the shrub but they were not there. At this point, her dog had stopped barking and stopped looking frightful. Ruth was confused more and became frightened, hurried her kids and dog to her car and drove home. When she got home, she informed her husband and family of her experiences today at the park and everyone brushed it aside believing the kids may have been nearby residents and may have dashed back home, you know, kiddies' mischief.

✳✳✳

Ms. Thompson having worked extra hours was rushing home to eat and take some over the counter sleep aid and get a good all-night sleep having been so busy in the office lately. She woke up very early and slept late to catch up with some work and earn her due promotion. There was an accident on the freeway that backed up the traffic bumper to bumper. It was so frustrating as she really wanted to be home and take a hot shower. It took forever for the highway patrol to come over and clear the road. Ms. Ruth ran into another gridlock two miles before her exit because of a road construction that has been going on for few weeks. She exclaimed to the workers, one mile away: stupid, can't you people do this in the midnights till morning? How long do we have to go through this? We need to get home to our families, dumb- dumb. She was frustrated. Eventually, she exited and continued driving home more relaxed but still anxious. Now, it was 8.30 p.m. and it was dark and quiet. She is used to flashing her long beam headlight intermittently in the nights to see what might be ahead before she gets there. She did this night and saw a baby, about 9 years old, by the side of the road and when she drove closer, she had a closer look at the baby, with blue eyes, neatly dressed, sat on the roadside in the pitch darkness, and was crying for help. Thompson slowed down, stopped, wound down her side window and asked the child who she was and what she was doing there at this time of the night? Where are your parents? How did you get here? The child could only be nodding, looking depressed and seeking for sympathy.

Thompson was momentarily confused, wanted to exit the car but something was holding her back. No other vehicle was passing and all you could see were pitch darkness as there was no functional street light until the next 500 yards. The insects were crying louder here and the frogs were screaming from a little lake nearby. You could hear the sounds of the nocturnal birds singing in the creepy quiet night. Ms. Thompson really wanted to get home but what of this child, she thought. A wild animal could devour her here as an easy dinner. She frantically searched for her phone, got it out of her purse by spilling her junky purse on the front passenger car seat, took the phone which was almost running out of juice and called 911. They answered, thank goodness! and Thompson relayed what she was seeing there. The 911 asked a lot of questions, including any other adult or parent, age of child, color of dress, exact location, what the child was doing except the cries, was the child able to answer any question? Height of child but child was sitting though; cross street; distance of any nearest home which is up to half a mile; was the child making any effort to walk to the car? answer was no. The operator was also talking to the nearest police squad patrol officers seeking that they get to the place as a rapid response. Thompson heard a siren coming about two miles away, left her information with the dispatcher, stayed a few more minutes watching the kid and drove off. She got home and forgot about the incidence or whatever you might call that.

The highway patrol officer pulled up a few minutes later and saw the child, called in that he had located the said child and will drop her off at the station and continue in his patrol.

Officer Bezos, a 10 -year veteran of the force, very efficient and dedicated, did his police work with love and compassion, an ex-US Army reserve, who decided to serve the community more by joining the police force including the high way patrol unit. He was an officer badge #942.His shift would finish by 12 midnight today and he was to embark on his long overdue vacation with his lovely wife and two sons in 2 days. He was a happy man and he loved his wife and kids dearly. He remembered when his boys were toddlers and how he used to play with them. He desired to have a daughter, daddy's girl, thought about how he would spoil her, learnt to braid hair so he could be doing that. He cherished the thought of when he could have her own daughter and the joy became overwhelming as he beamed with happiness. He prayed all the time for it and do prayer points on it too. He and his wife have been working on that and hoping that it would happen someday.

He pulled up in his police squad car, saw the girl and was surprised as to what she was doing there at this time of the night. He left his police car engine running, with the overhead lights circling. The whole environment was pitch dark, deeply scary and troubling. A wild animal could spring out and attack anyone here, especially with the recent sighting of bears and a mountain lion around this area. He quickly called the station and asked if anyone had reported a missing child and the answer was negative. He described the child to the operators, her dress, demeanor, and it conformed with what Thompson saw and reported. He walked closed to the girl and exclaimed, awwwww, you poor, very beautiful thing! Where is mummy or daddy? Who left you here, oh lord, stop crying, its ok. I will get you some chicken nuggets and take you home sweetie, its ok. Common, give me your hands but the girl stopped crying and was looking at him fixatedly, didn't extend her hands to him but became a little menacing. In a deeply evil and demonic hoarse voice, the girl, whose eyeballs suddenly turned bloodshot red, queried the officer:
"What are you doing here? Are you stupid? I am legion; I am Satan; I am that I am, the Lucifer himself. You are not very wise. I will devour you as a sacrifice to myself; I control the earth; I control your soul". Bezos was deeply scared and transfixed on his legs. He has heard of demons but never believed it or came in contact with any. He reached for his gun but found out that he left it in the car! The devil screamed at him: you think that your gun can kill me? You are more senseless than I thought. In a flash, the

devil stood up, with red blood eyes, turned into a half man, half lady, his fingers turned into a dagger- like object as she rushed over to Bezos and plunged the ten knife-like fingers in him, bit him on the neck at the same time and sucked up all his blood like a vampire. With a mouth full of blood, the demon started laughing and walked a few feet and disappeared. Bezos laid stone dead with all his intestines and entire gut spilling out of his stomach and a huge gashing wound on his neck. His radio was still on and the car engine running. Calls were being made to him from the station and the field but he was not responding. 911 called: 942, are you there? Did you pick the child?

please 10/4 urgently. We need you on an accident scene with a GBI, please come through. 942, are you ok? Still no response. They thought that maybe he slept off having been working hard in readiness for his vacation. They left him for another 30 minutes.

Later, Smith, an uber driver was going home after 19 hours shift in three counties. While driving on this desolate road this night, he saw a police car not parked very well but not surprised as they always violate all parking rules and regulations unperturbed. He drove close, and noticed that it was a marked highway patrol squad vehicle. The driver's door was open; the lights were on without the siren but the overhead lights were circling in full beam. Vehicle was vacant but the headlights were in full glare. There was no accident, so why is the car here? he thought out aloud. He slowed down, drove very closed and stopped and his jaws dropped as he saw the officer lying on his side dead, his uniform heavily soiled with blood which was still gushing from the open wound on his neck and the stomach and entire gut hanging all out. He pulled out his phone but it was dead as he forgot to charge it. He lives 8 miles away and he decided to rush home and call 911. He was so scared that he quickly ran back into the car but he couldn't find his key. He dropped it when he stepped out of the car to get closer to the officer. He was too scared to get out of his car which he locked himself in. The whole area was in creepy darkness and a police officer was killed gruesomely here. Who or whatever killed the officer may still be lurking in the bush somewhere. He mustered courage, ran out of his car, looked around and saw his keys, ran over and picked it up and raced back into his car. His hands were so shaky but he was able to start his car and raced home, violating every traffic rule to get home. He was very agitated and frightened. He got home in the longest ten minutes of his life, parked his car in the garage, walked into his dark sitting room still shaky. The memory of the pitch-dark environment, the ambience of the area where the officer laid, like what you see in a Dracula movie, would live with him forever.

Smith knew he would seek for counselling later but he was presently out of it as his brain needed a reset. He hurriedly plugged his phone waiting for 3 minutes and it came on. He dialed 911 and held the phone in his ear cursing because it wasn't connecting. He put the phone down and threw some tantrums in frustrations and anger. After a prolonged two minutes, he picked up the phone to dial again and found out that he never pushed the send button. Call connected and he relayed all that he saw to the 911 operator. He could hear the flurry of activities at the background as the operator was announcing "officer 942 down in a possible 187". He didn't understand what that means but he could hear and sense distress police responses from different police units, sirens were all going off rapidly and he could hear helicopters starting to buzz. The moment, expectedly, was very tense and scary. The operator held him on the line for a few more minutes and let him go. The operator thanked him and strongly advised him to stay away from the crime scene. Within the next one hour, the news was all over the whole tv networks and CNN. Smith turned on his television and saw the officer's body in body bag being removed into an ambulance, a lot of police squad vehicles, with full blowing sirens, scene cordoned off from half a mile. Helicopters in the air, including Channel 7 news. It was a very horrible development in a small city that has never been noticed for anything. Smith was very worried, like everyone else how Newtown has become an axis of evil things. He was waiting for the police visits and stayed awake, knowing that they would call him.

Meanwhile, Ms. Thompson slept off heavily and had no knowledge of what was going on in a scene that she started. Her phone kept going off but it was fully silenced as she does before she slept every night. At some point, all her family members slept off before the event came on television. At about 12 midnight, a knock was heard on the door but Thompson was in a lala land to hear the knock. Her husband heard it and opened the door to see two police vehicles in their front yard and some officers standing at the door. He walked outside to meet them. They apologized for the late visit, confirmed that this is Thompson's residence and inquired about his wife. She took some sleeping pills and dozed off and she needed the sleep. Officers thanked him and asked if she did mention seeing a little stranded girl today few miles out?

Husband said yes that she did inform the family of it during dinner. Husband expressed dismay how irresponsible some parents could be, leaving some toddlers to roam the streets in the night. He asked the officers whether the involved parents were found and the kid returned to them. He continued to ramble and stated that the parents should be stripped of the custody of their children and be punished. He was dismayed more by the location where the child was abandoned. The officers were watching and listening to him go off and off. They informed him that the officer sent at that scene was brutally killed and no child was located at the scene. The body of the officer have been removed to the mortuary. The place was now being processed as a crime scene as they spoke. They were there to talk to Ms. Thompson who called 911 to assist in the investigation of what appeared very puzzling to everyone. The officer, that was murdered acknowledged multiple times, of seeing the little girl as described by your wife. That was the last communication before he was mulled to death in a bizarre form.

The officer asked him to bring his wife to the station in the morning for a dialogue as they won't want to disrupt her sleep and they all drove off. Mr. Thompson confused, poured himself a big glass of cognac, sat down to process what these were all about. Is his wife in trouble; is she an accessory to the murder of an officer? What in the world is going on here? Why is his family involved in this craziness? In Newtown of all places? What is this town turning into? He turned the television on, switched to CNN and saw a breaking news, the killing was all over the news; Newtown is buzzing with press everywhere. The crime scene was heavily inundated by different departments of police units; the District Attorney of the county was there himself. One of the finest police officer killed in this middle of nowhere in a senseless manner. Is this a serial killing? But serial killers are not Dracula that sucks out blood of his victims. He stayed awake and continued to watch the news as it evolved. He was deeply disturbed knowing that the news media will soon be flooding his house and putting his family in these whole saga. His wife is a very private person and most likely will be depressed by this news. He walked over to their bedroom but she was heavily asleep. He walked back to the sitting and continued to watch the news. He learnt also that a passerby observed the dead body and called police. He wondered who it was, poor soul. He was caught up in a lot of thinking and he couldn't sleep. He stayed awake until very early in the morning when he slept off.

Smith couldn't sleep either. He was troubled of what he learnt in the television. This fine gentleman, a dedicated officer, mauled like this? Who killed him? Why? Was it a wild animal? Was it a serial killer? But look at his neck and tooth marks that doesn't appear human. He was as puzzled as the Thompsons. He tried to sleep but couldn't. He gave up and accepted his faith. His phone rang and it was a homicide detective from the sheriff station. He was asked to come over to the station in the morning to ask for Det. Godwin. He wanted to know why but all that they could tell him was that it was in relation to the murdered officer last night. He was not a suspect but needed to help them in the investigation. They thanked him for his civic help and hung the phone. Smith's confusion increased and he was troubled about these whole thing. Is he now a suspect, not minding their assurances? Was he supposed to have passed and go home as if he didn't see anything? Did he violate any law by walking on the crime scene? A lot of an unanswered questions. He felt very sad and deeply sympathetic to the dead officer. The street is tough and a lot of people don't seem to understand that.

As an Uber driver, he came close to being shot by drunken passengers twice. It is a tough world, a cat -eat -cat world, where vanities are pursued as if it is the end of the time. Man is wolf to man and humanity is full of evils. The things that mankind do to each other is unfathomable. Man to man is so unjust as sang by Bob Marley, very true. The bible said that the heart of man is wicked but I will add malicious too. How could this officer be hacked to death like this? What were his sins? What about his family and the agony inflicted on them by his loss? Does it really matter to world of evil? World of sorrows where humanity derives joy in the decadence of others. Life could be so unkind but we need to move forward. May the soul of the dead officer rest in peace. He vowed to assist in any way he could in catching the killer. He went into his bedroom, turned off the light and laid down, hoping that at some point he will doze and of course he did sleep off, dreamt of the event of last night.

✳✳✳

Ms. Thompson had a very good sleep, woke up in the morning refreshed, called her job and took the day off to rest more. She made some breakfast for the family but the husband was still sleeping which she found unusual because he was usually an early bird. The kids were still sleeping but she knew that they will wake before the food gets ready, or rather the aroma will jolt them out of beds. She wanted to turn the television to listen to the morning news but changed her mind. She went in to check on her phone and saw a bunch of missed calls from very late last night. She was puzzled as to who could be calling her that night. She listened to her voice messages and realizes that the calls were from the sheriff station. She was alarmed and she ran in to check on her entire family and felt very relieved. She continued to listen to the voicemails and kept getting the same messages a few more with a troubling urgency in the voice of the caller. She wanted to return the call but kitchen duty call took her away. She took few steps towards the kitchen and the same number called her again but with a man's voice.

Caller: This is Newtown sheriff station. Is that Ms. Thompson speaking?
Ms. Thompson: Yes, it is. I just checked my cell phone voicemails and found out all your prior calls. I was getting ready to call you people back. I am troubled by the frequency of the calls, coming from the law enforcement. Is there any problem, sir?
Caller: Hmm, there is a problem maam. You called 911 last night about a stranded little girl in highway 21 a little late last night, remember that?
Ms. Thompson: Yes, I did. What about?
Caller: The responding officer to the scene was gruesomely murdered in a weird manner. Another passing driver saw the crime

scene and called us in. Do you mean you haven't watched television since last night? Oh, it's been going viral in all the television major networks. We will need to see you at the station for a chat. We left a message with your husband last night. He didn't give you the message?

Ms. Thompson: what? My husband is still sleeping. You guys came here?

Caller: Yes, some squad cars went to your house but you were heavily asleep and they spoke with your husband and informed him of what happened with a message asking you to come into the station. We didn't see you and we decided to call again. The case is being handled by Detective Godwin and he is expecting you this morning. We are sorry for bothering but you know the old police work. This case has garnered national or even world attention and we need to handle it with utmost circumspection.

Ms. Thompson: Am I a suspect?

Caller: Oh no, you are not! you are just being sought to help us more in analyzing what you saw and circumstances surrounding the girl and her distressed situation. We want to extract as much information as possible to be able to investigate this heinous murder. It was only you and the passing driver who saw the deceased officer that were percipient witnesses to the event before and after the death of the officer. Your civic assistance, which you have already started will be heavily appreciated. Again, you are not a suspect or a person of interest.

Ms. Thompson: So, I don't need to bring an Attorney with me?

Caller; No. You don't have to. You are good.

Ms. Thompson: So, what happened to the officer?

Caller: We don't know anything except that he is dead and his body has been removed.

Ms. Thompson: What type of injury did he sustain?

Caller: We will not reveal that to anyone, old police work, maam.

Ms. Thompson: Rushing over to the sitting room to turn the television on, agreed to be in the sheriff station in the next two hours.

Thompson turned on the television and the CNN breaking news confronted her. Listening to the news anchor, she was jolted about what she was hearing. Everything was puzzling to her. She switched the channel to the local station and the same news was there. They, repeatedly, were showing a picture of a uniform dead highway officer with his body massively covered in blood. The news said he was attacked when he tried to rescue a stranded kid called in last night by a good Samaritan who was passing by and saw the child stranded. She kept getting more confused about this whole story. Was it the parents of the child that killed him? Why would they want to go that far? Was the child a bait?

The thought of that made her shiver remembering that a force held her back when she wanted to exit the car! She remembered a dream she had a few weeks back where she was trapped in car for no just reason. She couldn't open her parked car to get out.
She sat in the air-conditioned car for a little longer but the doors were not opening. She was forcing the door handle to loosen up and open, then her lovely dead mother appeared standing next to the door, signaling to her to stop her efforts and drive off. On seeing her mum, she desperately wanted to exit the car now to hug her mum but she still couldn't open the door. Her mother smiling, started backing away from the car, smiling and telling her to leave. She woke up a little disoriented, thought about it for a little while and concluded that it was a stupid and meaningless dream. She brushed aside the dream and forgot all about it. She even forgot to share that with her husband. It was that infinitesimal and baseless to her.

She now related that dream to last night and started perspiring more. She really wanted to open the door and go over to the little girl but something held her back. If the little was a bait, what was to be achieved by that? Why involving an innocent little girl? Whose child could that be? Why in this little inconsequential city occupied mostly by poor civil servants, a lot of them retired. What the hell is going on in Newtown? She waited a little while more for her husband to wake up and take her to meet with the sheriffs but he was so much out of it. Her kids were still sleeping when she freshened up and left to meet with Det. Godwin. She drove towards highway 21 but half a mile to the crime scene,the road was taped off and blocked with a detour sign directing drivers to another street. Feeling frustrated, she drove via the detour street down to the sheriff station. On getting there, she rushed over to meet with the detective who was fervently waiting for her.

Thompson approached the desk officer and introduced herself and indicated that she was there to see Det. Godwin. She was ushered into his office. Det. Godwin, stood up and shook hands with her and thanked her for honoring the invitation. They both sat and the talks started. Ms. Thompson, genuinely concerned, asked what was all these about? Because she has not been able to make any sense out of the whole drama. The detective asked her to relay what she saw last night, in relation to the crime scene, which she must also had seen on the television.

Ms. Thompson detailed out what she saw up to the point when she drove home. Every other thing beyond that were information she got from the television, like anyone else. She asked again, what happened last night. Det. Godwin, a 16- year homicide veteran from Washington DC who was specially asked to come in, flew in immediately last night and took over the investigation. He told Ms. Thompson that after her call last night, the nearest officer that they could get to retrieve the child was a highway patrol officer, Mr. Bezos, and he was dispatched to bring the child to the police station and continued in his patrol. Bezos got over there and saw the child just like you reported. Bezos called in multiple times that he was approaching the child, described her and it fitted exactly how you saw her. He walked over to pick the crying child up and turned up dead. Ms. Thompson asked, how and why? How did he die? The officer looked at her for a few seconds and quietly answered her: if we know how he died, we won't be calling you or inviting you here.

This is a needle in the haystack kind of case. We have absolutely no clue why someone could muster enough courage to heinously kill a law enforcement officer like they did knowing that the government will throw out all the necessary resources to find the culprits. Detective continued, it is not usually out of practice to reveal what we have to any person of interest but honestly, you and the passing driver, are not considered persons of interest and I will show you why. He pulled out a drawer and picked some pictures and handed them to Thompson, who looked at the pictures and reacted as if she wanted to puke, gasping for breath. Thompson yelled out: what is this?!! What happened to the officer? How could anyone do this to another person? Det. opined and stated that the injury may not have been caused by human being. He brought out another picture with a closer shot to the neck and explained to Thompson that the officer's blood was sucked out entirely from that huge gash wound in the neck. We have done a preliminary finger print match and it is not showing to be a human fingerprint. The dentition marks were checked out too and they are not showing to be either a human or any animal.

The FBI have a full equipped animal lab identifier in Indiana and this were sent over to them this morning. The saliva was also checked out and same result were returned. So whatever attacked and killed the officer was not a human and it was not an animal. The mystery deepened with these revelations. The stomach was severely damaged by ten finger- like forks, spilling out the intestines. A forensic test by two different pathologists showed that the objects has hairs in them, were fingerlike because a finger broke off and lodged in the stomach. An analysis of the nail and the hairs showed that the officer was not killed by any human or animal. More tests are being ran in other FBI labs and we will inform you of the outcomes. Det. Godwin thanked Thompson again and dismissed her.

Ms. Thompson left the office more confused than when she got in. The jigsaw puzzle increased and she was wondering whether it would ever fall in place. She was driving, rushing home to share this with her husband. When she got home, everyone had just barely woken up and looking hungry but that was the least thing in her mind. She sat her husband and the kids down and detailed them out about her visit to the sheriff and the whole discussions. She was deeply troubled. Looking at the tv without actually seeing it, Ms. Thompson was full of thoughts. Was this a demon at work?

She remembered the city clock incidence, as well as the dead Mr. Stokes. Could this be related to the same evil war declared on the city?

She did a lot of thinking but the whole thing was a cyclical foolhardiness. The dead officer doesn't have anything to do with evil forces and he may not even be resident in Newtown. But what about that beautiful girl? How could she be evil? She looked like a normal child with a normal baby cry! But why would she be there at that time of the night? Why didn't she walk away home or to some house? Why did her mum appear in her dream to save her for that night? Why was the force holding her back in her car? A lot of an unanswered questions. The thought of the darkness, the creepiness of the entire area brought out the chills in her. Ms. Thompson not being a very religious person had nothing more to do than to relax as her family adopted the same attitude and waited.

$$***$$

Smith woke up and saw that the news was still going viral in the television. He took a shower, checked his messages and went to meet with Det. Godwin who received him just like he did with Ms. Thompson. Their discussion virtually went same way and he was dismissed. Smith was troubled greatly by the pictures that he cried for a while in his car. He managed to drive home but it was so bad and torturing. When he got home, he kept on seeing the same story in the television that he decided not watch the tv in the next few days.

$$***$$

The Aristorian church and the Catholic Church were watching the activities in Newtown with renewed interest. In this church service today, Fr Angelus had decided that a greater part of their sermons and preaching today will dwell on the killing of the police officer a few days ago. The church started and the father cleared his throat and informed the congregation about his concerns as the latest tragedy in their small town. He asked the congregation about the news and whosoever have not heard of it. Some members said that they have seen the news but it looked like they had a serial killer in their midst. Some other opined that it may be a wild animal that has escaped from a private zoo. The priest asked them to explain why a wild animal will use a human being as a bait? Why would a serial killer use a beautiful small girl as a bait? Both scenarios didn't add up. Yesterday, Fr Angelus, who knew Det. Godwin from back in the days in Washington, paid him a visit over the case and felicitated with him, thanking him for accepting to help with the investigating the case, knowing his deep expertise in homicide issues. The detective firmly informed him that the officer was not killed by any human being or animal, showed him the pictures as well the forensic pathological reports. So Fr Angelus broke that to the listening parishioners who breathed out airs of exasperations, with gaping mouths.

A lady parishioner looking awed, stood up and asked Fr Angelus: did you say that the girl was blue eyed, wearing a neat white dress by the road side? And the father answered yes. The lady excused herself, went outside to make some calls. She called Ms. Ruth and fortunately she answered her call. The lady informed her about the issue that they were deliberating in the church now and invited her to come in and relay what she told her a few weeks. Ms. Ruth wouldn't have bothered to restate that but she saw this as an opportunity for vindication. Ruth was going for an appointment and was sitting waiting for the time to come up. She dashed out of the house and got to the church in time. She saw the lady friend, greeted her and they both sat at the back. The lady raised up her hand again and was allowed to air her view. She sought the church's permission to allow Ruth to address the church which was granted. Ruth was called to the podium to address the congregation; She greeted everyone and laid it out that she was only here for one reason, vindication. Her family did not believe the story that she was about to tell now but she was after all not goofy as she was teased by her family. She started; few weeks ago, I was at the park with my kids and our dog and…

When she finished the story, the whole church, including the priests, were jolted and now confronted with the stark reality that they were dealing with multi-faceted demonic attacks. Fr. Angelus yelled to the congregation, that they were dealing with a war of principalities that had started recently. Now, everything that the Detective told him started making sense. The officer may have been killed by a demonic beast that wanted to make its presence known by leaving pieces of evidence including the beastly nails that broke off inside the guts of the dead officer, the furs and the marks.

The church started praying for salvation and redemption. When they dispersed, Angelus called over Godwin for a dinner and a further clue to the murder. Godwin was ecstatic and rushed over to hear him out. When they sat down, shared some glasses of red wine and the discussion directly started as to the killing of the officer. Fr. Angelus gave a full narration to the detective about what has been going on here in the city in the last few months, the Winterbrushes, the attacks, the killing of Stokes which resembled this officer's killing, the evil dog, the dream of Monte, on and on. The same girl observed by Ruth that disappeared in front of Ruth was the same girl that Thompson saw. We are dealing with demonic powers, my brother, Angelus yelled out to Godwin. You are going to discover that this is not about fresh and blood but satanic principalities which is not going to relent. Godwin was confused for this revelation. This was not what he was going to put in his report but it appeared to be the truth. If he issued any such report, he will be retired forthwith and be sent to a mental home for God knows how long, as part of his retirement benefit. He remained dumbfounded throughout the rest of the night. He rushed off his wine and drove back to the hotel more disoriented than when he came here. He later drove to the office to review the report again.

Every jigsaw fell in place, especially after he spoke with Ruth himself. The question is how he was going to pursue this quagmire. He later went to sleep, scared himself. He called Thompson in the morning and invited her back to the office. Thompson came over and Godwin informed her about Ruth experience and gave Thompson Ruth's number.

The next day, Thompson called Ruth for a meeting and they later met that afternoon, exchanged their experiences. Thompson started firmly and formally confirming that the child was evil and not human. If she had gone to retrieve her like she wanted, she would have been killed by the same demon, feigning to be a child, that killed the officer. She started thanking her mother for saving her and prayed for the repose of her beautiful soul. She extolled her mum for protecting her in life and in death. Ruth started crying, with the reality that they were faced with unleashed demonic forces in their small city that held nothing. They started calling on God to intervene and send the Winterbrushes away from their city. They dispersed as friends and promised to be in touch.

✳✳✳

Fr Angelus had a meeting with Monte and they decided to have an all -night crusade by the side of road close to the Winterbrushe's residence. It was going to be a night of worship, with white candles, all members having done dry ten -hour food abstinence fast. They would sing the hymns all through the night like they did before, invoking the Holy Spirit to come down and destroy the evil occupants across the street. They assembled by 10 p.m. and started their crusade. Everybody wore white garments. They started with our Lord's Prayer in chorus. Holy water was sprinkled, some of the sprinkled waters reaching to the gate of the Winterbrush residence.

Inside their house, Philo and Oliver were watching the surprising development from the cameras, as usual. They called the sheriff office to report the nuisance in front of their home but the sheriffs hung the phone on them as soon as they knew who they were. They called again but the sheriff advised them to leave their town and hung the phone. Oliver called the prefect and he was asked to lay low and leave the fight that is raging. He was assured of a full protection to his entire family by the brotherhood. The prefect promised him that they would take out Fr. Angelus soon for his recalcitrance. The crusade raged throughout the night till early in the morning and they dispersed. Fr. Angelus was clearly seen walked over to the gate and sprinkled holy oil and water at the gate and inside the compound murmuring binding prayers. A black crow appeared from nowhere and perched at the gate pillars avoiding coming in contact with the sprinkled holy water. Father Angelus started yelling a command at the evil bird but it stayed there watching him for some time and then flew away. The battle line is drawn and Angelus knew that.

Newtown was still in the middle of summer, with a prolonged sunshine that now extends to 9 p.m. daily. Rainfall was months away. Tonight, the sun set at 7 pm and the whole inhabitants were surprised about that but they have accepted the weather as it came. Everyone was at home after watching the exciting Superbowl match between the Chief and New England Patriots. By 8 p.m., the weather started looking gloomy and a little bit afterwards, there was heavy thunder that ushered in a devastating rainfall that was torrential and frightening. It increased in tempo with a high wind that started blowing off roofs of some homes. The rain turned almost like a tornado and was very ferocious. Electric poles were uprooted and lights went out in some areas. Monte remembered his dream, got concerned, used his flashlight to locate his bible and started praying.

Fr. Angelus was out visiting some parishioners and Detective Godwin who was to leave town tomorrow. He drove back home into his parish compound, pulled up, started fizzling for his flashlight to scoop up his books, umbrella and his bible. The wind was increasing in ferocity and the rain became more torrential. There were some beautiful giant eucalyptus and oak trees in the church compound. The wind pulled out one of the biggest tree located just next to where Fr Angelus parked and smashed the tree into his car and crushed the car to less than half of its size, killing Angelus instantly. The rain continued to wreck more havoc in the town. The electricity nearest to the Winterbrushes, oddly, wasn't affected and they had lights all through the ordeal. That doesn't require any explanations. The whole town was heavily flooded and the connecting small bridge to the neighboring town of Arlington collapsed and got washed away by flood. The rain stopped in the morning. Angelus wife was very worried and did not see her husband pulled in when he did last night.

She didn't even know who to call that night. When it was morning, she stepped out and saw the wreck of her husband's car, she screamed out and Monte came out and both of them rushed over to the car while calling 911. Ambulance came in few minutes as well as the sheriff on duty. There were screaming and yelling. They peeped into the car and saw the outline of Angelus body decapitated by the tree. The fire service was called in and they were running a little late. When they came, they used the saw machine and cut open the car and retrieved whatever that was left of Fr Angelus. Neighbors have now converged and were all wailing when Angelus' body was retrieved. The ambulance took the body away and the sheriff spoke with his wife and Monte briefly and left for now. The city was in awe and subdued. Their very much loved Father is dead, killed by the evil rain of last night. Monte was speechless and withdrawn.

The whole town started another round of deep mourning for their beloved Father. The flag was lowered to half- mast in recognition of the extreme selfless services of the priest who has come to be one of them. There were cries in every home in Newtown mourning Angelus. There were gossips and fingers pointed at the Winterbrushes. The situation became more confusing knowing that Angelus was killed by a fallen tree. Could that have been the fault of the devils in their mist or is it a plain act of God? The question posed by a great majority of Newtowners were: why would there be a rain in the middle of summer? Investigation showed that it has happened only once in the year 1904 and it wasn't this windy and catastrophic. Why didn't it affect the suspected evil family? Are they that powerful? Where do this family emerge from? What is their anger towards us? Can't they just leave to another place where they could meet their match? Communal mourning, cries and agonies continued. The church council met to plan the funeral. The City Hall had a meeting to discuss the funeral too. A date was chosen by the church and communicated to the city hall who have decided to give the deceased a city burial. He , like Stokes, will lie in state at the city rotunda and the funeral ceremony done in the hall too. The family, still in shock have not decided where to bury him.

The initial church service before the main funeral was organized and led by Monte, who was deeply
distraught and disoriented. Fr. Angelus has come to be his spiritual mentor. He taught him the priestly
rope and that he did very resoundingly well. He was a good tutor and Monte was a willing pupil.
The church assembled and monte led them in prayer:
"Our father, who art in haven,
 Hallowed be thy name; thy kingdom come;
 Thy will be done on earth as it is in heaven;
 Give us this day our daily bread;
 And forgive us our trespasses as we forgive
 Those that trespassed against us;
 And lead us not into temptation;
 But deliver us from evil. Amen
Fr. Monte said: Can the congregation please say Amen one more time, please.
Congregation: AMEN!!
Fr. Monte continued in his prayers by reciting the following:
"Eternal rest grant unto him, oh lord
 And let perpetual light shine upon him
 May the souls of the faithful departed, through the
 mercy of God, rest in peace."
"God, thank you for being with us right now.
 We confess that we don't understand why things
 happen the way they do. We don't understand why death
 comes into our lives, but we do know that you walk every
 path of life with us. Remind your servant, Angelus that you
 are walking with him right now.
 Oh lord, our magnificent master, the maker and ruler of the earth
 The alpha and omega, the beginning and the end,
 The author and finisher of life; the I am that I am;
 The Almighty and Everlasting God; we appeal, we beg, we solicit
 That you allow the soul of Fr. Angelus into your Kingdom.

AMEN!!
Congregation: Amen!
"O God, whose beloved son took children into his arms
And blessed them; give us grace to entrust Fr. Angelus to your
Never failing care and love, and bring us all to your heavenly
kingdom;
Through Jesus Christ, our lord, who lives and reigns with you and
the holy spirit,
One God, now and forever more.
Amen!
Congregation: Amen!

Fr. Monte continued by admonishing the parishioners who visibly
looked wary that they should not mourn like the unbelievers,
reminding them that we are all passing through here until the day
of the resurrection, the day of final judgment, when Jesus will
return in glory and raise us all from the dead. That is the day that
the lord has made; that is the day of our reward and redemption,
according to 2 Peter, 3: 1-10; Mark 13.
Watch out that no one deceives you; false prophets will arise and
will perform signs
and wonders to lead you astray, if possible, the elect.
We do not know when Jesus will return; neither the Angels in
haven nor the son
–but only the father
Watch, be alert for you don't know when the time is Coming.

Fr Monte instructed the congregation to turn and read with him the
wordings of Psalm 35, which says as follows:

"Contend Oh lord, with those who contend
  With me; fight against those who fight against me;
  Take up shield and buckler;
  Arise and come to my aid; brandish spear and javelin
  against those who pursue me.
  Say to my soul, I am your salvation."
  Say Amen!

Congregation: Amen!!
Let us read psalm 23, do a little more sermon and disperse to continue in our Christian mourning.

Psalm 23, ladies and gentlemen, in faithfulness and a total submission to the will of God, let us read:
"the lord is my shepherd; I shall not want;
   He maketh me to lie down in green pastures;
   He leadeth me beside the still waters;
   He restoreth my soul; He leadeth me in the path of righteousness
   for his name's sake.
   Yea, though I walk through the valley of the shadow of death,
   I will fear no evil; for thou art with me;
Thy rod and thy staff they comfort me;
Thou prepares a table before me in the presence
Of mine enemies; thy annointest my head with oil;
My cup runneth over; surely goodness and mercy
Shall follow me all the days of my life;
I will dwell in the house of the lord forever".
Amen!
Congregation: Amen.
Fr. Monte asked the congregation to loudly yell after him the following:
"Even though I walk through the shadow of death, I will fear no evil; for thou art with me!"

Father Monte reiterated to the congregation that the town is under a spiritual siege that can only be broken and defeated by faith and belief in the holiness and power of the almighty God. They should not relent in their prayers and complete submission to the supreme command of God. God is still on his throne and this battle is for the lord. All we need to do is to follow the divine instructions and maintain our purities. A catastrophic satanic brotherhood invaded their town and presented a test of their faith. They will prevail if they want to but it requires resilient holiness and embracing of the teachings and ways of our lord Jesus Christ.

The Demarkians   Chidi Metu

Fr. Monte informed the congregation of his dream concerning the tornado that swept through the town and killed our dear Fr. Angelus, but it should be well with our soul, and talking about that, lets read our first reading today, Ecclesiastes 3:1-8:

"When peace, like a river, attendeth my way,
   When sorrows like sea billows roll…
   It is well, it is well with my soul.
   Regardless of our season in life, God teaches us
   to find eternal peace in Jesus;"
Further reading: Read after me:
"Dear God, thank you for being the God who never sleeps.
Thank you for always being here for me, even when I am not always here for you.
Thank you that you are love and that you want the very best for me;
Thank you for your promises and that you never change. I am feeling totally overwhelmed.
Please help me. Help me to rest in the fact that you know what is best for me.
Forgive me for turning away from you and trying to control the outcome in situations in my life.
The bible says that you are not God of confusion but of peace. Help me to rest in your love and to feel the peace which surpasses all understanding. Help me to feel your love and comfort. Help me to be
 still and know that you are God and that you will take care of me, just like a loving parent takes care of
their children.
Your word says to cast all of our anxieties on you because you care for us.
I turn all of my burdens and concerns over to you. Please guide my every step and help me to be attentive to your loving direction.
Monte continued:
Though Satan buffet, though trials should come, let this blest assurance control. No, Satan is not gorging himself at Golden Corral. Rather, he strikes repeatedly with relentless attacks,

prowling about like a hungry lion. Despite these onslaughts, along with expected trials and tribulations, this assurance of internal peace grants God control over our lives. It is through the blood of Jesus that brings about salvation, resulting in internal peace. Let the peace of the lord be upon and each and everyone of you now and forever more. May God bless you all as you leave here today, Amen.

The offering today will be handed over to the family of Fr. Angelus. Please do the needful if you can, as you are exiting from the church. And I will see you at the full funeral next week. Bye now, and again, mourn like Christians, embrace stoic acceptance, be brave and hopeful for the last day. May the enduring peace of the lord continued to guide and protect you now and till the end of time.

Fr. Monte walked over to the exit door, stood there and did a station of the cross on the faces of all the parishioners as they exited the church.

✳✳✳

The city hall was fully parked by all residents, clergy, parishioners, city mayor, council members, and friends of the town. Full service led by Monte was conducted in what was a very sober moment, with grief written on everyone's face. Eulogies were poured out by a lot of the attendees. Family of Fr. Angelus, dressed in all white sat next to the open coffin and were visibly very distraught. First procession of viewers of the corpse filed through. Second procession was called out...

At that point four black ravens flew to the roof of the building and stayed quietly for a few minutes and then the building started vibrating and the tremor increased in crescendo! The evil sound started blowing out loudly, to the surprise of everyone. The building kept on shaking violently to the point that the ceiling fan broke off and struck the people sitting directly under it and all the electric bulbs, even though not switched on, blew out with a smoke. The flat screen television used to publish the bible verses for the sermon as well as the hymns cracked and sparked with a smoke, broke out of the hinges and fell to the floor. The devil has come for a showdown, plain and simple, as they drew a battle line. The Demarkians are relentless evil and they could be very unforgiven.

Fr Monte was exclaiming: "Father Jesus Christ; Blood of Jesus, this is your fight; redeem us; protect your
children; father almighty, you can stop this; please stop the devil with your superior powers. I command
all these people into your arms, father".
The lord in Isaiah 41:10, you promised us the following: "fear not, for I am with you; be not dismayed, for I am your God; I will strengthen you, I will help you, I will uphold you with my righteous right hand."
We are strong and courageous as you asked us not to fear or be in dread for as the lord, you go with us, with a promise not to leave or forsake us. Lord you are the alpha and omega, the beginning and no end, the creator of heaven and earth, the unrivalled power with a dominion over all things, including the Satan. Show your presence oh lord, fight for us and protect us according to your words and promises. You alone can fight this war! You also told us in the book of Psalms, 91:1-4: "Whoever dwells in the shelter of the Most High will rest in the shadow of the almighty. I will say of the lord, he is my refuge and my fortress, my God, in whom I trust. Surely you will save us from the fowler's snare and from the deadly pestilence. You will cover us with your feathers, and under your wings we will find refuge; your faithfulness will be our shield and rampart.

The shaking continued and half of the roof caved out and people started screaming and stampeding out of the hall. The ravens flew down to the windows on different locations watching the people scattered and stampeding out through the exit. These birds were nothing new to the Newtowners who saw them as a bad omen that brought death and sorrows. Fr Monte saw the birds and approached them with holy oil and crucifix. He ran outside to confront the fearless birds, sprayed the oil on them but they were not ready to leave. He made invocations, brought out the crucifix from his pocket and flashed it to the birds and all the birds hurriedly flew away.

At this point, the hall was almost completely deserted except the family members and few parishioners of Fr Angelus who stayed back to assist the undertakers in wheeling the casket to the hearse. Monte mumbling prayers walked the rest of the people out and asked them to go home.
There was a big demonic laughter, a victory lap, that could be heard on the four corners of the town and it lasted for a while.

Winterbrush family knew about what has been going on. The toll of the school run, the dwindling business of the finance house because of low patronage and the pariah status of Philo at her job started hitting home. They never wanted to leave but rather stay back and teach these nosy and troublesome Newtowners lessons of their lives. He who fights and run away lives to fight another day. The Demarkians fights to the end. They don't back down, not at all. Regardless, they took a swipe on the idea of moving out of state as they toyed with it for a while, discussed with the prefect of the cult who consulted with higher leaders. The verdict: yes, they can leave if they choose to. They decided to move out to the west coast of the United States, possibly the breathtaking metropolitan Los Angeles where they could easily get subsumed with multitude of others.

They decided to seek for transfers from their current jobs to LA or get other better jobs through the help of the brotherhood. They found it difficult to get transfers and that aggravated their frustrations and anger towards the residents. They decided to stay back few more months if that was what it should take to find their bearings. After about 6 weeks, they got a call from the prefect instructing them to move in three weeks' time to their new jobs in the upscale city of Irvine, Orange County, a suburb of Los Angeles. They accepted and submitted to the instructions and started getting ready for the move out. The brotherhood contacted an agent to put the house in the market for sale as soon as they vacate.

The Winterbrushes moved to California in the middle of the night. Their vehicles were taken to the train station and they flew out in the private airplane of a fellow member.
The agents listed the house for the next two months but nobody showed any interest in buying it. The reason was obvious. The city blacklisted the building initially but later removed that to enable a possible good and innocent buyer for a closure with the evil that the former occupants brought to their town. They were still and will continue to deal with the relics of the damages inflicted on them by this family. The city raised the fund and purchased the house which was exorcised and cleansed by the church. Eventually the city donated the house to the church by raising the fund through the residents and friends of the town.

Fr. Monte was asked to be transferred to another parish but he declined the offer and opted to stay back in Newtown. He later sought to be relocated to the new house donated to the church, the Winterbrush former home. His request was granted and he moved in. He never had any problem living in it. Either through his spiritual faith or that the Demarkians had moved away from the town, taking with them, their evil powers and instruments. The town continued to mourn the deceased members, the damages that occurred in their lovely Newtown, the humiliations and the stigma brought into their town.

They learnt that other nearby competing towns referred to them now as devil's enclave with powerless churches! The city hall was rebuilt and the clock was changed as well as the public announcing system. The link bridge with their friendly city neighbor was to be rebuilt but the town volunteered to do the repairs as a show of magnanimity and solidarity. They even donated a little more money for them to repair their city hall.
The Governor of the state of Connecticut visited the city and donated state fund for them and rebuilt their gutters and drainage system that were damage by the storms. FEMA, the federal agency

for emergency reliefs sent in some money for relief. The city was repaired physically but emotionally the inhabitants were still ravaged.

Philip stayed away from the town for another 2 years to enable him heal sufficiently.

The investigation of the death of Officer Bezos ran cold as there was no clue except that the beastly attack was spiritual and that couldn't be included in the crime report. The case was officially classified cold and closed.

Det. Godwin felt disappointed that he couldn't unravel this painful killing, too heinous to go undetected. Is there really evil like that? What of if he strikes again? How do we crush it? Is it an organized body of satanic people? Who are they? and what do they want? Why was the officer a victim? Did he cross path with the cult? A lot of unanswered questions.

Ms. Ruth had this hollow feeling that this young couple came into this town, tore and tormented them and shredded them like a piece of clothes and walked away. Who were they? What was their wrath against the city of Newtown? Why didn't the church conquer and subdue them? She felt empty that even the clergy was shredded more. It became more embarrassing that the devil disrupted the funeral of the so-called clergy, man of God who was killed and ridiculed by the same satanic forces. The church that were portrayed as the prince in shining armor, the protector of the weak, became a toy in the hands of Satan and Satan won, as it appeared. It was as humiliating as it was sad. Men of God, where are thy powers? This posed a further threat to her casual and weak religious sentiments and belief. She could only but hope that the power of God will prevail someday and the satanic people receives punishment. She knew about the verses in the bible that states that the wrath of God is slow and very patient. That divine retribution and justice is not swift as humanity would expect. If that is true, then some day she will, hopefully, be alive to learn that the devilish ones are destroyed and the peace of the earth restored. Until then, she is disappointed and disillusioned by the failure of the church and the government in protecting them during these upheavals.

The memory of those, exceptionally, beautiful evil kids in the park kept on replaying in her mind. So, evil could look that beautiful? Well-tended kids in immaculate white apparels, with blue eyes, could be evil? So, it could mean that some of the striking beautiful people she sees everyday may not be humans after all? What kind of world do we really live in? where did those kids disappear to? Why were they laughing with such smiles, fine smiles and perfect dentitions? Why would God allow that to be happening in his world? What is this about the bible? By the way, why do we have a revised standard version of the bible? Revised from what? who did the revision and why? What was it revised from? Why do we have King James Version of the Bible? Who was King James? Why should he have his own Bible version? In one of her research, Ms. Ruth discovered that there were other disciples with their stories and epistles but were not allowed into the bible and the question is why? Even Judas Iscariot had his own gospel that was removed from the bible!

Her puzzle continued as to the followings: Satan was in heaven as an angel of God, a choir master, according to the bible. He disobeyed God and was chased down to the earth. On getting to the earth, he became so powerful. Why would that be so? Where did Satan get all that powers from? Why did God allow that? Why would he become an alternate to God? He was just a mere angel up in haven! If he was chased down to the earth, that should have converted him to a mere mortal! Why would he be allowed to wield that much power that he will be a direct challenge to the almighty God that created Heaven and earth, including him the Satan. If Satan is casted in the eternal pit of fire and in chains, what is he still doing on earth? Why is he ravaging the earth which is biblically described to be the God's stool? A lot more unanswered questions continued to plague her mind. Why would God allow this display of shame in the city hall recently? But again, let us hope on the redemption promised in the bible. Maybe Satan acts for the moment and to the gallery. God may have a final laugh.

The Demarkians   Chidi Metu

CHAPTER THREE

In the Hamptons, an upscale neighborhood of New York, often referred to as the Beverly Hills or Bel Air of New York. The Hamptons located on the eastern Long Island's south fork, is a string of seaside communities known as a summer destination for affluent New York City residents. It is marked by stretches of beaches and interior of farmlands, towns and villages with 18th century shingle buildings and estates hidden behind tall boxwood hedges. East Hampton is home to high end restaurants, bars and designer boutiques.

The Hamptons is usually described as the extension of the biblical heaven, in beauty and class. It is an enclave of the rich and mighty, the high rollers of New York, New York. It is breathtakingly beautiful. The cream of the New Yorkers lived there. The movers and shakers of the big apple state, New York, a neighborhood of status symbol. Like Beverly Hills, they said that you will go to heaven if you die in the Hamptons. The Hamptons sports club was a list of who is who in the last two hundred years of the great state of New York and beyond. Membership in it, if you can get in, was a two hundred thousand dollars' non-refundable fees, plus an annual renewal of one hundred and fifty thousand dollars. New members had to go through a rigorous admission process which included a two member attestations, criminal background check, credit reports in the upper 800s, a pedigree consideration, a minimum of a bachelor's degree or any certification from an Ivy League college or any of the celebrity colleges. The Rockefellers, the Cuomos, the Bloomberg's, the Ross family, the Blavatnic, the Koch, the Icahn, the Murdoch, the Perelman, the Soros, the Schwarzman, the Englander, the Bezos, the Shaw, the Newhouse, the Black, Mark Zuckerberg, on and on, stayed in the Hamptons club. Out of the ninety -nine billionaires in the state of New York, seventy were members of the esteemed club. It was just a conglomeration of the captains of the financial pillars of the big New York. Houses were not sold conventionally in the Hamptons, rather they were bided as in the vintage jewelries' auctions. An introduction showing that you are resident in the Hamptons came with an approval for a lot of things including credit approval. It was a rich man's world.

Mr. Edmonton, an elderly man, his wife and his son, Maxwell, Called Max, lived in east Hamptons. They were one of the movers and shakers of Hamptons. Edmonton was a real estate guru with vast experiences and was highly connected beyond New York. He made his latest trillions from land reclaiming engineering that gave him a 100 buildings oceanfront estate in the Hamptons. He was able to get his way through because he was a Demarkian and he had been around too. He knew and understood the real estate industry very well. He knew how to pull the strings and roll the dice. He was a savvy deal maker and could be very unscrupulous too. He was not a due process character, a stickler to the laws and rules as long he gets to the end of the lines. As a diehard Machiavellian, it doesn't matter to him how many rules were broken as long as the end justified the means. He believed, in his criminal and dirty psyche, that the laws were instruments designed to hold the less privileged down. He got most things done by phone calls only. He was an honest crook per excellence, honors among thieves, as anyone could interpret it. If you rip him off or crossed his path in a daring way, your body might be found floating in the Hudson. Killing and dumping an opponent could be a very privileged way to get rid of the challenger. He was a ruthless animal to the core, with an empty space where a human soul could have been located.

There were buildings owned by him with false basements not included in the building plan but cleared by the city planning departments. If you break his toe nails while matching on his toes, you will be impounded into one of the basements, tortured with your body parts missing when your corpse was to be discovered. His close business associates knew that and respected his space when it came to doing business and keeping the agreements and understandings. He was as cunny as a fox, an astute business man, could be very unscrupulous and a dollar meant a million to him. He believed that whiff of money smells better than a rose flower. In his warped brain, he believed that the world is for the rich alone. Like the music by the ABBA and Davido: "if you don't have money, hide your face". Edmonton, approaching the marked age of 80 years was clubber, a smoker, a functional alcoholic and an unadulterated womanizer. His lifestyle, in a ball park, was a complete violation of the entire Ten Commandments in the bible and he had no apologies for that. He believed that heaven and hell is an illusion, a fairy tale designed to confuse the fickle-minded. He believed that heaven is at the back seat of his multiple Rolls Royce, his private jets, two 75 feet yacht, both named individually after his parents, his houses in Hamptons, Beverly Hills, Bell Air, and Malibu. He derived pleasure in knowing that he was on top of the world.

Everyone was seeking his attention including politicians routing to ingratiate themselves in his favors because of the huge political donations he dished out to them. He loved vintage Cuban cigars. His guest houses were stocked with boxes of louis the xiii cognacs, with each box of twelve that cost about one hundred and twenty thousand dollars. His champagne of choice was the medieval Dom Perignon and Kristal, each running into hundreds of thousands of dollars per box. His beverages were shipped directly from Europe. Edmonton had in his storage champagnes and cognac fermented since the 1800s.

Edmonton represented vanity almost to a ridiculous level. He believed in the Machiavellian teachings that the end justifies the means. That nothing fails like failure and success smells better than a rose. His almost eighty years on earth was like writing out of point essay in an English language examination, a wasted eight decades that produced nothing except a perpetuation of evil and he had no pretenses about it.

He was of an average built but he took down giants that stood before him or challenged his supremacy. He was exceptionally arrogant and a mister Uppity. He carried himself with an air and a bloated head, a highly stuck up son of a jerk. He saw the world in dollars and cents. Academic education was part of it too because you can't exist in his world as an illiterate. His business empire was impeccably managed as any dereliction may not only lead to your job termination but could send you to his secret shark tank. He had a private zoo, filled with vintage animals, all with white furs. He was obsessed with the big cats, especially lion. He sat and studied the male lion, its courage, arrogance, power and strength. He believed that he was a human lion. He was a clear case paranoia, believing that he was better than everyone and that most people were out to bring him down.

Edmonton had his wife, an elderly woman, very quiet but dangerous too. In the last ten years, she withdrew into her shell, stayed away from the limelight. She liked watching television, mostly programs that bordered on the high and mighty, US politics, societal ladder -based programs, all those married women of Atlanta, New York. She liked the Billionaire real estate programs too. She shared almost same personality with her husband. She had over 100 vintage fur coats which she wore at home now as she got tired of running the towns. When she got tired of any of them, she burnt it. Magnanimity or kindness was not in her DNA. She was born a bitch and she remained one till the end of time. She had no business with anyone below her status. She was tall, long legs, very well built, enjoyed exceptional good looks, even at her current old age. She was an expert manipulator, used her good looks to the optimal level in dealing with men. She would tell you that she was not a whore in its simple meaning but that her affections are tied to the money in your wallet. Her parents were very religious as her father had his own small church in a rural town in the Midwest. Her mother was a well-behaved woman of virtue, a retired primary school teacher. They did the best they could to raise their daughter in Christian values but she was an apology of a child. She was very heady and rude. Being the child, she knew that her parents would be restrained in shoving her aside or she would run away which she repeatedly told them. They were very patient with her until she dropped out of college, accused of great bodily harm crime for almost biting off the penis of her cheating boyfriend. She was jailed for three years and when she came out, she opened an escort service in Washington DC focusing on the dirty married politicians. She ran an upscale outfit with pricey fees, leased a five -star brothel that could pass for a five star -hotel. All rooms were equipped with cameras and recording devices. For over a decade she serviced the perverse Washington power brokers including the gays in the closets and the straights, and all were recorded without the participants' knowledge. She had them by the balls but she was still making a lot of money and there was no need yet to blackmail them. Moreover, she could be killed easily by any of the victim power broker. She had her share of carnalities too, if the wallets were loaded.

A very astute business woman who believed that failure is death. His girls in the escort agency were well selected, fine, tall, shapely, college undergrads or college graduates. She embraced perfection and chose women with class. She cherished the ones from good homes who joined his escort business in utmost secrecy, for greed and vanity. She investigated all her girls, without their knowledge, despite their fake identities, discovered that some of them were from wealthy families. Some were kids of politicians including US senators. She found it a little puzzling that girls from such homes and resources were indulging in prostitution, but hey, all things worketh in her favor. She kept on recording them and storing up her dossiers for the future. She took a vow that she would never be poor and that guided every aspect of her life. When the time is ripe, she would get on their ass and make her demands, otherwise every tabloid in the world would get the videos. She needed to start soon or some of those politicians would retire into irrelevance and that would have been catastrophic, as you snooze and lose.

She ran into Edmonton, a senior college school mate that she dated briefly in her first year. They ran into each other in a club in Delaware and hell broke loose. They knew each other to be dirty – minded and crooks made from hell. The dots were connected and the blackmails started and they became rich. Suspecting that the FBI may soon be involved, they escaped to New York with millions of dollars. That provided the foundation for what they are today. A union of two evil minds who had no conscience at all. The rest is history.

Their son Maxwell was not like them in a whole lot of ways but a fruit does not fall far from the tree. Maxwell started off a good kid, attended elitist private high school in the east coast. He was an average student, reasonable sociable. He grew up in the early ages noticing the pervasive religious influence in the world. The escalation and advent of religious activities; the honor and reverence associated with that. He also noticed the downside to it, which, like anything in life, is prone to abuses. He was never taken to any church, so he was left in the dark as to the full import of religion or religions. He knew about the multitude of beliefs but Christianity seems to hold sway. He wondered on the ending of it all. What about the place of agnosticism and Atheism? Is there really God? If there is God, why do we have so much travails in the world? Why are kids hurt and killed? Why do evil men rule the world and have the best of everything? Why do good men experience much difficulties? Why did Jesus the redeemer allowed himself to be crucified gruesomely by a bunch evil sects? The world that we live in is in a mess and that does not conform to the teachings of all religious sects. Why do we have to die first to experience heaven? Did God bring us into this wicked world to suffer first before we are rewarded with heaven? Why would it be so? How did God come into existence? When is the concept of God going to be extinguished? A lot of unanswered questions. He watched television and sometimes observed all these, mostly out of his parents' house. Religion or its practices was not part of their house hold anyways. His parents always yelled at him to change the channel when religious discussions or sermons came up on the television. It kind of puzzled him that his parents were completely oblivious of religious principles or partook in the affairs of religion considering its overbearing influence in the world. His parents never broached up any discourse on religion. The mortality of life is a latent fear in everyone, but not his parents. They were stone-heart people of flesh and has no ecclesiastical affinities. If his mother was a devil, his father was Lucifer himself. They believed in the supremacy of money and that's all that mattered. If heaven was to be on earth, his father, in the pursuit of his business will consider it a prime real estate and would buy it or at least a portion of it. He got what he wanted, how he wanted it, with little or no inhibitions.

He was off to a secular boarding school and his father scolded him strongly and repeatedly, not to partake in any religious activities or he would get burnt. His father's explanations were that he should not be involved in that hypocritical craziness. His admonitions: "go after money and rule the world". He just doesn't understand why his parents seemed so obsessed with material wealth in this complicated world of agonies and pains. He was too young to comprehend all that.

When he graduated primary school, he was shipped off to a school in the Midwest where he met other students from wealthy homes. They seemed to be normal kids from normal homes. They seemed to have normal parents who raised or were raising them within religious pathways. He felt very odd and a little isolated. He felt ashamed but that was up to some point until he recognized the whiff of money. His mates in school noticed his evasion of religious topics, started picking and teasing him with that. They branded him with all kinds of names: "anti-Christ; son of Lucifer; devil; weird one; etc. He got used to it and always shared that with his parents who encouraged him to stay back and face an envious world. He didn't believe that those other kids were envious, after all, they were from wealthy homes too.
The Edmontons had many homes, even in the same area or nearby complexes. The father, had a private estate, massive and highly

exclusive, located by the beach of the Hamptons. That would be considered their primary residence, among other homes in prime areas of the country. Visitors were never allowed beyond the frontal massive building furnished better than any building in the history of mankind.

In the said exclusive home, they had a dog named zee and a cat named zeda. zee and zeda were not your conventional animals. They don't bark or growl. They were treated with utmost pampering and respected by his parents. They stayed on their own, at their own spaces, quietly and reserved. Their foods were served on different 24 carat plates and other very expensive hard wares. They were not being taken out for a walk but they seemed unperturbed by it. They had their own separated and furnished rooms too. They were not providing the conventional security associated with pets and they were not offering any companionship to the family but they seemed of critical importance to his parents. There was a very noticeable reverence of the animals by his parents. He was puzzled about all that but he kept that to himself after noticing that his parents were very unwilling to discuss the animals with him, which deepened his confusion.

They also had in their home a heavily fortified section of the house that was out of reach for everyone including him, Maxwell. He noticed that the parents went into that section in his absences. He knew that someday he would go in there and investigate the content of that room. It did happen and changed him to what he is today. On attaining higher teenage age, he was able, from prolonged planning, to obtain the keys to the entrance of the said secluded section of the house. His dad had a small bunch of keys that he never allowed anyone to touch or possess, not even for a fleeting second. On this fateful day, his parents had some much cognac, on a Saturday early afternoon and passed off drunk on the couches. He noticed the keys in his father's pocket falling out of it and he took it. He took the key to the Bentley car and drove off to a locksmith down the street where he copied all the keys in the bunch. He was very happy about it, especially after returning the keys carefully back to his father's pocket. He noticed that Zee and

Zeda, came out of the room and kept looking at him with restlessness, pacing around the sitting room. He walked away to the other sitting room. He later called Uber to the airport enroute back to school.

After some weeks, he came back home for a few days to meet with his parents who were vacation -bound to six countries in Europe. Their private Boeing 747, one of their air fleets, serviced thoroughly and all arrangements made with all their travel managers and concierge in Europe. His mother, a queen of vanity, had more fur coats and jewelries in her luggage than Elizabeth Taylor and Oprah Winfrey combined. They left for a 6-week vacation! Max moved over to the other wing of the home to take advantage of the services of the servants. The animals were fed by special arrangements without compromising the security and secrecy of the home.

On this particular day, while his parents were gallivanting around western Europe, Max decided to open the section of the house at their home. Initially it was tough getting in but he succeeded. When he walked towards the doors, zee and Zeda came again and became very confrontational and hostile. Zee was barking ferociously and menacingly walking towards him, showing for the first time a fanged tooth. Zeda was crying loudly and menacingly too, hovering around him. He was transfixed watching the inexplicable drama by these animals. That was the first time that he had noticed these weird and over pampered, good for nothing animals, behaving like animals for once. But he could not understand why they were unhappy with him trying to access that part of the house! He is human and they were not. He is a member of the family and they had their own rooms too. He walked away from the battle line, seeing that it was going to go down bad with these weird animals. He decided to do it again in the midnight. At about 1 a.m. in the morning, having drank a lot of cognac, which he wasn't supposed to, as a minor, he walked over to that section again. Twenty feet to the entry door, he saw Zee standing there, watching him like a lion protective of it cubs. Zee's eyes were reflectively red even though there was no direct light on its face.

The mouth was agape showing the fanged tooth again. An evil melody, not heard before in that house, and from no music set, came on and Max could hear that! Max backed out and walked back to his room. Max was confused further as to why these animals were reacting like that! What were they up to and why do the dog have fangs? Why do the fangs only show at confrontational episodes? Why were the eyes red in the dark? Where these animals evil creatures? So it seemed but he would find out sooner than later. He gave up on trying to access the house but kept the keys securely for another opportuned time. Max later went back to school before the parents came back from Europe.

Later, the school commenced a summer vacation and Max went back home. Out of the blues, the dad decided to go to the mall with his mum and the animals sitting in the car to catch some air. They drove themselves that day in their newest white customized Rolls Royce Phantom. Max was excited and jubilant. He retrieved the keys as soon as the parents left. In about 45 minutes, he walked over to open the door but it wasn't easy initially and eventually he succeeded and he got into the rooms. The same evil sound started playing again, without any musical equipment in the room. There were breathing sounds too as if a person is on life ventilator but with deep and hoarse inhaling and exhaling. All the cult's paraphernalia were in full view! The room depicted as a corporate head office of Satan.

The book of the Demarkians were all over the place. Their signs and symbols were ubiquitous and in plain view too. Max ran out of the room in fear and trembles. His parents were evil worshippers and he could now understand why they had secluded that part of their home to themselves. Their non- religious lives started making sense to him. Possibly their wealth too, if the demon could actually give wealth. The weird animals and their behaviors became explicit now. He confirmed that they were evil animals and all the dots connected. He became afraid of where he called home and the people he called parents. He started crying and asking why his parents should choose this path...on and on and on. But as it can be seen later, he towed the same line of existence.

His father came back home very happy but was puzzled about the restlessness of his animals at the mall, sitting in the car. Zee, at some point, even barked without any provocations. He sat down to watch television and was walking towards his room to grab a bottle of louis the xiii when his phone rang in a special set tone and he hurriedly picked up the call from his cult leader. There was a brief conversation on the phone and Edmonton's face became enraged. He walked up to his son and slapped him hard on the face, yelling at him and asking him whether he entered his private rooms?!! The animals were there and were ready to pounce on Max if the altercations escalated. Max was cowed by the whole drama. The phone rang again and Max could hear his father, very unusually of his character, said yes sir, yes sir, to the caller.

His father turned around and informed Max that they would be going somewhere in few minutes. Max objected but his dad reminded him that he wasn't seeking his approval but that he should get ready for a short visit to some place. Again, his Dad drove and they left and got to a highly secured building tucked in a massive gated compound with state of the art security equipment. They were buzzed in and a stern looking concierge took them to the back building fortified with its own security too. They were seated at the reception area and waited for close to an hour before they were offered water. These whole saga was jolting to Max, to see his great, super wealthy, cocky, uppity dad, reduced to a nobody by being treated shabbily in this extraordinary quiet and scary place. Who could be the person to wield such an influence to the Edmonton that had the world in his pocket? It has to do with the cult or the satanic power broker, and he was right.

After about another hour, a huge, well-built man, walked in and nodded to them to come into what turned out to be a temple. He looked at Max and introduced himself as the leader of a movement called the Demarkians. You were not supposed to know of it until you attained certain age and maturity but inquisitiveness kills a cat. You are not going to die but you will be initiated into the cult. You will die if you violate the rules of the brotherhood. We are not seeking for consent in admitting you into the family. Your father will explain the powers and reach of the cult to you and the stringent rules of engagements. Edmonton answered, yes my lord, I will do so. The man turned over to Edmonton and strongly rebuked him, reminding him of being a stage 5 of the fraternity and all the attendant responsibilities of keeping the sacrosanct rules of the order which he violated. The fraternity might demote him or hand down adequate punishment to him which might be a simple admonition. The leader expressed profound disappointment in the carelessness and poor indiscretions in not protecting their secrets in his possession.

Leader stated: Your incessant alcoholic obsessions had caused the brotherhood a breach of their innermost spiritual sanctity and in doing that exposed your only child to danger. You, alone, with your wife, were squarely responsible for any and all consequences of their indiscretions. He was asked to bring Max back in few days -time, Saturday by midnight precisely for his initiation into the cult. The leader turned over to Max and sternly warned him to keep his mouth shut about what he knows now and will know in future about their beautiful cult. He warned Max to make sure that he appears for his initiation as scheduled. If he fails to do that, he will die a very agonizing death. To allay his fears, he assured Max that they were just a brotherhood that looked out for each other and that they mind their business. It is an order of Lucifer but they were peaceful and highly secretive and exclusive. He reminded Max that his conduct brought him into all these. The Leader stood up, without talking to them any longer, started walking away arrogantly and without turning or bidding them good bye except when he turned and asked them to leave immediately as he walked into the back room and out of sight. Edmonton, looking very sober and defeated, walked his son out hurriedly into their car and left. The forty- five minutes -drive home was the longest journey that Max has taken in his life. It was built in suspense and inflammatory silence. A lot of things were going on in Max's mind, his school, his college, his future, and above all, to be a disciple of Satan! Edmonton turned and looked at Max, informed him that he won't be going back to school. He said to him that he would be home- schooled until he graduates high school next year. He further asked him to keep to everything the boss said or he would die, short and simple. He was reassured about the easiness of the cult as long as he keeps to their rules. The rest of the drive home was in silence.

On the weekend, Max was initiated into the cult formally. He was attached fully to his dad and the animals. His parents were relieved and were somewhat happy even though this development was out of sync for their very young only child. It was sadness and joy and it is what it is. When they came back from the temple after initiation, very early in the morning, about 3a.m., the animals were up and elated! For the first time, and to Max's surprise, Zee was happy, wagging its tails for Max and acting like a family friendly dog to him. Zeda was rubbing its body on Max and crying happily like a real cat. When Max sat down, the cat jumped onto his laps and recoiled and Zee sat under his knee. He was scared and embarrassed but his father assured him that it was okay.

Max was home schooled and he graduated and went to college. He ran his parents' businesses well enough but wanted political powers. He was introverted like his parents. He graduated ivy league college and had his ambition outside the family wealth. Edmonton, his father, loved the idea of his son going into politics having realized that being a Washington insider was not a bad idea, in terms of the connections, the money and the intimidations. He regretted having not joined politics but this opportunity for Max will not pass by. They started working on it and the fraternity was informed formally. Promises were made, especially with Edmonton being a high level member of the cult and heavy financier of the cult. Last year he donated two hundred million dollars to the cult, tax free. He abided by the rule of the fraternity totally. He feared and respected the fraternity knowing that his money and influence meant nothing to the powers of the fraternity. Moreover, the fraternity protected him and his wife during their early days of blackmailing a lot of big wigs in Washington.

He took his son to the temple and met with the leadership caucus of the order. The son was approved to go for the US senate. The fraternity will viciously bulldoze him to Washington and woe betides any challenger or any person that will obstruct the plan. The brotherhood will view that as an act of war and they never lose, at least not yet. The groundwork for the politics started, campaign team was formed, inducted and huge amounts of money, in seven digits doled out to them to start the groundwork. A Demarkian is on his way to the US congress.

✳✳✳

Dr. Julius Coen, in his late 40s, of a Jewish descent, grew up in splendor. He was born in Aristocracy and wealth, with a golden spoon. He attended up-ended private schools and later the prestigious Massachusetts Institute of Technology, MIT and Harvard University. He obtained his doctorate on quantum mathematics and other minors. He was elitist personified. He was creamier than the cream of the Hamptons. The family of the Coens were beyond celebrity as they had deep pedigree running into three generations of very well- read family tree, rich too in dollars and cents, gold and silver. Their religion was Judaism and they were very ardent at it. The family were primarily into oil explorations with prime oil wells in eastern Europe, Middle east and in all OPEC countries of the world. They own oil ocean vessels and were heavily involved in deep ocean and seas oil explorations. They were into offshore and onshore oil explorations. The Coens could stand eyeball to eyeball, shoulder to shoulder with any rich family in the world. They were a little bit into real estate but not to the level of the Edmontons. They started their son for the US senate, representing Hamptons and they believed that it would be a walk-over, but they were very wrong. Their path will cross with the powerful Demarkians and they would later realize, sadly though, that there was more to life than college degrees and wealth of money. The candidature was made public and Edmonton saw it on the television. He felt restless and informed the leader of the cult of it but he was re-assured to trust in the powers of the cult.

Electioneering started by all five candidates. Most other candidates withdrew when they noticed that a Coen was running. The Coen family was very powerful and extreme in their generosity to the extended community. They donated their lands for the Hampton parks. They single- handedly built a lot of the community's projects, the library, the contemporary museum of arts and culture, the town center ring road with water fountain, the billion-dollar entertainment center, among others. Even though the Hamptons were a rich man's cove but the Coens touched the lives of others kindly in the community. On the other hand, nobody would say the same of the Edmontons. It was actually the opposite except that they were one of the superrich too. Max and his dad thought out a scheme and started implementing the idea of hanging out in the public places in the Hamptons in an effort to fraternize with the local community. Rallies were held occasionally by both candidates, Max and Julius. Max was running as a Republican while Julius ran as a Democrat. Hampton is more democratic than republican but Max was not troubled by that. He trusted the overbearing powers of the brotherhood. A lot of campaigning continued and Julius was leading clearly in the polls.

Not connected with the trending election campaign but having got in tuned into the beauty of having out and mixing up in the public, with the crowd, Max, who was, in a relative sense, had a better heart and more socializing person than his parents, decided to take Zee for a pleasure ride in one of their vintage family vehicles. He first drove to upper Manhattans, New York, watched the marvelous and breathtaking New York skylines, the Rockefeller buildings, the Empire state buildings, the new World Trade Centers. He drove back to the long Islands, to Hamptons. Pulled up in the park, was drawn by the beauty of the environments, the beautiful people, normal in their lifestyles, doing their thing and all seemed to be having fun. He felt disillusioned for a few minutes and wished he could just be like them and live his life rich and simple. Some of them were up and about with their beautiful and expensive dogs and other animals. A man in short pants was seen in the company of others sitting in the park with a huge white Siberian tiger, on a strong leach. The tiger was very quiet and enjoying the environment. Max, for a minute forgot about his restrictions, drove further down, pulled out a resisting Zee out of the car and sat at the corner park and continued to suck in the beautiful life of the Hamptons, the life of the rich and the privileged. Zee was just obediently standing by his side until another dog walked by and started barking incessantly and Max had to leave immediately.

$$* * *$$

The election campaigning peaked out and Julius was still leading convincingly in the polls, followed by Max. The other two independent candidates were trailing far behind. The brotherhood met and decided to do something. The election was 10 days away and all candidates believed that Julius may win.

The Coens lived in their Coen exquisite estate called "The Elixir", located on top of the hills that slopes than to the ocean banks. They were enjoying the two landscaping worlds of the area. On this beautiful Saturday night, Julius attended a night party in the upscale part of New Jersey, alone as his wife and kids were in Africa vacationing in Ghana, Tanzania and South Africa. He had a swell time reuniting with his MIT and Harvard school classmates. It was a night of splendor. They talked about everything, their jobs, families, their spoilt lifestyles, Julius, obvious winning of the coveted US senate seat, their social indiscretions, the women, the vintage beverages, rambled on and on. The group represented the aristocratic hue of the east coast United States. At some point, Julius mildly drunk, left for home in his super customized Mercedes Ben, G- wagon, supercharged G63. He drove through the George Washington Bridge in New York, passed through the Holland Bridge, over the Hudson River overlooking the statue of Liberty, blasting his Joan Armatrading music tracks. He drove through the lower and upper manhattans and joined the long Island highway to the Hamptons on the beach. On approaching their estates, his car started slowing down and eventually stopped in the middle of the road. Julius found that shocking for a brand new, two weeks' old vintage Mercedes car. The engine and all the electronics packed up after a few minutes. He called his dad and informed him of the development and a driver was dispatched, with the father calling AAA for a tow. The lights in the car went off too, perplexingly. There was a little flicker of light from the street light, two hundred feet away. His wife called him coincidently and he spoke with her and the kids who were, obviously from the way they sounded, enjoying their vacations. Julius initially didn't want to tell his wife of his current predicament but changed his mind and informed her, if not for anything, for them to get off the phone to allow him concentrate on getting home first. The wife was a little troubled but she thought that it might be a little electrical issue with the car, with all the garbage technology in the new millennium vehicles. He continued trying to start the vehicle but to no avail.

Suddenly a cat and a black crow flew and perched on his hood, looking at him with the cat's eye turning yellow and the bird's eye red, all reflecting even in the dark, without lights. Julius was momentarily confused with all these weird animals with funny eyes in the dark perching on his car! Were they demons but Julius was too polished and elitist to believe in such rubbish. Julius called his father and informed him of all that was going on but the father asked him to stay put and that he already sent the family drivers out to get him home. Coen Senior said to Julius, I love you, son. You will be fine. Julius pulled his gun from the glove compartment, to protect himself if need, tried to open and step out but the vehicle doors couldn't open either! He got more alarmed and fearful. The cat edged forward but on the outside of the car. The cat made a few seconds eye contact with Julius and both animals disappeared. A few seconds later, the car came back to life, the engine started on its own, demonic voices and sounds came on, a deriding laughter calling him "Congress man Julius", more laughter and demonic sounds. The car engaged itself in a gear and sped out, in an auto drive, attained a speed of 160 MPH in a minute and smashed into a huge tree located twenty feet into the roadside and exploded instantly. The noise was so earth shattering that a neighbor thought it was a plane crash, called 911 on seeing the smokes from the fire. Within minutes, a fire truck was there to cut whatever remained of Julius out and extinguished the fire.

The drivers from the Coens came up there, saw the scene and called Julius' dad who, in the company of other family members, drove there in a jiffy. It was a gory sight to behold. The G-wagon was compressed to half of its size, blood dripping from it like a palm oil mill machine. The vehicle was badly burnt and Julius' body was half charred with his face showing intact. He died gruesomely and that broke his father who wept uncontrollably. The whole area was condoned by the highway patrol and fire trucks vehicles. The press could smell a news like a vulture with dead meats and they did smell this incidence. Channel ABC 7 helicopter flew in from downtown New York immediately when they learnt that the victim was Julius Coen, the candidate tipped to win the long Island US senate seat, and one of the Coens, a highly respected and celebrity family. The New York times vehicle was also there and it later turned into a beehive of press men and women. Reporters were seen at the crash scene analyzing the accident, with serious allusions of drunk driving or substance abuse. It was a puzzle how such an accident could have happened the way it did, even if driven by a drunken Julius. The neighbor that called police was called in and he gave his account of what he heard which wasn't very helpful to anyone. Julius was removed to the morgue and the vehicle towed away. The Coens left, broken and all crying. It was a breaking news in the CNN, all local networks, newspapers, journals. Later that morning, the leader called the Edmontons and they jubilated over it. The election was in 6 days –time. The winning was to be by simple majority and it looked like Max will coast to the congress but we will see. The fraternity has pulled it again and nobody dare interfere or obstruct with their plans.

In their sitting room, Max turned and smiled to his parents and thanked them. His father asked him for a hug and he heartily walked over and hugged his parents. His father jokingly told him to remember them in his new kingdom. In recent time, Julius has come to appreciate his parents and their decision to follow the devil. The dividends are incredibly warming. It would give all members a guaranteed homerun at all things. He was a proud Demarkian and his allegiance to the cult was entrenched forever. He developed reverie with the thought of being a US senator representing one of the richest constituencies in the world. He went and picked up a two hundred year old French Champaign and popped it with his Dad. He could care less about the source of their prosperity as long as they rule the world. He also cherished the idea of being protected by the cult while in DC.

A full-blown funeral was had for Julius and he was laid to rest. Julius' father, over a period of time, discussed with Julius mother, the calls and the messages that Julius relayed to him at the scene before his death. They did not share that with anyone, at least not yet. The whole thing doesn't make sense and they knew Julius drank a little alcohol. The autopsy report showed insignificant alcohol in his corpse. The brakes of the damaged car, even after the massive damage to the car, was found to be in top shape. The throttling system was still in good shape after the accident. The Mercedes plant did a full diagnosis of the car, on Coen's request, and discovered that it was in excellent shape. The car had no reason to pack up the way it did. The electrical systems were functionally in top shape. The new customized G- Wagon had a functional equivalent of aircraft black box built on its brain box. It was retrieved and played and all they could hear is Julius screaming and a loud demonic sound and laughter teasing Julius while the car was speeding to his death. The election came on and Max, expectedly, won and off he went to DC and was sworn in as a senator. The bible says that the foolish finds pride in vanities; the foolish enjoys ephemeral victories that only Satan could offer. Max was on top the world and he had his life laid out on success. He was happy and fulfilled.

Three months after his death, Julius started appearing to his parents in dream. Their dreams were very much alike in content. He would be seen crying and yelling at Max. He kept lamenting about his kids and his lovely wife, Eleno. He lamented about the election which cost him his life. He briefed his dad about the evil cult that sponsored Max and killed him when he was winning in the polls. He appeared so distressed in the world of the dead. He was spotted a few times by the cemetery attendees sitting on his tombstone backing everyone, disappeared when people were approaching. He walked around as a bitter and disgruntled ghost. He, as a spirit, wanted to wage a war with the Demarkians but they were too powerful for him, even in death! He finally appeared in the dream for his wife and gave her detailed information about their investments, the location of the key for a new safe he opened while she was away on vacation, the location and information on the safe, the content of the safe. He also informed the wife about a two hundred million dollars oil well deal that he closed few days before his death and gave the wife the phone numbers of the people to contact to consummate the transactions.

Elenor, called Ely, woke up in the morning sweating profusely, went straight to the location for the keys and found it just as she was told! She went on line and found the safe box address and drove over there and discovered everything that Julius told her precisely as in the dream. She followed Julius's instructions and closed out the deals but was confused about certain instructions on some loose ends. Julius appeared again in her dream the next night and clarified all that to her, consoled her, hugged her and reminded her that he loved and still love her. Julius told Ely that everything will be ok at some point, advised her to be focused on raising their kids and that he would be around for a little while more before he moved on to different plane where he won't be able to see or communicate with them anymore. He suggested to Ely to remarry if she wished as that will assist her in closure with him. He told his wife to hug his kids for him without discussing his appearances as that will scare the kids. He did inform his wife that he had appeared a few times sitting on his grave but that he would not be doing that anymore. Ely asked him to physically visit her and the kids for once but he declined strongly. Ely suggested for him to visit her alone but he declined saying that it won't serve any purpose because they cannot have any physical contact. He explained to Ely that their energies are not the same anymore. He intimated Ely about his effort to retaliate against the Edmontons and the cult but that they were too powerful for him. He regretted getting involved in politics and started crying, at which point, Ely started crying very hard with him and her kids woke her up. She continued when she woke up and the daughter ran over to call grandpa. Grandpa talked with Ely repeatedly that week but did not want to suggest a counseling for Ely because he knew that the dreams were real and that time would heal their wounds.

Julius appeared a few more times to his family and stopped. The Coens moved on with their lives. The community had already moved on too. Their new senator was in Washington DC, seemed to be doing a good job too. Max held town hall meetings with the constituent and community leaders. They gave him positive marks for performance. He initially, didn't live in DC because his dad gave him a brand new private jet that took him to the capitol every day. Max believed that he should get married at this point but there were some challenges. He had to marry within the cult family for ease of life and survival. He had to wait until that happens at its own time. He continued to roll high, like any other young and successful man. He started developing
his father's arrogance but cautiously though.

Senior Coen shared the circumstances surrounding Julius death, the cult, their activities, the birds and the cat, the car's black box and the weird noises, the dream appearances of Julius, his messages to him and other members of the family, to his senior sister, Mrs. Morrison. Expectedly, it was jolting to her. He sought and was assured of her keeping the information confidential for now. Coen, in excruciating pain and anger of losing his dear son, knew that someday, the world will be informed about this evil cult and their destruction embarked on, starting with the Edmontons. Before then he decided to reach out to Mr. Edmonton, Mr. big shot. He got his number from the sports club and called him. When he picked the phone, he introduced himself as Coen and asked Edmonton about his kids and other pleasantries. Rest of the conversation was as follows:

Edmonton; Waoh, what do I owe this call? The great Coen of the Coen majesty and empire, I am thrilled.

Coen: I hope you are having balls with your family, oh by the way, congratulations with your son's victory. I know the family should be proud of him, huh? Great.

Edmonton: tell me about it. I just came in from DC visiting and watching his honorable arguing bills that will benefit us here in the Island. I love my son!

Coen: Oh, I guess you do. We all do. We live for our kids. We love them. The worst thing that could happen to anyone is to lose a child. The feeling is crippling and devastating and recovery may never come from it, agree sir?

Edmonton: Yes, I do and I feel sorry for your loss.

Coen: No, you don't. It benefitted you, and not by providence.

Edmonton: What does providence mean?

Coen: it means things that did not occur by natural means and destiny.

Edmonton: I don't get it, sir.

Coen: No, you do.

Edmonton: How do you mean?

Coen: My son's death is not providential and you know what I am alluding to.

Edmonton: Your son died from drunk driving, sir. It was in the news.

Coen; There was no alcohol found in his autopsy.

Edmonton: He had an accident and died and, moreover, the alcohol may have dissipated before the autopsy. At the very best, he may have lost control of the powerful car and crashed to his death, could happen to any of us. My profound sympathies, great one.

Coen: I don't know how much I need your sympathies. They said that hell hath no fury than the wrath of a woman, right?

Edmonton; have heard that, don't know what that connotes. My fury is worse than that, if pushed.

Coen: I will tell you my own version, hell hath no fury than the anger of a parent whose child is murdered. All my son wanted was just a political office and you could have had that without killing him!

Edmonton: I don't know what you are talking about or referencing. Your son was driving alone and drove to his death, alone!

Coen: No, you are wrong. My son was not driving alone.

Edmonton: The report said that he was alone and nobody else would have survived that crash anyways. Are you saying that the report was incorrect?

Coen: The report wouldn't have contained your evil bird and cat, of your satanic cult!

The silence at the other end was earth shattering. You could hear the heartbeat of Edmonton on the other end. You could perceive his shock and surprise. You could feel the trembling shock on Edmonton on what he just heard.

Coen: are you there, sir?

There was continued silence and suddenly, Edmonton picked the phone and the dialogue continued.

Coen: was that a low blow? Did you think that you own the world and that nobody will ever know of your evil life?

Coen: I don't know why you should be surprised when your cult does not hide their activities and powers. I just called to let you know and that the world will know later.

Edmonton: Let me tell you this one time. If you call me again or broach up this to me again or anyone else, for that matter, you will die more gruesomely than your son. I don't think you missed any part of this clear message. Edmonton hung the phone quietly. Edmonton was still processing, to his surprise, about what he just heard from Coen. How, in the world did he know about what he just said? The brotherhood did not leave any evidence behind as the killing was perfectly executed. Did his stupid dead son call and reported the bird and cat before his death? Why didn't the cult jam his phone or suppress any vestiges? He will talk with the leader, he reasoned.

Edmonton called the leader and they had a talk about the whole incidence. The brotherhood will decide what to do and how to do it. It gave the cult concern because of the social stature of the Coens and the damages they were capable of inflicting on the business and aristocracy of the Edmontons, including the Senator who was beginning to make his mark in Washington. They found the development very troubling but it had to be dealt with decisively.

Edmontons, husband and wife talked about it for a while, with Mrs. Edmonton getting worried by the day as to whether the Coens could do any harms, that is if they have the capacity. Coen, at this point was so distraught that his own survival meant little or nothing to him. He might try to avenge his son's death. He had all that it could take to fight, if this was to be a mundane war but it ain't. He called and set up a meeting with the senior Rabbi of their church. In Judaism, spirituality is a major integral part of the religion. Their faith is predicated on the Old Testament of the bible. They don't believe in the Christian- claimed messiah status of Jesus Christ or the messages of the New Testament. They believe in the prophets categorized into three spheres as senior, medium and junior prophets, or old, middle and new prophets. They practice spirituality but towards God, but the Demarkians worship was directly to the devil.

On the meeting day, Coen met with Rabbi Abital and they had a prolonged talk about the death of Julius, the evil cult that took his life and ways to go about avenging his death or at least expose them. Sacrifices, according to their teachings were planned and executed. White fowls and pigeons, goats, oxen, sheep, were offered and slaughtered. The spiritual smokes exorcism was performed by circling the white fowls around Coen's neck for twelve times; incense was lit and flashed around him for cleansing and expungement of evil spirits, including, of course, the cult that threatened him. The Angels, especially Gabriel and the saints were beckoned to destroy the brotherhood. Dry fasting was conducted by church members and multiple prayer sessions were ordered for the peace and security of the Coens. The Rabbi did, on his own, deep midnight prayers for the member, a critical member of the church seeking their refuge. The situation was very precarious for the church and the community. A lot of spiritual incenses were burnt to ward off and chastise the evil spirits. The prophets and angels were summoned relentless to protect the Coens against what appeared to be great demonic forces. The ritual and cleansing continued but the cult was not done with them yet. An ecumenical committee of the Shabbat church was set up to address the issue of the attack on the Coens, especially considering the influence of the family on the Jewish churches. This spreads more, to the detriment of the Demarkians and they loathed that. The brotherhood was not happy about it and something had to be done fast.

A few days later, Edmonton received a call from the leader, who was very furious and summoned Edmonton to their temple. On getting there, a long discussion was held and the deliberation dwelt more on how and what to do with the Coens, who were engaged in an unmitigated smear campaign against the much esteemed brotherhood. The Coens did not seem to have learnt their lesson, or at all. The leader hinted that the cult will be very restrained in inflicting more harm to the Coens but that their flurry of activities were becoming a low blow to the brotherhood, and that has to be abated forthwith.

Edmonton left and drove home but very troubled. As evil as he had always been in life, he surprisingly, to himself, wished that the situation be reversed and that Julius wouldn't have been killed by the brotherhood. The Coens were very powerful and they were not relenting in their efforts to avenge for the death of one of their rising stars. He felt sorry for them fleetingly but on getting home, he relapsed to his old and normal dark soul. He discussed all that with his wife who was as stone cold-hearted as she had always been. The Edmontons could be anything but humans. Their life history is premiered on and predicated on evil and vile. The Coens could as well go to hell.

The primary residence of the Coens could be described to be out of the world. It was beyond exquisite and intimidating. The landscaping was breathtakingly beautiful and consuming. The compound consists of about 20 hectares on the hills, all adorned with flowers and vintage trees. The lawns were manicured to perfection as the gardeners, who had college degrees in horticulture, received premium salaries and allowances just to tend and maintain the landscape. There were giant and midsize trees that adorned the entire landscape. There were private streets, with reinforced asphalts that traversed the entire compound, all wired with the state of the art surveillance camera systems. There were street lights in the compound and connected by consent and contract with the Hamptons city hall, authorized to issue city citations for traffic violations within the compound. There were multiple buildings enclosed in the whole estate but the Coens' patriarch lived in the vintage building located at the south east corner of the estate. The building had beautiful canopy shrubs and trees in the front of it. Mr. Coen's house had a huge balcony that overlooked the estate. He loved to sit out there and suck in the beauty and splendor of his estate, a feat he was proud of. An accomplished man, that had recently been devastated and depressed. He sat out there with his wife all the time and engaged in reminiscence of their lives.

On this lovely Saturday evening, he came in from the church and had a long relaxation at the balcony, received few of his visiting close friends and allies, drank some pink rose Moet and Chandon Champaign. He felt relieved and dozed off in his Moda Italia leather recliner seat for a while. He woke up refreshed and rejuvenated. Coen had been a good man and he was a billionaire that had made no enemies in his financial ascension, which was very rare in the current world as it is. He was always conscious of how he related with all and sundry in his private and business life. When he woke up, it was dark and the weather was beautiful. He looked at the New York City sky line and got amazed as usual on the magnificence of the city of New York. He believed that life starts and ends in New York, New York, as he always called it.

Having woken up, he looked at the shrubs directly in front of his building and noticed that a wind was blowing on the shrubs and the small trees. He looked at the other parts of the compound and saw that the shrubs and trees were quiet. He couldn't make any sense out of it and the wind which was increasing in crescendo was only localized at that shrubs patch. The area, as common in the whole estate, had what looked like an artificial forest, with electrical lights built into the shrubs. There were no undergrown weeds and vegetation, so the view was clear and panoramic. Still surprised, he sat up in his chair, wiped his sleepy eyes and took a sober look at the shrubs again and the wind continued unabated. He walked across to the edge of the balcony to have a closer look as to this amazing act of nature and the drama remained the same. He concluded that, well it might be nature with its tricks. After all, we are humans and do not have the knowledge to understand something about the world and nature. He went back to his relaxation and poured himself more Champaign. Then he heard the whistling sound from the shrub and the high wind coming from the shrub as if seeking for his attention. He looked over again and what he saw was mouth-gaping! He saw, standing in the middle of the canopy shrubs, was a small girl, dressed in an immaculate white dress, with a blue eye that reflects like a neon light, impeccably clean glossy blond hair, with tooth that is snow white, even in the darkness of the night, a black crow, with glossy black feathers perched on her shoulders, like a Tarzan, smiling heavenly at him and waving at him. The Crow had bloodshot red eyes and was just looking at him too. He was transfixed for a moment and recollected himself but didn't know what to make of this and was at a loss as to how to handle this situation. A lot of questions went through his mind: who is she? And how did she pass through the strenuous security to gain access into his compound? Did she come with other adults and who were they? What about the bird, with red eyes? Why were they here and what do they want? At that moment, he remembered his son and the call he made before his mysterious death. The black bird and the cat! This is the evil cult coming to attack him. He called the Rabbi and relayed what was going on and he was instructed what to do. He ran and brought out some incense and oils and started some incantations. The little girl was undeterred and stood there for a while. The wind on the shrub never stopped and the evil sound and laughter came on and the demon rendered their warning, while laughing. In a very deep but clear voice the demon warned:

"I don't want to cause you more sorrows but we thrive in sorrows. I am the devil myself and I show no mercy. I destroy as I cause grief. I am the ruler of the earth and he who crosses me will be met with unending sorrows. You are trying my patience. I am warning you now and I don't repeat my warnings. When I come back, I leave trails of agony and ruthlessness. Back off from me, now, now!"

The whole drama quieted down, the wind stopped, the little girl and the bird disappeared and the dimmed shrub lights came on back fully. Coen was confused further and speechless. He started praying and asking the Angels to come to his rescue. His wife walked outside and saw him kneeling down in supplication and very troubled inquired as to what was going on. He relayed the whole drama to his wife who became even more confused. They believe that this was becoming too serious but there appeared to be no solution in sight. She dragged her distraught husband inside the house and closed the balcony door. It looked like their winter was going to be long. It was becoming apparent that their agony was just getting started but they believed that God is still on his throne. It was a difficult night to find sleep, which was understandable. The wife went into the private room and shed some prolonged tears while calling on El Shaddai to come to their rescue. They needed more strength to deal with this escalating trails of agony. They were still freshly mourning their child and now dealing with a satanic cult that were unrelenting in their onslaughts. They remained awake till daybreak and in a very deep sober state. They felt pathetically disoriented and gloomy. They knew that if they could hold on to their faith and their clean life lifestyle, that the day would replace the night. They read through the psalms of David and felt consoled. They later slept all through the day.

CHAPTER 4

Malibu is an upscale part of the greater Los Angeles metropolis. It had as its neighbors, Hollywood Hills, Bel Air and Beverly Hills. It is called the earthly heaven. Real estate in Malibu is for the rich and mighty whose incomes were in the seven and eight figures at the very least. There is no known word in thesaurus to describe the beauty of Malibu. There is a saying that the residents of Malibu breathe the purest air first and throws the remnants to others below the hills. There are winding scary canyon roads of Malibu as wells as chilling architectures built on the edges of the elevations and canyon points. The mountains and ranges are converted into magnificent architectures and urban civil engineering. Some Malibuans live in the valleys of Malibu too, a no less feat. One editorial in the Los Angeles Times quoted a movie producer as having joked, to live in Malibu and go to hell when he dies will be a news. Malibu is the world greatest class act. Like the Hamptons, it is a world of the riches.

In the hills and valleys of Malibu, an odd-looking building, castle-like, perched on the tip of a hill with a private compound, with the elevated back balcony facing the valleys of universal studio, Hollywood. The frontal part of the building had a patio and a relatively big compound with beautifully mastered landscaping. The building was located at the back of the compound with a long driveway, entire compound was very pristine and highly exclusive. The building was one of the Demarkian temples.

A wroth iron 20 feet gate painted all glossy black, with of course, surveillance cameras and stringent security, adorned the entrance to the compound. The building was obscured from the street, to avoid the prying eyes of the neighbors and the community. Building was an aristocratic masterpiece that looked very conservative but well maintained. The compound was always locked up when and without anyone being present. The mail box, the postal receptacles, utility bills meter were located a thousand yards from the main gate, on a private street adjacent to the compound.

Now and then, private cars, mostly vintage vehicles, Rolls, Bentleys, Bugatti, Ferrari, would quietly glide in and the gates would open and close with precision for them. They drove to the perched building and held their meetings, with candles and weird signs and language, in very low voices, of course with locked and heavily draped windows. These men and women, well dressed, highly educated, well-placed members of the society, were the Demarkians. They were, for the most part, of the aristocratic hue. They had a special handshake greeting, shook with right hand, doesn't matter which hand the member was endowed with, and rubbed their two thumbs together while shaking.

They punctually arrived for their meetings, greet each other a little, no social or business discussions, no family discussions or anything outside the agenda of the brotherhood. Most times, no food was to be served, so it meant that attending members needed to be on a full tank before the attending the meetings at the temple. Beverages consisted of vintage alcoholics and non-alcoholic and it was on a buffet basis. An intoxication at their meetings had severe consequences and so was any misconduct exhibited from the moment of entrance into the compound. Members, even though, were devil worshippers, were expected to maintain candor and dignifying presence when they were privileged to be in the compound or be in the revered presence of the conducting leader or prefect of the order. Violation of their rules had dire consequences and such violations rarely happened. Punctuality was taken very seriously as well as paying attention to all agendas for the day. The meeting hall got set up before the meeting started, candles in odd colors lit up, temple fixed with black and dark yellow clothing as a decoration of the interior. The leader started the meetings and conducted it to the end. As soon as the meeting was over, the leader, without exchanging any pleasantries, existed through the back door and members had to leave immediately.

✳✳✳

Ericson was a low member of the cult in Malibu, very rich and accomplished as a CPA. He had offices in Canon Street Beverly Hills, downtown Santa Monica, and on Wilshire Blvd., Westwood. He has been a member of the cult before he got married to his wife. The wife, Donna was a dentist and had a modest practice in Long Beach before he met and married Ericson. She was born and raised in the beach city of Long Beach, in the greater Los Angeles metropolis. Ericson previously was involved in an upscale divorce case, involving two kids and tons of community properties being fought over by him and his ex-wife. It was a very nasty case, highly litigated and ended in tragedy of his wife and the two minor kids.

Ericson never disclosed that to his new wife, Donna. Ericson and Donna had an initial first 4 years of a blissful relationship but Ericson, with a lot of cash to throw around, was a night crawler and a serial womanizer. Donna got used to receiving him back by odd hours of night. He came home very drunk and was very arrogant and standoffish about it. They couldn't even start a family because he was sexually, a disaster, at least to her. He was only and always obsessed with his job and street life. He had fleet of Rolls and Bentleys. He believed that he was on top of the world and untouchable. His wife could understand his wealth-related arrogance but his other attitude of superiority complex seemed predicated on something that she couldn't fathom out. Donna was determined to find out but what she did not understand was that her expedition and any findings therefrom, will spill a disaster and people were going to die in the process. She just didn't want a sleeping dog to lie anymore.

She started planning on how to embark on her discoveries. She hired a private investigator from an upscale Beverly Hills area, optimal in fees and performances justifying his steep charges. They scheduled to meet in the office of the private eye.

The private investigator, Dante, was a retired US Army Intelligence officer that received the best of the best trainings in US intelligence gathering and networking. He employed that in the pursuit of his private eye business. His equipment was state of the art, at all times. He had capable, well-paid staff that were thoroughly trained to discover anything from the end of the earth. They had the best eavesdropping gadgets, cameras that could capture events, pictures, motion and still from a one- mile distance and beyond. Their vehicles were equipped for reconnaissance and secret cameras installed at the perimeter of the vehicles. They had powerful Doppler recorders that could hear conversations held inside a fully raised vehicle windows and from up to 100 feet away. They had corrupt helpers on their payrolls from all major telecommunication companies including cell phone companies. They could interrupt satellite phone and similar equipment. They had military style encryption breaker equipment that could open encrypted messages on any and all equipment or platforms, including all social media. Their retainership fee was a minimum of a non-refundable fee of fifty thousand dollars. They achieved results and they were relentless in the pursuit of scoops and dirt. They also made a lot of money by stumbling into high news scoops for media houses on the collateral findings during their investigations. Dante was a true

Beverly Hills class service provider. You get what you pay for. His phone rang and Donna scheduled the appointment for next week Tuesday which she kept. She entered the office on the 5th floor of Dante's office and they had an hour meeting. He received Ericson's full data; his date of birth; their address; their phone numbers; the carriers of the cell phones; the make of the phones; how long Ericson have had the phone, how many lines he had; his social media types, if any; his close friends, if any; his office addresses, his type of business; his place of birth; his parents name; his siblings, if any; his bank names; etc. These were all filled out in the form that formed a highly confidential and classified information folder created by Dante's office. Donna wanted all dirt and anything on Ericson. She paid premium money from a secret account she just opened for this purpose. She was a disgruntled spouse who had nothing to lose. She believed that Ericson was a heartless asshole and that she was going to be a bitch to him, with the acclaimed wrath of a woman. The fury was a whirlwind and that Ericson would receive. She did not know the dimension of what her espionage will lead her to and what her husband Ericson was into. She never foresaw that she was stepping into a lion's den but she would find out in an ugly way and that would stink to high heavens. Donna wanted to know everything about the lives and times of Ericson outside their home.

She had endured enough, believing that she lost her youth and the chance of being a mother to this unrepentant idiot that had no respect for womanhood. She would destroy him by biting and sucking his blood. She never knew that Ericson was a Demarkian and that a war waged against the brotherhood was a dance of death. On this beautiful day in greater Los Angeles, the much respected city of Angels, Ericson, cautiously finished his work for the day, trying to avoid the traffic, drove out in his new and intimidating Jaguar S-type, custom built. He drove to the cult meeting in Malibu, playing his Kenny Rogers music a little loud while enjoying the moments.

Dante's job had started as he followed him in three different well-equipped vehicles changing drivers and communicating with each other, just normal investigative routine process. Ericson, consumed in his music didn't even notice that he was being followed. They followed him to the gate of the entrance of the temple and pulled over down the road and waited for him. He went into the temple and met with the leader, who dialogued with him for 20 minutes and dismissed him. On his way out the leader called him back and informed him that a tribulation is happening around him but that the brotherhood has seen it, know what it was and would take care of it. He was assured not to worry about it. He thanked the master and drove off. Dante and his staff followed him back to his house. They filed it in their report and dispersed. They tried running the profile of the building in Malibu, the ownership, the use, but they couldn't find anything of assistance in their quest.

The Demarkians meeting was coming up in two weeks -time and Dante had a whiff of it because they have fully tapped into Ericson's phone, followed him and found out all his sexual escapades, his social modus operandi, his thwarted and rotten lifestyles. They followed him to the clubs, got a picture of him with different women, in different hotels. and in the process found out that he was also a sissy! Ericson was on the downlow! They got pictures of him in the gay clubs, with compromising position of him and guys. Even in some instances when he had claimed to be out of town, he would be in an exquisite 6 star hotels tucked behind the exclusive parts of the upscale city of Westwood. He would be involved in sex marathon with extraordinarily good looking fine women and men from the topmost escort services that serviced the richest axis of Beverly Hills, Bel Air, Malibu, Hollywood, Westwood and Santa Monica. Those escort services did not entertain calls from any other part of the world. Their fees were in high five digits per day. Their male and female whores [

you dare not call them that!] usually, were currently, college men and women or college graduated, with continuous validations in the form of medical check-ups and authentications.

Ericson was a big time patron of all of them and they knew him with different stage names. Ericson had a secret bank account with consistent millions of dollars' balance devoted in paying for the escort services and his perverted lifestyle. Everything about Ericson was sleazy and dirty. He lived and breath evil.

Today he was in a hotel with a guy, brown glossy eye Italian, 28-year-old gay whore but officially he was supposed to be in New York as he indicated to his wife.

Donna Called him and the following discussions took place:

Donna: Hey, Hun, how are you?

Ericson: wonderful, New York is another heaven on earth, especially upper Manhattans!

Donna: How is the weather over there?

Ericson: fantastic. I just got in from the Empire state building.

Donna: Oh, yea, how was it?

Ericson: fabulous, I chattered a tour chopper and they dropped me on top of the building. It was something else, sweetie.

Donna: what else did you see in New York?

Eric: I rode the bike around major streets of the city. I went to the WTO on bike tours, went in and saw the names of the September 11 victims, felt so bad baby. How bad and heartless people could be!

Donna: what else you got to do?

Ericson: Tomorrow, I will be in the island to see our lady of freedom, the statue of Liberty.

Donna: Oh, by the way, my apologies for not being able to take you to the airport

Ericson: Oh, thats ok honey. I used the Uber xl, fun riding, nice Ethiopian guy, beautiful accent and we talked about Africa. I think it is time for us to visit Africa, the safe parts.

Donna: what did you eat today?

Ericson: I ate Jamaican food, brown rice with ox tail. I took a ride to the Jamaican Plains, lovely place, a lot of blacks, Rastafarians, with the creole and patois, oh lord I love to hear that English but I can't even understand most of what they say. Yea man…laughter. I love Bob Marley music and I was playing that in my Spotify, fully streamed.

Donna: Did you visit anyone yet?

Eric: Nope, you know I am not into friends thing. I am reclusive.

Donna: Are you for real?

Ericson: Surprise you asked that. As my wife you should know better. How many visitors have we had since we got married?

Donna: I don't figure that, not a lot but maybe because you are never at home to receive them. Have
you thought about that?

Ericson: I guess you may be right. Hey, how is Los Angeles?

Donna: Don't change the topic please.

Ericson: Lets jump right back at it, what's up?

Donna: So all the time you have been hanging out, you were not hanging with friends? Because you never invited me out!

Ericson: Hun, most of those are meetings, not social gatherings.

Donna: are you always come home drunk from the meetings? were the meetings held in breweries?

Ericson: The liquor is to buzz me up for alertness and we drank after the meetings, most times.

Donna: Hmmm, that's interesting, sounds like fun to me. Maybe I need to go back to college and study accounting. what do you think about that sweetie?

Ericson: Too late. What is that for? We have all the money in the world.

Donna: There is more to life than money. You come home, sometimes reeling of fine liquors and happy. You look fulfilled. I wanna be like you too, think about it. They say that a fun without a spouse in tow is wasted fun, do you agree with that, babe?

Ericson: Absolutely! Do you know how miserable I feel when I am out there without you?

Donna: But you don't invite me?

Ericson: because it has not been social outings, accounting practice, meetings, arguments, sometimes yelling and rancor.

Donna: Just like you didn't invite me to this New York trip?

Ericson: Same answer sweetie.

Donna: work, work, work.

Donna: work, work, at the Empire state building? Statue of liberty, Jamaican plains, etc.?

Ericson: You are becoming technical now, Donna.

Donna: Oh, beautiful, you rarely call me by my name. What happened now? Are you nervous?

Ericson: I think that maybe you need to go to law school, will be a good cross- examiner, hahahahaha.

Donna: Why would you say that? By asking you common sense question that a primary school child
could figure out?

Ericson: I see it differently.

Donna: How long are you out there for?

Ericson: 5 more days.

Donna: Are you auditing the Rockefellers account?

Ericson: I wish. I have forensic examination of some corporate books.

Donna: I am not an illiterate Hun. Forensic requires adversity and court case. Which case and which forensic analysis?

Ericson: You are wrong, forensic accounting does not have to require a court case.

Donna: So why would you be that long in New York? What about me? Do you want me to run the street, clubbing? Don't I deserve a life too?

Ericson: I have to do this and make money for us.

Donna: I have told you before that there is more to life than money, right?

Ericson: kinda, sort of.

Donna: You said we have too much money, which I agree with, more money than we will ever need in our life time. So why would you leave me here all by myself and you were never around?

Ericson: Hun, I thought you called to check on me and keep me warm on the phone?

Donna: oh I thought I was doing that. I am sorry if I lost it for a minute.

Ericson: That's ok as I can imagine. I can't wait to be in your arms soon.

[Donna muttered under her angry breath: You sleazy son of a bitch!]

Ericson: What did you just say? [he heard the comment]

Donna: sweetie, I wasn't talking about you. I was reacting to a tv program.

Ericson: oh the Epicenter series?

Donna: yes

Ericson: which season now?

Donna: Episode 5, Season 8.

Ericson: I need to watch more tv

Donna: If you are around and sober enough to follow the story.

Ericson: what you mean?

Donna: It means that you are not awake at home long enough to watch any program.

Sometimes, I wonder whether you even know who is the current president of our country.

Ericson: Tell me about it, babe.

Donna: About what?

Ericson: About my f****up life style, hahahaha.

Donna: You know it more than I do. But things always come out no matter how much we try to conceal them. We are what we see of ourselves in the mirror. Nobody will ever know you like yourself. Remember the saying, that we are the prime movers of our destinies. Meaning that we are in the driver's seats of our lives. The vehicle moves to the direction that we steer them to. Life is full of choices and the choice that we make will determine the life we live, the sanity and sanctity, right?

Ericson: Are you now a philosopher?

Donna: we all are one.

Ericson: I am not. My life is a simple open book, and I am happy for it.

Donna: Oh, you sure do. But I don't know about the openness of your book, if you can keep me here in Los Angeles and gallivant away to New York.

Ericson: Oh babe, I am so sorry. When I come back, we travel to Africa, I promise.

Donna: There you go, that's very nice of you. Thanks a lot, that's a good one. Hey wait a minute, I have an idea, I have my frequent flyer miles, first class that will soon expire, let me fly into New York with it in the morning. You can do your meetings and I will be in the room, at least we can do the sightseeing together!

There was a prolonged muted silence for thirty seconds.

Donna: Are you there?

Donna: Are you there, sweetie?

Ericson: I am here babe, just was in thought analyzing what you said.

Donna: why does it need an analysis?

Ericson: Its ok, I will change my flight and come back in two days.

Donna: Why would you do that? Because you don't want me to come to New York, huh?

Ericson: Not that. I don't want you to go through all that trouble.

Donna: It is a good trouble, Hun. I am flying first class.

Then a phone rang on the background, a male, with a sleepy voice started talking; Ericson could be heard making a muting shhhh sound to the male voice who hung up the phone, and cursed.

Donna: What is that voice? who was that?

Eric: That was the Tv

Donna: But I heard you making hush sound, right?

Ericson: No I didn't.

Donna: Are you auditing with other accountants?

Ericson, sounding irritated: I said No!

Donna: You beginning to sound angry, honey. Why is that?

Ericson: Because I don't know why you are badgering me.

■■■

Donna: How. I am your wife and you are in New York; I am missing you; You are lonely; I am keeping you "warm on the phone". So how could that be badgering?

Ericson: Never mind though. But I got go.

Donna: Not yet Hun. I am still being warmy [Donna smiled and stuck out his middle finger at the phone.]

Ericson: What else is going on in LA?

Donna: same ol; same ol

Donna: Did you hear of the last earthquake, 5.3 out of Lennox?

Ericson: where is Lenox?

Donna: Lennox is next to Hawthorne or Inglewood.

Ericson: where are all these cities? In Los Angeles County?

Donna: Oh, I forgot you are a big time, so big that you are detached from reality, huh?

Ericson: What's reality? That I don't know some third rated cities?

Donna: You refer to Inglewood as third rated?

Ericson: Yes, it has to be if I don't know it!

Donna: So all the cities that you know are upscale and first rated?

Ericson: I guess.

Donna: Ok Mr. Big stuff. If I may ask when did you make your first million?

Ericson: It's been a minute Hun. I don't maintain a record of poverty.

Donna: You are really arrogant and cocky; you know that?

Ericson: I guess; it comes with the territory.

Donna: You were not from a rich family, remember?

Ericson: Well, the clock has reset for me, ain't it?

Donna: Looks like it but vanities will never because you fail to see it as so, right?

Ericson: You are speaking in riddle, babe.

Donna: The things of life are vanities and they will not stop being that because you see it differently. Does that make sense to you?

Ericson: If I understand you correctly; you meant that my obsession with worldly vanities will not change their characterizations from being vanities, right?

Donna: Yes.

Ericson: Well, what you refer to as vanities are actually the essence of life. Money rules the world and you know that. If you have money, you can have the world in your pocket. Material wealth makes life easier and confi. Know what I mean?

Donna: Not, not at all, don't understand your drift, Socrates!

Ericson: The good things of life come from wealth and its vestiges. We scramble and hustle to acquire money so that we have access to those things, including you. If I was to be a cab driver, you wouldn't have married me, would you honestly?

Donna: Are you saying that I married you for your wealth?

Ericson: It is part of the packaging. No money, no honey, sounds a familiar phrase?

Donna: You are an asshole, for real. I went to college and had a good job. When I was asked to embrace my mistakes by a book of philosophy that I used to read, I embraced you, remember that?

Ericson: I thought you were joking that day?

Donna: No, I wasn't. At least you can see it now.

Ericson: Why do you view me as a mistake?

Donna: Switch the shoe on the other leg and you can understand what I meant.

Ericson: What do you mean by that?

Donna: Imagine that you and I switch positions. You need to step into my shoes to understand my pain. In your mind, you believe that you are a good husband but I guess that you have a conscience or have you sold your soul to the devil?

On hearing this innocent statement from Donna, Ericson, got very excited and his anger thermometer was climaxed in a second and he started cursing on Donna, calling her a bitch and all sorts of names. Donna was taken aback but she kept quiet while Ericson was roasting her. At the end, the discussion continued.

Donna: I don't understand your emotional roller coaster and why you went off the cliff over a casual statement that has been said from time immemorial. Your sensitivity to the reference: "selling your soul to the devil" has become a catchword for me and I will explore it more. Because I am perplexed at your reaction when I said that.

Ericson: where are we going with this discussion? Are you trying to put me down?

Donna: Nope. The last time I checked, you are still my darling husband [Donna stuck out her middle finger again to the phone.]

Ericson: So, tell me, are you unhappy in this marriage?

Donna: what do you think boss?

Ericson: I don't know, you tell me.

Donna: Why don't you switch the shoe and do your appraisals?

Ericson: Maybe I have to do that.

Donna: Oh, is that a maybe, honey?

Ericson: Is it mandatory?

Donna: Following your world, it is not, but in the world of sanity and equity, it is.

Ericson: Equity, how?

Donna: it is an English word with a simple meaning. You should know what it means because you went to college which is the primary reason I married you and not because of your wealth. If you continue to be
daft about it, equity means fairness.

Ericson: You sound frustrated and unhappy.

Donna: That's a gross understatement.

Ericson: I will see what I can do for you.

Donna: You cannot offer what you don't have.

Ericson: what does that mean?

Donna: A leopard that does not lose its spots. Animals do not lose their instincts because they are reoriented.

Ericson: You are getting me more confused wifey?

Donna: Hussy, it is difficult for you to change from who you are. Your internal make –up and wiring, your psych module, your perceptions about life, especially your troubling attachment to material wealth, makes it imperative that you are not and never going to be a nice person.

Ericson: Are you saying that I am not a nice person?

Donna: You are not very far from the truth.

Ericson: waoh, that is very troubling.

Donna: It should be. I am human too and it looks like I am not entitled to be happy. You monopolized
our marital happiness all to yourself. I have kept quiet all these while.

Then the same male voice was heard at the background talking to what sounds like room service, in very low tone. Few seconds, footsteps could be heard tiptoeing out of the room.

Donna: Is that the same voice at the background. The tv? I heard some footsteps, who were those?

Ericson: Are you hallucinating?

Donna: Maybe, I am. But I find it coincidental that the same voice was heard again after close to two hours of our discussions.

Ericson: Are you expecting a response from me on that?

Donna: If you feel like, doesn't matter anyways. Remember what I said about the leopard and its spots?

Ericson: I do, profoundly.

Donna: Oh by the way, I change my mind. I am not coming to New York. Stay back and enjoy your stay. I will see you when you get back.

Ericson breathed in relief: hurriedly said, Ok, we talk. let me get some sleep.

Meanwhile, Dante and his crews were listening to the whole discussions next two suites down the
hallway in the same hotel where Ericson was calling from.

The only thing that Donna knows about Ericson adventure and lies, having been briefed earlier by Dante, was that Ericson was not in New York as he claimed. She was informed that Ericson was there.

Dante at this point, later, felt that he had to give Donna a summary of his findings so far. He called Donna up and asked her to brace up for a very bad news. Donna's heart almost jumped out of her chest. She started precipitating and sweating. Dante informed Donna that his husband, is among other ills, a bi-sexual, and that the guy in the background was one of his favorite male whores.

There was also a female whore, a pretty college lady in the room and that Ericson is a threesome monger.

Donna screamed and the phone fell out of her hands, as she started crying so loudly and cursing. Dante was saying hello, where are you? I am so sorry, maybe I would have disclosed this in person; I am so sorry... Donna was yelling and crying and did not even hear Dante anymore. Donna, was calling on God to take her; why do you allow me to marry this evil man? God, I thought that they say that you are the perfect planner? Is it because I have not been worshiping you? Is it because I don't go to church? Oh my goodness, somebody tell me that this not happening; somebody should wake me up from this dream; No, no, no. no. no.nooooooooo!; my mum, my dad, y'all come and save me!! What in the world? Am I infected with diseases? What else is this evil man up to? Who is he? What else he has in his closet? She continued to cry incessantly and very loudly.

Donna went to the bar and drank directly from the bottle, a full bottle of a blended scotch whiskey, all by herself. She was exhausted, fell tired and slept off.

She woke up next day, a wreck of herself, with a migraine that seemed to be tearing off her entire head. She woke to the shocking realization that she was married to a gay man without knowing it. She felt retarded, disappointed in herself that she missed all the clues. She felt dumb that even when she noticed Vaseline lotion on her husband's private area, with his lame explanation being that he rubs Vaseline to cure dryness! She, in few occasions, smelt booboo in his panties sometimes but believed it may have been as a result of his hemorrhoid disease. She felt like an idiot. She could now understand why he showed little or no interest in their sexual life. But, again, Dante said that he is bisexual. In her mind, she asked, so what happens to the other female half? She got infuriated, stood up, in a melancholy way, asked again loudly as if she was demented: what happened to the other half! Am I not good enough? She lost it, started screaming: am I not good enough? What's up with that! asshole, idiot! You and I are going to be picked up from the drain gutter, when we finished fighting! This is it for me. She started crying loudly again. She rushed over and picked up their wedding pictures and all the pictures on the wall and smashed them on the wall shattering them. She wanted to set the whole house on fire but quickly restrained herself, knowing that the war has not even started. She also started nursing a homicidal feeling. She thought about arranging to kill Ericson but brushed it aside.

Donna continued her drinking to the point that her mentality started getting compromised, crying and laughing insanely. She could not believe that her life could get this screwed up so fast. She reminiscence on the day she met this evil, idiotic, sissy husband of hers. She reviewed her life with him and couldn't imagine if hell was worse than that. She was beyond sad and depressed. She knew she will need more than professional help to get beyond this problem, believing that no shrink could handle her issues. Ericson was a green snake in green grass but she is going to be a combined mamba and king cobra to him. She would go for his jugular; she would bite and suck his blood; she would be a demonstration of hell having no fury than the wrath of a bitch!
She started crying again, again and again and later dozed off till the next day. Her cell phone was dead and she did not want to charge it. She wanted to be alone, to clear her head and plan for the battle ahead. Her fight with Ericson might win an Oscar movie, at the end of the day. She yelled, Ericson, son of a bitch, you touched and bite the tail of a tigress, get ready for an Armageddon!

She drank a lot of milk to counteract the alcoholic effects, took some Excedrin migraine, ordered door dash of very spicy combo fried rice from an upscale Thai restaurant in Beverly Hills. Sat down, still cuckoo, but a little restrained, and waited for her food. She has not eaten in two days but she was not reasonably hungry. The food arrived, she did the best she could and ate some food, went back to her drinking spree. Later she called her sister, Claret, and detailed her out on every bit. It was catastrophic and her sister started crying for a prolonged period of time. Claret, a pediatrician based in St Petersburg, Florida, have always despised Ericson. She calls him arrogant s.o.b. and nothing more. She tried, at all times, to avoid seeing him. Claret had always maintained that there was something about Ericson that doesn't add up. She just doesn't understand why a human being would have the disposition that Ericson had. He treated his sister and everyone else like nothing. He was uppity, talked and acted as if he had the world in his pocket. He was completely deficient in humility and decency. Claret called their parents and relayed the whole story to them. It was a devastating blow to such a good and modest family. Their father invited all his kids to their current home in Miami, for a meeting. Like any parent, he understood all his kids and he knew what they were wired out to do in all situations. He understood that Donna was capable of anything if triggered. He wanted to abort that. Most importantly, as a doting father, he was still a dad that vowed to protect his kids from all harms, either within or without. He wanted to take back his daughter and revive her and make her happy again. With this information, her marriage to Ericson was over and so shall it be. If he doesn't get involved, something might hit the fan. He was an ardent Christian and the bible has always been his refuge. He planned to get his kids back to the lord who fights all battles and heals all wounds.

Donna didn't want to go to Miami but they love and respect their parents a lot. They viewed their parents as next to God and should be treated so. Donna, among all the kids, loved her father to death. She prayed to get a husband like her dad but wishes are not always horses. Her wish was there but Ericson turned out to be a cunny, diabolical, evil, perverted beast.

Donna mustered some strength and bought a first-class ticket on-line and flew out to Miami that evening. She took an Uber home into the arms of all her family, her parents, her siblings, all with tears in their eyes. They loved her so much and they shared in her sorrows too. They were bonded together and always shared in their joys and sorrows, together. Everyone whispered something in her ears; it shall be well, her father chimed to her ears.

For the first time in days, Donna was happy or had a semblance of happiness. She had not seen her siblings and her parents for a while. They were there in flesh and blood, not surprisingly, exuding love to each other. Her mum made her sit on her laps, running her finger through her hairs, and consoling her. Her father was squeezing her hands. She started crying again and the whole family, except the father, couldn't help it and they all started crying with her. It was so emotional and pathetic. The father brought his bible and put it aside for a later reading and communing with the lord. It has to be sometime tomorrow. The family continued their joyous time, the best they could make of the circumstances. They tried to steer their discussions, gossips and social talks away from the Ericson saga. They were all determined to make Donna happy, whatever reasonably necessary it may take. Donna understood the feel of the moment and tried so hard to move with the tide. She tried to stay away from alcohol considering what she has done to herself in the last three days but she needed the buzzy therapy of alcohol. She downgraded to just cold beers and water. She was just hanging in and pretending as if there was really nothing much to worry about. But self- deceit could be very aggravating to hurtful situations. Now and then, her mind flashed to her idiotic husband and what he, or is it she was up to now. When she thought of that, she had this evil smirk on her face. She had a vile in her soul and a darkness of mind that could melt a metal. Even though she was not a good actress, she continued to pretend and acted as if everything was okay and dandy. It is what it is though, as she extended her long immaculate fingers to pick another can of Heineken beer.

Her siblings found the ambience enticing and beautiful as they giggled about everything. They were having wonderful moments together or so it seemed. Now and then, they stole a glance on their sister, who seemed to struggle with an obvious inner turmoil. They were all hurting but they didn't want to show that to Donna. They needed to pretend as if everything was fine and under control, to motivate their sister from her emotional tsunami.

Donna, in fleeting moments, thought about Ericson and when he will be coming back to their house. She blocked him in her phone, email and all social media. It was hard to block him via email but she was able to find an app from the i- phone app store that allowed her to do that. That was just the beginning. She started thinking of going back to California as soon as possible for the great confrontation and showdown. The thought made her grind her teeth and she almost bit her tongue. The emotion started building up and she stood up to go to the lady's room.

Ericson, feeling exhausted from his perverted sexual acts and alcoholism and cocaine use, decided to check on his bitchy wife. All his calls were not going through. He tried reaching Donna via all social media but none seems to be going through. He tried Facebook messenger but realized that Donna blocked him. He became alarmed as to what was going on. He thought of using another phone to call his wife but decided that it wouldn't be a good idea. He remained puzzled about the situation for a while and later diverted his attention to the glorious white powder spread out on the bed stand. He muttered: go to hell Donna and stay there.

✳✳✳

Meanwhile Dante was gathering a lot of information on Ericson and his nefarious lifestyle. His eavesdropping revealed that Ericson was involved in Satan worship and that he may be a member of a brotherhood of an evil cult. He learnt that they will be having a meeting soon. Dante also learnt that Ericson has a secret safe in a highly and discreet part of Studio city, near Hollywood. Luckily for Dante, he had a hook-up in the safe storage place. He contacted his contact and they arranged for a meeting the next day. Dante called Donna and intimated her of his new findings including the cocaine use. Donna got maxed out being distraught. She thanked Dante for his good job. The die was cast anyways. Dante met with John and they arranged to allow Dante access to Ericson safe, to inspect everything in it and copy them, if possible. John and Dante agreed to accomplish that on Saturday when John was going to be working alone in the storage facility.

The leader of the Demarkians, having known about these ants and their activities, decided to pay attention and handle the situation without informing Ericson. Leader called Ericson and they spoke. He asked Ericson to go back home and stay low. He advised Ericson to make peace with his wife, if possible. Leader informed him that the brotherhood, since yesterday, have just paid attention to the black cloud hanging on his head recently. The operation of the cult and their activities are prone for a breach and the fraternity will intervene now.

✳ ✳ ✳

Dante, like other multitudes of the faith, was a sinful Christian, not being a practicing one. He had the affinity with his catholic faith. He, disappointedly, found it very difficult to keep the Ten Commandments and other biblical injunctions. He had the crucifix hanging on the rear-view mirror of his personal vehicles. He prayed only at the time of adversity. He had been confessing his sins up to certain point that he felt that God wouldn't listen to him anymore and he stopped.

Dante met with John and they agreed to access the safe tomorrow by 2 p.m.

That would be a herculean task as the cult didn't approve of such intrusion and they took that very serious. Dante drove out in his new BMW seven series and was playing his John Legend music, nodding his head and smiling, embracing his successful life. He touched his Rosary with the crucifix and kissed it. He started recounting our Lord's Prayer and the prayers of the saint. He pulled up at the rendezvous with John and waited for john. He lowered his car seat to relax and at that point, a cat, black and white in color jumped on top of his hood, lazily walked up to his front windshield, had a fixated look at Dante, made a consistent eye contact with Dante, opened its mouth menacingly to Dante showing the fanged tooth at both sides of its upper dentition, made a subtle cry for few seconds. The demonic music came up and started playing from nowhere and was getting louder and louder. Dante quickly checked on his windows and found out that they were all up and he quickly pushed the central lock buttons. The cat remained there for a while starring at Dante and Dante turned on the windshield wiper to strike the cat out of his car but the cat easily moved away from the wipers reach.

Dante was confused about why a cat should be on his windshield in a broad daylight and not making any effort to move. At that point, John Pulled up and the cat jumped down and disappeared. Dante and John talked and drove out to the safe place which is about a mile down the road. John did not want to leave his car parked at the premises. In few minutes, they got to the place and parked. Dante removed his Rosary, kissed it and put it on his neck, a practice that he normally does unconsciously. They walked into the locked building by John opening the highly secured door using his assigned codes and electric access card. They walked to the array of safes and were giggling and laughing. On getting to the safe belonging to Ericson, a black bird was perching on the safe handle looking at them fearlessly. They were very surprised as to how the bird got into the building? Why was it on the very safe they wanted to access? Why was it not flying away? They stood and watched the bird for a while but it wasn't making any effort to fly away. John removed one of his jack work boots from his leg and approached the bird in anger, raised his hands to smash the stupid bird but he wasn't prepared for what happened next.

The safe and the hallway started vibrating as if there was an earthquake. The black bird, the Demarkian bird, with its signature blood dripping eyes, swiftly attacked them ferociously. John was making all efforts to strike the bird with his shoe but it was a futile exercise as a force kept freezing his hand anytime he tried striking the bird. They started running away but the bird was unrelenting and was in close hot pursuit of them. They kept running and on getting to the general area, John slipped and fell to the floor and the bird rushed on him but John was able to ward it off and ran out of the door into the parking lot, just like Dante did. The door was closed and jam-locked before the bird could fly out. They ran to their car but the bird was there already, perched on top of the car door, waiting for them with its vicious eyes, with the demonic sound playing. Dante came to momentary realization that they were dealing with an evil spirit!

Dante pulled out the rosary from his neck and held out the crucifix as a screen while approaching his car. The bird, felt restless on seeing that and flew away. Dante and John, very upset, even though scared, and having realized the power of the crucifix, decided to go back into the building and accomplish their mission. They walked back in straight to the safe deposit box and opened it. Dante pulled out everything in the safe, open the first wrapped journal and saw very clear paraphernalia of evil worship. He looked in further and notice more disturbing contents. He brought his transportable memory copier from his bag and copied everything in that safe, put them back and they left. John turned back and reset the surveillance camera back to recording just as they left the building. John was dropped where he picked his car, drove off home puzzled and confused despite the explanations given to him by Dante. Dante has waged a war with the Demarkians and that was the beginning of his woes, may be.

Donna's depression continued unabated despite the family's effort to curb that. Claret was doing everything imaginable to stop her from gliding further down in her emotional turmoil. She could imagine what Donna was going through. She cried in secrecy too. Her instincts turned in and out of murderous too. The animosity towards Ericson surpassed vile. The Ericson that was known as a monster was an Angel until they find out more who he was. Ericson was a reincarnate of devil.

Donna's other siblings came out to be with her, kissing her on the cheek and holding her hands. The brother volunteered to go for her favorite Thai cuisine but Donna was far from being hungry. Her only appetite at this point was to tie Ericson in a stake and dissect him, like a medical student, with a clinical knife. She puts up fake smiles now and then but her family understood the deep agony, like a whirlwind going on in her mind. They were doing the best that they could to reclaim her but that was a herculean task. Her brother, Charles, at some point, even nursed the idea of paying Ericson an acrimonious visit but snapped out of it. The parents were deeper in thoughts and were invoking all the wisdoms in their aged brain to handle the situation. They talked about just extracting their daughter from Ericson without seeking for any community property from him. They felt so bad about the damages inflicted on their child who got married and expected bliss and blessings.

The father called all out and started preaching the word of God to them. Reminding the children who they were and their Christian background. He reiterated to all that he had continuously been teaching them about the troubles and challenges of life. The wordings of the holy book, especially the psalms will be your spiritual elixir on times of hopelessness and travails. He reminded them that there is always going to be sunshine after the rain. That the world got polluted from the Garden of Eden when Adam disobeyed God and was cursed...Ericson is a product of our imperfections and that he should be forgiven. He told them the wordings of Nelson Mandela who forgave the white apartheid South African oppressors who jailed him unjustly for 27 years. Mandela forgave them as soon as he left the prison gates stating as follows: "If I had left that prison, with anger and without the forgiveness, I will remain in prison forever". You are the first victim of your anger. Anger, grievance, vindictive thoughts, rancorous mindset, is a great burden to carry. There is no difference between you and your offender if you seek for and exacted a revenge. You have to be the change that you want to see. Anger and depravity of conscience violates all teachings of the lord and leads you to the wrong path. Raising you kids, I was very consistent in teaching you virtues. I brought you up in the ways of the lord, which is the right part. I have been very firm in my consistent efforts to steer you away from the vanities of life. When you fell out of line, I had always brought you back on the straight path. Your mother and I will not relent from such hallowed duties and obligations. Like anyone else, you will face temptations, trials and tribulations, but your approach in the face of all that is determinative of who you truly are. There is no shame in falling down but remaining where you have fallen is a humiliation. According to Socrates, in a letter to his son's teacher, he said: teach my child the powers of forgiveness; teach him that a dollar earned is better than ten found; teach him not to join the bandwagon when everyone else is doing so; teach him that the test of fire makes a fine steel…;

Donna's father paused to make sure that the last statement sunk in, repeated it again: "teach him that the test of fire makes a fine steel". Your life is hollow without tribulations. Remember the saying of the bible, in Ecclesiastes and other epistles: "It is well with my soul". It teaches you to accept things that you cannot change. You need to accept and move on. That we are mere mortals with little or no knowledge of this world, as well as this life. We are completely powerless in the enormous face of the trials and challenges of life. We are like the morning dew, a mist that could disappear in minutes. You cannot grieve like an unbeliever and people without hope. Ericson, obviously is not a good person because of the choices he has chosen to live with. He has chosen to be a follower of Satan and remember he had the right to create his life path and there is nothing anyone can do about that. We can pray for his redemption, as children of God. Remember that Jesus came to this world for people like Ericson.

Donna was beginning to get restless about the mention and forgiveness of Ericson. She wished that she could just exit from this meeting. But She shouldn't try that, as she knew better. They revere their father a lot and they believed that he was next to God, a good man. She tried to smiled and continued to listen to her adorable father, a prince of peace.

Her father continued in his admonitions and sermons. He looked at Donna and informed her that he could imagine her anger and even her disdain for his words but assured her that time heals all wounds. A lot of people are faced with very bad and heinous challenges in life but they don't even have a family like she does. They don't have a listening ear. That worsens the sorrow, when you feel isolated in your grief. My lovely children, you know that you are all that your mother and I have in this sinful and wicked world. We will always wish you, like Dolly Parton says: happiness but above all things, we wish you love. We are still living and on top of the soil firstly by his grace and secondly because of you. We share in your joys and sorrows. When Jesus was humiliated, tortured, nailed to the cross, very vividly represented in the movie, the passion of Christ, he looked up to the heaven and asked God to forgive his oppressors.

Nelson Mandela, a mere mortal like you and I did same. When his people, his fellow blacks in south Africa refused to forgive the racist whites, he told them, quoting him:" I have forgiven them. If I can forgive them, you should". This was a man, a young lawyer, married to one of the prettiest women in the country, had his beautiful world ahead of him, arrested and convicted for a trumped up charge of treason, like Jesus was charged with treasonable felony, and he was jailed for 27 years in an island prison, with hard labor, a concentration camp, if you choose to call it that. He lost everything, lost his youth, his law practice, lost being a dad to his lovely kids, released from prison at old age. He forgave his oppressors sincerely and demonstratively.

The platform of all good religious' teachings especially that of Christianity that I know of, is total and unconditional forgiveness. Like Socrates said to his son's teacher, these are tall orders, please see what you can do about them. I am not asking you Donna to see what you can do about them but rather to let go. I am extending that injunctions to all of you to forgive your trespassers as you will wish to be forgiven.

He continued by stating that they were going to have this meeting again before y'all go back to your residences. Before then, please be soul providers to our lovely Donna, "our queen of the coast" as we fondly used to call her. On hearing this name, Donna, for the first time had a hearty smile and hugged everyone. She loves her family infinitely.

Claret asked Donna to dress up for a –girls- all -night out but she declined. Claret said that she wasn't asking her opinion but, as a senior, telling her to dress up for the night, as it was an order!
They called lyft and jetted out to the Miami Grails, with a live band, beautiful crowd, fine music, beverages, wonderful foods. It was a wild night of fun. Donna did her best to stay emotionally afloat. Like her dad said, it was a tall order. They danced all through the night to bands and the DJ music. They got back home in the morning and crashed to the bed.

✱✱✱

Dante downloaded the copied materials and printed them out.
He started reading them and kept screaming curses on Ericson; You evil man; you s.o.b; You devil incarnate; a killer. And then he quieted down to read more and organize his thoughts too. He saw the Demarkian literatures and the memberships, their meetings and modus operandi; He read, to his greatest shock, that Ericson

Boulder was a fake man. His true name was Ericson Wilkerson, originally from Kentucky. He saw a newspaper clips about his murder trial in Kentucky. The damaging background information about Ericson, with his picture showing. He read in the clips as follows:

"Ericson was married to a beautiful woman some years ago; met the girl, Maggie, in a social gathering and one thing led to the other and they got married in a quiet ceremony. They started life together and had two kids, a boy first and a girl later. Family was happy or so it appeared to the external world. They had some bliss at some point until the late nights and money issues. Ericson acted weird and disoriented sometimes and his conduct was giving Maggie concerns. His quench for money, sometimes, appeared desperate. Sometimes he came home high and disoriented but there wouldn't be any smell of alcohol. She picked up his phone one day and the male caller said: hey baby, how you? Had enough fun yesterday? Maggie yelled to the caller, that's my husband, he ain't no baby! You called a wrong number silly. Maggie informed Ericson of the call and her response. Ericson admonished her to stop picking his calls which raised an argument that almost led to a fight.

Maggie, in anger asked him, why would the caller, a male call him baby? Ericson disdainfully looked at her and said: "do I look like a baby to you?" It was a wrong number, damn it. Ericson kept on with his financial rascality and his late nights. Maggie decided to investigate him and hired a low rated private eye, called Gordons. That was a disaster in waiting. The private investigator discovered that Ericson had a tie with the deadly Kentucky mobsters, the underworld kingpin of the region. Ericson was very close to the leader of the mob clan and was seen always hanging around him. The private investigator was following Ericson and his friends around but very carefully, as a detection would be a brutal termination of his life, possibly his wife and kids too will be burnt alive. The Kentucky mob family was very dreadful and mercy was not in their psych. On this Saturday night, Ericson and his crew, went to a club and Gordons followed them. In his drunken stage, Ericson went to the rest room and Gordons needed to use the restroom too, duty call. He walked into Ericson sniffing cocaine in plain view and had no pretensions about it. Gordons later left. Ericson was dropped off home by two vehicles.

Ericson and Maggie lived in a small three-bedroom bungalow in a small street where everyone knew everyone. Maggie was very friendly with Shasha, a Brazilian –American lady that worked with city hall. They attended church and other events together. They hung out together and talked about everything. Maggie had confided in Shasha about Ericson and his odd lifestyles and indiscretions. Shasha was worried too.

Maggie went out of county for a job assignment and would return late night. That day, Ericson, for reasons unknown, was picked up by another expensive vehicle driven by a driver and another man sitting at the back seat. Shasha, was sitting at her window watching the street when the beautiful car pulled up in front of their house. She became interested in who was pulling up and for what, at this time of the day. Ericson walked out of the house, all beaming with smile, walked across to the vehicle and sat next to the big boss sitting behind the driver. Shasha subtly adjusted the window to hid herself and had a better view of the vehicle and its occupants. He saw Ericson and the bearded man at the backseat engaged in a prolonged French kiss! Shasha quickly turned her phone camera on and recorded the event. Shasha almost shouted out, oh lord! She covered her mouth and kept watching as the man held Ericson like his girlfriend and the vehicle drove off. Shasha called Maggie and asked her when she was coming home and Maggie said that she would be home in three hours, much later than she thought. Is everything ok? Shasha said yes that everything was fine, just checking on you and will see you when you get here.

Maggie pulled in and went straight to see who Shasha carefully broke the news to her and showed her the video of the kissing. Maggie was shocked almost to the point of collapsing. She now started to make sense of the call and the male who called Ericso "baby". She rummaged through her brain as to all other activities of Ericson. She started crying loudly and unrestrained as she vowed to fight back. She immediately called Gordons for updates and she was asked to come over to the office. Maggie and Shasha was in the office in less than ten minutes, agitated.

Gordons informed Maggie that Ericson had ties to the mob and detailed her out on that. He informed her that Ericson is cocaine dope head too and informed her about his findings. He hinted a possible homosexuality but that he wasn't sure. Maggie told him about that and showed him the video from her phone, having transferred the video away from Shasha, to keep her out of the trouble that might come from it. She paid him for a job well done and left to prepare for war.

She picked up her kids and went home to wait for Eric. Few minutes later, she received a frantic call from Gordons asking her whether she knew of a million- dollar life insurance on her head as Ericson the beneficiary? She screamed no! Her kids, on hearing her agitated discussions on the phone, ran out to the sitting room asking, mum are you ok? Maggie started crying uncontrollably.

Ericson came back very late in the night and slept off, breathing hard and nervous. Maggie now understood that the cocaine is the explanation for his failing health and quests for money. Maggie dressed up in the morning and went straight to a family law attorney she found online. She paid for her legal retainer fees and stayed there for the divorce petition to be prepared and filed forthwith. She didn't want to leave the lawyer until the divorce was filed in court that afternoon. She paid the lawyer for the expedited service. She came home with a process server and waited for Ericson to be served. She called Ericson to come home right away because they had an emergency at home. she refused to disclose the emergency until Ericson got home. She sounded genuinely troubled. Ericson rushed home to meet an infuriated Maggie and a man at home waiting in the sitting room. The man handed Ericson the divorce papers and was excused. Ericson opened it, asked what was that for? What is the meaning of this? Maggie answered to him, what does it look like to you? Are you that retarded or has cocaine eroded your brain function that you can't read a simple document? Ericson looked surprise and confused and Maggie asked him to sit down. Maggie told him that the game is over. Narrated to him everything about his life, the mob, the drug use, the missing money from their account, his homosexuality with the mob leader, on and on. Maggie forwarded the video to his phone while talking to him. To protect Shasha, Maggie asked him, you did not notice a black car that pulled up by the side of the street when he was in the car with the mob man? Maggie continued; well, you wouldn't see me when your full tongue is in the mouth of another man! You shameless gay; you idiot. Watch the video yourself. Ericson watched the clip and kept quiet. I will fight you with the last breath in me; I will fight you to death; I will fight you to the ground, you slum bastard!

If you want to talk, I am all ears but let me start by telling you that you need to explain to the sheriffs why you took out a million-dollar life insurance on my head. You are a murderous crook, a monster in human form. While she was raving hard, the sheriff car pulled up and an officer walked up to the door, was let in by Maggie and he sat down. The officer introduced himself and his mission. He produced some documents and shoved them over to Ericson and asked him what he knew about the documents? Ericson breathed in and out and didn't say anything. The sheriff asked him whether he took out the policy but Ericson took the fifth amendment and asked for a lawyer. The sheriff terminated the interview and left, leaving a copy of the documents with the family. Maggie grabbed the documents off Ericson's hands and slapped him very hard across the face. Ericson stood up to fight back but the venomous looks on Maggie's face deterred him and he ran to his car and drove off. Maggie called the lawyer and asked her for emergency restraining other and child support pending the hearing of the divorce case. The lawyer jumped on it right away and filed it on-line same day.

Having been restrained in a temporal court order, Ericson left the house. The life insurance was cancelled and Maggie received full legal and primary custody of the kids, with high child support that cost Ericson sixty-five percent of his monthly income. That ignited the bile in him and he decided to bury the problems, with the help of the mob. Maggie was "robbed" after picking her kids and forced to drive to a cliff area. She and the kids were shot point blanks and their car shoved over the cliff. The car and all of them got burnt completely and their charred bodies were identified by tooth identifications. Ericson hurriedly buried them as he intended to have his problems buried.

Ericson was tried for murder, in the full glare of the press and news media and was acquitted of all charges. The sheriff, Maggie's family, the community, were all after him and he ran away unceremoniously to Los Angeles. few years later he met and married Donna and here we are with same pattern of behavior.

Dante read the whole clips over and over and realized that he and Donna had to be very careful indeed. He started researching more on the Demarkians and decided to take this up with his priest. He called him up, Fr. Johnson, and went over to meet with him. He relayed all information about the cult to the priest, left out Donna and other issues. They prayed about it and he gave him a vial of holy oil and advised him to try and get into the vineyard, knowing that God was the only savior he had in the circumstances. Fr. Johnson himself went on- line and the churches library to do more research on this cult. What he found out was mind- boggling.

Dante called Donna and inquired when she was going to be back to Los Angeles and she said that she would come in three days for a short while and leave to wherever. Is there any new dirt? she asked. Dante lied and said, not at this point but we need to meet. Donna volunteered to wire more money to him if that is the issue but Dante declined and repeated what he said. Donna said, oh I got it; you don't wanna be the agent of doom to me, huh? Destroying my vacation, huh? Well, you need to understand that I am not here for vacation. I am feeling a little better because I am surrounded by the people that will always love me, my parents and siblings. Over and beyond that, I am a wreck and a revenge seeker, hoping that my good parents won't overhear that! Again, I ask you, is there anything that I need to know more? Dante answered, none. They talked about known facts about Ericson and the strategies of approaching them moving forward and ended the discussion.

Donna was incredibly damaged physically and emotionally. He remembered that she needed to run complete tests for stds and Hiv 1 and 2. She called the public health office but they had a complicated protocol. Claret called her doctor and the test date and time was set up. Fortunately for her, she had nothing serious to worry about, except some troubling yeast infections and minor bacteria. She was placed on medications and she got better. She smiled again, noting that this is another positive for her in the recent times. She also did the covid-19 test again and was cleared.

Their father called them for another family meeting, spiritual communing before they all dispersed. He continued as usual with the lord's prayer.
Our father who art in heaven, hallow be thy name
Thy kingdom come….
He reminded the kids that there is no text or anything oral; any communication that is better than the lord's prayer. He stated the lord's prayer was an answer from Jesus to a follower who inquired from him as to how to pray. He instructed them to recite the lord's

prayer at all time, whether in distress or not. It is just not reciting it but living and practicing it.

He continued and asked his family if any of them had any question? And they nodded no; He took them up on their Samaritan status, asking each of them whose lives they have touched recently? Your life and your possessions means nothing if you do not touch the lives of others. Love and kindness smells like a rose. Your life becomes more meaningful when the mention of your name bring smiles on peoples' faces. I am going to end this meeting with asking God to extend his shield and banner of love, as always, to this family; to heal a fractured world; to bless everyone; to help us to forgive; to equip our minds with love and kindness. As a father, as parents, your mother and I, here today as always, till the end of time, beckons on the Angels of God, our lord Jesus Christ, to bless you immensely and protect you from all evils from over the earth and under the seas. Goodness and mercy shall follow you and your lineages forever. May God heal You, my daughter, Donna.
They started beaming with each other and ate the delicacies that claret prepared.

Father called Donna again into the room and asked her to let go. I don't want you to fight your husband. I know it will be difficult to continue in the marriage, especially with his sexual orientations, not minding his evil lifestyles. My word is this: don't get even, get out. God will protect you there. Leave in peace and let us know when you want your mother and I to visit. Donna hugs her father tightly and with misty eyes, told him that he and mummy meant the world to her. On their way to the airport, Donna surprising to herself and her sister, informed claret that she will heed daddy's advice not to get even but to get out. She will count her losses and rebuild. Claret did not say anything for a minute but later gave a surrendering nod.

***

Dante met with Donna and they went over the discoveries together. All that Donna kept doing was feeling limp and crying. Ericson was more than a handful but she promised herself that she would not relapse into her suicidal ideation anymore. She looked up to God as her bedrock and fortress. She asked a lot of questions about the Demarkians and learnt a lot in the process. She inquired of any possible life insurance on her head but Dante stated that there was none, so far.

Donna asked Dante to help her get a rental apartment in Orange County ASAP. She left for home to meet her husband and pack to a hotel. She needed the apartment expeditiously. She begged him to install utilities in his name. She desired that her identity and address be kept very private. She wanted a gated community with optimal security and access system. Dante jumped on it immediately and promised to reach out to her contacts in Orange County.

Donna got home and met with Ericson, who smiled and walked fast to her for a hug but Donna looked at him like a trash and wedged him away with her two hands and asked him: you serious about that? You really need a hug? You will meet your waterloo sooner than later and that's not gonna be from me, I promise you that. Sit down, let's talk.

Donna kept looking at him for a while and was lost as to how and where to start. She recollected her thoughts and asked him when he got home? Ericson said few days ago and Donna asked why did he return before his schedule and Ericson said that he was missing her a lot and he had to return home. Donna looked at him, felt like stabbing him with a kitchen knife but remembered his father's injunctions. She said to Ericson, oh that's very nice of you, my adorable husband.

Ericson: Oh, you don't understand, the six hours' flight from New York was the longest six hours of my life.

Donna: awwwwww, what an amazing man you are, thank you so much Hun.

Ericson: Can I at least get a hug now, babe?

Donna: Does this meeting sounds familiar to you?

Ericson: I don't get it. What do you mean?

Donna: does this meeting reminds you of anything, like a de javu?

Ericson: No. come on honey.

Donna: I am tired and spent. The last one week has been hell on earth for me; I am a wreck of myself and I am not surprise that you did not notice it.

Ericson: I was gonna bring that up but I needed to ask where you have been and why you blocked me totally from reaching you.

Donna: I wanted to give you a break for your escapades, and of course your job duties.

Ericson: escapades, did you say that?

Donna: yes, I did. you heard me clearly.

Ericson: I don't understand you, at all.

Donna: No, you do.

Ericson: what is going on?

Donna: you will know soon.

Donna: let me cut to the , sweetie. I need a divorce right away, doesn't matter in peace or in pieces.

Ericson: remembering the order issued by the cult leader to him asking him to make peace with his wife, got troubled with what he heard. Why divorce?

Donna: We don't have a life together anyway. I don't understand why the idea of divorce will appear

 surprising to you. Your lifestyle does not require a marriage to me.

Ericson: I am all ears honey.

Donna:

 I ask you again, Mr. Ericson Wilkerson, does this meeting look familiar to you? You evil bitch. Didn't you have a meeting like this with Maggie before you and your gay mob boyfriend , your lover, killed her and your two innocent kids, the boy and girl? Answer me, fool! You killed your own children to avoid paying child support! Your flesh and blood. You shot them point blank and shove them over the cliff as if they were pieces of trash. It was in the national news, so don't act so surprise! You took out a million - dollar policy on her head without her knowledge but it didn't work for you; you were tried and acquitted. You ran away like a coward that you are and came to Los Angeles and changed your name to Eric Boulder, forged documents to cover your true identity. You joined your evil Satanic cult, Mr. Demarkians, devil worshipper. You sought for wealth and they gave you a lot. You wanted protection and they gave you a lot of that.

Oh by the way, you never went to New York. You were in a hotel doing your usual bisexual threesomes with some young college boys and girls from your favorite escort services. You are a cocaine addict, a crack head!

You destroyed my life so you can as well call your cult leadership to finish me, to put an end to me like you did to Maggie. But just that you know; your escapades are going to be over soon; your cup is full and running over. An unannounced rain will beat you unprepared, watch. The world, even before me, had discovered the Demarkians and they will be destroyed in the fullness of time. You will be damned and sent to the deepest part of the hell where you belong.

I want to leave you with your ill-gotten wealth; I want to leave you to enable you come out of your sexual closet; I want to afford you an opportunity to do your drugs; I want you to have the opportunity of bringing in your satanic cat and dog.
We don't have a child together and I don't need spousal support. I will keep the money in my account; it is not a whole lot but they are much cleaner money. I do not want any payments or rewards from you. I don't want to have anything to do with you, ever gain or I will take your case to CNN and other media.

You think that the Demarkians are indestructible but you are wrong, Mr. Wilkerson. Evil will never prevail over good; it is a battle that will always end in the defeat of Satan, including you.
The divorce will be done and filed tomorrow. All you need to do is sign it and pronto, we are done. Till then, I need to be left alone while I am picking my clothes and personal belongings.
Ericson was dumbfounded and he kept quiet all through.

Donna went in hurriedly gathered her stuffs, kept moving them into her vehicle. She left the house and promised to come back. In about one hour she drove back and continued to move her stuffs, while Ericson was seen drinking whiskey silently. Donna left and yelled at Ericson that she would be back tomorrow. Like I said before how these whole things end depends on him. She has nothing to lose anymore. Donna informed Ericson that she would be back tomorrow with the divorce documents; she would call him on her way. Donna left for the day.

The next evening, Donna called Ericson and informed him that she was on her way. She got there with a court process server, met him and the documents were duly signed and later were filed. Donna called her father and laid out her divorce filings and what appeared, so far, to be a peaceful interaction with the devilish Ericson. Donna expressed that she did not know what Ericson got up his sleeves and that she wouldn't care about anything. Her father thanked her for her obedience to him and asked her not to detour. He started praying for her over the phone and they agreed to be talking every day.

Donna later left to meet with Dante. Driving through the crazy greater Los Angeles traffic, she was in deep thoughts but for the second time, she felt a little more at peace. She wondered what Ericson could be thinking; was he planning to send his evil cult after her? was he contrite of his evil life? how long has he been in the sexual closet? does he really have a family or not? why was he so evil in thoughts and deeds? A lot of unanswered questions that may never be answered. She kept on recollecting how they met and the little good times they shared together. She could not understand why Ericson, with the knowledge of his true self, made the decision to be married. It just doesn't add up or made any sense. You can have the sinful world in your pockets by being by yourself but why complicating that by getting married and destroying the life of another in the process? Is getting married part of the membership requirement of the cult? How could he kill his own children? That was the part that she couldn't understand! That made her adrenalin spike whenever she thought of it? How could one person have committed the enormity of these crimes and the so called long arm of the law didn't catch up with him? The law, truly, must be an ass. She felt disappointed in herself that she could allow this marriage to continue when the tell -tale signs were all over the place.

This is not her at all. What happened to me and my pride? she rhetorically asked and thought aloud. All her life before and after college, she carried herself so well, made wise choices and decisions and lived through such choices but how could she have failed so abysmally? Did she lose her intuitions? Was she subconsciously desperate to get married? What was the premium reason to end up with a trash like Ericson? Was she caught in his wealth, the flashy cars and all what not? That couldn't have been because she was raised in modesty and discipline by her family. They have never been a family of gold and silver. Stuffs like that meant little or nothing to her and her siblings. After all, she is walking away from all that now. So what was it? What was the catch? Was it Ericson's looks? No it couldn't have been; He was not particularly very good looking; He was just one of the average guys in the crowd. Maybe, because he was college educated, spoke intelligently well, dressed clean and savvy, complimented by his vintage cars and other evidence of good living. Could it be that the whole ball pack was thrown at her and she was caught off guard? Could it be that she was of age and ready to settle down? Is she entitled to the life's one error rule? Probably yes: but why would it be an error of such magnitude? A woman is a creature of maternal instinct, a home maker. Females don't usually make fatal errors in marital choices because they lose big and sometimes catastrophically, as in her case now. She continued in her thoughts and missed her exit. She decided to reschedule this meeting for tomorrow morning. She didn't want go this meeting in her current state of mind. She drove back to the hotel, while still engaged in her thoughts.

Donna, in her disappointments, kept on hounding herself for messing up her formally well- structured life. Why didn't she do a simple investigation about Ericson's background. That would have, somehow keyed her towards discovering his lies and prior disastrous marriage that ended in murder! What about her not investigating his background and family tree? How could she excuse herself for that? It sounds ludicrously ridiculous that she went into a life union with a man without an in-depth inquiry into his family background. With all the internet tools in this new world of information superhighway? Why was she so trusting and grievously stupid? What happened to all the stellar upbringing from her parents? She pulled up to the curb on Wilshire Boulevard and started crying deeply again, calling on her parents to forgive her, especially dad, calling on them to please forgive her for letting them down. I am so sorry but I will do better moving forward. She didn't want to think of the cult and their evil powers, whether they had a spell on her to have made her committed an atrocious and marital disasterous decision. She decided to step back into her Christian upbringing and seek the face of God, as that may have been the reason for her failure. She wanted to pray but she didn't remember the words of our lord's prayer. She googled it and recited it over and over again. She felt a magical relief of what may be a mental faith relief or an actual spirit of God flowing into her. She kept on muttering to herself: it shall be well: it shall be well with my soul. She drove home and was able to sleep better.

When Donna woke up, she called her father and had a hearty talk with her and her father advised on the ways moving forward. Her father appeared very thrilled on Donna's new discovery of the powers of God in terms of distress and the guiding influence of the Holy Spirit. Donna called Dante and drove over to meet with him which was a much better drive than yesterday considering the light traffic today. Dante was able to secure a beautiful apartment for her in Irvine. A gated complex, with multiple layers of security to access the pristine compound, a monthly face recognition access pass for the tenants; a twenty -four -hour security patrol; utility included with lawn services; a front concierge services. She loved it but she started getting concern about being able to pay for it beyond the next six months. She was now confronted with the stark reality that she was no longer rich. Of course, she will sell her premium Mercedes Benz car and get something smaller but how long will the money last? Is it right for her to walk away from Ericson without any spousal support or half of her community property? She could get over a hundred million dollars at the very least from that without much pushing but why would she seek money from the devil? How does that fit into her new life? She remembered her siblings and smiled. She will seek their support and she know they will gladly assist her. She decided too to get a job as soon as possible.

Dante and Donna went over the whole Ericson saga and decided to hold forth. Dante was paid fully including the Irvine home, which has to remain in his name for now. Donna was full of gratitude to Dante; Donna found a brother in Dante and she felt strongly about that.

✳✳✳

Ericson called Donna, after about six days, and the following discussions took place again:
Ericson: Hey, you unblocked me and took my calls, thanks for that. It shows that there is light at the end of the tunnel.

Donna: You will never cease to be an arrogant pussy, pardon my French.

Ericson: I am sorry?

Donna: For what?

Ericson: for my choice of word, now.

Donna: Just that you know, there is no tunnel connecting you and I; light and darkness has nothing in common.

Ericson: but both has been together for years, Hun?

Donna: I am not your Hun, get that into your head. We have been together because I didn't know you; because I had very poor judgment and made some fatal errors. Oh by the way thank you for the sexual diseases that you infected me with but I am ok now.

Ericson: how could that be? I am always clean!

Donna: sure, you were. How are your girlfriends and boyfriends? Are they members of your cult too?

Ericson: do you really need me to answer that?

Donna: why not? you called me for a conversation, right?

Ericson: yes, of course.

Donna: you don't choose what topics to talk about, right?

Ericson: Yes, but I feel uncomfortable with some issues you are bringing up.

Donna: I am showing you extreme kindness by talking to you and I believe you know that. So my question again before I hang this phone on your ignorant self is: are your perverted sexual partners members of the evil Demarkian cult?

Ericson: No, they not. The brotherhood does not control my private life.

Donna: How long have you been a gay man?

Ericson: Bisexual, you mean?

Donna: What's the difference?

Ericson: You omitted the females.

Donna: You have a very warped sense of your sexuality. You are in self -denial about who you are. I have a million things to say to you but I wanna pass for now or forever. I will change my number and all others and when that happens, I wouldn't want you to look for me or contact me. You need to move on in your world. Just like I told you, darkness and light has nothing together.

Ericson: I am talking to my banker to transfer twenty million dollars into your account tomorrow morning, at least to assist you in moving forward.

Donna: Awwwww, that's so wonderful of you. My bank accounts that you know of have been closed down exactly because of that reason, to avoid you and your stained money going into it. You don't get it, do you? You and I are from different worlds; you are in the dark; I have always been in the light; I kinda lost it inadvertently but I recovered it now; I am a child of God. Keep your money to yourself; You need every bit of it to run the streets; give them to your threesome sexual
partners.

Ericson: Are you kidding me! you rejecting twenty million dollars?

Donna: You are just an ass! You are just an unrepentant apology of a human being or is it a devil being. The money that you are offering me is far less than what you owe me in the divorce court and I walked away from all that. Doesn't that show your retarded self that I mean business. You believed that part of the reason that I married you was your money, huh? Well, as you can see, you are wrong. So, your twenty million is actually my money and not yours.

Ericson: How do I make it right?

Donna: Well, I don't have a problem with anyone's sexual orientation, at least civilly but I know that I still have the choice to choose to live with a man and not a coward man-sissy, like you. You should be proud of who you are, for once.

Ericson: Is that all?

Donna: Oh no sir; you are like a sea shell that has bacteria built-ups covering all the body. To clean you up will be almost impossible. You are as dirty as a skunk. If you are a car, you should be a total loss; your only place will be a junkyard in the ghetto. You are almost irredeemable but the kindness and mercy of

Jesus might save you. I don't know if that would be too much for God to admit to salvation.

Ericson: Am I that bad?

Donna: You are beyond bad, if you really need an answer. By the way, who are your family? did you kill them off too, I mean your parents, siblings, cousins, uncles, etc.?

Ericson: Please don't drift to that.

Donna: Why not? It is a simple civic question. I know that you told me that you don't have any but I know better now. You don't have friends from primary school to college? People that you grew up with?

Or did you just emerge from another planet a grown adult?

Ericson: Do you wanna meet for lunch?

Donna: No, thanks though.

Ericson: I am truly sorry for all the harms I did to you.

Donna: You are an agent of evil and I don't believe that devil can be contrite; maybe you are, still a human; I just don't believe that, I am sorry.

I got to go. May the spirit of God seek you out and redeem you. You need a lot of that. I am out, bye for now.

Ericson: very well, then, bye.

■■

CHAPTER 5

John Cushner, always looked elitist, well- dressed and carried himself with a disciplined air of dignity. He was a good-looking man, an investment banker extraordinaire, attended an average state college, from a middle income home. He Lived in Las Vegas, loved the strip a lot and gambled discretely big. He was, outwardly, a perfect gentleman but in reality, a devil in human form. Not as bad as Ericson, but he was equally of the same hue as him. He was single and seemed happy. He was not a habitual night crawler but he was out there. He had two homes, less than five hundred yards from each other, next street to the Las Vegas boulevard. But one of the buildings was completely shut out to the world. He was Demarkian and his cult life, including his dog, stayed in the secret abode. He bought the said house with forged but genuine identity of a dead college friend with his connection in the DMV. He was popularly called by his last name, Cushner or Cush. He was very crooked in a smart way and you would never catch him in his lies. He liked branded clothes, shoes, jewelries, which looked good on him. He drove two identical Porsche and a customized Bentley. He used the confusing identical Porsche cars to further his social lies and alibis.

He met with pretty Ms. Betsy William, a struggling Las Vegas Attorney, in a party at the strip. They hit it off and has been a whirlwind. He had other girlfriends but Betsy would swear with her life that her Cushner was not a cheating type. What bolsters her confidence was that Cushner, who she sometimes called Cush, doesn't even have time to cheat. But she didn't know that Cush was a slimy dirty-minded person that could go to any length to deceive even the smartest person. He derived pleasure in deceits. He had this infectious personality and a smile that lit up his entire face. Betsy had never known happiness as she was drowning in it now. Her friends were jealous of her, as she imagined, falsely or rightly. Cush got her a brand new Porsche panorama for her last birthday. She couldn't believe it when she received a one hundred and fifty-thousand-dollar vehicle with a complimentary Versace bag and shoes!

Betsy's mother came visiting despite the fact that she had cancer and was very sick. She was a real practicing Christian and raised her kids Jehovah witnesses. She was driven by a cousin from nearby Arizona to Las Vegas. It was almost a two -hour trip, but appeared longer because of her health. She got into Vegas and went to sleep. When she woke, her daughter introduced her to Cush who was present. The moment she walked into the sitting room to meet Betsy and her new boyfriend, she felt goose pimples all over her frail body. She didn't like how she felt and it got worse when she wanted to shake his hands. She went back into the room and waited for him to leave.
As soon as he left, Mum came out and the following dialogue ensued:
Mum: who was that man?
Betsy: He is John Cushner, a banker, has a college degree, originally not from here. He is on top of his business and life. He is very smart mummy. He has helped me in more ways than one. He is very honest and reliable. He fits into everything I want in a man. I love him mummy and I won't be surprise if we walk down every girl's dream isle, as she started beaming.
The mother is not feeling the same way, which was shocking to Betsy.
Betsy: Mummy, you don't like him?

Mummy: Mother's instinct, I don't despise anyone but I just don't feel good about him. There is something about him that bothers me. He is a fine young man, and looks very prosperous but my child, there is much more to life than the glitters. I will, hopefully, find out what it is before I leave. I can only but pray for you.

Betsy: Mum, you have always wanted me to settle down and have a family but now you are confusing me. I don't know what to make out of this.

Mum: I am not drawing any conclusions. All I said is that there is something about your friend that is troubling. You could continue with whatever you have going on, of course with my reminders that fornication is a sin before God. You were raised in the vineyard and I hope that the lures of this world has not derailed you into the flesh. The kingdom of God is real and the narrow path to it is real.

Betsy: Mum, mum, it is ok, I gatch ya, don't turn to mother Teresa here, as she started laughing. You still see daddy in your dreams?

Mum: she smiled heartily and exclaimed, my darling, my bread and butter, my adorable and protective honey, in who I am well pleased, your daddy, will never leave me alone. He visits me every day, no matter how short the dream was. He protects me, even in death. I am not afraid of death because he always reassures me that he is there waiting for me.

Betsy: Mum, you are not going there anytime soon. We, your kids need you here. We can't lose twice. So please don't talk like that. Tell daddy that we miss him but he should stop waiting for you for a few more decades.

Mum: Let the will of God prevail. I am very sick; I am terminally sick and you and your siblings need to accept that as a fact, honey. I didn't put the sickness there as I can only but hope that I have longer days and little bit more twilight. I have been around for seventy –six years, not too old but not too young either. My body is getting weaker and frail. Cancer is an evil disease and I hope that God will remove it from mankind. You should not worry about me. I am at peace with the lord and I am ready to go when I am called.

Betsy: Mummy, please, please, stop talking about going! You have to carry my children in your arms. My kids will call you grandma.

Mum: I will say amen to that. May the goodness of the lord protect you and be with you now and forever more, Amen. Please give me my medications.

A little later, Cushner came in and sat down in the sitting room. Betsy's mum looked at him and started a subtle interrogation. Hello young man, my daughter told me wonderful things about you. Thank you so much for your friendship with my adorable Betsy.

Mum: You are into banking, huh?

Cush: yes, I am.

Mum: I understand that you are doing well too.

Cush: in a relative sense, yes.

Mum: You are originally from another state?

Cush: yes.

Mum: family?

Cush: Yes, deceased parents, two siblings that stays in Los Angeles.

Mum: Family religion?

Cush: Catholic.

Mum: interesting. You attend church?

Cush: Not really. I am agnostic.

Mum: what is that?

Cush: a form of atheism where belief in the existence of God is predicated on God proving his existence.

Mum: Exclaimed, Jesus Christ!! She recollected herself and asked

Cush: so, do you see God in this planet earth?

Cush: Not in a long time.

Mum: what do you have to say about heaven and earth and its creation?

Cush: I don't know; maybe the big bang theory is true.

Mum: how did you come into the world?

Cush: I was born by my mother.

Mum: Do you believe in the existence of the devil?

Cush: kept quiet, was looking at mum, not having an answer ready, said he don't know.

Mum: Devil represents everything bad, as you should know. Lucifer, Satan, demon, devil, are all the same. He is evil and nothing from him is real or good.

At this point, Cush 's face turned purple in anger, looking very upset and disturbed, even though he was trying to mask it up, stood up and announced that he was leaving. Before Betsy could ask why he is leaving suddenly, he was at the door and Betsy walked fast and asked him: honey, why are you leaving so soon? Mum was only trying to hold a conversation. Cush maintained his pace to his car and drove out promising to see Betsy the next day.

When Betsy got in, she confronted her mum, with some anger and asked her why she was harassing her guest. She expressed a very strong displeasure to her mum about that.

Betsy's mum apologized and walked into the guest room to get some sleep.

Betsy was confused all through the night till the next day when her mum announced that her cousin was on his way from Arizona to pick her up. But not before she called Betsy for a meeting.

Mum: Again, how did you meet this man?

Betsy: In a party.

Mum: how long ago?

Less than a year or a little more.

Mum: have you met any member of his family?

Betsy: Not yet.

Mum: You should stay away from him, sweetie.

Betsy: Why? Don't tell me that you have decided to make my life miserable. I can't believe that. You wanted me to get married but now I just don't get this! Betsy hit her hand loudly on the dining table and

the milk poured in a cup spilled.

Mum: Clean the mess and calm down. Your parents are your most trusted allies in life and I want you to always remember that. The umbilical cord never gets severed, and the fluid of life from your father never dried up from you.

We will never be against you. I want you to fish but I don't want you to capture poisonous fish. This man, Cushner, is not a good person and I don't want you to find out the hard way. I have never seen any person that couldn't condemn Satan. He chose to run out of the house than to do that. You may not be hanging with flesh and blood but with principalities. I feel strongly against him. I will leave you now and will come back another time. I don't know how much time left for me here but remember always that I conceived you; that I am your mother; that I love you more than you will ever know. I wish you more than the best. Like I said, I will pray for longer days but if it is the will of our lord to call me home, i am blessing you today and always. Come here babe.

Betsy went to her mother and was hugged for a few seconds and her mother kissed her neck and rendered a short prayer. The doorbell rang and her cousin walked in and they all greeted. Betsy thanked him for picking up mum; thanked him for his dedication to his cousin, sharing closer relation with her mum than her mother's siblings. They drove out. Betsy received a call from Cush and he rambled on and on, lamenting on the treatment he got from her mum; claiming that her mum hated him. Betsy did all that she could to explain and debunk his mind but he remained adamant. They later hooked up that evening, on Cush learning that her mum had left. They went frolicking Las Vegas, the city of sin, as people call it. The most toured city in the world. If it sinful, then the world is a world of sin. It is indeed.

They gambled and drank all night. While playing and getting their free Champaign refills, Cush in a flash, disappeared while Betsy was engulfed in money line bets. Betsy turned around and did not find him. She continued in her bets and Cush reappeared and asked her to meet him in the car. They needed to leave right away. He received a call from a business partner that he is coming here but he didn't wanna see him. Betsy didn't feel like arguing, jumped up and they left via a longer route to his car.

✳✳✳

Martina, Cushner's other girlfriend, his heartthrob, in the same hotel hall, believed that she saw Cushner right now but how could that be? Cush was out of state and he dropped him off at the airport today, watched him cleared security. Martina turned around to apologize to a service girl she bumped into, spoke with her for a few minutes and just turned but Cushner wasn't there! Cushner was hiding behind a pillar watching her intensely, saw the confusion on her face; saw when she left and walked away. He was scared that she could walk up to Betsy to ask about him. His phone rang and it was Martina. He picked up the phone and feigned sleepy and tired, said the phone woke him up. Martina believed that and left for home, going south. Cush and Betsy went north to where they parked, even though it was a longer route.

Betsy's mum died the next week and Betsy was devastated. She was deeply distraught for a whole week and later went for the funeral. Cush gave her a lot of money to assist with the funeral expenses. Cush gave an excuse as to why he couldn't go, even though it was only a two -hour drive journey. While Betsy was there, Cush was with Liz, the third girl, in a condo that he bought for her. Liz was an incredibly beautiful blond with blue eyes and long legs. She had her own games too and could care a little less about her gallivanting boyfriend, Cushner. Cush was a cash man, so he was a good resource to be kept in the pool. She bites into his lies because she wanted to and not that she believed any of that. Recently she saw Cush in a busy nightclub in Arizona, frolicking with another girl, when Cush was supposed to be in Los Angeles. She did all she could to avoid him seeing her and later left with her man.

Cush thought that she was in Las Vegas, cheater, cheatee, as she laughed slutly. All through the week that Betsy was in Arizona, Cush was in Liz's house drowning in sin with the paragon Liz, as he called her. He told Betsy that he had an emergency one- week investment conference in Colorado. Betsy was too out of it to look into his lies. She never does anyway, because she had no reason to. Betsy came back to Las Vegas and continued with her life, including Cush. Her law practice has been doing marvelous and she started thinking of buying a big home from the upscale McDonald's Islands., home of the Vegas rich. And she did. She packed into her new home and kept growing. She owed Cush a lot, she thought. Cush gave Betsy more connections to fat legal briefs from the corporate Las Vegas and she started the social climb. Betsy was not the only recipient of the gift' and his other girlfriends had their hands in the cookie pot too. Cush had too much money to fund his gallivanting lifestyle. He joined the brotherhood long time ago and was ushered into unannounced wealth and counting.

Betsy loved animals but, like a lot of other people, she was concerned with the care and maintenance of them. On this boring Saturday, Cush was out of state,[she had his house keys and the cars were in the garage], she drove out from her house to the southern Las Vegas end but about a mile from the strip, she spotted a vehicle that looked exactly like Cush's car, sped up to catch up with it, was reading the number on the car which appeared same digits with Cush's car, and she started reading it again and just as she was about getting to the last digits, the car ran a red light and sped into another street, driving crazily away. She pursued the Porsche but couldn't keep up. She wanted to see who was driving the car, even though the glimpse of the driver from the back view looked like Cush 's hairline. She turned around and went to Cush's house, opened the garage and there was Cush's Porsche, cold as steel. She exhaled and started laughing, calling herself an insecure bitch!

She decided to buy a dog; She left for the vintage dog auction in the south. She bought an all- white- fur Bishon Frise, six months old, very quiet and without drama. Took the dog to a groomer for one week and then another month for audio lessons and commands. She picked up her dog, named it, whitey.
"Cush was out of town" again for a "business trip".
He called her from the airport to pick him up and in few minutes cancelled and claimed that he already was in uber coming home. Betsy was thrilled and wanted to go and wait for him at his house but he quickly said no to that, telling Betsy that he would freshen up and come meet her at her house. Betsy feeling disappointed
a little, agreed to that. Betsy was playing with her dog, been doing that for days now. Dog was very friendly to all her friends, her colleagues, wags her tail on all of them, licking their bodies, like all normal dogs do. Whitey never barked at anyone. It was just a pet, and not a security dog.

Cush pulled up to Betsy's house and walked up to the front porch, pushed the bell and waited. Cush had the keys to Betsy's apartment but he didn't wanna use it now, wanted to hug and kiss Betsy into the house. He was a smooth operator and got his game. Betsy heard the bell but she was in the loo. She yelled to Cush to let himself in but Cush pretended as if he didn't hear that. He waited for a few more minutes. Whitey on hearing the bell, walked close to the door and went berserk, barking loudly, drooling in the process, showing its full tooth and looking intently at the door menacingly, appeared ready to pounce on Cush as soon as he walked through that door. Betsy hearing the barking was very surprise and exited the restroom, walked to the dog to scoop it up but whitey wasn't in the play mood as it continued to bark relentlessly and clenching its tooth. Whitey was making a restless forward and backward movements and refused to be carried into the arms of the owner. Betsy got irritated and shouted at it: snap out of it, now! Shut up!! Whitey kept quiet and edged away a few feet. Betsy opened the door but Cush had already left. Betsy kept calling him but he didn't' t pick her calls. Betsy felt so bad and hated her dog for causing the problem. She, for a moment thought that she may have to sell the dog if this continues. But why would her dog react like this for the first time? It had always been a wonderful loving animal to all her friends. Whitey was just fed well so there was no reason for the tantrum that it exhibited now. So why did it react like it did?

Cush called Betsy back and asked whether she got a dog now? Betsy answered yes. Oh honey, you will love whitey, that is its name, very lovely and friendly. Well -trained and behaves well. I got it during your last prolonged trip to New York. Oh lord, I love whitey and I am coming over with it now. Cush intuitively yelled, oh no, please don't. I don't like animals, not just dogs. I tried to avoid them. Betsy responded: but he got to know you, sweetie, trust me. Cush sternly asked her to sell the dog but Betsy now beginning to get irritated declined that and reminded Cush that he should never try to run her life for her. They hung the phone and Betsy was infuriated at whitey and Cush.

She decided to watch basketball game, Los Angeles Lakers in a playoff game with Phoenix Suns. She poured herself a glass of Moet Champaign, nectar imperial. Her phone rang and one of her besties, Anita was on the other end teasing her about her winnings three days ago at Wynn hotel at the strips. Betsy asked her: what in the world are you talking about, gossiper? Anita said that she saw Cush from a distance gambling with a lady that looked like Betsy sitting next to him, drinking. She thought it was Betsy but before she could get closer they disappeared and she was confused. Is that not Cush, with his parted hair in the front, in night goggles and a baseball heart? Betsy laughed and informed Anita that Cush just got back into town from New York and that she was never in the Wynn hotel. They changed the topic and talked a little bit more and hung the phone.

Cush's issue and loggerhead with Betsy deteriorated further and they stopped seeing each other for a while until Cush called Betsy and they spoke about nothing. Betsy agreed to keep her dog with her friend for a while, will retrieve the dog later when she builds a house for it at the back of her apartment. She promised to keep the dog away from Cush. They met up and there was a lot of catching up to do. Betsy now remembered the Porsche car that she saw in the street and laughingly told Cush of her foolhardiness and how she was jolted and they laughed it off. She also informed him of Anita's claim of having seen two of them at the Wynn and they laughed it off too. Cush chipped in and said, oh, maybe I am cloned now, huh?

Anita invited both of them for Saturday evening game of basketball and Cush agreed to go with Betsy. They got there in excitements, walked in and sat down. Anita had a giant cat, with a diamond on its neck, always laid at the couch with Anita. As soon as Cush sat down, the cat walked away looking sad but Anita grabbed the cat and put it on Cush, telling it: meet my friends. Meanwhile, Cush's countenance had changed since they walked into that sitting room and saw the cat. What the cat did next was mind boggling. The cat longed at Cush with lightning speed and clawed heavily at his face, biting his neck in the process and ran away upstairs, crying ferociously. Everyone, except Cush, was surprise and jolted. Anita was so embarrassed and Betsy just didn't get it. Why would the cat attack Cush without provocation? Why would it bite him? And so viciously too. what has this man got with animals? There was a deep laceration on Cush's neck but Anita, a physician assistant took care of it, and they left. The evening ended sourly.

Cush withdrew into his shell and recounted how many times animals have attacked him like this. This was a cross that he had to carry as a member of an evil cult. Animals sees beyond humans. Animals are metaphysical beings and they are vicious to the evil ones. They protect their owners from such evil men and women like Cush. This was a concern that Cush had, having been informed of it by his friend that introduced him to the fraternity. He thought about it for days, knowing that animals are part of humanity and surviving them could be a hard experience. But if you are rich, you could navigate away from them, explained by his buddy, Franklin. He just couldn't get beyond the lures of wealth and connections as Franklin enjoyed. He has been doing well in his daily animal avoidance schemes but accidents do happen now and then. The incidence in Anita's home was just as embarrassing as it could get. He just explained to Betsy and Anita, that animals don't like him and he doesn't know why. Betsy, jokingly, looked at him and asked him: are you evil? Hell broke loose that day and he yelled at Betsy, with his eyes popping out. Betsy, just laughed and told him to catch a joke. Of course, you are not evil babe. You are a very wonderful, loving sweetie pie. Awwwwww poor boy, come here and spank me in the bedroom. Betsy dragged him to the bedroom and closed the door.

Betsy woke up and was very tired and decided that she would take the day off. She stayed back in Cush's house and ordered Uber eat of embroidered curry chicken food and a don perignon champagne, 1978 vintage. Life with Cush was heavenly but she needed to do something about his relationship with animals, Betsy thought. She got her food, ate heavily and dozed off and had a very scary dream. In the dream, Betsy was walking in a wooded forest area, surrounded by wide expanse of forests, all in a pitch darkness, walking and occasionally running with whitey on the pathway. She started getting tired after running a short distance, surprise of that knowing that she is very fit having always been going to the gym. She wanted to exit the scary forest but she couldn't and then her dead mother appeared as an apparition, trying to tell her something but she couldn't get out a sound. It looked like she wanted her to exit the forest immediately but she was happy going over to hug mummy but she was waiving her away to exit the forest immediately! A giant black dog appeared to her, she became cold with fear, as the dog chased down whitey and devoured whitey. She woke up sweating and almost immediately, Cush walked in and met her breathing hard. She relayed her dream to Cush who laughed it off, even though he knew that the dream was not an empty one. He advised Betsy to ignore the dream and live up her life awake. He said that he was not into dreams, just like he was not into religion. They started drinking and watching a movie together.

Cush left for Los Angeles for a Demarkian meeting, but lied to Betsy that he had a job-related meeting with his associates. Betsy dropped him off at the airport. He told Betsy that he would be away for four days. He was in Los Angeles for two days, flew in and called his girlfriend from southern Las Vegas, Martina to pick him up. Dressed in jeans pant and a hooded shirt, which he never wore when he was with Betsy, had on a baseball hat and dark glasses, they drove off to Martina's home where he stayed for another 2 days. Cush asked Martina to drop him off at the airport to meet a business partner for a meeting and that the partner will drop him home or he may use uber home. A soon as he got dropped off, Cush called Betsy who was actually waiting for the call having been called from "Los Angeles" an hour ago by Cush as he was "boarding" for Las Vegas. They drove to his house and talked about a lot of things. Betsy later said she wanted to go home and will not be sleeping here, with a smile, she said to Cush, the monthly pink lady is here babe, started laughing. I don't like being outside my house pinky, you know the cramps and stuffs, feel me? Cush nodded and she left, went to her office, picked some folders and went home.

Betsy went home and worked on some court cases, one of them being a high profile divorce case involving a society guy and lady, both of them, cheaters and sinners. They gambled in millions monthly and could care less about their financial and sexual rascality. These were two unrepentant dogs in its truest meanings. She represented the Respondent, Mario, the husband. She got the case via Cush because Cush and Mario were good friends.

Sometimes, she asked herself, how could my beautiful well-behaved and disciplined Cush be friends with this irresponsible couple that has no respect for decency. What the couple have not done was having sex with a snake. They were incredibly filthy and sleazy in everything they did. Now, they were out to bring each other down. She felt nauseated reading their documents and the entire case discoveries. They had two very spoilt teenagers that appeared worse than their parents. Betsy liked the case because of the money it spilled to her. The Island building, she just bought, was mainly financed from this case. She smiled again and did a thumb up for her boo, Cushner, a heaven sent.

She stayed awake till about 2 a.m. and slept off. She had another nightmare again. In this dream, she was walking in a very desolate road that seemed to lead to nowhere. She passed fierce-looking black dogs with blood –drooping from their eyes; passed some cats and black birds, with similar eyes. They growled at her but didn't chase or try to attack her. She walked further down into an open field and saw her mum in her burial dress beckoning at her. At the same time, Cush appeared and walked up to her, hugged her and asked her what she was doing there, and she, in turn, asked Cush the same question. Her mum, with tears dripping from her eyes rushed over and started pulling her away from Cush and asking him to leave her daughter alone, that she was an innocent trusting lady. She was not of your world, please leave my child alone! Both of them were doing a tug-of war with her in the middle. She was confused and disoriented. She was screaming at Cush to let her go now! That's my mum, stupid! The fight continued with Cush having an upper hand. A bigger force finally wrenched Betsy away from her mother and Cush took her deeper into the forest. Her mum was there crying and begging Cush to let her daughter go. Let her go; let her go; let her go; I am pleading with you!

Betsy woke up, so agitated and scared. She went for a drink but the entire house was in darkness, with little sleeping lights. The house was as scary as the scene in the dream. She was trying to understand the dream and make sense out of it but couldn't. Was my dead mother feuding with my boyfriend? Over what? They were fighting over me! Why was my mother so determined to pull me away from Cush? Even at her death? was there something about Cush that was hidden from her naïve self? Why did Anita's cat attack him so viciously? There has never been any other incidence involving that cat since then.

She decided to get her dog back the next day. She drove there and picked up the dog from her sister, benedict. Not her biological sister but a friend that turned to a sister. They talked for a while and the sister kept on hammering that this dog was peaceful and loving. Betsy informed her that the dog barked at Cush unrestrainedly. Benedict looked at her and said to her: If this dog barked at your Cush, then he needs to clean his ass more, tell him I said that. Betsy drove home and put whitey in his new cage at the back cozy room made for it. That seemed to take care of the dog issue for now.

Cush was in his other secret abode, practicing his evil worship, doing the incantations invoking the devil, with the demonic sound playing at the background. His huge black dog was there in the temple keeping vigil. His phone rang and it was Betsy but he ignored the call and turned off the phone when Betsy couldn't stop calling. He later came out of the house and drove off to meet with a friend, another cult member and they hung out for a while. He called Betsy back and lied about his location, promised Betsy that he would see her later. He came over to meet with Betsy and she relayed her dream to him. Cush brushed it aside, downplayed it and reminded Betsy that he never had a good relationship with her mother. That the dream was not unconnected with that fallout.

Betsy agreed and Cush quickly cashed in on that and changed the conversation to another thing.

Betsy wanted to go and see her brother that resided in New Mexico. She taught that it might be a good idea to visit Cancun for tourism. Cush declined that but Betsy continued pushing him to go with her, promising to molest him very well when they get there and he agreed. That was a mistake because international travels could be hazardous. They first went to New Mexico and stayed for two days and bought a ticket first to Mexico City and then to Cancun in the north. Sounds like fun, huh? Cushner asked Betsy, who responded, you bet.

They got to the airport and cleared immigration but there had to be extra searching because of the trip to the drug-infested Mexico City. Two fierce looking drug sniffing- dogs were sniffing all passengers down the line until they got to Cush and they growled, started barking and rushed over, pushed Cush to the ground and pounced on him and bit him in multiple places, tearing his clothes in the process. The assigned officers couldn't even restrain the dogs. Cush was taken to the infirmary, treated of his injuries and their luggage thoroughly searched but nothing was found. Their suitcases were torn and cut to bits but there was no drug in them. The officers were speechless about the dogs' actions. Betsy was a little surprise and kept asking herself how long will this continue? Betsy took Cush back to her brother's house and they had to go back to Vegas the next day. Betsy kept on asking Cush, why are the dogs attacking you all the time? Cush yelled back at her asking her to leave him alone. He couldn't wait to get home from all these bullshits.

The next day, they flew back to Las Vegas and Cush just went home, to the other building, to his temple, to express his frustration with the animal attacks. He wanted the brotherhood to do something about that! He was so sad that he stayed in that building for two days. Betsy was in Cush's regular building a few times but Cush wasn't there. He was not picking her calls either.

Betsy was infuriated and she stopped calling Cush and faced her job. Later, after a few days, Cush called her and apologized but held her responsible for the silly trip to Mexico that almost got him killed. They did a bit to repair their friendship and they did get back together. Cush left for home but instead went to Martina's house for the night, claiming that he needed a quiet time. The next day, he went to his office, broke off in the middle of the day and went to be with Liz.

Liz was with another man, forgot to park her car inside, as she does, when Cush arrived. He called Liz to let him in but Liz said she wasn't at home. Cush asked her whether she left with her car and she said yes thinking that she parked inside the garage. Cush asked her whether she bought another car and she said no. At that point, she looked out and saw her car in the driveway. She changed her story claiming that she left with her cousin in her car and that she didn't know what she was saying. Meanwhile Cush had seen her silhouette even though the light was turned off in the sitting room. Liz being as trashy as Cush, wasn't worried about him finding out of her sexual escapades. She knew of her intense beauty that was freaking men out. She has had enough of this lying playboy anyways. She has gotten some pricey items from him too. He could go, if he so wished.
Cush left and murmured that Liz had pulled a lion by the tail. He called Liz again and told her that. Liz infuriated, told him to go to hell. I have been putting up with your stupid lies and now you can't deal with mine. I saw you in Arizona club last two weeks when you were supposedly in another place. Cush responded to her that he was the cash man and that she should be at his service when he desired her. He wanted the house back. This made Liz more upset and she cursed at him. She agreed that she was at home and that Cush could go screw himself. She was not letting him in tonight or ever. She had moved on with her new boyfriend.

Cush left for home with a low blow again. This bitch was toying with a bomb. We will see, when the chips are down. He drove home to his official residence and drowned himself in Luis the xiii cognac, finished a bottle before 1 a.m.; couldn't sleep but he watched tv. What a week! The evil in him came up and he decided to fight back. The question was whether the brotherhood could descend low in punishing others for annoying members of the cult. That's childish and the brotherhood may even punish him for bringing such minimal social complaints to the attention of the prefect. He thought about killing Liz, in a mundane way but decided against it, doesn't worth it. If he makes a mistake, he will be executed or spend his life in prison. That bitch! He decided to let her go.

✳✳✳

Betsy went to sleep early today and was in lala land when her mum and this time, with her dad, smiling at her, with love flowing out of their eyes, held her and kissed her. She felt so loved. Her mother sternly advised her to go and buy a crucifix right away. They revealed to her that Cush is a disciple of Devil. They told her to stay away from him; that he would harm her at the end; that his wealth was of the devil and that she should back away and face her law practice. That's not gonna be without a fight but she would be fine at the end. He would want his money and gifted properties back but she should hand them to him, even without him asking. They told her about the dogs and the cult. They informed her that the cult will eventually be destroyed ecumenically. They played with her and left. She woke up in the early morning refreshed and felt better. She missed her loving parents. She went to a Christian store and bought a golden crucifix with a 24 carat chain and decided to be wearing that all the time. She came home, was a little cold today and tucked herself in her comforter and laid on the couch, watching basketball, the golden state versus the clippers, round of sixteen. She heard her door bell and went over to open the door and saw Cush standing there. She was surprised and asked him why he didn't call her to know if she was at home. Cush said, I know your lifestyle sweetie but check your phone anyway; can I come in at least? Oh sure shouted by Betsy. Cush walked in, grabbed Betsy for a forceful playful hug and kiss. On his body getting in contact with Betsy's crucifix, he yelled out pain and quickly withdrew from Betsy.

Betsy looked at him surprised again. What was that now? Cush tried to laugh it off and said that he had this health condition that, like a lupus factor that can attack him on certain body movement. Betsy looked at him and asked him why he never mentioned that before now? Why was it with her crucifix? She asked him to sit down, care for water or food or wine? Cush declined, feeling very uncomfortable. Betsy was playing with whitey earlier and forgot to leach it back in its cage at the rear of the building. The dog ran into the sitting room and started barking, rushed over to Cush and bit him hard on his shoe, charging on him more before Betsy took the dog away.

Cush wanted to go immediately but Betsy asked him to wait until she comes back from putting away the dog. Betsy came back and sat with Cush and turned off the tv and demanded to talk. Cush asked about what? Betsy said, about us. Cush said, fire, what about?

Betsy cleared her throat and told Cush about her last dream. My father who never met you is now involved in keeping me away from you. I need to be upfront about this: are you a devil disciple? Cush's face turned red and angry. He said: what kind of nonsense question is that!

Betsy asked the next question: why are the dogs and other animals biting you? why are you always singled out?

Cush: I wouldn't know; maybe you need to ask your parents.

Betsy: they don't have anything to do with this, ok? So leave them out.

Cush: They have everything to do with it, ok? Your mum hated me and you claim that she appeared in your dream to continue the hate. That's baloney, wake up.

Betsy: Did my father hate you too?

Cush: Ask him, I don't know.

Betsy: Why did my crucifix burn your skin?

Cush: You need to see a shrink. You are sick and I will have to walk out of this door never to see you again if you don't cut out these bullshits.

Betsy: Are you saying that my crucifix [hurriedly brought it off her neck] has nothing to do with your lupus attack few minutes ago?

Cush: You are really sick.

Betsy walked, edged towards him with the crucifix and threw it into his shirt. Cush reacted like a snake that has just been poured a raw acid. He wriggled in pain making weird demonic noises until the chain and the crucifix was removed from his shirt, by Betsy who pulled it out of his body. Cush laid quietly, slowly got up and sat still on the couch, subdued. He was speechless for a long moment, he looked ashamed and disrobed. He wanted to say something but the words couldn't come out. He wanted to leave but he was too tired. He sat down and started crying incessantly, pitiably. Betsy put the crucifix away, mustered some courage and held him because she loved him so much. She felt so sorry for him. She knew right there and then that he was in a lot of difficulties with his life.

Betsy informed him that she knew about the cult and the source of his wealth; promised to help him if he chose. He was so tired and powerless. He knew that if he opens up, he will die sooner and painfully too. He was in a deep quagmire. He was so tired and sleepy but he understood the reach of the brotherhood.

 A call came in and it was the prefect. He was instructed to go back home to his temple right away and await further instructions. He was confused further as to which side to gravitate to. He left without a word and went home as instructed.

CHAPTER 6

The Amazon rainforest, covering much of northwest Brazil and extending into Colombia, Peru and other south American countries, is the world's largest tropical rainforest, famed for its biodiversity. It's crisscrossed by thousands of rivers, including the powerful Amazon River towns, with 19th century
Architectures from rubber-boom days, includes Brazil's Manaus and Belem and Peru's Iquitos and Puerto

Maldonado. Amazon occupies an area of 2.124 million Miles.
It is scientifically established that forty percent of the world oxygen is produced by the amazon rainforest. The amazon is a continent of itself, bigger than some of the other continents of the world. Recently, a fire in amazon forest became a world pandemic because of the depletion it caused to the world oxygen level. The south American league of nations, with the help of the civilized world, in concert, sniffed off the fire to preserve oxygen and save the world's greatest ecosystem.

The Amazon, physically, is a world of itself but spiritually, it is another planet of itself. There are millions of pre-civilization societies inside the amazon. These countless peoples with weird and mouth- gaping cultures lives at the umbrella forest of the amazon. Some of them are still cannibalistic in their cultures. They hunted, killed and barbequed rival tribes as meals. Some of the cultures were centuries behind in terms of everything including Christianity or other religions. The actual animal wildlife in the amazon have not yet been discovered by humanity. Some animals in the amazon basin are yet not identified. The thousands of Amazon rivers present the world's greatest aquatic mystery. Some of the rivers and lakes are miles in depth, which is exceptionally odd for a river. Some of the Amazonian humans looks anatomically different from the normal world -established human anatomical outlook. A lot of the tribes of amazons were still in their natural coat, work around, live and interacted with each other stark naked. Some of them live in the trees of amazon. Some built their homes on the trees; some interwove their homes with the vegetative forest strands. They were mainly farmers and fishermen. Some of them ate raw foods and meats. They were very territorial too and can fight off intruders very viciously. There were incessant inter-tribal wars and prisoners of wars ended up on the dining table of the victors. Cannibalism was the way of life in the primitive Amazon. They fought with locally fabricated spears and knives.

The Amazonians were very deeply cultural and wouldn't tolerate any intrusiveness that tended to contaminate their ways of life. They communicated as animals and spoke weird languages that tilted more towards animal kingdom than human kingdom. They had very weird pet animals: lions, monkeys, birds, elephants. They farmed with their animals too; they wedged wars against their enemies, perceived and real ,with their animals. Like other parts of the world, territories were acquired by conquests in the brutal and ferocious tribal wars. The Amazonians did not speak one language as they constituted of multitudes of primitive peoples with primordial traditions, cultures and languages. They presented in light skins, dark skins, long hairs, nappy hairs, blonds, black hairs, brunettes. Some Amazonians were stout in nature while some were very tall and huge. An adventure into the amazons is an incredible experience, if you are alive to tell of it. The governments of the countries of the amazons stayed away from them. Incursions were met with death instantly. They killed first and foremost because an intruder was an enemy and secondly, the intruder was a food, especially if he or she looked different. A lot of journalists and adventurers had dared into the amazons and never returned to tell their experiences. The downed aircrafts or other captured means of transport were turned into objects of caricature by the Amazonians.

Some Amazonians are more civilized than the others, depending on their distance to civilization. A lot of the factors depended on the attitude of the country that lays claim to that amazon. The policies and engagement of the said country had a lot do with it.
Some of the tribes were more politically organized than the others. Some had leadership hierarchy and respect than the rudderless ones. Some even wore clothes and foot wears. Some of these developments were from religious and social adventurers. Geologists and anthropologists also visited the basin for scientific investigations. Some required elaborate arrangements for that to be accomplished otherwise the visitors would turn to dead meats. The mildly civilized Amazonians were easier to work with and they were less of cannibals. In some very few cases, some of them have reconstructed human buildings; wore clothes and had social amenities. The amazon is a world trapped away from the world.

The very spiritual ones were the deadliest to confront. Their practices were heavily dependent on sacrifices, mostly on human sacrifices. Firstly, captured adventurers who were viewed as enemy of the tribe, and secondly, the tribal convicts, mostly people who violated their rules and ways of life. They worshiped spirits and mysticism ardently. Their systems of worship, the artifacts, the sacrifices and the belief- system was complicated. Some worshiped giant trees buried in their jungles and believed that their spirits emanated from the trees and its branches. They offered sacrifices to the trees and do ceremonies around the trees. Their leaders live around some of the trees as a mark of honor and leadership rewards.

The Montas tribe were very notorious for their worships and cannibalism. They were more than a thousand miles from the nearest Brazilian civilization. The tribal animal held to the highest reverence was the lion. They lived and interacted with the domesticated lions. The lions, considered members of the clan, did not kill them too. The Montas were completely primordial in their lifestyle, cultures and traditions. The community cooked together and ate together. They cooked in giant pots, shared out the food, firstly to the kids, then their leaders, trickled down to the families. They lived under makeshift buildings in the canopy of the amazing amazon forest. They also lived on the trees. Their most favorite meats were the snakes of the amazon, antelopes and wild pigs. They hunted with spears and knives, among other hunting implements. They also hunted with their lions. The Montas were warriors, to the tee. In appearance, they skimpily dress in regalia of animal skin barely enough to cover their private parts. Other Amazon tribes, as stated, had similar cultural disposition in terms of cultures and traditions. They conducted their ceremonies in the quiet and serene basin of an endless forest that had a lot under it.

The Montas communed with the dead and the devil. They were extremely spiritual beings with ties to the greater spiritual realms. Their first worship were the sacred trees and, secondly their sacred rocks found in the hills and valleys of the Montas tribe. Legend has it that they have existed since the beginning of creations, spanning billions of years. They shun the so-called civilization with a strong spiritual and violent zeal. They have been in long precarious battle with the government of Brazil over their attempts to induct them into their own world and cultures. There was no accessible road to the Montas. Their sacred trees and stones were very powerful, with weird human- like figures seen physically communing with them. Their communing happens now and then, with a sacrifice of fat and robust wild animals or human adventurers, if they caught one. The prize, the sacrifice, was tied at stake, stripped naked, genitalia covered with leaves, for overnight, to allow their god to have full meal before the next day. They would eat whatever was left of the prize. Such meat rejuvenates them and acted as elixir to their health and well-being.

The Montas knew about humans from the other world, having caught some of them in decades past and continued to catch them, the stupid humanity that invaded into their world. They had open plains in their tribal territories where they farmed and conducted their civil activities. There were some areas of the territory that was only accessible to their spiritual leaders. They never, traditionally, allowed non-titled men or women, kids, and non-spiritual members of their clan, to come in one mile close to the area. The punishment for the violation of these sacrosanct cultures was death penalty. The area was large and expansive. They, Montas were always performing one ritual or the other. As a procedure, they invoked their spirits to grace the occasions. Their overall leader was a huge man with weird beards, always dyed pitch black with the local dye from herbs and leaf extracts. The leader was called Montasa, a very powerful man, their spiritual leader, the army general during his youthfulness but relegated his status as chief of army staff position to a younger person. The Montasa was next in command to their gods. The most revered deity lived inside the trees of the Montas forest.

They performed ceremonies every quarter of the year as a mark of recognition to their guiding spirits. They prepared elaborately for it too. The forest undergrowth was cleared of vegetation; big giant clay pots were dug into the ground for foods cooked fresh in the event arena. Animals were slaughtered crudely, hung on roasting poles, cut open and cooked for consumption at the party. Some meats were eaten raw as a special delicacy meant for the high echelon of the montas. The event would later be opened up for the whole tribe which occupied an expansive portion of that area of the amazon. Before the event, the spiritual leaders would meet and do the cleansing which involved a lot of spiritual activities. The involved members met in their shrines built around the trees of their gods, invoked the spirits, offered animals to it, spilled the blood of the animals to the spirits. In the incantations, they spoke special language to the deities.

On the day of the event, the community, all dressed in skimpy skirts barely covering their bodies, their entire body painted with black skin dye from their heads to the toes; their heads completely shaved and painted black too; women painted only their breasts' nipples and left the breast mound unpainted; barefooted of course, they tried to look like the spirit that they worshiped. They sang and danced, screaming all through the night. They danced around huge bonfires by circling it repeatedly, danced away from the fires and danced back to the fires. Some of the fire magicians or one with strong powers of doing extraordinary traits, would play with the fire, to the roaring of others. Some would swallow and spat out fires from their mouths; they would yell and scream, doing the impossible. The star hunters and farmers would exhibit their prizes, caught animals and fresh produce from their farms. The carnival were nights to remember, every quarter of every year. The tribal hamlets and their leaders organized and brought in their communities in batches. The Montas were close knitted and they were better off for it. They enjoyed the strongest security in their region.

Every male wore two bull horns and animal skins as an optional dress code for the event. Their masquerades would be on ground to perform at the event and entertained the community. The masquerades were depicted as spirits but they were in fact worn by human beings that mimic the evil spirits. The more heinous and uglier the masquerades looked, the more appealing and appreciated by the community, who cheered ecstatically. They danced to the music drums, wriggled on the dusted forest floors, jumped, performed like they were from the spirit world. These masquerades were very much revered as the offshoot of their spirits. They graced the night in suspense and fear; they graced the occasion too, profoundly. It was a taboo for anyone to conduct any investigation in trying to find out who was wearing any of the masquerades. The masquerades were believed to have the spiritual powers to order a spiritual attack on the inquisitive person, including instant death. When they danced towards the crowd, the crowd ran away to make way. Some of them had bloods of animals dripping from their masked mouths.

The spiritual leaders would be positioned in a little dignitary pedestal watching and directing.
They would be dancing, jumping and singing in their tribal

language that only them understood. Their commonest communications and singings were:

Kikikikikikikikikik

Agawu, wuwuwuwuwu

Kikikikikikikikikikiki

Agawam wwwuu wwuuuuu

Mponga da kikikkkkkkkkkkk

Agawu wwuuuu wwuuu

All of them will yell: kikikikikikikikiki and started jumping in ecstasy and profound excitement.

In their most powerful shrine was a deity that comes out physically to be with them. The description of this deity fits into the biblical and human description of the Satan. Towards the end of the event, the Image, their spirit, their deity, edged out into view, spitting fire from its mouth. The image was in a human form, about 7 feet giant, with very hairy body, huge hands, with seven fingers on each hand, and huge legs; large foot, a bigger head than that of the human. The eye was blood red, even in the dark; the nails of its 14 fingers were long and strong; bodily hairs were very bushy. When it was time for it to appear, it did so in arrogance and majesty, looked at the congregation and threw its hand in the air which produced a loud thunder in each direction that it threw its hands. It opened its mouth repeatedly and continued spitting huge fires, to the excitements of the congregation that yelled in appreciation. The voice could be heard from miles away. The spiritual leaders appear in awe of their lord. The image kept walking around the perimeter of the event, with intimidating strides, left huge footpaths on its trails. It said something and the community yelled back: kikikikikikik.

It threw its hand in the air and thunder would go off. Fire came out from its mouth, like carbon dioxide, whenever it spoke. One of the spiritual leaders would walk up to it with a full limb of the sacrificial animal and it took it and devoured it.

The montas were in a world of their own and they were enjoying every bit of it. This was one of the best moments of their primitive life in the jungle of amazon. They believed, like other tribes and communities of the amazon, that the world started and ended in the amazon. The event continued all through the night, even when the devil exited the scene. The Montas had positive inclination towards their deity, the devil. They didn't know of any other alternative. The deity, the devil, protected them and provided their needs, as it does to the Demarkians. It passed through the generations of their ancestors.

✳✳✳

Brazil is the most popular country of the Amazonian nations. They are the most prolific and the best in the game of soccer. They are assumed to be the richest among all the countries of the amazon basin. The cities of Rio De Janeiro, Sao Paulo, among others, were the most popular cities of the south Americas. Brazil was the richest country in that hemisphere and they were the pride of the amazons. The architectures were amazing; the commerce was mind-blowing; the sports industry, especially soccer was critically esteemed; the tourism industry was one of the most popular in the world. There were no middle class in Brazil. You were either very rich or you were very poor. Like any other society, it was dog- eat -dog life every day. It cuts across all spheres of life in the country. The power brokers were very corrupt and seemed to form a large clique of dirty-minded aristocrats. Some of them believed that they were not within the reach of the law. They were untouchables and privileged class of arrogant megalomaniacs.

Ronaldo was the governor of the Sao Paulo region; very wealthy, had fleet of cars, big mansions. He had very few friends, some of them odd friends. They were the Brazilian Demarkians. They were networked in the whole country. They ran things; they called the shots. They looked out for each other. They lived like other Demarkians scattered across the globe. They were evil satanic followers and they were not planning to stop. They were the only humans that had contact and interacted with the Montas. They were involved and participated in the quarterly Montas' event. They bowed and trembled for their devil master when he showed up. They flew into the forest in private small choppers for the event. The Montas never harmed or attacked them. They were equal disciples of Lucifer. The next event was coming up soon. Ronaldo got his massive private residence ready for visiting members from within and without the country.

As they started arriving, their names were submitted to the customs and immigration for special handling. They were cleared and escorted to Ronaldo's enclave. Ericson, Edmonton, Winterbrush, Cushner, others all arrived at GRU airport, enroute to Ronaldo's residence. This was a great time of the year as they all looked forward to it. They enjoyed the carnival event of the Montas. They enjoyed the overwhelming appearance of Lucifer on the nights of the events; the dances, the cultures of the primitive Montas; the fresh seductive appearances of the naked virgins; the creepy darkness and the bonfires. Some of them enjoyed the raw meats and the drinking of animal blood. The devil had given them so much prosperity and they couldn't pay him back enough! They all went back after the event and never discussed that with anyone. After the event, they flew back in the choppers, at least three, of it, to make sure that they had a means of getting out if any of the choppers was to be faulty or be destroyed by rival tribe. They would assembly back in Ronaldo's home and conducted further festivities before leaving Brazil for their respective destinations.

Cushner who eventually recovered from his situation in Vegas, went to Brazil and renewed his satanic vow. He sold his buildings and moved to the city of Henderson where he bought a massive building with an underground garage that could house four cars, and a secret bunker built on his specifications. It meant that he could hide in that house without another occupant knowing that he was there. He changed his phone number as soon as he came back to the United States. He laid low and cut off all communications with his girlfriends and other friends in Vegas. He stealthily went to his office and home. Now and then, he drove to the nearest Arizona cities for his fun. On this Saturday, he ran into Betsy at a eatery in Henderson. He was always sleek and wanted to avoid her but he couldn't. Betsy was not so eager seeing him too but she had found and embraced God after her experiences with Cush. She took a covenant to worship God till her end. She yelled out to Cush in excitement, real or imagined.

Betsy: Hey you, finally seeing you again?

Cush: I guess so. How you been?

Betsy: great, especially with my new found love of Jesus mighty Christ! How about you? How you been?

Cush: I am doing great as you can see.

Betsy: Looks could be deceiving, you don't think?

Cush: I guess you may be right but golden fish will never represent poverty.

Betsy: wealth and poverty are not measured in gold and silver. There is more to life than those, agree?

Cush: if you say so. Life without them is hell and purgatory combined. So what's up with you my used-to be- darling Betsy?

Betsy: Have you started sleeping well?

Cush: excuse me.

Betsy: Do you have a peace of mind now?

Cush: wealth is a sleeping aid. You lose sleep when you can't pay your bills.

Betsy: Nope, you know that is a baloney.

Cush: I know so. And I live so.

Betsy: Nope again. Life in Satan will never come with peace of mind. You and I know how that plays out,

Betsy. You forgot?

Cush: Betsy I loved you and I still respect you a lot. Be careful what you say, to avoid a wrath that you cannot handle, sweetie.

Betsy: What is in me is bigger, honey. I am not routing for a spiritual superbowl but tell your Lucifer master that Jesus Christ will blow him away like a candle.

Cush: A cow that spread out on a rail line might be very courageous but its wisdom is very questionable. You feel me, Hun?

Betsy: very well so. Your proverbial analogy is a misfit here. There is no cow on the rail. An antelope will never defeat a tiger.

Cush: I protected you before but your current attitude might expose you to a tide I can't control.

Betsy: awwwww, ain't you sweet. The tide of the Holy Spirit is bigger than a combined tsunami and underwater volcanic eruptions of the devil. A child of the covenant doesn't need protection from anyone. I want you to decamp to my side. The dogs and other animals will stop barking and attacking you. The crucifix will be your panacea instead of red hot iron on you. You won't be scared of the holy cross anymore; you wouldn't be keeping two identical buildings and cars for your deceitful social life and secret satanic cult worships. You will leave sin alone and cut down on your lies; you will sleep with your two eyes closed.

Oh by the way, it was you that I saw on the day with the other Porsche, remember? You did not go to Los Angeles on the day you claimed. You were with Anita. You went to the airport from Anita's house, I learnt of all that later. I also know about you and your spoilt fine but rogue friend, Liz and how she confiscated your house, well her house, that you bought for her. I got to know of all your business trips, Hun. I am not worried about stuffs like that. I am worried about your soul because you are not beyond redemption.

Cush: How you know all that?

Betsy: are they lies?

Cush: that's not an answer I solicited.

Betsy: so I am now your daughter that I have to answer in certain way, huh?

Cush: Oh lord! How in the world do you know all that?

Betsy: Sir, first of all, acknowledge that they are true.

Cush: They are and I am sorry.

Betsy: I have a crystal ball, honey. You don't have the monopoly of spirituality, do you? At least in mine, I don't seek that from Lucifer [laughings].

Cush: So how is your practice, coming on?

Betsy: great, can't complain.

Cush: I will have lots of works for you soon.

Betsy: because you ran into me here. You sold your buildings, your cars, changed your numbers, recreated your evil ways but didn't leave Vegas. That is not very smart Cush. The question is why are you hiding? You don't owe no body, or do you?

Cush: I am only trying to help.

Betsy: appreciate it brother but no. I am not prone for the devil's dividends. I gave all my wealth to charity to purge the tainted wealth and started all over again. I don't have gold and silver now but I am fine.

Cush: well, if you say so. Good meeting you. Can I have your number?

Betsy: for real, waoh, you really need that. Here it is.

Cush: I will keep in touch, bye now.

Betsy: bye Hun. Review all that we talked about. I am here to help you in recovering you from Satan. Just a call will do it. Bye.

Few months later, Betsy was attending a magic show in Bellagio hotel with her guests when she spotted Cush dejectedly walking out of the theatre. She ignored him and pretended as if she did not see him. She went to use the restroom and, on her way, ran into Cush who apparently was waiting for her. Cush looking very subdued, walked up to Betsy and they started a conversation:

Cush: hey, how you?

Betsy: you again, I am cool, has some guests, brought them here to have a feel of Vegas.

Cush: looked over and waived at the guests.

Betsy had never seen Cush looking that humble and subdued since they first met.

Betsy: Have you been okay?

Cush: Yes, I guess. Life is all about choices and we are stuck in our spaces.

Betsy: How do you mean?

Cush: listen Betsy, you are one person that has made the most remarkable impression in my life. I thanked my star every day for meeting you.

Betsy: I know you wouldn't thank God for meeting me, laughter; anyways stars are created by God. So why am I so important in your life?

Cush: You won't understand. You downloaded my life to me when you told me about my secret life. I was worried that the brotherhood would have taken you out but you are still on your feet, flesh and blood.

Betsy: He that is in me is greater than your cult. I believe that you could be retrieved from the grips of Lucifer if you are determined. Are you?

Cush: I have no idea or any interest about what you are talking about, sweetie. I am in Eldorado and it is a nice place to be.

Betsy: Not with the cry you did the other day. Not with your sleeplessness; not with the animal attacks; not with discreet lifestyles unbefitting to a young man of your age. Will you ever get married?

Cush: Yes of course when the time is ripe.

Betsy: "when the time is ripe" mimicking Cush sarcastically. You are 40 years old, has a lot of money, has the world in your pockets and the time is still unripe? I don't know what else that could sound more ridiculous. Let me tell you honey, our problem started getting solved the day and time we acknowledge them. You will never escape from a fool's island if you don't acknowledge that you are there. Self- denial is the biggest affliction to oneself. You are an intelligent man with a vision but you sought wealth inordinately but it is becoming too hot to handle and too cold to hold on. You need to seek the face of God and liberate yourself from the shackles of Lucifer. You can't stir the beehive and expect to have peace.

Cush: So what have you been up to, Mary, mother of Jesus?

Betsy: Oh I didn't know that such words could come out of your mouth, may burn like the crucifix. Anyways, I have been doing great as you can see. I am as free as the air. I am living my life and enjoying every bit of it. My practice took a dive after your exit from my life but it is well. Like I keep saying to you, there is more to life than gold and silver. A piece of bread from the holy Angels is more rewarding than a luciferous bakery.

Cush: Oh I have a gift for you, hoping we can hook up for you to get it. When will that be?

Betsy: Oh no, thanks but I don't need it. I have been contaminated enough by your past gifts, don't you get it? I love you as a person but your world is in the dark; I exist in the light. Darkness and light cannot meet. It will be my pleasure to pull you over to the light. Underneath the soiling, I can see a very good man in you.

Cush: I will be running now. You and your guests have a swell time.

Betsy: you have my number, call me if you need to.

Cush: Good to see you, always.

Betsy: pleasure is mine always. Remember, seek Jesus, embrace and grab him. You have no other choice. What goes around comes around, especially in your situation.

Cush: Bye now.

✳✳✳

Ericson still his old self, continued his dream of Los Angeles life, a night crawler, high roller, sexual extravaganza. He bought an upscale restaurant on the 4th street, Santa Monica, named Islets. Leased it out to a professional management company on a monthly leased fee. The restaurant has been doing well. The restaurant had upscale spa rooms; artificial ice rooms; discrete illicit drug balconies; whore rooms, both straight, gay and bisexual. The restaurant had Los Angeles top Disk jockeys all weekend including Sunday night. The Sunday night was transgender night with a side bisexual and transgender strip actors doing their things. The islets is the place to be, especially for the weekends. Ericson was very happy that he was talked into establishing this cove of sin by one of his friends. He laughed whenever he thought of it.

Life is sweeter when you make the right choices. Satan was being derided for nothing, Ericson thought. There was redemption in good and kind father Lucifer. The Demarkian cult had given him all that he desired and he was grateful for it. To hell with Donna if she feels any different. The members of the brotherhood had their own special lounge in the restaurant, branded the special room of the Elites. Everything was done differently in that lounge. On every weekend, six to seven digit figures were spent in that room by the cult members. The staffs were perplexed about the caliber and the amount of money expended by the patrons of the exclusive lounge. Sometimes, the lounge had their own entertainment which could be a life band.

Ericson continued on his sexual proclivities, his unhinged lifestyle and he was drowning in fun, so he thought. He went home at the conclusion of the club last Saturday and got home late. He slept all through the day, intermittently waking up and dozing off again and again.

✳✳✳

Cush drove to the park on this beautiful Saturday afternoon. He saw a lot of people walking in the park, seemed fulfilled and enjoying their time together. He felt envious and reflective of his life. He has been in self-denial knowing that he was deeply in a life of misery. He watched some young families and their friends running on the park. He felt like getting married, but to whom? Could the wife understand and accept the cult and the lifestyle? Could she put up with all the restrictions of the brotherhood? Could she improvise with the wealth he could afford her and tolerate the restrictions? How and where could he start? He thought about Betsy deeply but that was a mission impossible. He then switched his deep thought to exiting the cult? was that a suicide thought? It sounded like it and he knew that. He drove home and started drinking, avoiding calls from his new mistresses.

He dozed off and woke up in the morning completely fatigued.
He started thinking of his life again, this time deeply. He was going in and out about his continued membership of the cult; he thought about his material possessions, his life and the dangers of even thinking of abandoning the cult. The cult is extremely powerful and could end his life in a jiffy. He developed goose pimples on the mere thought of that. His mental agony seemed to be endless. In his mind, he started weeping internally. When he woke up, he saw a missed call from Betsy. He called Betsy earlier before he slept. He called Betsy back, just for a chat. Betsy picked up his call and they started talking as usual, their new normal of the battle of wits.
Betsy: Hey, junior Satan, how are you?
Cush was so upset with such joke. He started raining invectives on Betsy, calling her all sorts of names.
Betsy: Ok I am sorry for calling you that but you don't have to say all that to me. It looks like I am the only true friend or sister that

you have now. I am trying a tough love on you. You made a very terrible choice by joining the brotherhood and I am not going to patronize you anymore. If I have to tease you hard or call you names to get your attention, then I will employ that. You need to wake up to the realities of life. Money is not synonymous with happiness and I am sure that statement resonate more with you now than anyone else.

Cush: I feel you and I have been doing a lot of thinking too. I am very confused.
Betsy Excitedly screamed: for real?!! That's more than a flicker of hope. With that, I will remain undeterred in my efforts.
Cush: I have to go now. By the way, where are you now?
Betsy: driving home, have a party tonight at my friend's house. Wanna come?
Cush: No, sorry not in the mood. Thanks though for the invite. Hey, y'all have fun, ok?
Betsy: Sure, thanks.

✳✳✳

Betsy went to the party at Henderson, had a wonderful time and was driving home in the desolate part of the Vegas south side. The road was heavenly, super clean and well-attended. The lawns on the street neighborhoods were well manicured and couldn't have looked any better. The houses were well built and aligned with the street. The street lights were blasting in full stream. It was 2 a.m. in the morning and everywhere was quiet and calm, unlike the north side of Vegas. Betsy going on 50mph, a little above the speed limit but carefully driving to avoid attracting the police and a possible citation and arrest for Driving under the influence, DUI. As an attorney, a dui arrest and conviction may cost her law license. She slowed down to 45 mph, which is the posted speed limit and was enjoying her music and suddenly her car started jerking violently as if there was an earth tremor. She pulled over but the jerking remained unabated. From the blues, a giant black raven flew out and perched on her vehicle hood, characteristically of the cult, the bird stared non-stop at Betsy, refused to fly off, appeared fearless but deeply evil, with protruding red eye balls.

Betsy was confused for a minute and then she remembered the cult and quickly searched for her rosary and the crucifix, found it and retrieved it, flashed it to the bird, invoking the bible but the evil bird seemed unintimidated and continued to stare at Betsy. With a very deep hoarse voice, the demon started warning Betsy to stay off Cush or die. The demonic sound came on and increased in crescendo. Then there was this evil mocking laughter and the bird flew away. Betsy, jolted, drove home in jittery. She was scared but premised her faith in the powers of the holy spirit. She was, somewhat confused on the depreciated efficacy of the rosary and the crucifix. This was Satan himself and it requires a deeper battle. She drove into her compound feeling relieved until she flashed her high beam and saw the same raven and a black huge dog relaxing on her Porch. Her heart started beating faster again and she stopped, did not want to exit her car. She called the priest of her church and relayed the animals and the cult's activities. They started praying and invoking the book of psalms. She brought out her rosary and her crucifix again holding it out and started praying harder but the animals appeared unperturbed. She was too scared to exit her car; she was so disappointed on her strength of faith too. She summoned courage, drove past the animals and parked her car. As soon as she parked the car, the huge dog and Raven were by her car, looking intently at her. The bird perched again on her hood while the dog with blood shot eyes were looking at her as if it was going to pounce on her right away on slight provocation, but again the car was not open or accessible to them. But she was relying on that knowing that these were evil agents and a locked door couldn't stop them. She brought out the crucifix again and continued flashing it. The dog barked demonically asking her to put the powerless cross away or it will kill her. The dog, speaking in multiple voices, warned Betsy that they were just there for a final warning and were not intending to hurt her unless they were provoked further. The eyes of the animals were reflecting in the dark, ominous and deeply troubling. Her car started vibrating again for few minutes as the animals disappeared.

Betsy, in fear, drove to the church residence and slept there, so scared to stay in her house. The priest was teasing her by asking her: where is thy faith, young woman? Satan is real and evil forces are real too. You need to be truly equipped with the faith of the Holy Spirit to fight them. Running away from your house is a failure of that sacred responsibility. Go home and confront the demon if he comes back again today. Don't relent in your effort to save your friend, who is now your brother. Call him up and share your experiences with him. Invite him to see me if he could. Betsy got home, feeling confident and relaxed, invited Cush to her house. Cush drove over and they were sitting and relaxed. Betsy brought up the issue of pulling him out of the cult but Cush, looking scared, didn't want to talk about that but Betsy continued to push it.

Cush: Do you want to kill me? Do you really know the power of our master? You are toying with a fire hotter than a volcanic lava. I am not your regular Tom. Just allow me to carry my cross alone.

Betsy: I am happy that you know of the cross and its implications. Jesus carried the cross for all of us. You don't have to carry it anymore. My priest is ready to meet with you, if you desire.

Cush: You and your so-called priest don't understand the magnitude of what you are confronting. You need to back off or calamity will befall you. I made this choice myself and I should be allowed to deal with it. I made a stupid mistake but I am ready and willing to bear the consequences.

Betsy: All you need to do is to renounce evil and leave the rest to the angels of God.

Cush: Lets watch television please. Order some food please.

Betsy: I am a woman; I cook, okay; don't be rude.;

Cush: get me some food, mother.

They ate and talked until midnight when Cush left for home. He got home and continued to deal with his inner demon and his turbulent lifestyle. He tried to sleep but couldn't until 4 a.m. in the morning. When he woke up, he felt so desolate, wanted to call his other girlfriend for a hang -out but recently he found himself withdrawing from that lifestyle.

He called Betsy again and asked to visit her but Betsy said she won't get in until morrow morning. He hung the phone and started drinking heavily. In the night, maybe with the influence of alcohol, he decided to exit the brotherhood, even if it means that he dies. He called Betsy and asked for the priest's phone number. He got the number, called and spoke with the priest and they agreed that he should come to the church that late night. Cush drove out in anger and frustration to meet the priest. Less than a mile to the church, the cult unleashed their powers on him. First, a very strong wind started blowing and he continued to drive hoping that he may be saved if he gets to the church. The wind turned into thunder as he was pulling into the church compound.

In the big cathedral church building was a huge crucifix placed on top of the roof. Next to it was a 5-foot iron casted thunder protector rod. In a heartbeat, the rod swiftly disengaged from the building and plunged like a spear into the heart of Cush pinning him to the driver car seat causing an agonizing instant death.
The priest who saw Cush drove into the compound, was watching the spectacle from an open window, with some lit candles that were being set up for the spiritual warfare. He heard, the noise but it was a little dark. He went for a flashlight and shone the light and screamed at the carnage that he saw. He quickly called Betsy, called his fellow clergy, called 911 and the police department. Within minutes, the fire truck, the ambulance, police squad cars, all arrived to see the graphic death scene.

Betsy drove over and saw it too. Cush's dead body was gruesomely strapped to the car seat, with his eyes popped out in fear. The entire vehicle was littered with an unusual amount of blood. The killing rod went with dumbfounding precision through his heart and protruded to the back of the car seat.
That was the end of Cush. Very pathetic and deplorable story, the type you see in a horror movie.

The Demarkians   Chidi Metu

CHAPTER 7

The Demarkian confraternity had seniority and levels of membership. The order, unlike most order cults, was extremely powerful. There were five steps of membership in the fraternity, steps one through five. The fifth step was for very senior members of the order. They shared a lot of privileges with step four too. The Demarkians believed that a human was made up of body and spirit. On death, the spirit disengages but stays around for a while. Just like the zombie philosophy, they believed and practiced the recalling of the spirit of a dead person, especially the levels four and five for a final meeting before the spirit was let off. It was mandatory with step five but optional with step four. The option was to be exercised by a local leader in charge of the region where the dead resided before his or her death.

Mr. Augustus Chambers was a very seasoned and senior member of the California bar, with specialty in medical malpractice litigations. He was admitted to the state and federal bar in 1968. He had maintained an impeccable law practice till his death. He was known by all medical facilities within the greater Los Angeles area because of the number of years he practiced law and the number of medical facilities and doctors that he sued and won. He was viciously prolific in dealing with erring doctors. He made more than millions of dollars in litigation practice. He did not have a friend when it comes to assessing and accepting a case. He employed the same attitude in the court, spanning decades of successful litigations. Chambers was a very tall, slender man, carried himself in glamor. He maintained a complete five floor office building in Beverly hills. He lived in Beverly hills too. He dressed in black suit most times, with a bowler hat. He walked with the aristocratic swagger of an accomplished old school lawyer.

Chambers, an Irish Caucasian American, of the third generation of the chambers pedigree, represented success totally. He was divorced forty years ago, without a child and never remarried. When he turned seventy- five, few years ago, he willed all his properties to his alma mater, Harvard law school endowments. His social life was weird and disoriented. He had round the clock concierge services in his house. He had very few friends that visited him now and then. His childlessness never bothered him. He was obsessed with his law practice and Dom Perignon Champaign. He was a core recluse in his lifestyle. He did not talk a lot except when he was tearing medical personnel up in the courtrooms. Chambers turned 82 years and age crept in and started damaging his pelvic bones, among others. He walked with a walking stick and still staggered sometimes. He had no pet, unlike other Demarkians.

He grew up in Boston, attended most of his education there. On passing the glorious California bar exam, he relocated to California and almost immediately started living in Beverly Hills. He was a top ranking member of the cult. On his 81st birthday, some cult members came over and they had a feast. A private jazz band was invited and they played all the afternoon and early evening. The amazing jazz music was so thrilling that some members slept on the couch in his massive and gorgeously furnished house. The cult brought in their own food and beverages, most times. Today they did. The entire bartenders, the concierge, valet parking attendants, had no clue who they were serving and dinning with on that day. The party went well, of course with such wealthy bunch of megalomaniacs in attendance.

Chambers continued in his retirement and not having anything to do ushered in some sicknesses. He received optimal treatments at Cedar Sinai hospital Beverly Hills. He used John Hopkins Hospital too. The medical sciences kept him alive for a while. One morning, while descending the stairs, having eaten a mango, with a huge kitchen knife in his right hand, forgetting to hold to the stair rails, Chambers tripped and fell on the knife. He was going to put the knife away in the sink downstairs. With an early on-set of dementia, he forgot to hold the rails as advised by his Doctors repeatedly.

The only house help with him that Saturday morning was Frank and he was working on the garden at the far end of the compound when this happened. When he came in, he saw Chambers' lifeless body in pool of blood. He called the 911 and reported the incidence. He was asked not to touch the knife or anything around the dead body. He was instructed to step to another part of the house until police arrived. He obliged and stayed away from the body. The cops came and created a possible crime scene, looking at the knife sticking into the corpse. The ambulance arrived, processed the body and removed him to the morgue.

Frank was interrogated by the police on the scene and he relayed what happened. They took him to the station and continued with the interview to determine if this was a homicide case. They later allowed Frank to go but on call for further investigation.
The cult members were distraught on hearing of his death. Chambers had no known family or next of kin. The only friends that he had were the same cult members. They met at the temple and started planning his funeral.

Chambers was a step five member of the order and he had to be accorded a last respect. His spirit had to be recalled for a chat with senior members in a special ceremony. They already know how he died but he was still going to tell them that. Moreover, he had to make a short farewell speech to the brotherhood. His spirit would be recalled with special incantations in an elaborate ceremony to be performed three to six days after death, if there were no inhibitions. In this case, there was a little inhibition on the case as it was being investigated as a possible homicide case and the police not allowing the body to be removed out of the morgue, even after the mandatory forensic autopsy was conducted .But the Demarkians were too powerful for the police protocols. The overall sheriff of the county of Los Angeles, and the cream of the greater Los Angeles were under the thumbnail of the fraternity.

On the early night of the next Friday, senior members of the cult, all dressed in black suits, black shirts and black ties, acting as family members, went to Harrison and Ross to retrieve the body. They took the body in the casket to his house and the driver of the hearse was given a bundle of one hundred dollar bills and asked to come back by five a.m. He was puzzled and started to protest. One of the members gave him a phone and asked him to talk to his boss who was on the other end of the phone. The boss of the funeral home asked him to abide by any and all instructions given to him. Some other members gave him more money and he left in happiness.

The house keeper on that day, Ms. Juliet, was asked to go home and come back next night and a bundle of money was given to her too. She left as instructed. The cult members waited until the chosen time, locked up all doors, closed all curtains, turned off the lights and most other lights in the building. This was a very solemn event and any interruption by any junior member of the cult or a non -member could mean death for the person. They wheeled his body into his secret chamber and stood surrounding the casket. Mozart music started playing in the background. They lit their satanic candles, a member brought in one of their fiercest cult dog and crow. The dog stood by the side of the pedestal of the casket while the crow perched on the window pen directly at the head of the casket.

The leader walked over and did some rituals reflecting the ethos of the cult. They opened the casket and started making some invocations, calling on Lucifer to recall Mr. Chambers spirit for the final ceremony. They continued this process for over thirty minutes until the building started to shake mildly ushering in the presence of devil himself. The members, looking very stern and out of the world, were patient and all were fixated on the dead body in the casket. Mr. Chambers, received the best pathological care and he looked as if he was still sleeping. The members looking at him steadily, waited for another one hour. There was a mild wind that started blowing and papers on the desk started flying around. Other small objects started falling off the tables and chairs. The usual cult sound came on and voices speaking muffled languages and sounds that could not be deciphered, came on but members looked unperturbed. This has been the way and manner their master comes into their presence. They were used to it. A very huge dark cloud enveloped the room for some minutes and disappeared. Everything became quiet and sober immediately.

The leader took over, made some incantations, and Mr. Chambers body showed a movement and his corpse gradually started sitting up in very slow movement. They were looking at him unfazed. Chambers sat up fully but was still in a zombie state starring at one place. The dog and the crow started making some low but demonic noise. The leader flagged at them and they kept quiet.

After about five to ten minutes, Chambers with his eyes not moving, turned his neck and smiled at everyone in the room. His hands remained at his groin area just like a dead body he was. But he could smile and turn his neck. The leader asked him to render his messages but he couldn't talk but rather starring at the members like a sitting zombie. He later opened his mouth and started talking. His voice sounded as if he was from a very far distance talking on speaker phone to the members. He kept on smiling and thanking them for the respect and sacrifice of their time. He said that he died a natural death which, of course they knew. He told them that he had no beef with anyone and that they should bury him in Los Angeles. He asked the leader to take steps in exonerating Frank from the investigations, informing them that Frank was a wonderful servant, like Juliet. He informed the cult he donated the building to the cult via the leader. He implored the cult to please give large sums of money to the house helpers. He thanked the cult for all that they did for him in assisting him during his life time. He smiled at them again and said that he was ready to be buried. They thanked him and bid him farewell.

Chambers slowly descended back into his former position until he laid straight and the casket was closed and wheeled back into the sitting room. The members started drinking until the driver of the hearse came back and took the body back to the morgue.

The funeral ceremony was first conducted at the temple exclusively and later at the cemetery where he was buried quietly. Members re-converged at the temple for a continued cerebration of life of a life-long and dedicated member of the brotherhood. Other business of the brotherhood was discussed including the frivolities of Ericson. The members dispersed quietly into the dark night.

CHAPTER 8

The Demarkians continued on their exploits. Their powers and activities appeared unhinged.

The next story is about Mr. Adamson, a Demarkian, a senior member of the city of Los Angeles regional planning department and he was in serious feud with Ms. Coker, head of the Human Resources department. On this day, the two departments had a meeting and it just couldn't go well because of the rancor and animosity of these two tough individuals. There were multiple complaints about the treatments, work place violations, against Adamson, brought in by employees in his department. Adamson was a racist, uppity and arrogant individual who believed that he had the world in his pocket, a signature personality encouraged by the brotherhood. He was a product of Princeton College, savvy in a lot of things though. He was very thrifty, only when others were involved. His frugality does not extend to his own enjoyment of anything. He was a me, myself and I, kind of a man. At 52 years, he had been divorced twice and doesn't seem to be gravitating towards a third marriage. He was a Mercedes Benz Freak as he exhibited his leased different classes of the latest sporty Mercedes Benz vehicles. He was an integral part of the city's section as the head of the department, controlling about 200 employees and a chunk of the city's budget. He conducted departmental meetings with dominance and intimidation. He read the riot Act to his subordinates and any opposition had been met with severe consequences including termination. In the last five years that he took over the department, the city settled about seven law suits relating to wrongful employment practices and terminations. The city council have had many meetings with the Mayor to terminate him but all to no avail. The citizens of greater Los Angeles had called for his termination but he had Abraham as a father. The reason was simple: Mayor of the city of Los Angeles was a Demarkian and the brotherhood protected their own. Adamson continued to have field days in the way and manner he discharged his duties and he was getting away with it all. Adamson could be nice when he chose to be. He had some few friends and he let them in only to a limited space of his life. He was very structured in a sneaky way.

Adamson had a serious gambling habit that had accounted for his failures in life. He was never at home or pay attention to things that were important and he was unapologetic about that.
Ms. Coker was a tough lady. She was only 40 years of age, attended Boston College and University of southern California, had her doctorate in social sciences, among other accolades. She was very good looking and had been married to her husband for 5 years, without kids. They would tell you that they were working on it. She took in on the 5th year of the marriage and lost the pregnancy. Her husband died later which devastated her and hardened her more. It was a very difficult time for her but she forged on.

She was very free-spirited, full of life and very confident about her accomplishments and her abilities. She flaunted her shapely long legs, impeccable deeply tanned skin texture, a killer body shape, very pretty, and she enjoyed taunting men with her beauty. She was every body's sweet heart in the city hall. Her compassionate personality was shown in everything that she did. She didn't hide her disdain and loathing of Adamson. He called him an asshole among other invectives whenever they go off on each other. Their relationship was messy, beyond cat and mouse.

The city was currently engaged in the construction of few local bridges; drain canal repairs; planting of trees, among other major projects. There have been series of meetings involving the finance department, planning department, the human resources department, among others. The meetings were stalled twice because of the attitude of Adamson who showed little or no respect to opposing views, including that of Coker. The meeting was scheduled for today to approve the submitted plans and the funds necessary to execute the projects. Adamson was practically, as always, telling others how and what needed to be done. Coker looked at him for a while and the argument ensued:

Adamson: My opinions and conclusions are pivotal and I wasn't expecting any of you to raise any objection or issues as to them.
Coker: Well, just like I have always told you, you need to purge yourself of the huge malady of arrogance. I don't know how your brain works but I am pretty sure it needs to be overhauled and reset.

Adamson: Young lady, you need to watch your words. Stop sticking your fingers in the mouth of a tiger.
Coker: What I see is a retarded man, a human being with a faulty brain box. The only relationship between you and a tiger is that both of you are animals. I don't think you need me to educate you on the differences between humans and animals. Or do you?
Other members in the meeting were all beaming and smiling, enjoying the roasting of this idiot, Adamson.
Adamson: I am not used to being challenged by nonentities like you. I wasn't raised like that. Give me a break, please.
Coker: Your behavior is an evidence of bad breeding. You need to be taken to a car wash and have them detail you out. You are sickening and annoying. My presence in any of our meetings will always lead to this until you are cleaned out of the numerous debris attached to your personality.
Adamson: his face turning purple, fuming, yelled at Coker to watch her words or be destroyed.
Coker, upset herself because they haven't been able to accomplish anything in their recent meetings because of this bozo.

Coker, with a sarcastic smile on her face told Adamson that he was not fit to head any department in the city hall, as he was grossly incompetent. You couldn't even run a home, with two failed marriages, all your faults.

Coker: Oh by the way I forgot to tell you. I have a gambling rehab center for your habits. I don't even know how you are able to pay your bills.

Adamson: We will see. When the chips are down, we will know who is who.

Coker: There are no chips, except your gambling chips. You are full of shit, Adamson. You need a lot of enema. Adamson couldn't take this any longer and he stormed out of the room to his office and later left for home. On getting home, he drowned himself in alcohol and woke up in the morning feeling like a train wreck. He called off work for three days, feeling very despondent and disillusioned. He stayed back home, his cars locked up in the garages. His girlfriend, Rosemary, called him multiple times but he wasn't picking her calls. Rosemary came by one morning and peeped through his window, saw Adamson's weird cat perching on the couch but there was no sign of Adamson. She stood around for a few minutes and left. She felt irritated that this cocky man may have been avoiding her calls just for the heck of it! She left in anger.

Adamson reminiscenced on his failed marriages, found consolation in his warped mind that he wasn't the cause of the failures. In the first marriage, he loved his wife but filed for a divorce when he caught her with a neighbor's older son having sex in their guest room. He travelled out of town but came home earlier, having been suspecting his wife of infidelity. He walked to the porch and heard whispering sounds coming from the room. He quietly walked in on them. He pulled his gun, was on the verge of wasting them but changed his mind for a quick second. He took pictures of their nudity which he used to get an easy divorce and a big civil court award on a loss of consortium law suit against the lover boy.

He didn't want to marry again but changed his mind few years later and married another lady, a pharmacist. Initially the marriage worked because she tolerated his arrogance very well and seemed to rise above his flaws, his baggage as she used to call it. They continued to live in peace until he found out that his wife was bisexual, in heated lesbian circle of friends, engaged in the practice of free fall partner sex exchanges. It was devastating in all angles. He divorced her and decided to live single and die single. To hell with the bitches, sucks his teeth whenever he thought of that. These experiences contributed to the deterioration in his character.

He deliberately chose to ignore his contributions to the reasons for the failed marriages. He was wired to believe that he was always right and everyone else were unwise fools.

For Coker to taunt him with his personal life was a low blow. It was declaration of war and she was going to be punished severely. He later, with bitterness, called the local prefect of the cult and it became a cult issue. He even discussed all that with the mayor who was very infuriated with Coker and decided to set traps for her to fire her but until then, he advised Adamson to do the needful and contact the leader which he did. The leader collected as much information as needed on Coker and even learnt that Coker's birthday was in two days- time. The cult decided to take her out on that day, as a birthday gift. The cult didn't usually get down to this level of retribution but they considered Coker's attacks very deep and intrusive. They looked out for their own, especially a depressed member who could develop suicidal ideations. The brotherhood could not afford to lose a member for a reason that could easily be taken care of.

✳✳✳

Coker lived in Palos Verdes Peninsula, Pv, a rich suburb within the Los Angeles County, considered in some way as part of greater Los Angeles.

Today, Coker came to work, dressed to kill, full of beautiful spirit, received lots of compliments, reminding everyone that her birthday was around the corner, with dinner and elaborate ceremony planned by her friends. The day was Coker's birthday and she was determined to enjoy every part of it. She couldn't call off work because of her busy assignments, believing too that she could get home in time enough to attend to her birthday hang-out as planned.

It was winter period in Los Angeles and it gets really dark by 5p.m. Coker was stuck on the 405 freeway with the usual snail and frustrating traffic. She calmed down, trying to avoid anything that would spoil her birthday spirit. She got home behind schedule, sadly. She drove to the front of her house beaming with smiles that she eventually made it home for her night out! She walked up to her porch and noticed that a black crow with huge beaks was perched on her porch starring at her sternly. The bird was not making any effort to fly off with her approaching. Coker stopped, petrified, for a moment, especially having noticed the abnormal eyes of the evil-looking bird with reflective blood red eyeballs. She picked up a piece of wood to attack the bird but it flew away. In trying to strike it, she lost her steps and failed to the ground, almost sprained her ankle. She got up from the ground and walked into her home a little disoriented. She sat down to suck in the incidence, puzzled as to what had just happened? She called her boyfriend, Henry, and her friends and informed them that she would be running late for the birthday dinner.

She related to Henry what had just happened to her, especially the puzzling eyeballs of the bird. Henry was puzzled too but didn't attach much weight to it, asked her to speed up, noting that the night was for her and it really doesn't look well that she kept everyone waiting. Henry suggested to run over and pick her up but she declined. She mustered the courage and dressed up and was about to leave when she heard a noise at the back of the house. She opened the door, she saw a menacing black cat, with fangs fully exhibited and had similar menacing eyes as the bird. She was momentarily jolted again and became scared. She maintained eye-to-eye contact with the beastly fearless cat for a while and she then ran into the house and quickly locked her door. She developed instant migraine and took some pills with shaking hands. She was concerned with taking the acetaminophen and codeine tablets, knowing that she was going to drink some alcohol that night. She needed the tablets to be able to function that night. She was still shaking and confused and was out of it for a while. Some ominous music continued to play at the background. Coker called the 911 and complained about the harassing animals but she was advised to call animal control. She was initially reluctant in doing that, sensing that these were not normal animals but later she did and it took about 25 minutes for them to come but the animals were nowhere to be seen. She used that opportunity to escape from her house and drove to the party venue. She called Henry and relayed all these developments and Henry got more perturbed. Henry teased her, asking her whether she was already drunk without being at the event? That was not fair baby, he teasingly said to her, to assuage her mood. He started laughing loudly, to Coker's irritation. She was too out of it for Henry's silly but sensible jokes. She needed that anyway, at least to maintain her sanity and drag her out of this nonsense. She did not feel well at all. Tears started building on her eyes and she blurted out: "on my birthday, damn it!"

She continued to drive erratically, a little disoriented, having drank two full glasses of whiskey during these animal harassments, hoping that the eagle-eyed Los Angeles Sheriff or the police, especially the Torrance police department, wouldn't see her driving. A driving under the influence arrest and conviction will do a damaging blow to her career and her personality. The thought alone rushed adrenalin in her body and she wanted to pee badly but she later got out of it. She drove through the beautiful city of Torrance, via Hawthorne Blvd, through the Pacific Coast Highway to the north Palos Verdes estate.

She found herself relaxing connecting through the mountains and valleys of the Rolling Hills part of the peninsula. She started getting into the party mood again and called Henry and relayed everything to him. Henry was relieved and happy. He announced that to all the attendees that her queen was en route and that she was in the estate now.

Coker driving through the winding dangerous roads of the peninsula, got jilted on remembering that Tiger Woods just had a very bad accident and fell into one of these valleys suffering life-threatening injuries. She slowed down and became more careful in gliding through the endless snake road surrounded by deep valleys and mountains by the side. She occasionally used her high beam lights for clearer vision, knowing that driving in the dark was a nightmare to her. On getting to Silver Spur Avenue, she flashed her full lights and caught a clear glimpse of two very good looking kids, well dressed but appeared in distress. She was reluctant to stopping for the kids, with her full beams on, she stopped and rolled down her side windows and looked at the kids. She heard the kids well and clear asking for assistance and sounding distressed. The kids were saying to her: our mum died in there, the kids about ages 5 and 6 years, pointing to a very dark shrub about 200 feet away. The shrub was at the edge of a very huge crater and valley nearby. Coker was confused as a lot of things were running through her mind. The whole environment was dark and very poorly illuminated. Just the usual signature environment of the Demarkians when they wanted to strike but Coker didn't know of them. A lot of things went through Coker's mind as she saw one of the kids shivering, in a very angelic voice, asked Coker to take them away to a safer place. The other kid started crying, very pathetically.

Coker's phone started ringing and she wound up her windows to take the call. She pulled up a little more, and now, she was sandwiched by, at least a thousand feet deep valley on both sides of the curb where she parked. The few street lights in that location were very dimmed by the demand of the residents to create and boost the canyon appearance of the area at night. The residents live about 700 yards from each other in this very exclusive city of Pv Peninsula. In the quietness of the night, Coker answered Henry's call and relayed what she is witnessing there in the last three minutes. Henry advised her to drive out of that place fast and call the police for the kids. She kinda realized her folly and was just about to drive away but noticed, within seconds, that the two kids have turned into two huge black cats, same one she saw earlier at her house! She became fidgety and informed her boyfriend of all that. She, in a panicky fashion, struggled with her car doors and pushed the central lock down, even though they were already down. The cats, in a flash, rushed over towards her car. They jumped on the front windshield and was staring at Coker with those scary eyes.

Coker's mum, a retired school teacher in North Dakota, was feeling sick as she had been down with a bad flu in the last few days. She took some drowsy medications to assist her in sleeping too. She slept very well on taking the medications. It was late in North Dakota, being two or three hours ahead of California time zone. Coker's mum was already deeply asleep having called her daughter earlier in the morning and wished her a beautiful birthday. On this night, she had a nightmare about her daughter being pursued by evil forces. She saw the animals in her dream but couldn't place the reasons for the attack. She saw her beckoning for her help, crying mummy, mummy, please help me! She also saw children waiving and calling her name, fine kids but weird in some ways; evil in different metamorphosis. She saw her daughter, Coker, later lying in state in charred body, in death and in a funeral ceremony. She woke up scared and concerned.

She looked for her phone and started calling Coker who was on the phone with Henry. She couldn't switch over to talk to her mum. She believed that her mum was calling to find out what she had been up to with her party and merrymaking. She would call her back later morrow but now she needed to get out of there and Henry was helping too. Her mother, of course, was calling to inform and warn her of her dream and to take good care of herself.

Mum have been on her neck pressuring her to remarry, persistently reminding her that the female biological clock runs fast. You have mourned your husband enough sweetie and you need to move on, she would say. The beauty of a woman is like morning flowers; it withers fast in scorching sun. I want a grandchild, if you could; I am pleading with you. Coker would laugh and exclaimed, mothers and wanting grand kids, old cliché. She loved her mum to death but she was at the top of her world now and another husband might not be as nice as her former husband. She would think of it later. But sometimes, she shivered a little when she thought of her age and the state of her womb at over forty years. Well, it is what it is. The world is growing away from the archaic concept of the institution of marriage and child- bearing, anyways.

The mum called Henry but Henry for the same reason, talking to Coker, couldn't switch over because of the serious and dangerous moments then. Mother was jittery and confused. She called Coker's best friend, Ariana, who informed her that they were assembled there waiting for Coker. She did not know anything more than that. Mum asked her whether Coker was running late and she answered, yes, very late, and it was her birthday. That panicked and aggravated Mum's thought of the danger expressed in the dream. Her daughter was full of life and running late on her birthday was not her thing and that certainly didn't smell like a rose. Something was definitely going on and whatever it was stank to high heavens. She started praying, calling on God and the angels to rescue her daughter. She started pacing up and down her house. She did not understand what was going on but it, for sure, wasn't good.

While still on the phone with Henry, the menacing cats stayed on the car, characteristically of the cult attacks. In panic, Coker inadvertently pushed the red end button on her phone and cut off the call. She tried to call henry back but her hands were too shaky and the phone fell out of her hand into the under- seat crevices. Oh Lord, she exclaimed. What the hell is all these!

She drove off the car, being disoriented, through the curves of the winding roads and just on getting to the worst turning of the canyon road, one of the cats turned into a huge menacing beast blocking her view. She also noticed that she was no longer in control of the car's speed, as the vehicle quickly lost control, drove off the cliff and descended into the deepest part of valley crater with trees, spikes, in pitch darkness. The side window broke and her purse and her phone flew out into the dark abyss. The vehicle spiraled into further speed, somersaulted repeatedly and flew fast and hard into the valley. It made a big bang but surprisingly didn't burst into flames, even though it was smoking in fumes and dust. The car was reduced to less than half of its size and Coker's body was mashed almost to dismemberments.

Henry was on the phone when this happened up until the car went over the edge. So at the very least he was apprised of the accident and it appeared fatal, based off on what Coker was relaying to him at the time. He was jolted and screamed in fear attracting the attention of others that were waiting for Coker. They rushed over to him and he detailed them out on the whole communications between him and Coker. Everyone was in awe and in concert, and they decided to go on a search party. Henry called the 911, the police and discussed the incidence with them. They agreed to meet to the closet last point in Palos Verdes, near Silver Spur Boulevard. The police started a cell tower tracking of the phone communications between Coker and Henry and were able to trace the last port of call which was still near the same place. There was no mark or tell- tale signs of a car crash on the area but they all continued to search the area, using vehicle headlights, flashlights, skid marks which were non -existent.

Henry went home feeling very distraught and devastated. He just couldn't sleep. This whole scenario made absolutely no sense at all. Why would anyone want to hurt Coker? The greatest disturbing part of the whole saga was the unusual and unconventionality of the hazard. What was this about black birds and cats, little kids appearing unescorted by any adult at odd locations and odd times of the night? Why did they pick on Coker? was she a member of any evil cult? By the way, are stuffs like that real? Were these mere illusions? Was Coker hallucinating or paranoid? Did she develop mental problems that he never knew about? Was it a genetic issue, that they had mental health challenges in their lineage? Why wouldn't she share that with him, embarrassed to discuss that? Does she have multiple personality? Oh, no she doesn't, he thought out aloud. Coker was a very resoundingly normal lady, beautiful in and out. She had no spiritual inclinations but rather an open-minded person, jolly good lady. She was full of life and very mundane. she was a honey pie and he wanted to propose to her in few months but now... He became more disoriented and confused as his head started pounding with a high migraine. He went and took some pills and sat down in front of a television that he wasn't watching. He was fighting back tears. But cry for what? She might still be alive somewhere.

His Mind detoured again and he started reviewing his relationship with Coker, thinking of recalling any suicidal ideation, in conduct and verbal expressions by Coker but he couldn't recollect any. Was she hiding in the closet about anything? Not that he could think of. At some point, it appeared as if he was even questioning his own sanity. He was losing it and real fast. He had this forlorn look on his face and mind of vacuity and wandering thoughts. He was an emotional wreck and he started wondering whether he could ever recover from this and how.

Henry's phone rang and it was Coker's mother. He picked it up, after series of missed calls from last night and they had a long conversation wherein Coker's mum detailed out her dreams and the very clear messages in it. Coker was further devastated on learning that, almost coming to the conclusion that Coker was dead. Henry, with no hold barred, opened up and educated Coker's mum on the dialogues between him and Coker. Coker's mum screamed out and started yelling incoherent words about her daughter. She cried very loudly, started mourning her child and making statements to that effect. She sounded very distraught and emotional. She sounded as confused as Henry and other Coker's friends. The whole drama was completely out of whack and bunkum. She cut off the call without any closing statement.

Henry made calls to the search party and they assembled by 6 a.m. at the same location. They started searching more carefully now as the dawn has set in fully. There was still no skid mark in view. The forests in the canyon valley appears undisturbed. The Highway patrol and LAPD officers came on the scene and the search continued for another three hours, extending into the whole neighborhood, concentrating more on the valley. Henry, still dazed and disoriented, with an empty look, sat on a nearby curb when he noticed a black bird flew out of the remotest part of the deepest end of the valley about half mile deep. He stood up, with heightened interest, walked over to the edge of the valley and looked but still could not see anything. The same bird, now in company of another bigger raven, flew by and dived straight to the giant trees and shrubs in that part of the crevice. He walked up to the officer and was relaying his suspicions of that part of the deep end, citing the birds as evil birds connected with Coker's death. The officer, confused about the senselessness of his assertions, asked Henry who he was and his relationship with Coker. He inquired from Henry whether he was asserting that the birds could have killed Coker? Henry answered yes. The officer exclaimed and said, wonderful! How do you know that Coker is dead? The officer asked? Henry gave him the details of his communications with Coker and Coker's mum. The following conversation continued:

Officer: are you saying that these birds killed Ms. Coker?
Henry: Yes, based on what I explained to you earlier.
Officer: How?
Henry: They might be evil birds.
Officer: Those are ravens and Crows that are seen everywhere, son.
Henry: Not these ones, sir.
Officer: with a sarcastic grin on his face, called another officer to come and share in the ghost, or is it, Lucifer story.
Officer 2: Hey, soothsayer, what is your angle?
Henry: I have relayed all that I know to your colleague and you guys have the prerogative of not believing me. I never claimed that I am one hundred percent sure but just an opening to investigate, that's all.
Officer 2: walking off muttered to himself: you are either stupid or retarded.
Officer: Son, have you slept since last night?
Henry: not really sir, been hard on me and our friends.
Officer: drinks?

The Demarkians — Chidi Metu

Henry: No sir as that will twist me more.
Officer: But you are sounding twisted and cuckoo already. You need some sleep. We will take it from here. Leave the black birds alone. In fact, leave the animals alone. It is a crime to hurt any animal, you know that?
Henry: I sure do. I am sticking around.

At that point, the birds flew by again and flew back into the valley, as if they were drawing the attention of Henry or the search party to Coker's location. Henry yelled to the officers who walked over and listened to his baloney again. The officers sternly advised him to leave or they might arrest him for obstruction. Henry felt so bad and walked away to sit in his car. He sat in his car for a while and started crying profusely now. He got a little better with the venting and his head cleared. Henry, in a better state of mind, suddenly remembered that he had a power military stethoscope, with day and night visions, that he bought recently on Amazon. He got excited and rushed over to his trunk and brought out the equipment. The clarity and magnification strength of the equipment was state of the art. It had the trappings of the US military as it was made for them initially. He set it to daylight, set it to the highest resolution and far distance setting and peeped in. What he saw was beyond comprehension. At the floor of the valley, showing broken tree branches, laid Coker's vehicle, badly crushed and the two birds perching on it and looking straight at him. He screamed, dropped the equipment and started crying loudly. Other friends started rushing over to him where he laid on the ground crying like a toddler. He couldn't explain what he saw. He was just pointing at the canyon valley and his equipment. Friends called the officers to come over and the older officer came back again and asked Henry what he was still doing hanging around and causing mischief. The officer said to Henry: son, I understand that you are distraught in not knowing what has happened to your girl but you need to understand that we got a job to do and that does not include being a shrink. Now, whatch you got? A cat running around, huh? Henry sat up, picked the equipment, gave it to the officer and took him to the edge of the canyon and asked him to look. The officer looked and let out a

huge breath, screamed: "what the heck?!!" Police instinct kicked in and the officer said, Son, are you sure you telling us all that you know about this case? Oh lord, young lady; look at the crushed car; oh my, oh my, look at the black birds again. What are they doing on the car? Oh, why are they looking at us like that for? Are y'all Lucifer birds for sure? I finna find out now.

The officer walked over to his car, brought out his long service rifle with telescope, loaded the gun and walked over to the spot. He aimed the gun at the side, some inches from the raven perching on top of the Driver's side door of the car, pulled the trigger of the AR 11 powerful gun. The gun shattered the shrubs but the birds were not perturbed and didn't move. The birds continued to look at the people watching the spectacle. The officer shot again and still same reaction from the birds. He thought of shooting on the birds direct but that will send him to prison and end his career. The officer looked at Henry repeatedly, and in confusion said to him: son, this your Lucifer shit looks like it is real. These birds, men, are not normal birds. What in the world is all these about? The officer walked back to his squad car and called for a helicopter back up; police retrieval equipment and described, via the call, what was going on. He called his colleagues who had already left to announce that the vehicle was located. Within 25 minutes, the whole canyon was swamped with law enforcement vehicles, police and News media choppers, ambulance, fire trucks, different police units. The city hall on hearing the news about their senior staff, sent the best of their best fire engines and equipment over to the place. Henry, realizing that he was not losing it after all, felt relieved. At some point he came close to agreeing with the officers that he was going cuckoo. He laid back in the car and watch the rescue effort unfold.

The CHP special recovery chopper flew down to the location and lowered their specially trained distressed officers by the side of the car. Flew up and brought more officers down to Coker's car. They were able to hoist the vehicle and brought it to the top on the roadside. Meanwhile, officers have cleared everyone, all bystanders, including Henry and others to a considerable distance.

A flat- bed truck was waiting to remove the car from the accident scene. The car was placed on the ground and a check of Coker's mangled body confirmed that she expired a while ago. They didn't bother to cut her out as they took delivery of the vehicle straight to the highway patrol office nearest to them.

Henry and Coker's friends were unrestrained in their grief. It was so sad and depressing. Henry drove behind them to the station. Even though he knew the answer but he asked and was informed by the older officer that Coker has died from the crash. He advised Henry to go home now and come back to see him tomorrow. He gave Henry his card and reminded him to make sure that he comes in tomorrow. He advised Henry to invite Coker's family to come and identify the body and possibly take possession of her corpse.

✷✷✷

The whole exercise was captured in the local channels, 4,5,7,9 news. A lot of people saw the news and were disturbed by some traits of the story. The first one was that Tiger woods, the celebrated golf star and the darling of Americans, had a plunging accident into a canyon in the same or nearby area recently. He was lucky to survive the accident with some fractures. People were asking what the government intended to do to barricade those dangerous canyon roads. Next question was why haven't they done it before now?

Another disturbing part of this story is the weird component of it, stating the involvement of the black birds. The story was given to the media, in details, by Henry and somewhat corroborated by some police officers, especially the ones that fired the shots at the birds and the reactions of the birds. A cell phone investigation also confirmed that Coker had a long discussion with Henry on the prior night laying credence to Henry's claim about all that Coker told him. Moreover, Henry and his friends were there even before the cell tower confirmed where the accident could have happened. That showed that they knew before the officers as to the possible location of the accident. Coker's phone and purse were recovered too. The story kept Los Angelenos in awe for the next few days. Coker's mum came into town and claimed her body.

Adamson ardently followed the whole story in the media. He seemed very happy and fulfilled on Coker's death. The brotherhood is where to be, he exclaimed. They have rescued him again and put a smile on his face. He was enjoying every bit of it. He has now proven to Coker that she stuck her stupid finger in a tiger's mouth. He who laughs last, laughs best. With that, he jumped and mimicked Michael Jackson's kick- dancing, rushed into his wine bar and brought some Dom P, high vintage and celebrated his evil victory.

The workers at the city hall, especially the Human Resources department, were thoroughly hurt by the death of their lovely Coker. She was an ideal leader and fearless at that. She will be sorely missed, and for a very long time too.
Her funeral was conducted and a repass done at her house. After her burial, her mum left for home.

* * *

Henry still puzzled about the way and manner of the death of Coker consulted a card leader, named Suna, in the ghetto of Los Angeles. He found out about her in internet web yellow pages. He initially did not trust her abilities, considering that she appeared to be a hoodie rat. But it was only a fifty dollars session and they agreed to meet later that afternoon.

Henry met with Suna and they talked for a minute. Henry paid the money while Suna started shuffling some tarot cards. The cards will tell me why you are here and the services will be addressed accordingly, understand? Henry answered, yes. She started reading the cards and mumbling to herself. She read the cards for a few minutes and started frowning her face as she read them. Her countenance portrays increasing concerns and then she stopped suddenly. Asked Henry to spread out his hands. She held Henry by both hands for a few minutes and she let them go. She looked hard into Henry's face and said to him: there is a problem. Did you lose a loved one recently? Henry said yes and mentioned his girlfriend. Suna picked up the cards again and started reading them and suddenly dropped them as if they were burning her hands. She turned to Henry and asked him how his girlfriend died? Henry said he didn't know and that's part of why he was there. Suna looked at the cards fixatedly for a while as if she was in a trance and raised her face to announce to Henry that there was a problem. She said that she saw her girlfriend in a very distressed situation on the other side of the divide. I can see her surrounded by too deep darkness and I can barely make out her structure. She has long legs, a white lady? Henry, impressed said, yes that's her. Suna kept on reading the card and suddenly dropped them again and informed Henry that she saw her smeared in a lot of blood and deep cuts all over her body. She asked Henry, did she meet with an accident? Henry, getting more impressed, said, yes. Suna kept quiet for a while and was in a deep trance and started speaking deep Jamaican Patwa, making some incantations, rush off to the inner room and came out with sticks of different incense, different colors and smells. She lit the sticks and some red and black candles too. She was now getting too agitated and reciting more incantations, pacing around the room. She abruptly stopped and walked over to her seat and sat quietly. She looked at Henry and informed him that she couldn't see much. If he wanted her to dig deeper, it was going to cost him five hundred dollars at a minimum. Henry already impressed, quickly agreed and asked whether he could pay now? Suna said yes but the session will continue morrow and that she needed to do some spiritual research at the wee hours of today. Suna only accepted cash payments having been audited by IRS tax office twice. Henry ran to the nearest ATM in the area and came back with the money. They agreed to meet the next day by 1p.m.

Henry couldn't wait to be back with Suna. They sat down again and the clairvoyance continued. This time, Suna was all Jamaican and deeply spiritual. She was being directed by the spirit but it could also mean being directed by all powerful dollar influence because Henry gave her additional two hundred dollars in tip. Suna continued and at some point jumped up from her chair and exclaimed: your girl was killed by a satanic cult. She had a beef with their member. "Do you know who that person is?" Henry, looking jolted said no. Suna continued to shuffle with the cards, ran into her inner room and got a big bottle of jack Daniel whiskey and poured a full glass for herself, offered Henry but he declined. She started sipping the hard liquor and getting more into the spirit. At some point, she started vibrating and stopped, took a huge sip of the whiskey and told Henry that the cult killed his friend. They are very powerful and vindictive. You will rather choose to march on a mamba and a viper at the same time than to step on their toes. They are very unforgiving when it comes to their own. They use birds, crows, ravens, cats, dogs, evil animals, as their protections and points of attacks. One more thing, you can find a book about them written in 14th century in the Los Angeles archive library in downtown. Good luck young man. Step up your spiritualism and buy a good rosary and crucifix. Good luck, sir, as our session is over.

Henry left there shaking literally and in fear. He felt inebriated with the whole information. He had no doubt in her mind that this woman was real and knew what she was saying. He sat in his car for a prolonged period of time and engaged in deep thoughts. Who was the person that Coker had an issue with? Over what? When and for how long? How can he find out? Is he safe investigating this? He thought about going back to the police but these are not subject to any kind of legal proof. He felt frustrated, especially with the idea that Coker was in agony in the land of the dead. Whoever orchestrated her death was still punishing her even in death. If he knows the person, he might exert a revenge and that for sure will be lethal. He felt very upset and drove home. He stopped at a religious store on Hollywood boulevard and bought the suggested religious paraphernalia. He got home, went straight to his bar, drank for a while and slept off. He saw Coker in a dream looking dreadful and subdued. She was crying nonstop and very bitterly too. She kept on trying to mumble a name to him but she couldn't get the name out. He woke up more troubled than when he went to sleep. He started talking to himself, felt more frustrated and yelled, fuck it, throwing and shattering the wine glass in his hands on the walls. He sat down and started crying again and again, dozed off till whenever time.

The next day, Henry went to the Library and searched all day before he could find the book. The content was breathtaking and scary. He learnt about the demarkians and almost peed on himself. The world is full of mysteries, he shouted. So things like this actually exists in the world? So there are people that actually live and worship devil? So devil is real then? Then God should be real too, huh? He asked himself a lot of rhetoric questions and turned on the tv to divert his mind away from these but he was far from sanity to watch tv or live a sane life, at least not anytime soon.

He searched through the amazon to see if he could find any literature on the cult but none was found. He did find some spiritual books bordering on Satanism, exorcism, Holy Spirit, rapture, etcetera and he bought some of them. He brought out a bible and for the first time since he was 17 years started reading it. He later went to talk to the catholic father of the Los Angeles church, Fr Dominic, and shared everything with him. He was expecting to see him jolted but he was there smiling all through his story. At the end, Dominic asked him whether he believe in God? Henry said, well now I do, seeing the whole thing as it plays out. I wasn't into Godism before now though, my apologies, father. Dominic said that Christian evangelism are actually for people like him and worse ones too. He shouldn't apologize at all because he had, like a lot of others, reasons to doubt the existence of the creator. Dominic drilled him on the realities of the things in the bible and that evil and holy spirit do exist after all. Henry asked him why he did not seem surprise about his story and Dominic told him that his callings were in the realms of spiritualism and he shouldn't be jolted by that. He continued by informing Henry that he dealt with the conflicting forces of evil and good every day. He lived by blessing people and by fighting principalities and powers daily. My son, you are no different. I am like a doctor and you are a patient and you will get treated or advised spiritually. In fact, to surprise you further, I, like other clergy, within and without the

United States, knows of the Demarkians confraternity. Henry screamed, what? Dominic, calmly continued, yes we know about them and we know that sometime this year, they will have their once in ten- year world converge in Los Angeles. The Vatican, the Church of England, other ecumenical, know about it and we are preparing for the war. The lord has revealed that they will, this time, be destroyed and Satan will be bound in the abyss for billions of years again. We are all working towards that, my son. You will be part of that war but you have to seek the face of God and embrace him. The Demarkians are very powerful and diabolical in their ways and means. Lucifer himself appears at their battles. Taking out your girlfriend should have been a piece of cake for them. Your girlfriend, not a wife I guess, may have stepped on the toes of one of their members and their prefect ordered a hit on her. Their animals are actually evil agents and not real animals. They also use cute little kids seen at odd times, at odd places, appearing distressed. Those are not humans and we announced this in the church but people still get caught up with all that trap. I am sorry for your loss but you need to join the charismatic bible society to purge you of a life of sin and shield you with the armor of Elohim, the almighty God. Henry felt like a little toddler, naïve and stupid, if you might. Righteousness is the only weapon that defeats evil. Even if it fails you, God might have a different scheme for your soul. Again, son, my profound condolences for your loss and I will now give you some prayer points. Do those prayers, including our lord's prayer all the time whenever you can. Have your rosary always with you, in your car and on your neck even if you dress over it. Stand up, let us pray before you are let out. Father Dominic started praying and quoting the bible. At the end, he brought out a vial of holy oil and did a station of the cross on Henry's forehead.

Henry got home and felt much relieved and ate some fried rice and shrimp for the first time in days. He felt energized and, in that spirit, turned on the tv and watched the news. After that he, switched to HBO and started seeing strings of horror movies but he just couldn't get to watch any of them. He equally didn't want to see any love story because of him and Coker. He eventually settled for a thriller movie called "extraction" which blew him out! The movie was so nice that Henry wanted to see another similar movie but slept off in the middle of it.

CHAPTER 9

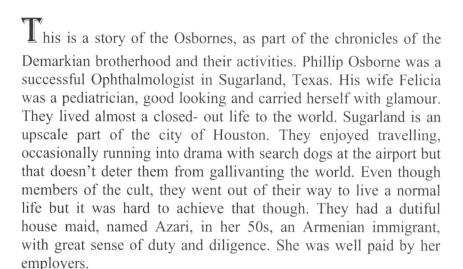

This is a story of the Osbornes, as part of the chronicles of the Demarkian brotherhood and their activities. Phillip Osborne was a successful Ophthalmologist in Sugarland, Texas. His wife Felicia was a pediatrician, good looking and carried herself with glamour. They lived almost a closed- out life to the world. Sugarland is an upscale part of the city of Houston. They enjoyed travelling, occasionally running into drama with search dogs at the airport but that doesn't deter them from gallivanting the world. Even though members of the cult, they went out of their way to live a normal life but it was hard to achieve that though. They had a dutiful house maid, named Azari, in her 50s, an Armenian immigrant, with great sense of duty and diligence. She was well paid by her employers.

Dr. Osborne had his office located in the choicest part of Sugarland and he was always swamped with patients. He was just a success story or so it seemed. His wife, Felicia, was a senior partner in a medical group located in another part of Houston. She was a firebrand, attended elitist school, great grades and very bright, a daughter of a Demarkian. She was very close to her dad and it was easy to have initiated her into the cult. She was kind and very smart. Her husband too shared in some of those qualities. Despite their efforts to maintain normal lifestyles, there were some oddities about them. They turned down most social invitations. But on this day, a med school colleague of Osborne, Dr. Hughes, invited him to his daughter's graduation party at his house at a suburban Houston. They tried to dodge this invitation by claiming, among others, that they don't drive in the night but Hughes offered to have them picked up. They mentioned that they might be at an opera event but Hughes checked and informed them that the concert was cancelled. They eventually felt cornered and accepted to attend. Felicia was trying different dresses, took a long time to make up and making a choice of the shoe to wear. Her husband was getting restless and at some point, he exclaimed, God thank you for making me a man! Women are so annoying but I guess...shut up when the wife called him into a room to assess her looks. Azari was surprised that they agreed to attend a party, a rarity indeed. She didn't ask where they were going, strictly not part of her job. Felicia instructed Azari on things to do until she slept and leave in the morning. Her job related only to house duties. She was strictly instructed not to bring any religious materials into their homes as they were atheists. Her off day fluctuated but it was usually Sundays and Mondays. Azari, a divorcee, was to have no visitors, not even her children.

The Osbournes had a black and brown fur cat, named Petis, weird pigmentations, brought in as an adult cat. Azari puzzled, asked why an adult cat, with odd looks, had two small fangs, very dull eyes but could be very vicious if upset, wandered around the house but stayed on its own most of the times, liked to perch on the window pane, never come to Azari or rubbed its body on Azari, like normal cats. Petis ate when food was in the its plate, hated to be beckoned for food, made it infuriated. Petis walked over and ate food and went away, with eyes abnormally fierce in the night. Azari recollected when Petis was locked out in the night one night, she started looking for it with a flashlight and spotted it lurking on the beautiful shrub at the back, relaxed, not cold and the flashlight picked what looked like bloodshot eyes. As soon as that happened, an ominous sound played for a few minutes, Azari scared dropped her flashlight inadvertently. The Osbornes pitched a fit when they learnt of that and almost fired her. Azari hated the cat and she thought that the cat knew. There was something about the cat that doesn't add up. Azari walked up to it one day to scoop it but it got irritated, showed her fangs, jumped down from the window pane and walked upstairs to another window on the hallway. It used toilet like humans and made no mess in its trails. Azari later learnt from an old widow that lived few buildings down the street, had a big fur cat with diamond on its neck, confronted Petis, a much smaller cat and was torn up really bad by Petis that it died the next day. The widow was surprised about the strength of this cat. Widow later found out that the Osbournes owned the cat. The widow even intimated Azari that she had spotted, twice, a black raven perching on the outside wall, with Azari on the inside and they stayed like that for a long time. Azari wouldn't know about all that because she was always busy with her works. Petis is only friendly to the Osbornes as it behaved like a normal cat to them. Sometimes, Azari heard ominous sounds around the house but couldn't make out what it was.

A limo was sent to pick the Osbournes up and the driver patiently waited knowing that such patience could be very rewarding. A concierge limo stocked with vintage beverages and full recliner seats. The driver, dressed in white suit, was very courteous and friendly. The driving was excellent and when the driver got to Hughes home, he exclaimed in appreciation: "In my next world, lord remember me, like you did to them", he laughed quietly. It was a convergence of elite attendees, med school mates, doctors and their families coming from out of towns. The food and beverages were upscale too.

While the Osbornes were at the party, Azari became inquisitive and took a huge risk. The Osborne home was a four -bedroom duplex. One of the rooms was permanently locked, with strict instructions to Azari not to enter there as it held properties that they considered sentimental and personal. The Osbornes cleaned the room themselves, when Azari was on her off duties. The key was always with Osborne and he never left the key to lie around. On a day, there was a water leakage from upstairs and a plumber was called in who wanted to access the damage point from the locked room but the Osbornes declined and asked the plumber to go in through the roof or knock off any other part of the building but not the locked room. Azari found that perplexing! Meanwhile, petis during all these time, with a stern face, perched on a nearby window watching everyone with keen interest, showing its fangs to Azari on few times that they made eye contacts. The plumber later left murmuring in anger that they wasted his time. Azari was asked to call in another plumbing company who on a very steep fee, accessed the damage from another side of the building and fixed the leak. Azari's interest got heightened on what that room was for; the odd cat, petis, the lifestyle of the Osbornes, their reactions on how and where they got the cat from, lack of social life and no visitors, despite their social ladder.

When the limo left for the party with the Osbournes, Petis laid quietly on its couch. Azari was watching tv crime scenes, crime Id, on the mysterious death of a priest in San Diego. Azari remembered that she forgot to put a cleaned flower vase upstairs. Felicia was an orderliness freak. She wanted her stuff kept well. Azari paused the tv, ran upstairs to fix that up and noticed a bunch of keys on the walkway. She picked it up and wanted to rush back downstairs to continue her documentary program but a thought came into her head, to open and access the room! Hoping that the right key was among the bunch. With her heart beating faster, she started trying all the keys on the door. While doing that, Petis came up, became restless and kept gnarling her fang tooth at Azari. That could only aggravate Azari's inquisitive mind. The ominous sounds came on and a black raven flew and perched on the window, with glowing red eyes. Azari was momentarily stunned being the first time she had seen the bird up close or even at all. Azari determined to access the room, tried the keys and one of them opened the door! What she beheld in that room was a house of horror. Demarkian literatures, paraphernalia, artifacts, black clothes, weird objects, pictures of Lucifer himself. She pulled the biggest book out and took a picture of its cover and some of its contents. She ran out of the room in a flash, breathing hard and rapidly. On exiting the room, she was attacked by petis swiftly with a scratch on her neck areas and cuts too. She fell to the ground, summoned courage, walked into her room, parked her stuffs but was too scared to leave right away. She started hearing the evil sound more clearly and louder now. She came to the jolting realties that the Osbournes were devil worshippers. She, being an ardent Christian, felt that she betrayed her faith grievously by being with these evil kinds. She called her eldest daughter and relayed her experiences and discovery and informed her that she was coming home. She also called her friend and left her a voicemail. She ran to her car which, luckily, was a few feet away from the door, and locked the doors. She had a ford escort, a little old but in great condition, refurbished engine, new brakes as she took great pride in maintaining her car. The car had a GPS system mounted on the dashboard; Car interior was neat and polished. Azari lived 30 minutes away from her job. She doesn't like driving in the night or during inclement weather except if she couldn't help it. She started the car, calmed herself down, tried calling her son but her hands were unsteady. Petis, may have exited when she opened the door, jumped on top of her hood and was gazing at her steadily. She yelled at it: you agent of Satan, I command you in the name of Jesus to back off! Petis remained but jumped away when Azari drove off.

She drove out into Interstate 45 hoping to avoid weekend late night traffic jams before she hits Freeway 610 but for some inexplicable reasons, she ended up in interstate 288 that leads to the outskirts of the town. While exceeding the posted speed limit, and a little disoriented, weather turning cloudy with silhouette of ugly beasts appearing in the dark, in her views, strong wind blowing, creepy darkness and turbulence, her vehicle surged on its own for 160 MPH. With failing brakes, she drove into the shoulder of the freeway, through a thick forest for five hundred yards, striking and uprooting shrubs and other vegetation. She hit a tree and stopped. One of the uprooted trees broke off and forcibly stabbed her to death gruesomely. The damages to the environment, the nature of her injuries and death was mind- boggling. The signature Demarkian cat perched on the hood of the car for a while and disappeared. Her daughter waited for her to come home but she never got home. It had been like hours since she drove out homebound, for a journey of thirty minutes, at most. Her daughter kept calling her phone but at some point her battery died and calls were going into her voicemail box. Her son later retrieved her voicemail and rushed home. With his sister they decided to search for her but no result. They went to her job but nobody was there. They reasoned to wait till morning.

The Osbornes got to the party that night, alighted and walked towards the house. There were a lot of people but event appeared very orderly. Philip and Felicia walked in and spotted a huge crucifix at the pivotal point in the sitting room. They looked at each other and decided to walk in the other way. They met with the host who embraced them and turned to introduce them to his classmate, Fr. Edison, a priest adorned in priestly regalia with across hanging on his neck and did the introduction but Phillip was tactfully backing off to avoid his torso contacting the priest. Phillip and Felicia were heavily discomforted. The priest started explaining to Hughes that he couldn't get home to change to party attire and they laughed about it. Hughes was a strong financier and supporter of the church, apart from being his classmate. So he had multiple reasons to be at the party. The Osbornes acted fast and disappeared into the party. They sat at the farthest part of the awning at the back of the building. An opening prayer was conducted but they did not actually participate even though they stood up like others. They sat close to a neighbor's fence and the neighbor's dog was going berserk trying to break out of its chain. No amount of yelling or commanding could make it stop barking until The Osbornes relocated to a farther part of the compound. Other dogs were also barking in unison and support. They smell devils nearby and they were behaving like dogs do and the Osbornes knew that. Introductions continued, old acquaintances, school mates, classmates, med school mates, but the Osbornes claiming tiredness stood away. The good music, beverages were going on. Edison, still feeling uneasy about this couple because of how his body felt when he shook Philip's hands, kept throwing a glance at them. He asked Hughes who they were and Hughes explained to him. He watched them all through the party and noticed that they were not part of the event really. There was something about them that was not right. A guest, Daniel, came and innocently sat with them and introduced himself, a radiologist, lived in Sugar land too, married with kids and downloaded his life in five minutes to them but they didn't have much to tell him. Daniel continued rambling, no thanks to alcohol, talked about church activities, evils in the world, the end time, Christ second coming, the apocalypse. The Osbornes were getting visibly uncomfortable. When Dan left to use the restroom, Felicia finally went off on her husband claiming that they wouldn't have come here. They almost got into it but Dan reappeared and continued his chats to unresponsive Osbornes, who were just nodding. They had only been there for less than two hours and they decided to hang in more. Daniel continued to talk about the beauty and the redemptive qualities of the teachings of Jesus Christ as it relates to the sins of the world. He changed the topic to medicine and patients, Philip a little relieved, participated a little. Everyone was dancing and getting drunk and the Osbornes decided to join in the fun. They started drinking and dancing and felt better for it even though that didn't stop the priest from glancing at them.

At the end of the party, Uber too them home and they found out that Azari was not there. They called her number but it went to voicemail. Everything seemed in order. Petis didn't run to them as usual. It stayed back and gnarled it teeth at them, looking upset. It later came to Felicia and jumped on her laps
for some minutes and wandered off. They went to sleep after switching off the lights.

The search party on Azari commenced the next day but was not yielding any result because the search focused on her regular route home. But contrary to that, Azari was directed off course by the devil to the other part of town, to her death. She was discovered by a trucker who pulled up by the freeway shoulder to check on his truck and observed the interrupted vegetation and decided to probe into it and found Azari. The highway patrol was called in and a check of her id revealed her family and next of kin.

The police arrived at her house and announced what they found out and all hell broke loose. The family took over from there and started preparing her burial. The Osbornes heard of it, came over to her house and expressed their grief, looking puzzled. Phillip had deep thought and then figured out that this was the brotherhood at work. He remembered finding his keys on the hallway when he got back. He connected the dots. He wanted to call the regional prefect but decided against it, knowing that he might be scolded for such grievous carelessness. He wrote Azari's family a large sum of money to cover her funeral costs. That ended the story of Azari.

✳✳✳

The Christian community becoming increasingly aware of the confraternity and their havocs, started garnering interests and efforts to fight them. In doing that, biblical insights were sought as to who they were:

Jude 1:6: "And the Angels who did not keep their positions of authority but abandoned their proper dwelling-these he has kept in darkness, bound with everlasting chains for judgment on the great day"

Was Satan one of these angels? Couldn't be because he was chased down to the earth.

Revelation 20:1-3: "And I saw an angel come down from heaven, having the key of the bottomless pit, the abyss, and a great chain in his hand".

That refers clearly to Satan being chased down to the earth where he is now wreaking havocs.

These and similar points of worships were mandated by the clergy community to fight the evil cult by understanding who they were and how to approach them. The catholic communion and the ecumenical in and around Texas initiated a coordinated effort to confront the cult. The modus operandi of the cult were studied, noting that their membership cuts across the high and mighty.

The regional meeting of the Texas ecumenical developed a strategy to execute a spiritual war against the cult. Fr. Edison read a book in the library and learnt much more about the cult and shared the information with the church community. The Demarkian spirits were primarily locked in evil stones located around the world. The developments and natural tampering kept on releasing the spirits of Lucifer locked on this stone. That is part of the legend which might run contrary to other anthropological analysis as to the origin of the devil's cult.

Fr. Edison was in the forefront of the crusade against the cult, holding meetings, rallies, services, educating the church community about how to fight and defeat the devil. Fr. Christo, friend and colleague of Edison, very pious and a revered member of the catholic community, a member of the opus dei, prayed all the time, asking God to intervene. Being a Visional, it was revealed to him that Houston will undergo an evil spiritual attack this week. Cats, dogs, other evil animals were revealed to him. He invited other priests, including of course, Edison to discuss how to embark on prayer shields to protect Houston or the world in general. Prayers involving all clergy and parishioners commenced.

Edison still thinking of the Osbornes, called and received the work place address of Phillip and decided to pay him a visit. He drove over there, hanging his rosary visibly on his neck. He decided that he must try to hug Phillip when they meet. He covered his shirt up knowing that Phillip may decline seeing him if he was to know who he was. He was ushered into the office and he, citing Houston weather as an excuse, removed his shirt revealing his cross and regalia as a priest. He noticed that Phillip flinched on seeing that but smiled. He introduced himself as he was walking up to Phillip for a hug but Phillip was retracting away from him like a ghost. He tactfully insisted for a hug but was rebuffed. So who are you and what can I be of help today? I am Fr. Phillip, friend of the Hughes, remember me now? At the party? Phillip remembered him as soon as he walked through the door but continued to feign otherwise. No clues sir, he responded. I was at the party, met a lot of people but can't recollect anyone, Phillip stated. Edison refreshed his memory about meeting a priest right at the entry of the door but Phillip, becoming impatient maintained his lack of recollection. With a courteous smile, Phillip asked him again what he desired for his visit? Edison brought up religious discussions, the angels, the messages of Jesus Christ. Phillip turning red, informed him that he had no time for any religious talks now and that he could stop by the church at the close of the day. He asked Edison to drop off his address on his way out but noticed that, by Edison's posture, that the meeting was barely getting started. He breathed deeply, felt calm and relaxed and asked Edison to offload. Edison, gaining confidence, asked him whether he believed in God? Phillip retorted to him: are you my parents or my guardian angel? Why are you asking me all these? I am here to treat and heal the sick and I really don't have time for this now, sir. Edison smiled, asked Phillip, why he did not take part in the prayers at the party? Phillip responded that he did his best. He looked at Edison and asked him why he was here? Edison calmly informed him that he was here to save his soul from eternal damnation. He continued and laid out comprehensively what he knew about the Demarkian cult and their powerful memberships. He informed him of the dogs, cats, crows and other evil animals used as the devil's tools.

Edison point blank asked Phillip Osborne that he was being chastised by the dog in the community when he came there. He also informed him what he felt when he shook his hand. He went on to explain to Phillip that he felt same today when he shook his hand and his effort in trying to hug him with the crucifix which he avoided craftily. Edison informed Phillip that from all indications, that he was a member of the Satanic cult. Phillip freaked out and asked him: "is that why you were obsessed in watching my wife and I at the party You were being just a freaky asshole, not minding your business!" Edison laughed heartily for a few seconds and asked excitedly: So, you remember me, huh? I knew you were pretending when denied having any clue about me. Phillip looked at him steadily for one minute and warned him to stay away.
Phillip: Don't be a rubble rouser, Fr. What? I forgot Your name.
Edison: Edison.

Phillip: Don't stand before a moving train, I am just warning and alerting you. Just continue with your call and leave others alone.

Edison: I was trained not to mind my business. I am a flock of God, a fisher of men; a fisher of lost souls like you; I serve a redeeming God. In our space is peace and tranquility. We represent light and glories. We are the children of God. Dogs, cats, birds don't attack us. We don't hurt anyone rather we bring hope and redemption to the hopeless. Devil is catastrophe and represents everything bad. Peace eludes you here on earth and at the last day over there, when you chose Satan, as you have done. It is not too late, my brother. If trying to redeem you is your concept of a moving train, I will be a Godly king Kong to that train. You are a child of God but you need to come back to his space and know peace.

Phillip: That is an act of war as you have drawn a battle line against the brotherhood. You brought this upon yourself. Now, get out or I will throw you out.

Edison: I will leave you now, brother, with the redeeming peace and love of our savior, Jesus Christ and all the angels of God. May the lord be with you and your lineage forever. May the holy and shining light of Jesus extract you from the evil jaws of Lucifer. God be with you. I will find my way out and sorry for this intrusion.

Phillip: Fuming and boiling, sat back for some time, calmed down and left the clinic for the day. He got home and called the prefect of the cult. War was, therefrom, declared on Edison by the cult.

Few days later, In the dark early night, Edison got home from a meeting of the clergies. He pulled up into his compound in the church and parked. As soon as he got out, he started hearing the evil sounds and understood then that there was a problem, most likely, the cult has come for a war. He brought out his chaplets and started praying. He looked up and saw four fierce- looking dogs on his porch, menacingly glaring at him showing their abnormal fang tooth. He stopped in his stride and increased his prayers, recanting the psalms of David. The dogs, now six of them, walked over and surrounded him while approaching him quietly with their blood-shot eyes. He started yelling Jesus; the son of God, rescue your servant! Rebuking the evil dogs who for a minute were restrained in attacking him but watched him intently as if waiting for an order to attack, the evil sound increasing in tempo, evil laughter, mocking and mimicking, busted out from nowhere. Even in the dark, he noticed a black cloud formed in front of him and a gigantic human figure with beards and two short horns appeared, with a body filled with hairs.

The Lucifer himself had to kill Edison in a war of the spirits. The devil's eye was reflectively bloodshot, dripping of bloods, he was about eight feet tall, huge hands, huge fingers and toes. He stared at Edison for a few seconds, laughed menacingly and yelled out an angry statement that came out in multiple voices. With very deep coarse voice, with huge fang tooth, rebuked Fr. Edison for startling a bee's hornet, for sticking his stupid fingers in his mouth. He laughed with smoke emitting from his mouth, yelling : I am Satan; I am the great that I choose to be; I control the earth; I destroy as I choose; Your holy book tells you about my powers; I am hell myself; I have the universe and the four corners of the earth under my command; I am destruction and calamity; I am the dreaded evil; I am the guillotine; I come not in peace but in pieces; it is my way or the highway; you will suffer and pay a huge price for daring me; I am not confined to the Abyss as your stupid book tells you; I am darkness myself; you messed with my servant and you have invoked my wrath; you are nothing to stand before me; You are less than an ant; I will masticate you,[fire blowing out of his mouth, more hairs came out of his body, the head horns got more elongated ,showing anger and fury]; I am the almighty Lucifer with infinite powers; I control the thunders; I control misery; I offer misery and pain; I am apocalypse myself; I am revered and worshiped; I am the real alpha and omega; I have no beginning and no end; I drink bloods of any animal, including humans; I leave trails of destructions; I cherish pain and agony; I protect my flocks from idiots like you; I am going to punish you severely and set you as an example for your colleagues; I will devour and kill you all and chase your miserable spirits into my kingdom where you will be laden with pain in perpetuity; your bible tells you that the earth trembles when I roar; I am over the universe and beyond;

At this point, a very beautiful little blond haired and blue eyed boy appeared dressed in satin white, stood by the devil's side, beaming, with eyes changing in colors but mostly remaining bloodshot. The little boy laughing satanically while looking up at the devil. The little boy's eyes occasionally locked with the animals' eyes and he smiled at them.

Edison responded: you vile; you scum, ugly being from the pit of hell; you renegade, dirty; you regurgitate; I am of the lord; I command you, I bind you in the mighty name of Jesus; I destroy you; the dark cannot claim what the light does not surrender; the bible commands you not to touch his anointed and do no harm to the God's prophet; you despicable being, chased down in shame from heaven; You are a loser and a failure. Whoever dwells in the shelter of the Most High will rest in the shadow of the almighty. I will say to the lord, he is my refuge and my fortress. Even though I walked through the valley of shadow of death, I shall fear no evil for he is with me. Goodness and mercy shall follow me forever and I will dwell in the house of the lord forever. Scums like you cannot stop that.

Edison very agitated now looked up to heaven and continued: contend oh lord with those who contend against me; fight against those who fight against me; take up shield and buckler, arise and come to my aid, Brandish spear and javelin against those who pursue me, say to my soul, I am your salvation; o my God, I trust in thee; let me not be ashamed, let not my enemies triumph over me. yea, let none that wait on thee be ashamed; let them be ashamed which transgresses without cause; Save me like you saved Meshach and the two from the lions; redeem like you did to the Israelites from the Egyptians; strike my enemies with thunder and trepidations; Lord I am not fighting with flesh and blood but against principalities; Come down from your majestic throne and take control. You are the beginning and no end, the alpha and omega, the I am that I am; the almighty Jehovah Elohim; the creator of heaven and earth; the only power that there is; what you don't know does not exist; you asked me to worship and follow you and I abided, now is the time to protect me and defeat Satan standing before thee here. Incinerate him and send him to the endless pit of hell where he was chained; you told me that he who follows you can thread on snakes and serpents; the devil has never and can never win a war against you. Let your magnificent presence be shown here, to protect your servant. I know and trust in you, my father.

The devil commanded the animals to devour Edison and they pounced on him, pushing him to the ground and the struggle started. They were biting and clawing him. Edison kept screaming, Jesus the savior; brought out the holy oil in his pocket and spraying it at the animals, invoking God and the Angels to come to his rescue; the holy oil burnt like acid on the animals and they ran into the thin night. The Devil stayed back yelling at Edison with tormenting voice. Edison sprayed the oil to the devil but that infuriated him more. He rushed over and scooped Edison with one hand, pulled out a sword-like nail to stab Edison but Edison was still calling on God to rescue him.

At that point Fr. Kettle, a colleague of Edison, drove in visiting him to discuss the cult thing and saw the drama. The Devil saw him and dropped Edison for a minute, turned towards him. Fr. Kettle brought out a huge crucifix he always had in his person, brought out his own holy oil, and stood for the devil's attack. Fr. Kettle started praying and calling on God to intervene, citing biblical quotations as Edison did. Kettle started taunting the devil calling him names. The devil lifted Kettle who was spraying the oil on him. Getting more infuriated, devil turned around and struck Edison who stood up to assist Kettle. At that point, Kettle placed the crucifix on the beast's face and it burnt him like a hot iron and the beast dropped him and disappeared with a loud noise blowing strong winds on the trees; other evil cohorts disappeared too.

A neighbor called 911 and Edison was removed to the hospital. Kettle was okay and he went home.

CHAPTER 10

The chronicles of the Demarkians continued with the story of Mr. Wilkingson. He was suburban, born and raised in Riverside County, a neighboring county to Los Angeles, California. He attended Lake Elsinore high school. He was a very brilliant student but very nosy and feisty. He was thrilled by the teachings bordering on mystery and spirituality. He read a lot of books on spiritual teachings, learnt and practiced spiritual magic, the wonders of the earth. He was embedded in learning what he termed alternative forces of the universe. He read the bible all the time, practiced all the teachings of the seven books of Moses, picked out the inconsistencies in the bible, especially on the Old Testament. He practiced sacrifices, sorcery, spiritual invocations, some of them he performed at wee hours and in discreet locations. He was dangerously inquisitive and probative of the spiritual realms. At some point, he conducted and showed keen interest on the powers of the Satan. He questioned the origin of the world and developed his own theories.

He went up to the mountains and practiced the 40 days fasting without the family knowing where he was. All search parties couldn't locate him. He came down, malnutricious, dehydrated, emaciated, scraggy and refused to go to the hospital. Later he recovered and believed that he was clothed with the power of Holy Spirit. He brought in a deaf relation and commandeered him multiple times to talk but it didn't work. He was so disappointed with Christian faith that he devoted more time in the research of alternate powers and control. He was embarrassed and failed in his ambition to enroll in the monastery for priesthood. He didn't read for a while. His room was disheveled and scattered which was a depiction of the state of his mind at all times.

His rooms were filled up with spiritual materials and literatures. He stayed awake all nights reading and practicing his interests.
One day, Fr. Capacino, a senior catholic priest, spiritual advisor for his family, an opus dei member of the Catholic Church, visited his home and they got into some discussions which later transformed to arguments about the inconsistencies in the bible and the failure of his faith, citing his reasons. Wilkingson believed that the concept of Jesus Crist is a fiction considering his research and timelines of the activities in the book, not to consider the failure of his effort to cure the deaf cousin of his. They continued to meet for weeks. He was caught in the strong consideration of whether to go to college and study economics or enroll as a priest. He liked Lee Iococa and his likes. He dreamt of attending Harvard business school. His siblings were all in colleges and his parents used that in their arguments against him attending any training on spiritualism, having seen his interests and what it does to him. He later decided to be a priest and enrolled in the seminary with the help of Capacino. He was studying advanced theology and he planned to get to the doctorate program. He was very stoic in his studies and was deeply interested in exorcism. His practical mindset about contest between angelic and satanic powers continued. He viewed that contest with scientific mind, a tussle that must be demonstrated as an open battle. He shared that with the seminarian teachers and all explanations were not cutting it for his complicated mind. He disconnected with his friends, his girlfriend, practiced celibacy, rarely talked with parents, always quiet and reading. His mind, though, was restless.

The Demarkians   Chidi Metu

He took a pilgrimage to Jerusalem to study and apprise the New Testament, searching for the areas cited in the bible to determine their actual existence, places like Judea, Bethlehem, geometrical distances, burial place of Jesus, the Golgotha. He came back more confused.

He continued in his doubts, in the second year in the seminary. He read the Time magazine interview granted by mother Theresa relating to the hollowness of her commune with the Holy Spirit. Theresa essentially stated that her prayers revealed emptiness and that was found troubling by a lot of Christians all over the world. He read a lot of articles on the opinions of the atheist community in reaction to Theresa's assertions. He thought about the exhibited powers of devil and it seemed thriving and practical. He kept on reading books on satanology. He started gravitating towards Satanism, didn't like it, felt guilty of it but he couldn't stop. He discussed that with fellow students and teachers. He discussed that with Fr. James, his spiritual mentor in the monastery. Other students were now acquainted with his mindset and flowed with him most times. He liked horror movies like Omen series, exorcism. Against school rules, he watched these movies on his laptop.

When the school was on a two- week vacation, he left and sneaked over to Texas, to attend the satanic church and learn their ways. He attended their church and observed their practices and processions. He got back to riverside a very quiet and more confused individual. He was always teased by fellow students who called him "weirdo". He continued to delve into satanic cults and literatures, their powers and influence on the world and that was what he had always wanted. He wanted to be on top of things and call the shots. He liked dominance and to control others. He adored the power of money greatly.

He started thinking strongly that priesthood doesn't actually seem to be his thing. It was too dull and abstract to him. He started reading the deep spiritual books on Satanism found in the library of the monastery. He stumbled upon the Demarkian cults, a dusty book lying on the shelf for God knows how long. He read about the cult seriously and was thrilled about their ways and practices. They permeate across the strata of every career including the finance world. He was obsessed with their enormous evil powers and influence. He spent all his leisure times on the cult's literature, asking questions on the library attendants if he could locate more books on the cult, claiming that he was doing a thesis on them. The news about his new obsession spread out and his spiritual advisor had meetings with him on that. He later left the Monastery unannounced but not surprising to anyone. He learnt of the hidden Demarkian temples in few cities and he went to seek out the Los Angeles temple. It was difficult for him to find it or know the actual location. He stayed back at home but his parents confronted him with all that but he denied them claiming that he wanted to explore the world more. He continued to search for the temple and as luck would have it, he learnt of their location but couldn't get in. He followed a member driving out to his office and breached a lot of protocols in reaching him. The member met with him in a park and getting convinced that he was a good candidate, took him to their leader.

He later got a job in a Demarkian-controlled bank and he rose through the rank fast and in less than two years, was made a manager of one of the big branches in Santa Monica with hundreds of millions in liquid assets, a busy and upscale bank, with the patronage of the high and mighty. He was assigned a huge dog, named kimo given to him as a puppy in the temple and he groomed the dog to adulthood. The dog, as usual, stayed at home most times. He was at the best time of his life.

Meanwhile, Fr. James, in the monastery, was very curious about him, his personality, their discussions and dialogues, his interest on the evil cult. He was shocked that a young man that rose to be trained as a priest could do a complete turnaround leaving the holiness of such call to follow Satan. He started showing interest on his life since he left the school. He knew about his ascension in the bank and was not surprised at all knowing that the reward of evil is usually swift. He tried a few times to meet him at the bank but Wilkingson saw him as a distraction and avoided meeting him. His parents met with Fr. James to discuss their son and the choice that he made. He educated them thoroughly about the cult and their son's sudden wealth. He bluntly told them that their son had cosen a path of destruction.

Wilkingson's parents, after many trials, met with him in his house and went over his life and the choices he made. They asked about the evil dog, his rise to money and his obvious wealth which doesn't really mean much to them. You have chosen Satan over the almighty God, a decision that we found very appalling and dumb. He with God is with majority. Affinity with devil always end in sorrow, my son. You have poured gasoline on yourself and all that we are doing to remove the lighter from your hands. Devil cannot offer you prosperity, know that for sure, boy, Wilkingson's father said to him.

Fr. James was able to get to see Wilkingson who decided to deal with this for a very last time. He walked into his expanse office, tried to shake Wilkingson's hand but he declined that. He asked him to maintain a distance while they sat and talk. James kept preaching to him to revert on the path of righteousness. He quoted biblical verses to support his grounds. He rebuked him for his poor choices and advised him that the devil will never offer anything good to anyone. It is a matter of time. The blessings from God, like any good thing, is not swift but it will come in the fullness of time. He brought out his holy oil and Wilkingson felt so upset and threatened to shoot him, as a bank robber, if he refused to leave, and now! James apologized to him, explaining that his intention was good and redemptive. He blessed him and left the office. Sometimes, Wilkingson brought his dog to the bank and left it in his office.

Bank robbers have robbed the bank twice before Wilkingson took over the bank. A group of hardcore, ex-military friends, have been robbing top banks in greater Los Angeles. An FBI special unit was set up to forestall and catch them but they seemed one step ahead of the unit all the time. These robbers were very experienced and methodical. They wore special masks once they got into the bank. They didn't shoot up the bank or made unnecessary noise. They didn't shoot or kill nobody unless pushed hard. They were very polished and spoke college level English. They were dressed in fine suits and shoes. They came into any bank with guns, ammo, explosives, that could withstand an army platoon. They drove top flight rugged and powerful cars, all stolen on the day of their robberies. They checked out the banks for days before the robbery. One of their modus is to kidnap a child of the store manager of the bank and held the child in another location as an added security in bargaining their security out. They didn't always do that, as in this case, Wilkingson had no wife or child and lived a closed life. They learnt from their inside source that the bank had close to a billion dollars delivered today to the bank. They wanted the whole cash and any person that stood on their way was dead meat. They called themselves "the bad sons". They drank, smoked and sniffed cocaine before any operations. They monitored the cops through their powerful police scanners that they used. They had a gateway position in two different parts of the exit route, whichever walked for them.

On this day, about 11a.m., after the money was dropped off, they walked in casually like any patron of the bank but they wore covid mask and baseball hat leaving almost all their faces covered. As soon as all of them were in the bank, they quickly removed the masks and put on the full mask with "bad sons" written on all of them. They fired a warning shot to announce their presence. They asked everyone to lie still on the floor and collected their phones. By the way they talked or carried themselves, you would know that they were not kidding. They were professionals and very experienced too. They collected all the money at the counter and dumped them in the giant duffel bags they brought with them. They locked the entrance doors and turned off the lights. They put "emergency closed for covid" sign that they brought with them, on the front doors. Some people walked up, saw that and innocently walked away.

Wilikingson did not know what was going on until his dog drew his attention by behaving erratically, including jumping up on his desk. The dog ran towards the camera monitor and stood under it. Wilkingson looked and saw what was happening. He brought out his gun, while calling the police to report the robbery. He called the local leader of the cult and he instructed him to allow the dog to deal with the thieves. You need to understand that guns cannot kill the dog, remember that. He was asked to walk kimo to the door and let it out and he did just that. Kimo looked like it increased in size and was making some funny deep noise, not associated with any animal. Kimo walked into the banking hallway, showed its full fang tooth and bloodshot eyes to the first robber. The robber, with an uzzi military rifle aimed at the dog and fired but the gun didn't fire. He shot at it again and the same thing happened. He aimed the gun at the ceiling and it fired. He was scared and he started backing off from the dog that was now rushing at him. Other robbers came up and was firing at the dog but same result. Kimo jumped on the first robber and bit off his entire right hand in one swift bite. Further bit him and almost dismembered his shoulder. He ran after the second banker and bit off his two hands in few seconds. He chased the other robbers but they already ran out into the waiting hands of the security agencies surrounding the bank.

Wilkinson was watching the whole saga in his office monitors and was jolted by what he saw. The bank patrons raised their heads, watched the spectacle too and were deeply confused as to the powers of the dog. Why was the gun not shooting it? Whose dog is that? Was it the law enforcement dog? Was it cyborg dog created in the lab? But it looked natural.

The FBI, LAPD, other security agencies stormed into the bank and condoned everyone out, keeping them in custody until they watched the video and saw who were the robbers before they let others out. They shivered when they saw what the dog did and screamed. Some of the patrons in custody got even more dumbfounded realizing that the dog was not from the police or FBI.

The dog went back and laid quietly in Wilkingson's office as if nothing happened. The officers walked to talk to Wilkingson as the store manager and saw the dog. They were scared but they stood there looking at it. The dog didn't even pay any attention to them. There was no blood in its mouth anymore. On inquiry, Wilkingson told the police that the dog was his. He couldn't explain why the gun didn't fire. He joked and said to the officers" maybe it is a dog of God" The dog turned ferociously growled loudly making the officers to flinch. Wilkingson started laughing and the dog seemed to get more infuriated by his laughter and Wilkingson apologized to it and walked into the banking hall with the law enforcements. This was unlike anything anyone had ever seen.

The news of the capture of the bad sons were breaking in every major tv network. The leader instructed Wilkingson to hurry up and take Kimo home. Don't allow Kimo's picture to be taken by anyone. If you can't take him out now, go home and come back for it. It will wait for you. Don't grant any media interview, if you can. Lay low and remain low, until this blows over. Call in sick, if you could.

Fr. James saw all that was going on in the tv. He called Wilkingson's parents and they informed him that they were following the news too. They talked about the dog. Wilikingson was a media star and questions were raised about this mysterious dog that couldn't be killed by a conventional weapon. What dog was that? Robocop? The police, Army, FBI, denied any connection with the dog.

Fr. James invited other fathers and explained everything to them. The students were informed too and sooner than later the media learnt of the Demarkian dog and branded it "the devil's dog". The fraternity was very upset with that and they traced the source to Fr. James. Wilkingson was contacted by the general leader of the cult and extolled him and the bravado of the dog, kimo. They informed him that his faith is under attack and Wilkingson reaffirmed that Fr. James was behind it all. He was ordered to cut off everyone for now, including his parents and he agreed. His father came to the bank multiple times to meet with him but he couldn't see him. The entire family have been fully informed of his involvement with the cult and his sudden rise to wealth and fame. Wilkingson later met with some officers of the cult and the leader and they discussed thoroughly father James. The cult officially declared a war on him.

Fr. James had a house in Phillip Ranch, a hilly suburb of Los Angeles. He lived alone in the small bungalow, two bedrooms with his brother occasionally stopping by to see him. James, as a fully ordained catholic priest, was fully resident in the Monastery but comes over to his house when he could, which was more often recently. He was a nice and loving man, devoted his pious life in the full service of the church.

On this day and time, winter in California, it got dark fast. He lived in a gated community in the ranch, exceptionally quiet and creepy. In the night, the lights and the skyline of the greater Los Angeles was seen at the valley below. He came home, took a shower, made some dinner bread toast, with egg and decaf coffee, was getting ready to sleep early and wake up early too to pray and do some work. He needed to be in his quiet home to be able to attend to his numerous works, without any distraction from students. He did not tell his brother of his arrival in the ranch. Their parents were dead and they were only the two of them and they loved each other deeply. The brother normally brought a thai spicy combo fried rice from his favorite restaurant in Los Angeles. But he could do without the food this weekend.

Fr. James had this uneasy feeling that something was not right since he got here. He prayed over it. The cult was getting ready for war. The evil birds came on and perched on his roof making the demonic sounds as usual. James have had that house for over ten years and had never heard such noise from birds at this time of the night. Regular birds were sleeping by now, he thought. One of the birds flew to his window to announce their presence. The bird made eye contact with James and stayed put, refusing to leave. James now realized that the Demarkians were there for war. He called and relayed that to Fr. John at the monastery. They agreed to stand their ground and engage the cult. James brought out his holy oil, his rosary with crucifix, the bible. He started praying and calling on God to take over. In few seconds, an image in human form, average height, with a masked face, two menacing dogs on his side appeared in the middle of his sitting room! James yelled at them: I know who you are. You are the evil Demarkians, the agents of darkness. You came to attack me but you made a wrong choice. I am a lamb of the almighty God. I am a product of the divine mercy of God. Your powers are for the unbelievers and people not clothed by the blood of Jesus. What do you want now? The devil, in deep voice, informed James that they came for his stupid soul. Two black birds appeared in the room too and perched on his tv table looking at him, all with bloodshot eyes, as if they were sizing him up. James getting charged up started praying harder and asked them to leave immediately. A gold staff appeared in the hands of the devil and with a swift gesture he motioned the staff to James and fire hit him burning his garments. James was able to quench the fire and continued to invoke the Holy Spirit but the devil was undeterred. James sprayed the holy oil on the devil and he looked at him and laughed. Asked James: is that all you got? You will die a painful death tonight. James responded: you will be banished back to the abyss where you came from. With faith- based courage, he moved towards the beast with the big crucifix but the beast attacked him again with the fire which stopped him in his stride. He continued to approach the beasts trusting his crucifix. He picked up the bible and doused the fire with it, opened the middle and held the entire book embracing on his chest with his left hand while having the crucifix with his right hand. The beast and the dog rushed him to attack him but he held the crucifix in his face which made them stop. James, holding the cross, walked fast to the beast and the beast snatched the cross out of his hands and it burnt his hands so bad that he dropped it and disappeared with his animals. James picked up the crucifix and started praising God fervently, singing the hymns, rock of ages, Amazing grace, I surrender. The light has triumphed over darkness. It is well with my soul. He later slept with the bible and the crucifix on his chest. When he woke up, he called his colleagues in the monastery and told them everything. He did the same with Wilkingson's parents. He left voice messages to Wilkingson about his failed attempt to kill him. He reminded him in the voicemail that the power of God has proven again that it is superior to the power of Satan. He asked Wilkingson to retrace his steps and come back to sanity and light.

Yorba Linda is an upscale town of about sixty -seven thousand people in Orange County, California. It is accessed by 91 freeway going to Riverside County. The Bedfords, family from Minneapolis had two sons, Meka who was physically challenged and Teddy. Teddy was academically sound and that's all about him. He was a nerd, liked to study nature and animals. He watched, mostly,science and animal channels on tv. He rarely went out to socialize. He attended the upscale UCLA in Los Angeles, graduated in psychology major. He was always neatly dressed and his sense cleanliness was a red flag for mental challenge. He had no girlfriends, very formal and a little weird. He is totally obedient to his parents. He hated going to church, despite his parents being ardent Jehovah witnesses. He loved science and regretted having not studied pure sciences which he later found intriguing. He loved California, for multiple reasons, including the beautiful friendly weather, the sunshine, the mountain and valley ranges, and above all, people mind their businesses here. On graduation, he went home to see his family.

He discussed his career with his family, his intentions to study pure sciences later or go to medical school. Parents wanted him to stay back in Minnesota to assist with his deformed brother but he declined selfishly. He hated the life at his hometown, the gossips, the unannounced visits, the communal informalities. He found the local people dumb and unambitious. They yelled instead of talking; they talked about religion and church which repulsed him; He was like Wilkingson in some remarkable ways. He approached life with scientific mind. He reviewed the Lucifer and the powers that are ascribed to him. He read the holy books of other religions, Hindu, Buddha, Islam, others. The story of Jesus pissed him off. How could he, Jesus, have allowed himself to be humiliated and killed by some charlatans when he had the power to incinerate them!

He found a job at Yorba Linda after graduation, at a Crystal stairs private tutorial school. He showed efficiency and dedication as if his life depended on the job. He had no other life or friends and could care less about all that. He loved to work overtime assignments with very little remunerations. But surprisingly, he liked expensive vintage stuffs and sometimes wished he could change his life and redirected it.

He liked to use Yorba Linda library a lot. He had a triangular lifestyle and part of his problem was poverty. He just could not afford the things that he wished that he would get. He prepared class works on time, very focused, overzealous, graded his class works, took calls from students 24 hours a day, seven days a week. His fellow staffs teased him a lot and made him roast topic in their school comic weeks. He later got another good paying job in an investment firm in the nearby city of Fullerton. His assignments brought him in contacts with high rollers in the community. He rendered efficient services to them, especially this arrogant man, Clifford. Clifford was aristocratic, dressed real nice and drove fancy cars. He had the swagger of the rich, huge financial portfolios, managed mostly by Teddy. He was detail oriented which actually drew Teddy to him. He started paying attention to Teddy and liking him. Cliff occasionally gave Teddy wads of hundred dollar bills in appreciation for his dedication and humility in doing his job. He took Teddy out on lunch someday and questioned him on a lot of things including his pedigree. He later found out that Teddy was a nerd and that poverty contributed to his deficiencies. He drilled Teddy on religion and surprisingly found out that Teddy gave little or no hoot about Religion. He also discovered that Teddy liked good stuffs. On Teddy's birthday, he gave him one of his Rolex watches and that watch never left Teddy wrist except when he took his showers. He wore the watch to sleep. He also learnt that Teddy was agnostic and with a mind of spiritual practicality. He took Teddy under his wings, gave him more assignments, more investment funds and promised to make him big, which he did. He turned Teddy away from anti-social dispositions, hung out more with him and bought him a brand new Mercedes car. Teddy became a medium roller. Cliff kept on studying Teddy, edging closer to him, kept on routing to how Teddy would react to the revelations of the Demarkians. He finally asked him if he would be interested to study and possess deep knowledge about a brotherhood cult? Teddy said Yes but Cliff, on purpose, didn't follow through for sometime, to ignite Teddy's interest, which worked.

He opened up one day and informed Teddy of the Demarkians, told him where to read up materials about them, the discreet nature, the enormous powers of the cult and their rules. He didn't go too deep as he was taking his time and leaving Teddy to find as much information on his own. Teddy researched and discovered the amazing Demarkians, which resonated with him heavily. He believed that this has been his missing limb. He asked Cliff a lot of questions about the cult and got expansive answers with a caveat to be discreet, a violation of that could be fatal. Cliff discussed with local leadership and they approved of pushing the boy more into the brotherhood. Teddy, having tested good things of life, started yearning for more. Cliff gave him more money in his portfolios so that he would rake more commissions having attained some level of investments.

Teddy took an MBA class from university of Southern California, a top flight, ivy-league like school. Bought an S-class Mercedes Benz, moved into the high class area of Yorba Linda. His relationship with Cliff progressed and he was asked to resign and start his own investment firm which he did call Tbedfords Investment, Inc. Cliff transferred all his investments from all companies to Teddy's company. He also brought in his friends and cult family to Tbedfords. Cliff promised to turn the company into a fortune 500 outfit and he did. Cliff took Teddy to the temple and he was sworn in and he took the deadly oath of secrecy and admonitions. He was informed of the restrictions attendant to the membership but he obliged and agreed to jump in. Teddy became very rich and started getting 7 to 8 digits annual income from investment portfolios. He was given a key to the Demarkian lodge, temple and libraries. Above all, he was given a dog and was briefed on the dog and how to handle it. He named the dog, Sacha.

He bought a huge house at the Fullerton Hills, area of the rich and mighty. The place, expectedly, is very pristine and classy. Everyone lived at least 500 yards from each other. The houses were surrounded with cottage fences and well-tended trees and shrubs, like in the Hamptons. He bought another big duplex for his parents in Minnesota and set up a five -star grocery business for his parents too. He hired a company to provide a 24-hour caregiving and assisted living for his brother, Meka. Teddy kept growing in business, socialized more now, had a girlfriend, Turner, but never wanted to settle down. Turner was barred from accessing some parts of the house in Yorba Linda. The cult dog, as usual, wasn't paying attention to her. Teddy graduated USC and declined Turner's suggestion for a party of church thanksgiving. His parents visited him and were very impressed by his financial turnaround. They congratulated him for his achievements and left for home. In three years, Teddy grew in wealth and influence within and without the cult. He rose to be a step 4 member in the cult. He acquired immense spiritual powers and his life was embedded in the cult.

On a Saturday night, on Cliff's invitation, Teddy attended a party in Laguna Niguel, drank a lot of spirits, louis the xxxiii high vintage cognac, mixed with some Perrier jouet, a deadly combination. Party lasted till about 2 a.m. and Teddy drove home recklessly. In an Uncontrollable speed in his newly acquired porch panorama, supercharged, lost control on the hills of Yorba Linda, drove into a huge tree, uprooted the tree and shredded his car and his body. His corpse was barely recognizable. The police, through his girlfriend, invited his family and they all came. Cliff met with the family and informed them about his close relationship with Teddy. He updated them about his business and handed his properties to them. He assisted them in closing down his business and his bank accounts. They gave his girlfriend some money and left for Minnesota to prepare for his funeral. Family deliberated about where to intern him. His mother, very emotional, chose Minnesota to enable her visit his grave. Dad opposed it and suggested that he should be buried in Yorba Linda and they all eventually agreed to that. They contacted Cliff who asked them to step aside and allow him to plan the funeral. They graciously agreed to that, without knowing the reason for that offer. The cult met and planned the funeral. The dog was removed by Cliff and returned to the lodge.

The funeral was conducted low key and the cult members were there in full support. But there was a ceremony to be performed by the cult for the repose of the soul of a high grade cult member.

On the night of the first day of interment, some oddities were observed on the Teddy's tomb. Dogs, cats, crows perched on the Tomb. It was also windy around the tomb. Light bulbs around the tomb blew out and the cemetery worker gave up replacing them. The animals made odd sounds, with reflective eye colors, sometimes bloodshot eyes. The birds were seen perched on the tomb every night until morning. Sometimes they hung there quietly without any noise, ran away when the attendant approached, and assembled again as soon he left. Cemetery worker started getting scared of the activities and always looked over to the tomb. He brought his dog to work on this night but his dog refused to conduct the patrol with him, stood behind his office door and was barking incessantly. Attendant wanted to drag him towards the tomb area but the dog was so scared and drooling that Attendant left it. On the 7th day after the burial, at midnight, attendant flashed his light on the tomb and noticed the same animals, and an image of a human, in pitch black flowing garments standing by the tomb backing him. He rubbed his face to make sure he was not hallucinating but when he opened his eyes, the image had disappeared. He was confused and he called the police, thinking that it might be tomb robbers. The officers pulled in but couldn't see anything and advised him to stay away from alcohol, after noticing an empty bottle of forty ounce old English in the trash bin. Next night, everywhere was quiet and cemetery was calm but worker in fear was focusing on the tomb and couldn't give the cult the needed opportunity to do the closure ritual for Teddy. They had only 3 weeks to do that after his burial. It continued like that for few more days and a man named Clifford appeared to the cemetery attendant and made a weird request for him; few friends of Teddy to meet over at the tomb by midnight and do some traditional rituals, originating from their ancestral home outside the United States. The attendant declined and asked them to put it in writing. They did and the cemetery management declined that. The quagmire continued and the situation became more troubling.

Teddy was a special step 4 of the fraternity, with a complete submission to the devil during and after life. If he was not detached from the devil within the given period, his spirit will become rebellious and destructive. His eternity will be greatly disturbed, which it was doomed for anyways. In the life of mystery, he would face multiple judgment for the choices he made over here before his death. The belief of the fraternity was that the purging would detach him from here and move him to eternal order. As silly as it sounds, it appeared to be true considering the activities associated with Teddy later. His possessed spirit would ravage for years unprovoked and nobody could stop that. The clock continued to tick and the fraternity was running out of time. Consequences like this comes with the territory of being a Satan disciple and it is what it is.

Cliff and co went back and offered the cemetery worker hundreds of thousands of dollars to enable them conduct the ritual but he declined it, getting worried about who these people were and their intentions.

✳ ✳ ✳

Meanwhile, the Bedfords, their grocery store closed, were mourning and receiving guests, neighbors, consolations. Ghost of Teddy started showing and weird noise evidencing his presence were noticed in the house. Teddy's assigned bedroom showed that Teddy has been sleeping there every night. The beds showed usage every morning even though the mum fixed it every night. The beds made squeaky noise in the nights as if someone laid on it. The toilet closest to Teddy's room showed evidence of usage in the nights, with flushing sounds heard. Light snoring could be heard in the room at night sometimes but the dad looked in and noticed the bed empty. The family started feeling that they may be the ones losing their minds over his death. It was a very tough period for the family. But when they continued to hear footsteps and the piano playing at midnights of Teddy's favorite songs, then the family knew he was there all along.

Dressing iron was, on few occasions found plugged in and it was red hot. His mum would call on Teddy asking him: "Teddy, baby, is that you? Are you here? What is going on?" she would start crying for her son. The family brought in Fr. Morrison, to assist the family spiritually. They joined forces with him in addressing the problems. Teddy's family decided to visit Yorba Linda with Morrison, on a Sunday, to pray at Teddy's grave. They picked up their rented vehicle from the airport. On their way to the cemetery, a crow perched on their car hood and was looking at the priest intently until they got to the cemetery. On walking over to the grave, a funny-looking cat appeared from the side of the cemetery and walked boldly to the tomb and climbed on it, with the crow too, looking intently at the three of them. The priest sensing the presence of the devil started praying as the animals continued to cry and made desperate distracting noises. Morrison brought out holy oil and sprinkled it on the tomb and kept praying more. He tried to sprinkle the oil on the animals but he couldn't lift his hands to do that!

It became clearer to him that these were evil animals and that something was amiss. Otherwise, what were the birds doing there and obstructing them? None of them had an answer to that.
They got to Teddy's house in the evening, unlocked it, cleaned it, went out and got some foods, came back and noticed that the house was in full darkness despite the fact that they turned the lights on before leaving the house. They tried switching on the lights but to no avail. They found a flashlight and inspected the house and its surroundings. The whole neighborhood had electricity except Teddy's house. They reasoned that his light may have been cut off for bill issues.

They went to sit at the porch to analyze these whole sagas and noticed that the same bird and cat came on there too, and now with a scary dog with funny fur pigmentations. These were real agents of darkness. The priest and the Bedfords went into prayer frenzy again. The animals, never attacked them but went away after sometime. As soon as they left, the lights came on miraculously. This puzzled them more because none of them turned on the lights or touched the switch. The priest, in deep thought, started mildly to interrogate the Bedfords about their son's lifestyle, his ascension and the source of his wealth. They had no answer for him.

The next day, they contacted Cliff and he came over and they talked about a whole of things including selling the house and taking possession of the remaining properties of their son. The house was listed for sale in the MLS right away.

The family went back to the tomb that Monday afternoon but could not see any animals there and the priest led the family in prayers but a little later, a dark, dusty, minor cyclone-type of wind came on, with evil sounds. The bible was snatched out of his hands by the wind, with his oil pouch falling to the ground. The Bedfords were screaming, "Jesus"!; the priest pushed to the ground by the strong wind was reciting psalm 23 and eventually regained his composure, yelling prayers and binding the devil. The attack stopped and they left for Teddy's house. They drove home confused and perturbed. The priest, with irritation, voiced out to the Bedfords that their son was involved with devil but the family asked him to please stop saying that, claiming that their child was a good son. He was not evil and couldn't have been. But they knew that they were not being honest about those representations. They knew their son and his inclinations. They felt ashamed and the sudden wealth and other things started making sense to them. They got back to Teddy's house, held hands and prayed together, ate and watched tv. They poured each other some red wines as they all needed it. They went to sleep later, a little late. At about 3 a.m. the family kept on hearing footsteps on the wooden stairs, went to check but they couldn't find anything. Mr. Bedford knocked on the priest's door to inquire but found him praying and left. The priest heard of the footsteps and thought it was them that were walking around. And suddenly the tv came on a little too loud for the time of the day and the mother rushed out of room, turn on the stairs' light and what she saw was gut-wrenching: standing on the lowest part of the stair, in full glare, was Teddy backing her. Teddy wore the shirt that she bought for him on his last birthday before his death. Mother called on him and yelled for her husband and the priest. She informed them of what she just saw. They looked but Teddy was not there. Teddy's father and the priest admonished her for having a little too much to drink. She had remained fifteen years sober from alcohol having had a history of the bottle in the past.

Teddy's house was sold a few times but it turned out to be heavily haunted by Teddy's spirits, as piano kept on going off in the night, footsteps, coughing, toilets flushed and snoring heard at different times of the nights. The cult bought the house and locked it up.

Back in Minnesota, Meka had a terrible nightmare. In his dream, Teddy appeared in a fresh dark garment, waived at him from a distance, later came closer to him but stayed a reasonable distance avoiding eye contact with him. Teddy informed him that he was in torment; how he was lured into an evil cult that gave him money and powers but he now couldn't find a rest...He explained the dogs, the cats, the ritual and the rest of them. He said he was very cold where he was. He informed Meka about the failure of the cult to perform the ritual but suggested to Meka to visit a certain library and study the Demarkian book; get a certain exorcist involved; reminded Meka that the fraternal order was very powerful too. He wanted his body to be exhumed, his spirit conjured up at certain time and purged and that his corpse would never decay as long as he was trapped in his current location. His appearance still looked like a zombie, with the morgue make-up, claimed that he was cold, hungry and tired. He started crying loudly and Meka, sweating woke up and screamed intuitively. His parents ran into his room, held him down and inquired what was that? He explained the dream to them and the mum fell to the bed and started crying.

The Bedfords decided to go on a little weekend vacation to St Paul city nearby. They lodged in a hotel, tried to relax but it was not easy as they were deeply troubled about their son. They went for a softball game tournament at St Paul, with sizeable people in attendance. Soda, hotdogs, popcorns, were being sold. Spectators were in high spirit enjoying the game, except the Bedfords. At some point, Teddy's father looked across the field and got some chills. Standing there, clearly in plain view, was Teddy, with same shirt as seen by his wife. Teddy was looking directly at him and at some point threw a hand sign they shared when Teddy was growing up. His soda fell out of his hands and he recollected himself, told his wife what was going on. The wife and Meka looked across and they all saw Teddy! They were transfixed to their standing positions in awe. Meka cried out: "oh my God! so ghost is true?" the spectators standing nearby heard him and followed his gaze but they didn't know what to look for. Teddy's dad followed Teddy as he was walking towards the woods and dad started running to catch up with him but it looked as if he would never achieve that, even though Teddy was just walking. Dad started yelling his name asking him to stop but Teddy disappeared. He was yelling at Teddy asking him why he chose to destroy his life and now tormenting his lovely family that raised him well for a choice that he made alone. He kept on yelling to him: do you need help? What can we do for you? We will follow your directives to Meka. We are still your family and we love you regardless. Dad, in exasperation, fell to the ground and started crying. Passersby and innocent bystanders were confused looking at him. They thought that he was, maybe on the fringe of insanity. They hurried back to the hotel and left for home. Dad dozed off and saw Teddy in the dream who confirmed that the messages he passed to Meka were true. He explained to the father about the cult and apologized about the drama in Yorba Linda, claiming that he was not in the position to stop the attacks. He requested from his father to make the hard efforts to exhume his body and the do the needful. He apologized to him for all his bothering and stated that they were all that he got. He informed him that he was gonna run into oppositions from the city of Yorba Linda and others but that he had to push. He also informed him that the biggest opposition would be from the cult and might be life threatening. In this dream discussions, he never made any eye contact with his dad. Dad woke up and called Fr. Morrison and they met, had a detailed talk and started planning on executing them. Morrison went home, in preparation, engaged in fierce fasting and prayers, seeking the face of God against this evil cult that was ravaging the Bedfords and other families in some other places.

Bedfords contacted local health department in Minnesota, contacted the city fire department and received all clearances. They arranged and paid the funeral undertakers too. They offered reasons for the second reburial to the city. They paid for a plat in the cemetery and applied to the funeral home to be given a prior full day traditional privacy communion with the corpse uninterrupted, paid for it handsomely and it was granted. The priests, with few family members, would be there as that was agreed upon. The Bedfords now had the opportunity to invite their friends and relations for a befitting and regular burial and repass. The community was confused though and they asked questions. A lot of unanswered questions remained. Was it required by the insurance company before they could pay out the benefit? Is it spiritual? Was it for him to be closer home for remembrance and flowers? On and on queries.

The Bedfords ran into stringent problems in Yorba Linda as the orange county fought them with all they had, to stop the exhumation request. They applied to court in an expedited hearing, advanced their reasons and the court granted them the request, with a caveat, that they must put some health precautions in place. The body was exhumed, with the supervision of the health department as ordered by the court, taken straight to the morgue. The casket was opened and Teddy's body appeared exactly as it was on the day he was buried. The corpse showed no dent or any sign of decomposition. The pathologist still treated the body with formalin and other preservatives.

Everything was prepared for transportation to his home state. The city was heavily involved with all that. The body was transported to the Long Beach airfield where the chattered twin engine private plane was waiting. Fr. Morrison and the family were there in circle praying, invoking God to take control as he did in Egypt, as he parted the red sea, as he redeemed mankind... The Bedfords were visibly shaken; Dad brought out cigarette and lit, having not smoked for 25 years. His wife started crying more. They loaded the body and took off in the early darkness of the night. Aircraft attained the assigned altitude of thirty-two thousand feet and stabilized. The plane was quietly tearing into the night as the night got darker and chilly. The plane continued to tore up the sky with supersonic speed to Minnesota. Two hours into the trip, the turbulence started and the pilot announced for the seatbelts. The air tower report on that area did not show any turbulence on their radar though. The turbulence increased and the pilot communicated with the aviation tower and sought to be transferred to another aviation corridor but it was denied as the radar did not show anything warranting such transfer. Plane started jerking, and pilots were advised to depress to twenty- eight thousand feet which they did. They were detoured to another route which added additional 45 minutes to the journey. They dropped the altitude a little suddenly to avoid the incessant jerking. The sky was still clear but the plane was going crazy by the seconds. Knowing what was going on, the passengers started praying, yelling as if they were in a prayer retreat. One of the pilots on hearing that came out and saw them, surprised. The satanic sound came on and got louder as the devil was focused on crashing the plane. The pilot ascended back to the former altitude but the jerking continued. Now, the passengers realized suddenly why the Satan left them alone on the ground. The pilots were doing everything to stop the plane from going down in the middle of nowhere. The oxygen supply dropped as the cabin pressure decreased substantially but the passengers were too to disoriented to put oxygen caps them on. The priest helped them in hoisting them on their faces before putting his. Few minutes later, one of plane's engines failed and pilots issued an s.o.s to the nearest airport in South Dakota for emergency landing clearance. The plane never slowed down and they were running out of gas too, which was okay because they couldn't land with gas in the tank. They were cleared to alternate between twenty- five to thirty- five thousand feet before the emergency landing. Dakota airfield was going haywire as fire trucks, ambulance, police cars, were positioned in place. The plane continued its craziness, showed the pilots in deep struggles, sweating, yelling to themselves, cursing out obscenities, but fifteen minutes to land, everything stopped. Morrison continued to pray and called on God not to fail them. The second engine of the aircraft came back on too. Pilots reported to the towers to be cleared for their Minnesota flight and it was granted. The problem now was whether they had enough gas to get them there. The plane ascended but on attaining the altitude, the headlamps started blinking and Morrison went into the pulpit and started praying, sitting with them. The pilot, in anger and indignation, yelling at him: "what the hell is going on here? Who are you people? What's all these about, men?" after a few seconds, and for the first time, the Demarkian raven, with oversized beak, red shot eyes, appeared on the windshield and was looking at them without making any effort to fly away. Pilots were confused because at thirty – five thousand feet, birds don't fly that high! Why is the eye red anyways? The plane's electrical system started going in and out and Teddy's mother started crying, calling and scolding her son for putting them through this because of his stupid, selfish and inordinate ambition.

Priest started spraying oil on the windshield of the plane but he was asked to stop and go back to the passenger section. He left but continued his prayers. Finally, everything stopped, with the last bit of gas, they landed in Minnesota. God had prevailed over devil, hallelujah. The plane landed and the casket was removed to the morgue and they went home, ate and refreshed. Teddy appeared in his father's dream and hugged him and reminded him that there were more battles ahead.

Fr Morrison, joined by Fr Adamson and other clergies, got ready for the next agenda which was the exorcism and burial. They knew that it was a tough task. They drove with the Bedfords, except Meka, to the morgue and walked in to the body already rolled out into a private parlor. Wife, a little dramatic but dad strong and was ready to end all these nonsense, today and tomorrow. Curtains were drawn, doors locked, casket opened and the expungement rituals started with the singing of the hymns and prayers. The priests had their rosaries and crucifix, as well as their vials of oil. Fr. Kissinger brought out his oil pouch, poured some in his hands, in trying to do a station of the cross on Teddy's forehead, but on first contact with his body, got his finger deeply burnt and he yelled out in pain. Funeral home attendant heard it and ran over but the door was locked and he was asked to ignore that. The prayers continued but it appeared that the fathers were avoiding touching Teddy's body. Kissinger mustered courage, repeated the exercise again but this time, his fingers stuck to Teddy's skin for a few seconds and he pulled out and fail to the ground in severe pains. Ice blocks and holy water were placed on his hands. The process continued and just suddenly, a levitating strong wind lifted Fr. Adamson and struck him to the floor violently and he hit the pedestal of the coffin tripping it over making the corpse to fell out face down on the floor on top of a scared Adamson. Bedford was greatly troubled by this and he cried for his son, felt momentarily hopeless. They were all looking at the body confused as to how to put it back in the casket. Morrison, in prayer, asked the younger priest to assist him in putting the casket up with Teddy in it. That was a victory for them. Morrison determined to carry out the final rite, put the oil on his hands and did the station of the cross on Teddy. As soon as he did that, loud demonic sound came on, the entire building started shaking and increasing in intensity, demonic voices warning them to steer away from his eternal disciple. Having not been purged on a given period, he stayed with his for eternity. Building continued to shake and the evil birds and cat appeared on the window interior, watching them. The vibration was heard by the attendant who ran over but couldn't gain access into the parlor. He called his boss and left him a message.

Black smokes enveloped the entire room and Satan was in rage, commanding them to leave. Teddy's corpse levitated and stood airbound for a while but Morrison and his crew remained in deep prayers undeterred. Devil speaking in multiple, incoherent voices, reminded them that Teddy wanted his wealth and protections. Mother yelled at the devil: "he is my son!" Devil yelled back: "not any more". His soul is mine now and till the end of time. Devil asked mum, shut up and submit. "Don't you see what I am doing to your priests? Can't you see that I am more powerful? Hahaha, hohoho," laughter of the devil. Morrison and Adam kept on rebuking the devil and spraying the oil in the air. The smoke and vibrations stopped momentarily. Suddenly the evil kids appeared and stood by them watching them with a smile on their faces. They commandeered Teddy's casket to descend and it did. They stood at the two ends of the casket watching the priests intently. The kids were caressing Teddy's face affectionately and smilingly. Turning around with eyes that have turned bloodshot and voice hoarse and deep, turned to face the priests, directly on Morrison and Adamson standing closest to them, threw their hands in the air, in a gripping motion, making the two of them riddled with strangling pains as the kids turned their hands. They fell to the ground screaming Jesus! The kids kept on squeezing them as their oil pouches and their bibles fell out of their hands. Other priests continued in their prayers and the battle raged on. The kids stopped and later started walking towards the priests asking them in mockery, to scoop them up, that they were little kids needing attention; that they were hungry. They started laughing and did a high five with each other. They continued to approach the priests who brought out their crucifix and placed them in front of their faces as shields. The priests sprayed them with the oils and they, obviously overwhelmed, with one of the kids catching fire from the oil, disappeared. The priests continued to pray and spraying more oils on Teddy's corpse in the casket. The exorcism continued for another twenty minutes as a thick black smoke suddenly gushed out of Teddy's body, vibrating the coffin and the environment. It was all over. It was all over as Teddy was re-buried and the whole drama and dreams stopped.

Back in Houston, Father Edison was in the intensive care unit, icu, receiving treatments for his traumatic injuries. His assigned doctor was Dr. Wong, an amiable senior physician that practiced medicine with love and compassion. He was a family-oriented man, worked one week in, one week out. He received Edison in one of his week on. Next week, he was off and a floating Doctor was substituting for him until he returned. The department had a nursing station, somewhat exclusive because it was an icu unit. There was an elevator close by the nursing station. You have to walk by the elevator to get to Edison's room at the hospital. Few visitors, mostly his fellow priests, and parishioners came around to pray with him. They had to be accredited at the nursing station before they were allowed into Edison's room.

On this day, Nurse Rita, personal assistant to Dr. Wong, was on duty assisting the floating Doctor, as Dr. Wong was out on his off days. Rita and the floating doctor attended to Edison on a Friday. Edison was doing great even though he was still on iv therapy and further diagnosis. He was, sometimes, heavily sedated to relax his muscles and heal his invasive wounds and fractures. He received constant physical therapy too. The war with the devil was not over yet and Edison knew that as he had premonitions of it. He always had his bible and rosary nearby. Sometimes he locked them up in one of the bedside drawer. He normally prays and asked God to build a wall of Jericho around him, to keep anything that was not of God away from him; to bind all evil spirits away.

Later the same Friday, Dr. Wong, was by the bedside of Edison who was very drowsy from medication therapies. The doctor fiddled with the iv infusion lines and was removing the oxygen supply line. He was dressed in a white flowing doctor's jacket. Rita, about twenty minutes ago, had attended to Edison and left for other ward rounds and was going to return back in two hours. She was not supposed to come back to Edison room but she forgot her stethoscope and needed to retrieve it. She was with another patient in another room down the hall when she remembered the item. Initially, she was oblivious of Dr. Wong's presence in Edison's room as she was busy attending to another patient and chatting with other colleagues. She walked back to pick up the item and was surprised to see Wong in Edison's room backing the entry door, fiddling with the infusion lines. She excitedly yelled at Wong: "waoh, see who is here! Family man of the year! "

"This is amazing, on your off day! Bless God. What do we owe this honor sir? You missed us so much?" She started laughing. Rita walked closer to tease and chat with Wong but he was evasive and tactfully turning away from her, with a difficult smile. Wong greeted Rita with a somewhat different voice, while avoiding eye contact with Rita. This was not the usual Wong …did he fight at home? Why is he here anyways? Wong walked past Rita and walked into the hallway and disappeared. Rita surprised, walked down the corridor, same direction that Wong walked but couldn't see him anymore. He ran into another nurse and asked her if she saw Wong and the nurse said no and teased Rita, asking her, what have you been drinking? Wong never worked off days except on emergency calls only, likes kicking it with his family, you know. Girl get over it. Go get some nap. Rita still confused, looked around, more puzzled, as she went back into Edison's room. She found the tampering on the lines and noticed that Edison was now breathing hard and jerky. Rita called code blue and another Doctor and some nurses rushed into the room. Rita relayed what just happened. The Doctor examined the iv lines and noticed dangerous tampering, raising a lot of questions and dialogues.

The medical director, who happened to be within the hospital premises, was called in and same puzzles were observed. Rita was thoroughly interrogated by the medical director but she maintained her story. The Medical director asked the human resources to provide him with Wong's phone number and he called and spoke with him. He inquired of Wong's family, kids, wife? Wong, excitedly as usual, asked how the hospital and his patients were? He asked the medical director if there was any problem with him calling him? They chatted for a while and the director cut to the chase and asked him whether he was in the hospital today? Wong said that he had not been in the hospital for the past 6 days. Director put the phone on speaker phone and asked the same question again and Wong gave the same answer. Director explained to Wong what Rita claimed to had just happened in the last hour and Wong declined being there today.
Rita was interrogated more at the director's office, was later relieved from work until further notice. Rita started crying, felt defeated and went home to her husband and kids.

Weeks later, Edison was later transferred to the general ward and assigned to Dr. Sayama, a tall Japanese American, with board -

certified internal medicine practice. His normal schedule was morning/ afternoon shifts. Today he came, exchanged pleasantries, reviewed Edison's records and was puzzled about the incidence involving Wong's name. He examined Edison's wounds, the healing, soft tissues, felt good and announced to Edison that he would be going home soon. He asked Edison if he desired to still be sedated now and then but Edison declined that. Sayama checked the iv lines, injected more norco into it for pain. He left to do more rounds and after that, do some medical reports and would stop by to see Edison. With that, he did a thumbs up and left the room, advising Edison to call the nursing station if he needed anything.

Nurse Patricia was Sayama's assigned nurse on that floor. She worked into the room, started a discussion with Edison. Patricia was an ardent catholic and finding out that Edison was a catholic priest, she developed interest in his care, optimizing her attention and always looked in to make sure he was okay. Nurse Chris, a black guy, born a catholic, been a nurse for a while, loved his job, was an lvn, was asked by Patricia to help in overseeing the welfare of Edison. Chris was very friendly with Sayama, both loved to talk about football and basketball, as both were strong fans of the 49ers and Houston Rockets. Chris walked by Edison's room, decided to talk with him for a minute, and saw Sayama standing by Edison's bedside, fiddling with the iv lines. He excitedly greeted Sayama but Sayama, unlike him just nodded at him and spoke less with a body language asking Chris to beat it. Sayama, in his right hand, had a syringe with an injection in it. Sayama was not making any eye contact with Chris, focusing on his activities. Edison was watching Sayama with keen interest, especially with the last incidence with Wong, knowing too that Sayama left less than an hour ago after having had a long talk with him. Sayama was cold and unfriendly. Edison inquired about the injection in his hands and Sayama claimed that it was an additional norco to numb his pain. Edison never complained to anyone that he was in pain and advised Sayama not to infuse that into his iv line. He obliged Edison but continued to fiddle with the iv set up. Edison was beginning to get restless and started asking Sayama why he came back so soon and what changed.

Chris phone rang at that point and he stepped out about 100 feet to answer it. Down the hallway, talking excitedly on the phone, was Sayama walking up to Chris and smiling heartily. Chris cut off his call and told Sayama: I didn't know you have a twin brother, a doctor too, in this facility! C'mon men, and you are supposed to be my friend! Sayama, looking surprised, told Chris that he didn't understand what he was alluding to. Chris explained briefly about the other doctor in Edison's room. Nurse Pat walked into them talking about that and teasing Sayama. Curiously, all of them rushed over to Edison's room. Sayama was petrified to see his replica in the room fiddling with the iv line. Sayama asked him: who are you sir? Edison now confirmed his fear and jumped out of his bed in pains and started searching for his crucifix, yelling to everyone to back off. He continued to yell at them that the other Sayama is a devil but they couldn't understand what he was saying. Chris walked into the room bravely confronting the "doctor". Pat was close to fainting as she maintained a reasonable distance. Sayama stood there confused with loss of words. Edison started yelling spiritual incantations and shouting at Sayama and Chris to back off! That's an evil spirit, please run away. This is my battle and it is of the spirit, please go! The evil Sayama started laughing with a demonic sound and voice, typical of the cult during attacks. More nurses and doctors, ambulatory patients filed out to the area to behold the incredible spectacle.

The medical director was called in and he rushed and saw what was happening and remembered Rita. The two Sayamas were there in plain view. The devil walked out quietly into the hallway, with his eyes turning blood red and showing a fang dentition. He laughed at them and informed everyone that he is the devil, with small smokes coming of his mouth. More people came into the hallway and the spectacle continued but stampedes were caused whenever the devil turned to face any direction. Edison came out and confronted the devil and a repeat of the first fight ensued. Edison was praying and sprinkling the devil with oil calling the name of the Demarkians and asking God to destroy them in totality. Devil lunged at Edison but he held the crucifix on his face and he stopped. The devil stood still watching everyone and later disappeared.

Director went into his office but was too scared to stay inside. He called the HR department and some managers to meet him on the hallway of his office. He relayed to them what had just happened which shocked all of them. Message was sent to Rita and Wong to come down to hospital right away. Rita was apologized to strenuously and recalled with past full pay, a promotion and increased pay rate in her new ward transfer appointment. She was still deeply hurting for the humiliating allegations and insinuations that she may have been stealing the hospital's hallucinating medications from the meds locker. She decided to continue her search for another job. Wong, like anyone else, was dumbfounded. Edison requested to be discharged to his home and it was granted. He decided to wage a full spiritual warfare with this cult. He did just that but the war didn't happen immediately.

CHAPTER 11

England 2018. The British aristocracy and the vanity of mankind; the desire to be in the hue of the uppity; The lure of wealth and the power to intimidate and subdue others; the superiority complex and the price for it. Humans are social animals that are seeking to be better than others, most times in their demented imaginations. Europe, they say, is the world. The continent represents civilization and modernization. England has always been an encapsulated civilization and mystery of spiritualisms.

At the outskirt of London, United Kingdom, 175 miles in the city of Hertfordshire lies a quiet, more than 450-year-old stonedhouse known as the WHITLESEX CASTLE, dwarfed by a studded-stoned high wall of about 20 feet high, a swinging double fortified, archaic wooden gate. The walls and the frontal parts had ubiquitous climbing Hydrangea and wisteria flowers. On the side was rose flowers, clematis flowers and a multitude of other types of beautiful all- year-round decorative flowers. The high walls were same at the perimeter of the building, exquisitely maintained. Observing the building from outside could only show the topmost part of the third floor of the three story building tucked away deep into the relatively three -acre compound. The house was heavily stuccoed in classis archival European designs and style. The lawn inside was green all year round. Compound was manned by an elderly white haired Caucasian man who rarely showed his presence. The whole place had the ambience of a monastery without being one. The first story of the building was an underground; the second floor was on a street level and third floor was actually seen from the street level as a second floor. The building presented an architectural optic illusion. The building, an exhibition of the hue of aristocracy, was solidly built more than four centuries ago but very efficiently maintained in great shape. The woods at the doors and windows were highly ornamental; the interior décor was padded sound proof, designed to enhance and maintain tranquility. The whole place was inundated with flower vases containing rare flowers in butterfly outlook, exuding aromas and flagrances, especially in the nights. The furniture was of premium qualities, medieval styles that were waxed and polished every year in the last 400 years. The flooring was a glimmer of glamour extraordinaire; the entire compound represented steep prosperity in class and aristocracy. The roofs were heavily reinforced to withstand the inclement weather of United Kingdom especially the winter period. Beautiful, vintage classic vehicles drove in and out in certain times of the year, with a fleeting minuscule showing of the occupants of the vehicles.

The Chef and the kitchen attendants stayed in the kitchen area, quite a distance from the huge banquet halls buried in the basement of the building. The halls, four of them, had different sizes and each of them required a special entry code to be accessed, just like the entry gates. The entire building had huge ensuite rooms and lounges even at the basement. The second floor had zero access suites. The only people that had access to it were the members in attendance. Mr. Anderson was the only liason, a concierge between the kitchen and the general staffs and the members. Cleaning of the halls especially the exclusive parts of the Whistlesex was done by Anderson. Violation of restricted area is catastrophic and Anderson let the staffs knew about it. Even in the exclusive portions of the inner chambers was somewhat out of reach to Anderson. The last employer/ liaison like Anderson, named Tibo that tried to violate this rule almost got his eyes ripped off by a vicious cat that appeared from nowhere and lunged at him. He never came back to the castle. He lost an eye and never disclosed the source of his injury even to his wife as doing that would have cost him his life.

There was a food tester too named Wilberforce as all dishes were meticulously tested at different times, including finally by Anderson, before presented to the members. The beverages were brought by the members, very wealthy English aristocrats, so it seemed. They dressed in hand made shoes, fitted designer suits, Rolex watches; Breitling watches; very expensive jewelries, handmade ties. They were usually quiet until the meeting doors are closed. They never came out or exited the meeting halls until their meeting were over. They seemed perfect gentlemen and ladies; very educated and classy. They held and conducted themselves in glamour even after heavy consumption of alcohols. Classical music played in the background in low tunes even during their meetings. They were never heard quarreled and acted unruly in their meetings. Their leader sat on the stage and directed their meetings; no cameras were allowed into the meetings. There were no phone calls or phone discussions; there were no breaks too. Two huge weird-looking menacing dogs sat on the stage with the leader during their meetings.

Most of them wore bowler hats and custom-fitted suits, carried air of arrogance with some measures of affluent exuberance. These were the real English aristocrats, accomplished in any sense. Some of them were legal luminaries, Queen's counsels; Some were high ranking members of the revered British parliament. Some of them were high in the social ladder. They drove vintage cars, optimal classic in the British tradition.

They visited this town twice to three times yearly. They spent millions of pounds sterling to maintain the said building without any visible utility of the building. These Englishmen were the Demarkians, the disciples of devil and they felt comfortable about that.

The city of London is aesthetically beautiful with century old castles as in old Europe. The medieval buildings are maintained in top shapes. Life in London is organized, with the impeccable train systems and the ubiquitous double decker buses and the black cabs. London is a reflection of class for the world, especially the Anglo-Saxons. Summer Vacations in London is a remarkable feat and it attracts a lot of tourists. It is intriguing to see the right hand side vehicles and the left hand side traffics in the narrow roads and streets.

The central London booms with tourists walking by to see the Parliament building, the big ben, the Westminster Abbey, the London bridge, the tower bridge; the London eye, the county hall; Trafalgar square with the pigeons; the Prime minister's office on number 10 Downing street; the Buckingham palace, Queens place. This is the beautiful London, the pride of every English man.

Lord Winston, a high ranking member of the British Parliament, called a British MP, in his mid- seventies, a permanent member of the Westminster Abbey, top notch politician. He lived a quiet but very affluent lifestyle. He drove an antique 1935 Rolls Royce with very clean interior décor, heavily glossy chrome on the dashboards and the doors and a hundred percent leather interior. He lived by himself but unlike other Demarkians, he was amiable and loving to everyone. He greeted people if and when he was out and about. He had a red nose pit bull named danger, a cult dog. Danger was almost 4 feet high, doesn't drool, usually very quiet and had its face down most of the time, avoiding eye contact with anyone. Winston rarely brought it out anyway, for obvious reasons. Danger was a very obedient dog to Winston. It sometimes got bored but never showed it to the master but Winston knew and felt sorry for it sometimes, with the consolation that, after all, it wasn't a normal animal. It was an evil in the form of an animal. Winston understanding the implication doesn't bring danger out except sometimes very late for a quick walk. Danger avoided other animals methodically too. Even the times that Winston had visitors, Danger walked away to the back room. Danger doesn't bark but it was an extremely dangerous animal with enormous evil powers.

On this day at London, Winston, made a very poor judgment by taking a restless danger to central London. He first took it to the MP building for a short period, left it in the car while he was in the building. He later came down and walked over to watch life and activities of the tourists and others at the Trafalgar square. Life was good as people were roaming the area with the happiness and contentment of the summer. Couples were kissing and a lot of people taking selfies with their phones, with some yelling on the phone, "I am now in London!" The roller skaters were busy rolling around in styles, and people of all shades, sizes, shapes, were seen basking in London summer. Winston and danger were enjoying it too, from where they were seated.

Danger laid recoiled between Winston's legs, edged to the back to conceal its presence the best it could while watching the world of humans and real animals. There was nothing remarkable about Winston and danger. Winston was busy waving at the Londoners who looked in his direction.

Two sisters on short pants, with one of them sexily cut revealing some part of her panties, were boisterously walking their three dogs, a Rottweiler, a small size pit bull and another smaller dog. They walked towards Winston in trying to avoid a rough roller skater. Winston and danger became alarmed seeing them walking towards them. Danger edged back, in retreating form, under Winston's legs under the bench, while Winston made effort to conceal danger more. The three dogs, on getting closer to danger became suddenly troubling, barking ferociously which was initially ignored by the ladies knowing that dogs hate each other and could be very territorial. Winston started getting concerned because he knew what was going on, which could potentially escalate dangerously. He kept on instructing to Danger to remain calm. He couldn't take danger away at that point because that would draw a battle line. He was hoping that the ladies would pass so he could go home but the dogs were unrestrained, viciously. He started asking the ladies to take their dogs away but they couldn't do that as the dogs, in concert, rushed and one of them took a swipe on Winston's leg. That infuriated and received the murderous attention of danger. Danger ran towards the dogs swiftly and devoured the pit bull by ripping its throats up in seconds, rushed over to the other two, shred them to pieces, like a prize dog, with incredible strength and speed. A lot of bloods dropping from its mouth as people were now running and walking fastly away. A lot of people were calling animal control. Danger seemed very upset and was ready for anything, not listening to Winton's order to follow him out. It was menacing and ferociously out of control. The ladies scared but very angry too, were yelling at Winston and cursing him and the dog. Danger initially ignored them until one of the ladies picked up a huge stone and threw it at danger but it missed. Danger growled at them and ignored them but didn't want to leave. The scene continued to get inflammatory for few more minutes.

London police first appeared and were talking with Winston about what happened and Winston explained the fight, trying so hard to hide his identity. They asked Winston if Danger was a prized dog, looking at the way it tore up the other dogs in minutes. Prized dogs are not to be exposed to a fight like that as that would have been a felony crime offense.

The animal control truck with some officers arrived immediately. They assessed danger and its menacing disposition and boldness, not showing any sign of backing down. Danger was still, now and then, mauling one of the dogs that were still showing a sign of life. The officers were trying to figure out how to take danger down, considering its size, stature and the menacing looks on its face. Danger continued to ignore Winston who was yelling at it to go home. It was a big spectacle as hundreds of people were watching from a safe distance. Three of the officers approached danger and one of them in trying to headlock the beast threw a pole with strings loaded noose at Danger. Danger's anger got aggravated and in a lightning speed rushed to the officer and practically bit off his entire right hand and the situation became more riotous. Trafalgar square and the whole of central London turned into a frenzy of the survival of the fittest as there were stampede everywhere. More police and law enforcements, with sirens, were rushing over to the scene with their guns drawn. Winston disappeared in the crowd and drove home but danger was just beginning the fight.

London police armed with rifles and pistols started shooting at danger but the bullets were not really cutting into its body, rather the impacts pushed it to the ground and it came back up, growling menacingly and running towards the police officers, while the signature demonic sounds came on. Danger not showing any exasperation, breathing like a human being, with loud heartbeat, was approaching the shooters who started edging away and taking protective positions. The police kept on shooting at danger that kept on getting more infuriated. Danger claws got elongated and more hairs appeared on it body and it increased in height and looked feisty to kill now. It rushed the police squad and was able to catch up with one of the unfortunate officers. Danger, like a lion, bit him at the neck and suffocated the officer in seconds, leaving a huge gash on the dead officer's neck. At this point, the whole security personnel knew that this wasn't a regular animal and back-ups were called for police chopper and London SWAT team with their armored truck. Danger started running towards the west of London as more police came in the air and started shooting more and more but danger was not fazed by the glazing bullets. Danger ran into what appeared to be a house, outside public view. Police on public announcement were asking people to go home as the whole place was swamped with the media, including CNN London. The house was barricaded to trap in danger as hours passed. When danger came out, it looked unperturbed and clean, with no blood spatter on its body! Danger wanted to show Londoners that it was an evil beast and they needed to see the power of Satan. They continued to shoot at it but it turned into a huge beast of about 7 feet, stamping its chest in victory while getting shot, made a huge deep laughter and disappeared in a thick black smoke. Everyone, including the law enforcement, lost their sense of compass in trying to escape. The news media recorded most part of this in video. It became breaking news all over the world in minutes.

Winston was at home and watching everything in the news, very offended, with a large glass of whiskey in his hands. He didn't even know when danger came back in and laid quietly on the corner. The prefect of the order was fuming as he recalled the dog the next day and Winston was issued a cat instead.

There were a lot of tv analysis about the central London event. The public were puzzled as to what the dog that turned into a beast was all about. Who was the mystery man that brought the dog to the hub of London? Was it a cyborg from Russia? Was it an evil beast? But a lot of people all over the world don't believe in what they consider a spiritual bullshit made for the tv movies. But why did it disappear? Why didn't it disappear without hurting others? What happened to its bloody mouth? If it was a lab creation, why didn't the bullets get into it? But it had blood that showed on it. What has the world turned into? A lot of unanswered questions until the Vatican called in and fully briefed the British government about the Demarkians and a global ecumenical effort by the Christian community to fight and destroy the cult. Some clergy were invited to CNN London for a roundtable talks that dissected more the new razzmatazz.

$$***$$

A wooden house in the middle of a forested neighborhood, in an extremely, quiet and suburban town of Edenton in North Carolina. It was unusually dark in the night in the town. The house looked like a haunted home filled up with angry spirits of the deads making weird noises in the dead of the nights. Tourist campers, with keen interest, in the nearby forests, watched the house with telescope hoping to see walking deads as in Michael Jackson's thriller music video. Some of the campers were interested in visiting the house and passing the night in it. Conversation between two camping brothers were on- going over there, with some childish excitements, yells, do some dramas, drink cold beers and act like ghosts, laughed over it. Maintaining the insistence, one of them rode his bike over to the house to see the house up close but was rattled away, after some minutes, by a huge mamba snake that climbed out of the house.

The house looked creaky and abandoned, filled with rodents, bird nests, rotten woods with fungi, insects and huge spiders, with strong smell of ecosystem oozing out of the house. The house has frontal balcony, a decrepit flower vest hanging on it giving it the appearance of a Dracula cove, broken chairs, rotten and broken stairways leading up to the balcony, jammed windows, cracked woods on the whole periphery of the building. The house had an unknown history of ownership. It looked like a house of horror in the night. It reminded one of the house in the said Jackson's thriller music video movie.

The Edenton community had about five thousand residents, occupying about 25 houses, each home being at least 700 yards from each other. The homes and neighborhood were barricaded by giant eucalyptus trees and heavy vegetation. The houses had trees surrounding them and some branches hovered into the roofs. Pockets of deep rivers, streams, and lakes surrounded the entire area of Edenton. The town looked like what you read in fairy tale books about a town in the middle of nowhere. In the nights, the town became virtually non- existent as there were very little lightings seen in the entire perimeter. The waters were very natural in terms of purity that you could see fish and other animals swimming in clean pure water of Edenton. Bacs of the huge trees, fallen branches, would be seen in the water. It was, almost to a chilling level, incredibly pristine in Edenton. Birds of different colors and sizes were seen flying around in this amazing nature's cove. No fishermen or anyone would be seen tapping into this magnificent but scary natural ecology here. Edenton was nature in its purest form.

There were no tarred roads in Edenton but rather dusty trails that mostly allowed the passage of one car at a time. There were bike routes, a post office, two market stores, a little church, a village square with a small building functioning as the townhall, a huge bell that chimed every hour when it chose to work. Once in a while a neighbor will be seen rowing a small boat through the quiet waters and streams, under the serene canopies of the forested waters. Edenton, its world, was beautiful indeed, especially to the weirdos.

One day, a van appeared in the dilapidated building and parked for a long time. A huge man, about 6 feet, 4 inches tall, 260lbs with an obvious powerful muscular physique, wearing a hooded shirt, was seen walking around the horror house, walked on the stairs to the balcony, opened the decrepit doors and went inside with a flashlight, even though it was in the day time. There was some noise of the man attacking the snakes and other rodents and animals.

The nearest neighbor to the house, Ms. Hardwater, a very nosy person, 73-year-old widow, with no child or family, surviving on her social security monthly payments, lived about one thousand yards away from the house. Armed with her usual telescope that she used to observe nature in her neighborhoods, she noticed the strange man and his boldness, walking around fearlessly like a marauding Pirate. She started, avoiding detection, from an angle allowing direct access from the trees and shrubs, watching the man and the house with an intrusive obsession. She was wondering what a rational person could be doing in such desolate building that may have been abandoned for ages. She wondered what this young man could be looking for in a town mostly inhabited by retirees.

The mystery man seemed to be the new owner and he drove a cargo van, clean with some neatly arranged work equipment at the top. He normally drove in and out and had no schedule. He walked in and out of the house, with the long police flashlight in his hands, sat down sometimes with cans of Budweiser beer and a transistor radio, weirdly nodding his head to whatever he was listening to. He always had a machete beside him to fight off the reptiles and rodents. He later started bringing in wooden planks, paints, sands, gravels, cements and other stuffs, to fix up the house. He started work on the house, removed all the rotten woods and dug out a lot of sands from the obscure and barricaded side of the building. It appeared he was constructing a basement on the property. He worked on the garage and kept bringing in a lot of materials, all by himself and at different times, including odd times too. That perplexed Hardwater who kept on asking herself why this young weird man was all by himself doing such project. Who was he and what was he up to? She vowed to find out. Sometimes, he worked all through the night, cutting woods, digging the ground and mixing gravel and cements, always dressed in hoodie clothes. She wondered if he was the new owner or whether he rented the place or was he an adverse possessor? She considered calling the sheriff but restrained herself, after all what was her business? The sheriff station serving Edenton was about 50 miles away. She felt that Edenton was a forgotten place and she never saw the cops here anyway. The Sheriff had only 3 officers with head officer named Sheriff Williamson, [Willie].

The mystery man continued working on the house, doing a lot of diggings, for another week. Hardwater decided to pay the new neighbor a visit. She rode her bike over there and met the stranger who was busy cutting woods and pretended as if he was not aware of her presence for a few minutes. Hardwater greeted him loudly and he stopped what he was doing, not perturbed or showed any excitement on seeing her, smiled grudgingly and said hello to Hardwater. They chatted for a few minutes, studying each other. They talked about this and that and she rode away. Stranger continued to work for another two hours and later left. He came back later and continued working till late night. Hardwater, on a hunch, believed that the digging and the explanation offered was suspicious, decided to call Willie. The next day, Willie drove over there in the afternoon and met the stranger who was, as usual, busy doing his work. Stranger looked up and saw a police cruiser driving up to him and got agitated. He knew right then that this old woman didn't mean well.

Stranger and Willie greeted, conversation:

Willie: Hey, how are we today?

Stranger: doing great or pretending so, laughs. What can I do you for sir?

Willie: I am Williamsom but people call me Willie.

Stranger: Good to know that, Quiet town, small and peaceful. I like it out here though.

Willie: Oh I can see and you got right into it. By the way I didn't get your name?

Stranger: I am Paulo, pardon my manners.

Willie: It's ok. So are you the owner of the property or renting?

Paulo: I am the new owner. Trying to put it back in shape and make it a home. I am originally from Phillie but I like it out here.

Willie: Glad to have you with us. We is good people and we kinda do our thing nice and right, feel me?

Paulo: Kinda gatch ya, sheriff.

Willie: A lot of diggings, hope you are not turning into a badger? Laughed at the joke.

Paulo: We see, am trying to, like I said, make the house habitable.

Willie: I believe you acquired plan approvals for all the work?

Paulo: Yes, I do sir.

Willie: You an Engineer or a handy man?

Paulo: I am neither but I am gifted.

Willie, looking at the van with working tools, turned and said to Paulo: "you had all these tools for just being gifted?"

Paulo: I guess you could reason that way.

Willie: sounding a little sarcastic especially seeing this man that wore a concealing hooded shirt in the hot summer, said: as long as your habitability doesn't make you burrow too deep into the soil. Anyway, have a nice day. I will stop by again to say hi.

Paulo: That's cool. Bye now.

Willie drove still watching this intriguing character from his vehicle rear-view mirror.

Paulo feeling a little angry about this visit, suspecting that Hardwater called the cops on him, decided to deal with that later. He continued his work and completed all he planned in the next few weeks and moved in. He lived alone and there was never any visitor. He had no fixed schedule, drove in sometimes by midnight and sometimes at very odd hours. He was always putting on his hooded shirt. He seemed very strong because sometimes he was observed removing very heavy bags and objects from his van, especially in the wee hours of the night. Hardwater had sleeping problems compounded by age and could stay awake all night. She had a combo military style adjustable telescope with clear vision for day and night. Paulo had presented her with assignments and she was enjoying it. She watched Paulo day and night with keen interest but cautiously too because there was something odd about this young man. Paulo seemed emotionless and hard. She normally turned off her lights while watching Paulo. She also oiled and serviced her gun in anticipation of any attack from this creepy man.

On a rainy midnight two days ago, Paulo drove in. A rainfall in a midnight in Edenton, a heavily forested sleepy town, lonely and dark, very spine-chilling, was a personification of fear. Why would this young man drive in by this time of the night in a cargo van in an eerie surrounding environment? He was dragging out a huge duffel bag that seemed to take a lot of efforts to be removed into the dark garage. The entire building had minimal lightings too and the windows were never opened, drapped out with thick curtains too. Does he have a tv? Wife? Kids? Paulo would disappear from the house, sometimes for days or weeks and drove back in unannounced. He sometimes sat in the balcony with his radio, ate, drank and disappeared into his house and later drove out.

Willie and his two deputies had two squad cars, trying their best to remain efficient while doing nothing in this sleepy part of America with zero crimes or old police work. Sometimes, they even locked up the station and went for barbeque or drinking spree. They did mountain and trail hiking or used their boats on the waters of Edenton and its environs. They received free donuts, buggers, coffee from different small eateries. Everyone knew everyone in Edenton. In the small church, they talked and gossiped about everything, including Paulo.Hardwater went hard on Paulo and alerted the community about her suspicions of this young man.

Few months later, an all- points- bulletin, apb, came in announcing the finding of dead young girls floating on the rivers of the next town, their bodies were mutilated, sexually molested. In nearby counties about 100 miles away, more dead young girls, appeared to be prostitutes, were also discovered, same modus killings, with their breast nipples cut off and their breasts carved open, their necks slashed. This continued in the nearby states of the Carolinas. Victims were young females that were in hiking, jogging, doing other field activities, travelling hikers, broken vehicles on the freeways, showing typical serial killer situation. It simply showed that the entire state and nearby states had a diehard serial killer in their midst. He or she needed to be discovered otherwise they would be removing dead bodies for as long as the killer wished.

Sheriff Willie and his colleagues were getting disturbed, having been redundant for years. They had even forgotten how to process a crime scene and conduct a homicide investigation!
Some of the victims were placed on the location of the crime while some others were transported into different locations including the waterways. Willie called for homicide detective assistance from the state and the investigation started across state lines. The interviews were conducted and Hardwater quickly fingered Paulo. Willie and the detectives visited Paulo but he was not there for two weeks, which threw them off, strong alibi, and they removed their attention from him.

Paulo was a methodical criminal and Edenton community did not understand who was in their midst. Paulo located a convenient spot about 1.5 miles from the edge of the town overlooking his Edenton home and kept vigil watching his house with a powerful long range industrial telescope that he obtained from an undisclosed source. He wanted to understand his neighbors more, particularly Hardwater, the old nosy witch. Watching his house one day, he saw Willie and the detectives visited his home and he smiled. He saw them walked around his house, inspecting the garage area and other perimeter, with what appeared to be a cadaver dog.

Few days later, he sneaked into town in another regular looking sedan car but was pulled over by the police in a routine search that they started since the killings. They saw the telescope and asked him about that. He answered that it was just a toy for his hunting expeditions in the forests. He drove to his viewing location and watched his house as usual but there was nothing and he decided to leave. Just as he was about to go, he saw a movement, the old witch, Hardwater pulled up in her bike, hid the bike in the woods, tiptoed to his house, walked around, brought out a camera from her trench coat and was taking pictures of everything around the premises! She was seen trying to break into the house via a side window but Paulo built in a strong barricade in all doors and windows and ceilings too! She was seen planting what looks like an all –weather wireless secret surveillance camera in a tree branch nearest to the balcony. Paulo was enraged as his face turned red and he made his decisions. He drove off to Durham where he had some businesses to take care of.

Another body was discovered 145 miles away from Edenton. She was a pretty blond college girl, found almost naked, brutally raped, with her throat slashed and a missing right breast nipple. The detectives now branded the killer "the nipple killer" and the entire Carolinas and neighboring states became alert. More detectives from all local police, county sheriffs, state police, high way patrols, FBI, were involved, and heavily too. They had to catch the nipple killer. Federal detectives specializing on serial criminals were flooded into the Carolinas and the war had started.
The killer stopped for months, laid low and everyone got relaxed. Paulo came home one afternoon and Hardwater saw him pulled in and decided to pop in on him. She rode her bike over to the house. First thing she did was to make sure her camera was still there and it was.
Paulo: Hey maam, you again, how are you?
Hardwater: hey dear, how you been, haven't seen you around for some time. Where have you been?
Paulo: up and about. What's up? what can I do you for?
Hardwater: Are you aware that dead bodies had been flooding the Carolinas?

Paulo: Waoh, is it. That's not nice. What's up about that? When and how?

Hardwater: been so bad that the FBI is here heavily as well as other security agencies in this region. They call the evil killer nipple killer, and she laughed on saying that name.

Paulo: Nipple killer? What's that?

Hardwater: Most of the victims were young ladies and their nipples were always missing. Looks like the idiot did not get enough nipple from his mum or wife. What in the world is he doing with all these nipples he has collected? Sick-ass weirdo. They will catch him and fry his ass, that I am sure of, we will see, stupid coward.

Paulo: Well, its good seeing you but I got to run inside as I am tired. We talk another time.

Paulo went inside and Hardwater looked at his camera again and left.

Hardwater, now a little close with Willie, called him and informed him of Paulo's presence that afternoon. Paulo sensing a visit from the law enforcement quickily drove out of town before the sheriffs and others came calling. The sheriff and the FBI rushed over with cadaver dogs but there was nobody there. The woods around the vicinity was gain thoroughly searched and neighbors were interviewed about Paulo. Paulo was watching all these activities from his observation spots and he felt very distressed.

✳✳✳

Hardwater felt a little bit under the weather today, that time of the year for her sinusitis allergy flareups, with all the trees in Edenton. She took a pm allergy medication to get some sleep too. Became very drowsy and dozed off deeply at about 10p.m. She was in lala land when a new black sedan, 4 -cylinder car silently drove into Edenton by 1 a.m. The driver pulled up by her house, turned off the interior light of the car before opening the vehicle door, alighted silently and went over to her window. Being a criminal, he manipulated his way into the house, walked in a foamy shoe to Hardwater's room and strangled her to death effortlessly, covered her back with her comforter as if she was still sleeping and exited the building.

✳✳✳

Weeks turned into months again and nothing happened. The Carolinas were safe again; whatever happened to the serial killer? Paulo came home again, removed the camera from the tree and relaxed in the balcony. He was happy listening to the music when Willie and another pulled up and asked him: hope you don't mind our presence here? Paulo responded, hell, no, any time sir, grab a beer and they did. The conversation started dwelling mostly on the killings and his whereabouts, his reactions to the killings. They asked him if he would allow them to search his house. Paulo felt irritated, asked the officers, why? Have you any probable cause for that? Did you search the house of others? Why mine? I just barely got into town. They apologized and changed the topic. They observed some scratches on Paulo's hands and inquired how he got those scratches? Paulo responded that he does handyman job for himself and others. Willie had a closer look at the scratches and told Paulo that the marks doesn't look like they came from any tool. Paulo laughed sarcastically and told Willie that he did not know where he was going with his comments but he should stop harassing him. It sounded like a subtle warning. He asked them to leave and he advised that they should not come back for another visit except with a warrant.

Willie and his colleague drove off and was beginning to lose further interest in Paulo. It occurred to Willie that he had not heard from Hardwater or seen her in the last few days or more. She never called him for updates on Paulo. He stopped by her house, knocked, yelled out her name but no response. He knocked on the window and the doors but no response. He found that a little unusual but they left with Willie leaving his card.

After a week, Willie called her number again but there was no pick up and her voice mail was full. He got alarmed and decided to drive over there. He knocked harder on the front door, yelled her name, walked around the building for inspection but didn't find anything abnormal but the police instinct kicked in as he was about to leave. He decided to look more and went around the building again. And then he found that one of the back windows had its latch carefully breached. He looked closer on it, got alarmed, went to his car and got a glove and a flashlight, put on the glove and went back. He fiddled with the window and it opened. Very alarmed now, he called for a back -up for his deputies and they drove over to the house. They flashed the light into the house but everything seemed okay. They deliberated whether to jump in and investigate or get a warrant. Better judgment prevailed and they went for an emergency warrant from the local court, 70 miles away. They came back a little late in the evening, forced open the front door and gained access.

The sitting room and everything seemed normal, no evidence of suspicion until they got deep into the house and were confronted by the stench of Hardwater's decomposing body. It was in early stage of decomposition. They covered their nose and walked to see her body and ambulance was called in to remove her body. Questions were raised; was she robbed? But her purse was still there with some money in it. It appeared nothing was removed. How did she die? Was it natural? But there was a broken latch. There were fading finger marks on her neck. Who would like to kill her? She had no known family too, so sad. She was just an old lady, a widow that lived a quiet life in a sleepy town. Willie's mind flashed to Paulo but he quickly dismissed that. Paulo never knew that Hardwater was reporting on him. He was also out of town when she passed. What about the crazy killings in the Carolinas? She did not fit into the profile of the victims of the nipple killer. They kept searching, checking all the crevices of the house, checked under the bed and found her dead cell phone. They left for the station and reported this to the state headquarters.

Few days later, the autopsy result came out with a conclusion that she died by strangulation. The whole town was panicked and came back alive again. Meetings were held between the law enforcements and the local communities. Safety instructions were issued to everyone to lock their doors in the night, get a dog if you don't have one, apply for a gun permit and get a good gun; be wary of strangers in the community; report any and all unusual activities. Tough times but y'all need to be tough people as we don't know how many serial killers were on the prowl.

In Minthill, Mr. Linford Jackson and Lisa Jackson lived a quiet life, by themselves, in a bungalow, both worked in a local bank, minded their own business, didn't receive visitors or visited anyone. They had a huge brown dog and a white cat. These animals rarely came out of the house. They were Demarkians and they lived to the core principles of the brotherhood. Their parents were Demarkians too. They rarely come outside or walk in the park with their animals because the reactions of other dogs or even birds were unpalatable. Lisa was a very pretty lady in her 30s, with long shapely legs and fine built. She was just an exquisite looking young lady and she knew that.

Paulo liked to stay in Minthill, another quiet and beautiful city. He considered living there but chose Edenton because it was closer to nature to stay over there, with less population and more peace. He loved to drive around Minthill, lodged in a local motel for days and sometimes for weeks, with forged documents that were arguably genuine. He even opened a bank account with the forged and stolen identity of crime victims. He loved to watch beautiful women from his motel room and in the process developed obsession for Lisa.

It doesn't matter to him that Lisa was married at the time. He watched her daily with his powerful telescope. Linford was not a match for him if he needed to attack him but he snapped asking himself why would he attack him? On this Sunday night, everybody was at home, the Minthill park was desolate and Lisa was very bored, having been home for the whole week. In agreement with her husband, she took their dog for a walk to the park, which appeared deserted and safe. Paulo noticed that Lisa was outbound and gathered his instruments for a sexual assault if need be. He, for the first time, laughed and beat his chest and yelled to himself: you are the nipple killer, son of the devil. He started laughing like a deranged beast that he was. He remembered all his stored nipples at his secret compartments in Edenton. He might have Lisa's nipple in that jar by tomorrow morning, can't wait. The dog wouldn't pose a problem. He was a US marine and could kill the dog in less than a minute. Paulo in ecstasy, rushed down the stairs of the motel, with his bag in tow and stumbled into another guest and one of his killer instruments fell out of the bag and fell on the reception area of the motel, in full plain view of everyone. Embarrassed Paulo, the guest, and the receptionist looked at the instrument with dried blood in it, for some brief seconds.

Paulo quickly scooped up the instrument and said he was rushing for a friend's night barbeque and burn fire, got to his vehicle and drove off towards the park. He got there and waited for Lisa. He planned on how to take out the dog with a special implement and his army skill. He planned to sedate Lisa and take her to a place where he could live and rape her forever. He was just a dangerous psycho. He considered all locations, maybe in his Edenton's secret basement. He drove his van to the park and hid it in an obscure part. Minthill town was asleep and in peace. It got darker in the park as some lights were faulty and he stayed on those part of the park.
There came Lisa, strikingly and stunningly beautiful with a swagger of a sassy lady of confidence. She looked like what you see in good Hollywood movies. She didn't look scared. Her dog was in tow. Lisa walked about 100 feet towards him as he exited from the corner of the woods, greeted Lisa and was approaching her asking her for a chat time. Lisa smiled and nicely informed him that she was married and was just out to catch some air. He approached Lisa menacingly and tried to grab her, pushed Lisa to the ground looking through his bag to find his sedating injection already drawn and prepared, but the dog appeared from nowhere with an incredibly swiftness, with bloodshot reflective eyes, a fanged dentition, lunged on Paulo, with the evil sound playing at the background, in a swift , bit Paulo on the shoulder blade and ripped it off so badly. The dog's nails were out for a kill but Lisa got up and rushed to remove the dog away from Paulo who was crying and bleeding so badly. Lisa Kicked the duffel bag away

while calling and inviting her husband to the scene. Paulo was there begging for Mercy when her husband arrived and called the sheriff who arrived in less than three minutes. Paulo was cuffed and taken away to the sheriff station. His cup had run over, it seemed.

Paulo was treated in the hospital; as multiple surgeries were performed to reinstate his arms to his shoulder. In recuperations, as a suspect, he was placed on one-on-one police surveillance. He was a person of interest and they needed to find out who he was and what he was doing in Minthill. At the station, his duffel bag was inspected and shocking discoveries were made. Murder implements, binders, handcuffs, mouth-gagging tapes, sedatives and syringes, injection needles and pouches, key bunch with over one hundred keys in it, a wrench, keys to his van, which was earlier located by parking violation officers and impounded to a police parking location and not processed yet and they had not run the license plate yet, flashlights, a jigsaw, different identity cards, hotel receipts. These findings were announced to the whole of Carolinas and the FBI dispatched some officers to Minthill. They came over there the next day and met with Paulo. They asked him his address and he gave the Edenton address. Willie was contacted by the FBI and invited over to Minthill.

Willie arrived the next morning and saw Paulo on the bed and was shocked but recollected himself. Paulo was actually sleeping from the effects of his drugs when Willie arrived. They all waited for him to wake up. Willie looked into the bag and found a remarkable pendant that he had observed on Hardwater, with her deceased Husband's picture in it. He opened it, confirmed it, and almost fainted. He drove out to the nearest liquor bar and bought some whiskey. He knew it was against the ethics of his job but he could care less about that now. He needed to hold himself back from sticking his .38 special into this fool's mouth and splatter his stupid brain all over the place. 30 minutes later, he went back into the room to see Paulo awake. Their eyes locked for a few minutes. Paulo surprised, said hello Willie but Willie ignored his greetings. Willie walked closer to Paulo, wanted to ask questions but didn't know where to start. Willie asked Paulo whether he drove his van here but Paulo initially did not want to answer the question for the first few seconds but nodded his head and said yes. Willie asked him where he parked the van and Paulo said at the park. Willie asked the officers if they know anything about the van and they answered negative.

The officers called the station and parking enforcements to locate the van expeditiously as it might be a heaven for homicidal evidence. They made some calls and found out the location of the van which was towed immediately to the station.

Willie, the FBI, others went to the station to search the van, excitedly. They started the search and saw normal working tools only, nothing suspicious. They searched through the compartments and found nothing incriminating. They evacuated the whole contents of the van and noticed a perfectly reconstructed secret compartments, broke it open and saw disturbing murder tools. There was a jar with preserving chemicals containing female breast nipples of different sizes and dimensions. The officers all yelled out in unison, "the nipple killer"!! They jumped up in happiness and gratitude. Having become convinced that Paulo was the nipple killer, they went back to him with the jar and other forensic evidence. Willie walked into the room and screamed at Paulo: "You evil coward that attacked and killed innocent young women! You slimy bastard; you killed Hardwater; I feel like ripping you open here and now. You sick son of a bitch. You have come to the end of your demonic road".

FBI formally took over the case and the Minthill drama was all over the US major network. CNN brought their best anchors to the scene. The town went agog with festivities, interrogations, interviews, documents reviews, who was Paulo; what was he doing in Minthill? The Jacksons were interrogated at different times before they ran out of the city for a few weeks' holiday. The press was camped outside their homes waiting for them for weeks. The cult prefect asked them to lay low where they ran to in Iowa until they were cleared to return back to Minthill. A good thing has come out of Babylon. The Demarkian has become useful twice in a row. They said that the Satan can quote the bible or could do good deeds. Was this one of them?

The investigators went to the park, pictures, video were taken. Tv stations were in the park interviewing people who were not even there but claimed to have be involved in beating Paulo. As a matter of fact, one of the city loafers claimed that it was his dog that assisted Lisa's Dog in biting Paulo. He said that he punched Paulo to the ground. All kinds of stories, real and imagined, were trending at Minthill. FBI interviewed the hotel receptionist, the guest that was bumped into who claimed that he chased Paulo out to catch him but that Paulo outran him. They were shown pictures of the equipment and they singled out the one that fell to the ground. The hotel worker hinted that Paulo demanded for a particular room at all the times he had been in that motel. The officers then knew that he planned this well in advance.

The FBI and all the security team working on the case reviewed how many victims that were found in the whole of the Carolinas and beyond and which ones were close to Minthill. The locations, dates, the modus, the identity of the victims were compiled and they all happened when Paulo was around in those areas within the state. He was a very organized serial killer. On Willie's invitation, they went to Edenton for a search of his house.

News already leaked to Edenton community about the findings and Hardwater too. They assembled in commiseration at Hardwater's place and prayed, held a religious vigil for her soul. There were so many cries, and the press, like vultures were there.
Someone eventually leaked more information to the press. Identity of the Linford and Lisa Jackson were revealed and their pictures flashed consistently on news. There was more news analysis, breaking news repeatedly as more bodies were discovered. Missing photos of family members were published hoping that Paulo would disclose their locations. Families of the disclosed ones were all in disarray and confused. Endless calls were bombarding the FBI hotline created for it.

Paulo was interrogated but he wanted a lawyer. Before a state lawyer could be assigned to him, he decided to cop out. He spilled the beans totally and in great details. He went with the officers to Edenton and they went through the concealed basement that he built without permit. He had torture chambers in it, super cleaning mortician chemicals that cadaver dogs couldn't smell; pictures, torture books, some live videos of his raping of some victims, deep freezers, a tv, a couch, sex toys, handcuffs, tapes, chains, sedatives, noodles, bunch of dirty and bloodied female underwears. There was another chemical jar containing female nipples, bigger than the one found in the van. It simply showed that there were much more victims that the security agencies knew about.

Paulo took them over to the Hardwater apartment and detailed everything out to them. He informed them of his surveillance and why he killed Hardwater. He told them about his telescope and Hardwater's secret camera planted in his house. He took them to the sites of all his discovered and undiscovered victims. He disclosed the victims not yet known and took them to where he buried them, including some buried on his basement at Edenton. He gave details of how he kidnapped a 25-year-old girl during a rainstorm, walked her to his van and sedated her. He drove her home, taped her mouth and sedated her more, spreading her leg very wide without underwears and taping her legs to the poles, went to sleep. He raped her for two weeks on a row and later injected her with a heart freezing chemical that killed her. She was thrown into a river 75 miles away. All her victims had their breasts nipples amputated as souvenirs. He explained that he killed Hardwater for poke nosing into his business, including trying to break into his home in one occasion. A lot of bodies were later exhumed on his directions. It was a very dark period in the Carolinas.

CHAPTER 12

THE GRAND FINALE. THE FINAL SHOW DOWN.

By revelations in the global Christian community via biblical forecasts and repented members that didn't live to see it happen, the Demarkian confraternity would have their centennial converge in Los Angeles on October 31st 2020. It was also the Halloween night known in the western world as the night of the witches. It would be the day marked for Satan to take over the earth and rule till eternity. Satan had broken the chain of the Abyss in the pit of hell, millions of years ago. The converge was a chest thumping event where the satanic powers of the cult would be felt in the world once again. It was to be a revival meeting where the cult took stocks of their achievements, enroll more members with continued promises of power and prosperity; reiterated their supreme powers; admonish failing members; repeats their vows to their almighty Satan; appoints new leaders and prefects; review all the activities of the cult in the last one hundred years; spread their evil gospel to the nooks and crannies of the world; appoint evangelizing coordinators to spread their powers and influence to willing participants and offer them powers of joining the brotherhood. The converge offered members the opportunity to meet with each other and make new friends. Above all, the devil would be there in flesh and spirit, roaring as ruler of the earth and beyond.

Biblical quotations on the onslaught of the devil: "And I saw the beast rising out of the sea, with ten horns and seven heads, with ten diadems on its horns and blasphemous names on its head. And the beast that I saw was like leopard; its feet were like a bear's mouth. And its mouth was like a lion's mouth. And to it the dragon gave his powers and his throne and great authoutity. One of heads seemed to have a mortal wound, but its mortal wound was healed, and the whole earth marveled as they followed the beast. And they worshipped the dragon, for he had given his authority to the beast, and they worshipped the beast saying, "who is like the beast and who can fight against it? And the beast was given a mouth uttering haughty and blasphemous words, and it was allowed to exercise authority for forty-two months…" Revelation13:1-18 "And the great dragon was thrown down, that ancient serpent, who is called the devil and Satan, the deceiver of the whole world-he was thrown down to the earth, and his angels were thrown down with him" Revelation12:9

The Christian world were getting ready to fight Satan, destroy him, or at least send him back to the pit of hell, the pit of abyss where he would be chained again for billions of years. It was a tough task but has to be done. The world belongs to God almighty, the creator of heaven and hell, the beginning and the end, the alpha and omega. Satan was just a renegade angel that chose to torment the world but his reign in the darkness would end again on the converge. "and the devil who had deceived them was thrown into the lake of fire and sulfur where the beast and the false prophets were, and they will be tormented day and night forever and ever. Revelation 20:10

These were among the sermons and prayer points developed through strenuous ecumenical efforts to confront and destroy the devil on the D-day. It shall come to pass, they vowed. It will be tough but it has to be done. Satan and his followers had to be banished from the earth. The pope announced and said: we shall be ready. Do your wars from all pulpits of God, from your Godly temples wherever located; from your bedrooms, from your offices; in your vehicles; call on the lord and the holy angels from now till the 31st of October instant, to destroy Satan and banish him from the throne of Jehovah. It will be a testament of your faith as a child of God. This is the time, and the hour of redemption is here. We have lived with these sons of darkness since the beginning of time. We have received their wraths and wickedness for time immemorial but the light of the Holy Spirit will shine on us and redeem the world using all of us. Pray and fast if you could; maintain holiness and purity of your body and soul so that we can achieve the feat. In doing so, may the almighty God bless you and lead you to victory. The American Evangelicals also issued a communique to its millions of followers, asking them to follow through with the ecumenical injunctions, as this would be a test of the Christian faith and the powers of the holy spirit over the spirit of darkness.

✶✶✶

Los Angeles International airport, LAX, is one of the biggest and busiest airports in the world with flights arriving every minute on the clock, January through December of every year. The airport is massive in size and its operations. There are also multiple airports serving southern California: Long Beach airport; John Wayne airport in Orange County; Ontario International airport; San Diego airport, and others.

To everybody's surprise, the flights to these airports were filled to the brim. The tickets were overbooked both domestically and internationally. The car rentals saw the same upsurge without having an explanation for it. As a matter of fact, they marked up their rental rates but the reservations were swift and booked. Even air-conditioned vans were all booked up. The four to six star hotels were booked up solid. The hotels and some motels in metropolitan Los Angeles were all booked and paid for a week earlier and left vacant by the patrons. Everyone was in awe as to what was going on, except the dedicated Christian community that knew about the up-coming Demarkian converge somewhere in upscale part of town.

In Bel air, with the highest elevation of landscape in Los Angeles, the richman's cove, there was a surprising hectare of land untapped and untouched, which was surprising for such neighborhood with the costliest real estate in the world. The said land was prime and overlooked all Hollywood, Beverly Hills and Universal City. It was a breathtaking piece of asset. But since May of 2020, heavy duty equipment was seen excavating, digging, and installing huge pillars and platforms, extending from the canyon valleys up to the mountain ranges on top.

There were too much excavations and sand dunes. The brick work alone can only compare to the rebuilding of the world trade center buildings in New York. Hundreds of millions of dollars were being spent on the project that was blocked away from the world. The involved cities were overly paid for the permits and inspections. The ownership of the entity was never disclosed and no building billboards were erected.

The Police were paid millions to provide round the clock security around on the perimeter of the project. Works went on the project twenty- four hours a day, with the floodlights used in the night. The contractors were not visible to the public and the whole place was barricaded from the public. The platform and the project will accommodate more than five hundred thousand people comfortably. On completion, a private street will be routed to it, with multiple giant gates and security. Already grown giant oak trees and palms were already planted around the perimeter to block the public view of the place. The architectural designs alone running into over four hundred million dollars was marvelously done to protect the identity and the activities that would be conducted in the edifices built on that land. This was the Demarkian converge arena coming up in October. The devil has money to throw around and this was part of it.

The churches eventually found out about the project and decided to hold a vigil in front of it on the D-Day. Pamphlets were created; announcements made in the churches for committee volunteers;

Placard bearers; night vigil participants; prayer warriors; placard bearers in front of the Beverly Hills, Be Air city halls condemning the permits granted to devil worshipers relating to the project even though they knew that the law allowed permits to be legally issued to applicants. The churches also purchased Billboard commercials, neon light commercials on the freeways and major streets; dropping fliers on the streets, posting posters in greater Los Angeles, informing the public about the upcoming satanic world converge.

People were admonished to be in their houses from the night of the 30th of October as the devil would like to show its presence in Los Angeles. The struggle continued and every side was getting ready. The chief of LAPD trained his men for that night. He met with the local church leaders on security concerns but was informed that the war is not a war of flesh but a spiritual one involving prayer vigil only. It was not a basketball final but a battle of darkness and light. Light is always about peace but darkness relates to evil and insecurity.

By October 24th, the cult brotherhood members started trooping into southern California as booked and planned. Los Angeles became crazy as all major freeways were jammed morning to night. Hotels went haywire, including Airbnb that were also fully booked. The limousine services made a kill as they were engaged all through the day and nights. There were too much dramas in the airports between the security dogs going off and attacking some "innocent" arriving passengers. The activities of these dogs were surprising to the airport officials until some of them read the billboards attacking the Satan cult members and why the dogs attacked them, in line with other educational brochures preparing everyone about the invasion of LA by evil people.

By the 31th afternoon, all the attending cult members were camping in the massive edifice at Bel Air, getting ready for their convention. The churches were getting ready too, having marked out a Bethel church across from the convention place as their meeting ground in the morning of the 31st till next day. Hundreds of volunteers assembled with their rosaries, bibles, crucifixes, holy oil, holy water. Some of them had fasted for weeks asking God to show his presence by destroying Satan and his followers. The weekly weather forecast showed that Los Angeles area would have sunshine days and dark evenings with good weather. This forecast was for the entire week of the 31st. Normal life in Los Angeles, therefore continued, except that people were warned to go home and stay home but the warning sounded too abstract for Americans, in their ways of lives.

The weather forecast for the 31st was that it was going to be warm in the evening, with night temperature of 60 degrees Fahrenheit. Darkness was to set in about 6.30 p.m. that day. There was nothing adverse about the weather that day. By the hour of 3p.m, to everyone's surprise except the Christian world, darkness befell all over the entire Los Angeles. The traffic was on a snail speed in the freeways and streets, almost to a chaotic level. Suddenly, a tremor was felt in the town which never recorded on the earthquake ritcher scale as an earthquake, which Los Angelenos were used to.

Another major tremor came on and cracked the 110 freeway, dismembering the over-passes on downtown Los Angeles, with vehicles falling down 400 feet to the freeway bed below and some of the vehicles getting inflamed as people were burning to death in agonies. The huge multi-storeys overpass of the 105 freeway by the 110 freeway broke off in its entirety plunging hundreds of vehicles to over two thousand feet below. Fire was everywhere as there were multiple vehicular accidents on 405 Freeway. Trees were uprooted including the palm trees of Los Angeles, with some of them smashing into peoples' home, causing hundreds of casualties.

There were thunder and brimstones as trees were mysteriously set on fire. Many church building were cracked by thunder and some of them set ablaze by the thunders that were relentless. The high rise buildings, the skylines, were threatened as some them almost caved in to the tremors. The oceans of the beach cities were roaring in anger and overflowing its banks causing a mild tsunami.

It was just deeply chaotic as sirens were heard everywhere as ambulance and police were seen everywhere protecting law and order. Lights were off in the greater part of the metropolitan Los Angeles as electric poles were uprooted to the grounds with a lot of people dying from electrocutions. Nobody could understand what was going on at the moment but most ascribed it to earthquake but it wasn't. The Devil just arrived LA and announced his presence. The damages or the turbulence did not come anywhere near the converge place for the cult.

The vigil members seeing what was going in the tv, were praying hard calling on God to take over, to destroy and stop the devil from winning. Their Bethel church building started vibrating hard and unrestrained but they kept on praying and calling on the angels. They trooped outside with their candles and chaplets and continued to call on God in the high heavens to end all these now! They were using a high sounding microphones encouraging each other and not to submit to the shenanigans of Satan and that they would have the last laugh. They held hands together in prayers and singing the hymns. They were ready to do all that it took to defeat the devil tonight. They were calling the devil derogatory names and promising him back to the abyss tonight. The Satan followers were asked for the last time to exit the converge and cross over to salvation as it was never too late. They were informed that they would be destroyed with the devil tonight if they refused to reject Satan. Bible verse was read over and over again extolling God, his supremacy and dominion over the earth.

Inside the converge, the Demarkians were oblivious of the outside. They were cuddling, eating and drinking wines and beverages. They were happy to be there and reaffirm their vows to the devil in exchange for his protections and prosperities. These people were from different parts of the world. The event continued with the control and direction of the leadership of the cult. By 3 a.m., the devil roared loudly that the Christians even heard him and started yelling on God to destroy him. The devil, a huge beast with indescribable features, appeared at the converge live and direct, looking at his followers and laughed in appreciation. The members bowed to him, knelt down in worship and respect and the devil laughed again in apprecive gesture. It roared like a beastly lion and started speaking in an incoherent tones and language but his followers could care less about that as they continued to bow to him in reverence. The vigil Christians continued their own crusade, just as the whole world were in deep prayers at that moment making the same supplications asking God that this was the time! At about 6 a.m. in the morning, the Demarkians felt the first sign of trouble as the converge center started vibrating with increasing crescendo.

This was weird because they had never been through anything like that as they believed that they ruled the world. They have never been on the receiving end. The converge building continued vibrating as the Christians noticed and was hailing the holy spirit for coming to the redeeming war. Devil could be heard yelling in anger and claiming dominion over the earth, threatening brimstone to the world and destruction of any and all other powers. Suddenly, a huge fire was seen descending from the sky into the converge arena and lit the whole place. Cult members were crying as they were dying in agony.

The churches, holding vigil all over the world, felt it and were singing more praises and praying harder and harder in adoration as God almighty was destroying Satan and his disciples. The beast that showed as Satan was set on fire and he cried endlessly in agony and couldn't disappear as usual. As this was going on, the Demarkians all over the world were in turmoil as some of them died in agony while others were slowly incinerated with their dogs, cats and birds. Their temples were smitten with fire and lit to ashes. A lot of things happened at that moment and thereafter in the world as the entire cult structure were dismantled and destroyed. Some cult members fell sick mysteriously; others committed suicide; on and on and on. All the relics of the cult, the stones of the cult that unlocked their powers were destroyed globally. God demonstrated his dominion over the earth till the end of time. Satan was banished and chained again in the Abyss, or so the Christian world believed. There is peace in the world again.

THE END.

THE SEQUEL TO THE DEMARKIAN STORY

The power of the devil represented the power of darkness that lacked reliance and dexterity. A devil could turn its claws against his followers in a heartbeat, moreso when it was being consumed by the power of light, power of the most high.

In defeat, Lucifer turned against his kingdom and caused some terrible losses to his followers. The following are the ending story of his notable disciples in the story.

The Winterbrushes met with inexplicable paralysis for a few years, with two of them ending up on wheelchairs. Oliver got drowned in a pool when an unseen force held him strapped on the chair and rolled him into 8 feet deep end of a convalescent home swimming pool. His wife, Philo, lived for more decades in torment until she had a heart attack and passed on later.

The Edmontons, including their political son, Maxwell, had a very bad plane crash few days after the destruction of the cult and their bodies were completely incinerated by fire. They were alive after the crash but were burnt alive, hollering in pains. Their vast assets were escheated to the state of New York because they had no next of kin.

The Osbornes committed continuous errors in their medical practices and lost their licenses to the state medical board. Phillip later committed suicide by hanging himself. The wife, Felicia, developed serious mental problems that made her scream non-stop 15 hours daily for more than 5 years until she hit her head on the wall one day and died.

Ericson died about six months after the end of the cult. Developed suicidal ideations, he jumped the Golden gate bridge into the freezing waters of San Francisco.

Donna's Dental practice picked up very well and she later married Dante, the private eye and enjoyed a blissful marriage, blessed with three beautiful kids.

Betsy's law practice and life blossomed too. She got deeper into the Christian vineyard and became a pastor. She later got married to another rich pastor and had kids. She kept on seeing her smiling and beaming parents in her multiple dreams.

Paulo received five death sentences and two life terms, with the judge making these remarkable statement to him as follows:
"Mr. Paulo, life is all about choices and you made yours. To call you an evil person would be a gross understatement. You are worse than Lucifer himself. You brought so much sorrows to a lot of families and communities. You took away that which was very precious to the families. If there is reincarnation, you will be executed five times as long as you keep on returning through any unfortunate womb to this our world again and again. The same thing applies to the two life terms, which you must serve if you continue to reincarnate back to the world. I don't want to appear comical but I would have suggested that you will be buried with all those nipples that you had in the bottles stuffed into your evil mouth, to your eternity.
The law is very lenient to you as we could not do worse than this. Take him away."
This judgment went viral in the news media and all social platforms for a long time.

The Demarkians   Chidi Metu

ABOUT THE AUTHOR

The writer, Chidi Metu Esq., is a Nigerian- American practicing lawyer based in Los Angeles, California. He is a trained journalist and a gifted writer, outside the shores of his educational trainings. He was the Deputy Editor of Amandala Newspaper, Belize. Story telling is a flair that he had from birth and now he is determined to share his gift with the world. Not for the gold and silver, he enjoys writing as hobby. He has other products on suspense, action and Horror, including other genres. Lay your hands on those other works and be the judge of his skills.

His works is shoulder higher than any renowned world Authors as he combines his skillful writing, amazing sense of imaginations, his legal trainings, his experiences, having practiced law in three different continents including presently Los Angeles, California; his immense experiences in the criminal courtrooms and the police investigative processes; the crime profiles and the forensic analysis of crime.

Mr. Metu is married with four children.
Review by Dr. Kissinger. [Los Angeles].

OTHER WORKS BY THE AUTHOR

- ENFANT TERRIBLE
- DEVIL'S NEXT OF KIN
- ELEGANT EVIL

Printed in the United States of America

Made in the USA
Middletown, DE
30 August 2022